I0590096

Guardians of Alistile

Risen from Ash

Copyright © 2025 by Samantha Vargas

All rights reserved. No part of this book may be reproduced in any form or by any electronic or mechanical means including information storage and retrieval systems—except in the case of brief quotations embodied in articles or reviews—without permission in writing from its publisher, Samantha Vargas.

This is a work of fiction. All of the characters, organizations, and events portrayed in this novel are either products of the author's imagination or are used fictitiously.

Cover Design: Bewitching Book Covers by Rebecca Frank
Internal Book Art: Jennifer Z. DeHart
Editing and Formatting: Charla Ayers

Author: Samantha Vargas
Title: Guardians of Alistile: Risen from Ash / Samantha Vargas
Description: First Edition |
Identifiers: ISBN 979-8-9932025-0-1 (ebook) | ISBN 979-8-9932025-1-8 (paperback) | ISBN 979-8-9932025-2-5 (hardcover)
www.samanthavargasauthor.com

Books by Samantha Vargas

Guardians of Alistile

Risen From Ash

The AshBorn (Coming 2026)

The World of the Gods (Release TBD)

Journey into Shadows (Release TBD)

A Broken Curse (Release TBD)

The Rise of a King: Prequel (Release TBD)

Queen of Fire (Release TBD)

Dedication

FOR MY CHILDREN

One day you will stand before the crossroads of who you are meant to be.
Choose with courage. Claim it as your own.
On that day, the world itself will bend to the power of your becoming.

FOR MY READER

Darkness lies thick upon the world.
Question it. Challenge it.
And in doing so, you will carve your own light.

Trigger Warnings

Though mild in manner, this book may have some trigger warnings and content not suitable for particular audiences. Should any of the below be of concern to you, as the reader, please think cautiously about moving forward with the read. Your mental health and safety is of the utmost importance!

- Narcissistic Abuse and Emotional Manipulation
- Imprisonment & Psychological Torture
- War, Violence, & Death (including battle casualties and grief)
- Blood & Injury
- Language & Crude References
- Child Abduction (implied past events)
- Animal Abuse (Brief, not gratuitous)

If you or a loved one is suffering from narcissistic abuse, know that I see you. You are important and you are capable of freedom! Help is available! If you suspect you're experiencing narcissistic abuse, or if you've left an abusive relationship and post-separation abuse continues, call National Domestic Violence hotline at 800-799-7233

"You know that place between sleep and awake,
The place where you can still remember dreaming?
That's where I will always love you,
That's where I will be waiting."

—JM Barrie, Peter Pan

Prologue

The bed was deliciously warm as Connak's eyes fluttered open to the soft golden light filtering through the woven walls of the oasis home. Dry heat clung gently to the air, carried on by the scent of sunbaked earth and distant flowering palms. Even in the heat, life pressed in around him, green and persistent. The city of Holbeck was surrounded by looming red rock pillars, nestled in the middle of the realm of Alistile. Those pillars were guardians to the oasis, protecting the city from sandstorms and sandwraiths—a fancy word for a desert pirate.

The contrast of the earthy richness and the dry, mineral sands around him wafted through the windows of Connak's Holbeck residence as he stretched and turned to see Tavren lying next to him, her big, brown eyes encompassing him. She stirred and placed her hand on his chest. "Want me to get some sandroot stew?"

He wrapped his arm tighter around her rough skin. Scales had begun to form around her face, fresh purple hues shimmering along her hairline. He breathed in the scent of aloe and smiled. "You know I hate that stuff. Can we stay here for a while?"

Tavren hummed, her body vibrating against his.

He knew he had to leave Holbeck soon, but for now, he let her warmth sink into him, soaking through like he could carry it when he went. Tavren never minded. She understood who he was and that he had duties in his own land, preparing for a war that had stalled for twenty-three years.

She buried herself back into her pillow and hid her scales from the sun. Connak moved to follow, but something tugged at the edge of his mind. It came with familiarity, something that had been there his entire life, but he'd been able to ignore it before. Now, it scratched deeper, threading at the base of his skull all the way to the deepest parts of his mind. What once felt like a whisper pulled invasively at him, tugging him toward something he couldn't see. He clenched his fists into the sheets and tried to root himself. Tavren was right there, dammit, and Connak didn't want to frighten her. He risked a glance. Her eyes were closed as she breathed gently against the linens.

Whatever control he thought he had over his mind burned away. Connak prayed Tavren wouldn't notice as his internal wards failed and his surroundings shattered like glass as he barreled toward the call. He needed to relax. His body was tense, sending a splitting headache behind his eyes. He rolled his shoulders and pulled in a deep breath. His mind was projecting, though his body remained in Holbeck. He'd be safe, as long as he didn't stir the wrong creatures.

His consciousness flew across the desert until he found a towering stone wall protecting a gray and lifeless city. His jaw tightened, tension rising in his shoulders. He knew this city. He'd been thrust into it by his people and forced to find his own way out as a child. So much for not stirring the wrong creatures.

Now he was back and questioning why. He wondered if the King of River Storm had finally raised that army of the dead he'd been working on. He found his answer when his mind thrust forward violently through the wall and met a pair of eyes, icy blue and piercing. They were wide and slightly upturned at the corners. The ice-blue irises glowed against the contrast of her thick lashes. They were frozen fire set into glass and the only thing he could see at first. Connak startled at how close they were, like they were waiting for him. Slowly, the rest of the body appeared to reveal a woman. Very much alive.

Pity. An army of the dead might have been more fun.

Connak studied this woman. She looked sad, sitting at a table with a wine cup. Her hair curled in soft, smoky waves, fading from dark brown roots to an interwoven pale ash that shimmered like moonlight on cold metal. It fell past her shoulders, hovering over her face as she let her head hang. Her skin was sun-kissed and radiant with warm, golden tones.

Seeing her was like fitting a puzzle piece together that he didn't realize was missing. His mind jolted with sparks. He was meant to find her. Did she know he was here? Could she feel him as deeply as he could feel her? He dipped his hand into her presence, wondering if she would react. It didn't appear that she could see him yet. But she called him…why? He cleared his throat. "Hello."

Her head jolted up, and she looked around frantically before her eyes settled on his. His back stiffened, something primal flickering through him. She parted her mouth like she wanted to say something, but then her brow furrowed, and her eyes glazed over. She couldn't see him anymore, but the more he looked at her, the more he felt the faint bond that tugged at him his whole life. It gripped him so tightly now, like the roots of a tree grasping soil for life.

A hand brushed his shoulder, jolting Connak from his focus, and his mind spiraled away from the woman. His eyes acclimated back to the brightness of the harsh sun pouring into his room. Tavren sat up in bed and rubbed his back. Her touch startled him, destroyed him, because she would never understand what he saw. He only understood pieces of it himself, and only from what they told him back home.

River Storm had a way of burying things. Not just people, but memories, too. The city wrapped its cold fingers around the mind and twisted until the truth unraveled. That's what it had done to him, smothering his past so thoroughly that he hadn't even realized what he'd forgotten.

But the Eternal Mother never let go.

The goddess returned pieces of him, little by little. And now, called by the pull of that woman…it was as if the goddess threw open every door.

He remembered.

He didn't want to admit it, but he remembered her name, her place in the prophecy, and the reason they were all here. She was a ghost hiding in the seams of history. The moment he acknowledged that, he knew he had to go back for her. She was woven deeply into the tapestries of his life. The stories were clear. She would haunt him until the day that he died.

Chapter 1

—Kienna—

Kienna lit her hand with a flame that burned so hot her skin almost peeled through the protective spell around her. The power surged through her as the king fed his magic into the room, pouring it into her and Danek like a current. They were conduits to his magic, his control. Without him, there was no magic.

The frigid battle room was built of bare stone. High ceilings loomed overhead, offering more space than comfort, and a constant draft whispered through unseen cracks. The scents of iron, steel, and sweat clung to the air with the sharp tang of spent magic, as if lightning had cracked through the walls and left its ghost behind. The taste of smoke lingered as a bitter reminder of flamework recently cast. Footsteps echoed in the vast emptiness, voices too, if they dared speak. The walls were bare except for the weight of expectation etched on them. Scorch marks laced the ceiling, and old cracks spiderwebbed through the ground from past magical blasts. The room was built for fighting. For survival.

"You won't win," Danek warned, adjusting his grip on his dagger.

Kienna's lips curved with a half smirk—one she wore before she did something lethal. She was never strong with the king's magic, but this day felt different. She stared at her opponent with cool eyes, watching the dark curls on his head wave with the wind incited by her flames. Strands of her hair loosened from her braid and swept across her face.

Danek's deep green eyes studied her, sweat dripping down his light mahogany skin. A killer, the ladies called him, but not because he was dangerous on the battlefield. In fact, Danek was a healer and an apprentice to the wind, but he liked to pretend he was strong enough in these duels.

"Begin," rang King Vaerin's voice. He stood in the shadows on a narrow balcony tucked near the door, partially hidden by the winding stairs that led to it. The alcove was cloaked in darkness, but faint threads of magic pulsed from his palm as he controlled the room like a puppet master pulling strings.

Kienna and Danek bowed to their ruler before stepping around each other, waiting for the other to make a move. It would be him. She was sure of it. If he could use the wind to his advantage now, while the flame still burned deeply, he'd be able to capitalize on the magical wards around the room that were feeding them. It didn't take long for Danek to do exactly that. The wind surged and swirled the flames around her arm instead of into her palm as she intended. Though it did not physically burn her, the heat hurt, nonetheless. She didn't waver. Couldn't let him see her weaknesses yet.

Coming out on top was easy for Kienna if their battles required pure strength and strategy. But fire magic? Fire wasn't much of an offence when her opponents wielded the sun, stone, and wind. It was too easy to snuff her out. Plus, she had to be angry to summon it. Which was never a problem, but then the king would pull it from her if she misstepped. So, anger didn't get her far, and it was messing with her head. Then there was the fact that the king fed her less magic than the others. She was always fighting with scraps.

She ripped the flame off her arm and pushed it into a ball, hurling it toward him at an immense speed. The fire peeled off her skin like it had always belonged there. Power surged through her, fierce and electrifying, filling every inch of her until she could hardly breathe. She shaped it into a burning sphere and hurled it at him with everything she had. It knocked Danek off his feet. Kienna's heart raced with excitement as she prepared herself. Standing there on the edge of battle was like standing at the edge of a cliff and preparing to jump.

Danek stood as she bolted at him with speed only the divine could match, and she grabbed onto his shoulders and leapt into the air, wrapping her legs around his torso and pulling him backwards onto the ground. Kienna prepared for impact, tightening her grip and holding him by the neck. He dropped his hips low, twisting his shoulders into Kienna's body, and kicked off hard with his heels. He slid sideways beneath her grip in a tight reverse motion, shrimping backwards through the pressure. The instant her hold loosened, he turned sharply inward, shoulders rotating first and flipping their positions.

Now, Danek was above her, chest heaving and arms pinning hers against the stone. Her lips curved upward. This was her chance to show the king she could be strong and wield magic like she was supposed to. No more weakness with the gifts he bestowed. "Gotcha," she said.

A tug pulled on Danek's lips. "Pretty sure I'm the one with the upper hand."

"Sure." Kienna lit her hand again, and a ball of light, not fire, flew out and hit Danek square in the chest. He shot backwards onto the ground, and Kienna flipped herself for distance and rose to her feet. She summoned a spear. It ripped off the wall of weapons and found its way to her. It was time for Danek to meet his doom.

And he would have, but Kienna had made a mistake. The ball of light she summoned didn't come through the approved channels of magic that King Vaerin allowed. She pulled too much from the king and too fast. He only allowed her to use fire, and she found a way past his barrier of magic. She couldn't help it. It'd been building intensely inside her, and leaving it unused would have been a damn shame.

She'd pay for it, one way or another. The king was already pulling the magic away, draining her energy faster than she could hold it. He had done this since the beginning of her magical journey. When she'd finally sorted it out, he stopped her, never allowing her to be strong. Kienna knew the best step forward was to try to save face and put a flame back into the spear, but Danek was on his feet now. He conjured a spiraling wind and knocked the weapon out of her hands, stunning her into silence.

She had to think quickly, but what the hell was she supposed to do now?

Her magic, along with the protection spell on her skin, was depleting faster than usual, and there wasn't much more she could do for defense when Danek still had his power. White fire tore from Kienna's hands; a desperate, untamed flicker of emotion made into flame. As she began to panic when it grew too hard to hold onto, Danek snuffed it away. The fire sizzled into a smoky afterthought.

The vibrant blue aura of Danek's hands siphoned the power from her trembling palms, leaving her drained. Her jaw tightened. The king pulling his energy away from her this early into the battle made her skin want to explode. She crumbled to her knees, each breath a ragged gasp as searing flames of exhaustion clawed at her lungs.

They'd just started. This would be a short battle if she couldn't pull it together. Her eyes darted around the room, jerking her head to determine if she should summon another spell. It's what the king wanted—to force them into training their magic and not their skills with a blade. Kienna would have loved to do it, too, but the king only allowed her to use fire, and she grew bored of the heat.

She tried a new spell she'd read about that required incantations and not the use of elements, but Danek, too, tore that from her grasp as it was beginning to spark with life. He hurled the magic back, hitting her square in the forehead. The skin above her temple split, blood dripping. Her hands tensed against the floor of the training room. Her eyes flicked to the stone statues lining the walls that guarded the weapon racks full of enchanted blades. She should have gone for those instead of the damn spear that held no magic at all. At least those weapons would have proven more useful, but her ego got the best of her. Kienna didn't need enchantments. She should have been able to kick Danek's ass without them.

"Is that all you've learned? You're getting too predictable, Kienna." Danek kept a strategic distance around the room. His feet danced haughtily in circles, his golden green eyes piercing her every move.

Kienna glared up through the threads of her hair dripping over her face. Strands streaked in silver smoke stuck tightly to her forehead, dampened with blood. "Well, if Our King would give back what he took, I could show you predictable."

The king's eyes blazed an intense fiery red, crackling with the magic coursing through his veins. The aura infused his body and loomed over them as a reminder of how strong he was. King Vaerin's jaw tensed, the red glow highlighting a scar near his lips that he wore like a victory. Though he stood in silence, a shadow dawned in his eyes. A stab pierced Kienna's mind, a warning far too familiar as she and the king found themselves butting heads more often as of late. The warning gripped her thoughts like a vice, sharp and unrelenting, even if she felt her words were mild. But King Vaerin didn't appreciate the look she gave him or the impending insinuation that her failures were his fault—even if they were. Still, the message was clear. If she spoke like that again, she'd find herself regretting it.

The sound of her hitched breath echoed off the stone walls around her. With a shudder, she tore her gaze away from King Vaerin and forced herself to stand up. She scanned the room, searching for her spear. It lay flat on the ground ten paces away. Her head throbbed with the bleeding gash, but she refused to allow the pain to distract her. No, she would use it for her benefit. Winning was all that mattered now. She winced, allowing her hands to tremble and her breath to come in and out in uneven huffs. If she hunched over just right, she might earn a few points through psychological warfare.

Danek softened a little. She knew he would. Even if the battle was tense and King Vaerin would scold him later for it, Danek hated seeing pain. No one knew how to spot this weakness, but Kienna leached onto it and used that to her advantage as strategically as she could.

He reached out his calloused hand. "I can heal that cut for you."

Too easy. She almost pitied the sorry bastard. He cared too much, and he fell right into her trap. Kienna jumped at the opportunity. She grabbed hold of his wrist and pulled him to the ground, knocking enough wind out of him to make up some time to get to her weapon. The enchanted stone floor rippled beneath her feet with the shock of his body as he flung out magic. She needed to get the spear, graze him, and end this damn thing. Her footsteps rang sharply against the stone as she reached down to grab the weapon. It was clunky in her hands, but this gave her a slight advantage against the magical attacks when she could create a little space while striking her opponent.

Kienna stumbled, blood now dripping down over her eye. The sting alone, blurring her vision, should have made her stop. The cut pulsed like a heartbeat, and the amount of blood covering her made her pause. It was worse than she thought. Kienna tried to keep moving, one clumsy step in front of the other. She had to reorient herself before Danek decided to keep going or King Vaerin decided for them. The king didn't believe in mercy in the middle of battles, so she marched onward.

"Seriously, Kienna, I think you need a break," Danek said.

Her laugh vibrated her chest like a warning drum. She couldn't accept defeat now. This would only paint her as weak, and any sign of weakness in King Vaerin's eyes was a spell for catastrophe. She didn't want to be the catastrophe that cracked the barrier. That would lead to River Storm's collapse, and everyone inside their heavily protected realm would die. That's the mantra King Vaerin instilled inside her and the others.

"Keep fighting." Kienna summoned another crackle of energy through her hands.

She pushed out her fire, and her vision blurred. An image of Danek jumping behind her caught in her mind, then faded and shifted into something else—a woman screaming in the square. Was she having a vision? She caught herself stumbling over her own weak attack. So pathetic. Danek dodged it, and his gaze cut sideways. He was pissed.

Still panting, she twisted her body with all her might, jabbing the blunt of her spear toward Danek. The wind from the strength she pushed into the weapon shifted the dark strands of hair on his head as she almost grazed him. He smirked, rolling his eyes, and then he stepped toward her carefully. "Try again. Maybe you'll get lucky next time."

Kienna narrowed her wide eyes, the glacial blue darkening as storm-gray rings formed around her irises. She threw her spear above her head and stopped it in midair. It took everything she had to hold it up with magic. As Danek halted to watch it float, Kienna charged like a stampede, the spear spinning furiously toward him. He didn't even flinch. His shoulders dropped with a long, tired exhale. Then, Danek blasted the spear out of the air with his glowing palms. Shards of wood and metal shattered overhead.

Kienna could only stare at the exploded pieces in the stone. Running to the enchanted weapons would take too much time. Danek was merciful but not dumb. There's no way he'd let her grab one. She spent too long thinking. With an opening, Danek drove his foot into her chest. Her body caved to the ground as she heaved, desperate for air. A cough escaped from her aching lungs, bouncing off the chamber. Kienna flipped onto her knees.

Stomach turning, she held her breath, trying not to lose her lunch. Her fists slammed into the ground in front of her. The black reflection of shattered metal revealed nothing but frustration. She'd been so used to victory before magic. Even Broan, their stone-walled giant, couldn't stand up to her in hand-to-hand combat. What she lacked in strength against the big man, she made up for ten times in speed and agility. Now, she found herself continually bested, and the cold, coiled stare of their king slithered across her skin. Was this some sort of exercise to humble her?

Kienna screamed. She did everything right. Studied all the books. Put in extra time with the soldiers to better her techniques. Bowed to her king when she was supposed to bow. Kept her thoughts to herself…most of the time. How was it not enough?

The feeling of uselessness boiled in Kienna's blood. Feeling so hollow after giving everything she had made her want to explode. The fire inside her rose, ready to spill over into the world around. She was done with this.

Kienna clenched her fists and steadied her breath.

Someone was going to feel this rage she struggled to contain.

Chapter 2

—Kienna—

"Maybe next time," Danek said.

Kienna's cheeks flushed, and her jaw tensed as tightly as her fists. She raised her hand to strike Danek, pushing him to the ground. Danek tensed and then scrambled up.

"Enough! Hold your temper," King Vaerin's voice boomed from the balcony. Magical seals flared around the room in his presence, and something slammed inside of her mind. "If you must resort to cheap shots when he's already beaten you at the end, then you're already dead. The key to surviving is winning. If you can't win, you're better off dead anyway. Am I clear?"

Crystal clear, though the cheap shot still felt good. Kienna didn't dare to meet his stare; otherwise, she'd be guilty of rolling her eyes too deeply. She gritted her teeth, "Yes, sir."

She inhaled sharply. Danek offered his hand again. Though tempted to slap it away, she let him help her up. Her chest throbbed too much to resist. A boot-shaped bruise would surely mark her torso by nightfall. Wincing, Kienna nodded at Danek. "You fought alright."

"You seem distracted." He held her hand for a moment longer. More quietly, he leaned in and winked. "I can still heal those wounds later if you'd like."

"You're dreaming." She rolled her eyes and yanked her hand away.

Danek smirked but straightened, offering a courteous nod to Kienna. He then turned toward King Vaerin, bowing deeper. With a final composed glance at both, Danek pivoted gracefully on his heel and exited the room.

Kienna flicked her eyes again. Even the way he left was annoying. Of course, Danek would exit like a diplomat, as if the king's scrutiny had barely touched him. Why should it? He was the victor. His boots echoed faintly until they disappeared altogether, and the room fell silent. Her king's glare burrowed into her while shame prickled along her body. Her performance was subpar at best. The thought of disappointing him yet again only worsened her mood.

Flames brightened along the sconces, casting a warm light amongst them. Kienna glanced down, too frustrated to see the dismay cast on King Vaerin's face. She caught her reflection in a shard of metal. Smoke-brown hair with silver undertones toward the end framed her features in tousled waves that had fallen from her braid. The wounds etched around her frosted blue eyes mirrored the fatigue heavy in her bones. Bruises formed along the sharp angles of her cheekbones, each one a reminder that she wasn't enough this time.

King Vaerin walked slowly down the balcony stairs and approached Kienna. The flesh around his cheekbones pulled taut in a sneer, and the scar above his lip caught in the light as he ground his teeth together. She expected him to scold her. He should have. She deserved it. And he would have if it were any of the other Guardians, but there were times in their relationship where he softened toward her more than the others.

He never explained why, but Kienna wasn't certain she cared. Part of her enjoyed the extra perks of being a favorite, even if he had a weird way of showing it, like handing her a snack and then telling her not to get fat. But she still sensed his watchful eyes carefully guarding her at times, sneering if she did something too well.

Slowly, Vaerin's scowl softened, the magic dimming from his eyes. The red glow faded from his scar. "What disturbs you?"

Kienna wiped blood from her cheek, the burning pain sending tremors through her muscles. She would have needed stitches, but Vaerin lifted the wounds away from her body without any effort at all, leaving her skin flawless.

His magic brushing up against her carried a wrongness she could not shake, like it shouldn't be coursing through her veins, as it coaxed her flesh back together. She groaned. "You shouldn't keep healing every cut."

"You should be grateful to be touched by the magic of the gods."

He was right, of course. His magic was a gift from the divine as a keeper and protector of the living. He was gracious enough to share it with the Guardians. Plus, Kienna didn't mind the benefits of never having to hold onto the pain of her battle wounds for long, but then there was the awkwardness of Danek to tend to. And Broan's snide remarks. King Vaerin never healed *them* or spent time like this with them.

"The others notice I never scar."

"Then you should have let Danek heal you. At least then, you could keep your scars." King Vaerin flashed a hint of rage. It subsided as quickly as it came, but the sudden shift had already dampened the room.

His words rang true. She should have just been grateful and let it be. She had to toe the line around his shifting mood to avoid sending him into a wrath that could only get worse. King Vaerin turned toward the door. Kienna lingered and followed him into the hall. The king's advisor, the Warden of the Crown, stood where statues and treasures lined the corridor to honor the king's highest accolades. She liked to study them in detail on days she spent in the castle, wondering who he depicted in unfamiliar statues. She had once asked him who they were, but Vaerin often changed the subject to topics that had nothing to do with the wars he fought. She learned not to bring it up again.

The king stopped in front of the tapestries. His warden pulled him into the corner, whispering about something over the river. Kienna paid it no mind. She should have been leaving anyway, but it was her turn to stand in front of the public the next day and give a speech about River Storm's glory, something she did *not* want to do. He wouldn't let her out of it, of course, but maybe he'd get his scribes to write the speech for her. So, she waited, and while she did, her eyes fell on one of Vaerin's favorite paintings, one of her and the other elite Guardians as children, the night they were brought home from the ruins of the southern lands.

She had been found as a newborn in the remains of a tree, nearly burned. How she didn't burn to death was a miracle. All she had was a blanket around her and a branded K on her thumb. Sometimes that K pulsed fervently, an ache similar to grinding bones. Kienna brushed her fingers along the waxy texture of oil paint. The cracked varnish caught under her fingertips.

Moira, as a young child, stood beside the king as well as Broan and Danek, who were just toddlers at the time. They say Moira was found near the waters of the sea far beyond River Storm when the Great War of Liberation had just started. Danek and Broan were found in random villages beyond, all saved by the king and his army, and then placed in the orphanage to grow up. In the painting, Vaerin sat in a royal chair, flawless in posture and composed to the last detail. His dark hair draped to his shoulders, impeccably tamed and brushed straight back from his sharp, bony face. Youthful in appearance, there was something in the stillness of his features that shimmered unnaturally, like magic had smoothed over the years but couldn't quite hide the strain beneath.

In the portrait, the king wore a high-collared black tunic laced with maroon threading, and jeweled chains crossed his chest in precise symmetry, similar to what he was wearing now. He was holding Kienna proudly next to another baby, Baila. Baila was the only Guardian born inside the River Storm barrier and raised by a family of her own. Kienna, too, had a family, lucky enough to be adopted the day she came to the city, but it never shed the ache of not knowing her real parents.

"Don't you have somewhere to be?" Vaerin broke Kienna's trance.

She startled. "The others won't be at the barrier until sunset. Moira says the sun near the horizon gives her a better magical pull."

"Shouldn't you be studying the elements, then?" His long fingers tapped impatiently against a metal statue, clinking through the hallway. He wanted them to study the art of magic as if knowledge alone would make them stronger. As if mimicry could make them gods. But *he* was the god. The magic was never theirs. It was King Vaerin's. He held every thread of it, feeding it to them in careful doses like roots feeding a tree. Their power was borrowed and conditional. He never let them forget it, so studying it was a waste.

"No." Her voice cracked through the anger burning in her chest while she glued her eyes to the painting she had seen over a hundred times.

King Vaerin snapped his fingers. The hall filled with another flame, glaringly colder now. A sharp twinge pierced Kienna's head, forcing her eyes on him. Her breath caught deep in her lungs. "Then why are you still here?"

She gathered her thoughts quickly, pushing through the trembling bits of herself. "My speech, Your Grace. I haven't written it yet."

"Of course you haven't. You think I'd let you speak without my transcriptions?"

"Oh," Kienna stumbled, heat rising to her cheeks. "I thought… Moira says she writes her own speeches."

King Vaerin laughed, but not because she was funny. "Moira is graceful and gentle. You are not."

It was true, but it still made her angry. She was always angry. That's probably why he gave her fire. She was a hot head, trying to prove herself, and fire was the easiest element for her to be able to control without needing to find peace within herself to do it.

"Is that all, then?" Vaerin asked.

"Well, if you're asking—"

"I wasn't, really."

Kienna sighed, fighting internally to keep her composure and her face calm. "Okay, but if I may, why did you pull your magic away from me when I was just getting started? I should have had that fight."

Vaerin's eyes squinted, a flicker of a red streak flowing through his scar. "I'm hurt that you think I would do that."

She wanted to roll her eyes again. "If it wasn't you, then why was the magic lagging?"

Kienna knew the answer. She had endlessly heard it, but every time he said it, a blade twisted in her gut. It was her fault, he'd say. She didn't believe in herself enough to yield it the way it should be. If that were true, then maybe she wasn't cut out for this anymore and—

Wait. How did she get from blaming him to blaming herself? She shook her head and grunted, but another pinch to her temples stopped her. "I just don't know what the point of it is anymore. If I hit a wall every time I try to channel deeper into what you gave me, then why even have this power at all?"

Vaerin's jaw shifted, likely biting back a sharper reply. Silence stretched between them, only filled by the faint rustle of robes through the hall and the distant sound of torchlight crackling. His eyes didn't leave hers, but they cooled like steel settling. "Come. I'll show you, *yet again*, why we do this."

She'd already pushed her luck enough to know she better not protest, so she let him guide her through the corridor. The hall stretched ahead in solemn silence, its stone walls lining the narrow windows that let in slivers of pale, gray light. Deep maroon and burnished bronze tapestries hung heavily on the walls, their colors dulling with age. Near the end, the scent of the corridor shifted from cold stone and torch smoke to the faint trace of distant water. The archway opened widely, and they stepped out onto the terrace.

The river sparkled to the west, winding through the bustling city. The soldiers stood at the very entrance of the northern mountains, checking in ships and identifying merchants as they came and went. Only northern merchants were permitted entry under this strict surveillance. To the south lay the forbidden lands in which their very existence formed.

Kienna's eyes traced the south entrance, barricaded and blocked by a towering stone wall and metal gates to deflect any underwater attempts of entry. Magic pulsed through the stone, humming with a faint glow. Above it all, the Orb shimmered, an invisible dome of energy encasing the entire city. The wall was the barrier, immoveable and warded, but the Orb was the true shield. It stretched over River Storm like a massive sphere of woven magic, rising from the barrier itself and curving overhead, protecting them from anything that might come from the skies or beyond the South. She and the Guardians oversaw infusing and strengthening it. A tight hatred shivered down her spine.

Vaerin pointed below to people in the square, hanging banners and laughing amongst themselves. "They look to you for hope. Anyone can learn to fight, but it's the magic they need."

"How am I supposed to protect everyone down there if I can hardly use it?"

"You'll never keep up if you continue to resist your path, let alone with such ingratitude." Vaerin's words cut her with sharp precision. "Remember why I gave you all magic in the first place."

She hesitated to answer, ready to fight back, but fighting Vaerin was like going to battle in a thunderstorm with metal armor and hoping not to get struck by lightning. He was right anyway. King Vaerin held the weight of the world on his shoulders before he graced them with his magic. He'd been the one forming the barrier, building River Storm, and making sure everyone behind the wall had enough to manage their lives.

This was all to protect his realm from what lay beyond in the South. Soldiers who survived in Vaerin's War of Liberation spoke of such atrocities they'd seen from time to time: savage creatures with skin like torn leather and mouths full of too many teeth, clawing their way forward to get a taste of the power that pulsed in the king's veins. They all wanted it and would stop at nothing to get it. His magic was the only thing that kept them safe.

Kienna tensed and then softened. "My King, I know you've given me everything. Perhaps if you could filter me less, I could be what you need me to be." A savage warrior. A magical goddess. The possibilities were endless. "Right now, all I get are faint visions and scattered bits of fire that drain me before I even start. I can't be useful to you if you don't let me channel it."

King Vaerin's attention snapped to Kienna at the sound of visions, eyes twitching as he considered this. He chuckled. "Tell me, child. What is magic to you?"

She hesitated, thinking through his question. To him, magic was everything. It defined him. He held all the power through the magic coursing in his blood. To her, magic had always been a burden she had to constantly fight with him over. Kienna shook her head and shrugged. "Fire is easily bested, and visions can't knock someone down. I'm not even good at seeing visions anyway, so what good is that in a battle? It's distracting, and it pulled me from the fight with Danek today."

"What *do* you see?"

Kienna turned and stared at the wall. Jagged spires of red and gold flickered faintly in the distance. Its tiny glow shimmered against the Goldmere River like light trapped in glass—or protection in a cage. "Random things that never come true. I even saw the barrier fall once." She looked down at her boots. Specks of her blood were settling into the leather. "But I've told you this before. Then you gave Baila and Broan more power to harness strengths where you thought they might be weak, so the visions stopped. I try to see more like you ask, but it's like smoke. The more I push to see the future, the hazier it is. Then my brain hurts, so I stop."

Even now, the haze buzzed faintly against her mind like crackling electricity. Any attempt at magic deeper than the flimsy incantations always flooded her with the smoldering fire. She thought that magic shouldn't hurt that badly to use. But it did.

"Hmm," Vaerin hummed. His deep gray eyes lingered on her like a blade beneath velvet. He exhaled, taking in the tang of iron and stone. "And what of the barrier? Are you unfit for the task of sealing that, too?

"No," she said through her teeth. "I can complete my duties, Your Grace."

"Good. Speaking of the barrier, is it strong? Can you push through the haze to see it still standing now?"

"I can't see anything about it." Kienna scoffed. Had he not been listening to her? Did he not care that it hurt to try to see the future? She pushed his question away. "I imagine it'll hold. It has for all twenty-four years of my life, and I doubt anything out there can fight against how powerful *you* are."

A gleam sparkled in the king's eyes. "Perhaps. But remember, the world beyond River Storm wants us gone. We are but one section of the realm with very few allies."

The understanding that Kienna would be building that barrier for the rest of her life hit her like a fist to the gut. If she stopped, anything beyond could weaken it by tinkering.

She'd never been able to see beyond the wall, but Vaerin's deep concern still rooted itself within her. His paranoia didn't used to be this strong. It changed when someone from within River Storm's walls broke through the barrier and left for the southern lands. Probably dead by now, if the vile creatures were really out there. From then on, his fear rose every day. If someone could break out of the barrier, would getting back in be as easy—or possible? The Guardians worked tirelessly to make sure that didn't happen. It was the incident that sparked King Vaerin's justification for gifting magic to the Guardians. They tended the barrier daily so no one would ever threaten its integrity again.

King Vaerin placed his hand over Kienna's temple. Her mind pricked and then eased with the pulsing over her. The haze thickened for a moment and then cleared. Kienna blinked back, examining the king in front of her. She remembered she'd been there for a sparring match as usual, but any emotions that came with it suddenly floated away.

"Go now. You still have work to do."

Kienna lowered her head, the weight of her thoughts lifting with the gentle bend of her neck. The sky painted itself with muted hues of orange and pink as the sun dipped lower toward the horizon, casting long shadows across the ground. She stole one more glance outside, the river glistening with strange shadows. The air itself shimmered wrong, like heat rising from stone.

Old whispers used to circulate the city of cursed shadows that once lived beyond the wall. They said the West could be cursed enough to hold them, too. No one spoke of those creatures now, and Kienna was glad about it. Those people who used to share those stories were no longer around to recant them, and she'd be forced to take care of anyone else under the pretenses of treason.

Shivers crawled along her neck, and a tremor started in her hand. King Vaerin watched her carefully. Kienna dipped her head, the hitch in her breath catching along the cold stone as she turned to leave. Duty called, after all. The Guardians would already be at the barrier waiting for her, and not showing would be her own act of treason.

Chapter 3

—Danek—

River Storm reeked of burnt iron, the smell of magic covering even the faintest smells of the natural world. Danek waited outside the castle for Kienna, hoping he would be able to catch her before setting off to the barrier to pour another seal of protection into it. She was bound to be upset after their battle. Danek knew how much she hated that he and the others were stronger at magic than she was. She was the Starborn, after all. Kienna should have been stronger with a title like that, but she didn't compare magically.

He didn't quite understand why they did this day in and day

out. If King Vaerin was so strong, surely, he could do this on his own. Danek pushed his thoughts away. The surging guilt of even questioning his king tugged deeply at his heart while he searched for appreciation instead.

He grew up in the orphanage after the War of Liberation, when King Vaerin rescued children from the ruins beyond the southern border. If it weren't for the king and his strength, he probably would have died as a baby. Though the orphanage was no walk in the park, with children scarce of food and proper clothing, it was a better childhood than death. Plus, getting called to the castle as a chosen Guardian with Broan had its perks as well. For one, Danek found ways of sneaking food from the castle for a time to make sure the kids could eat. He couldn't do that anymore, though. King Vaerin had chastised him one too many times for being sneaky, and he'd been one step too close to a night in the dungeon.

Outside on the square, people walked past him. A few stopped to bow and smile at Danek. He returned the favor, but each time, his skin crawled with leechbugs—those pesky creatures that tormented merchants near the square on rainy days and would make the skin tear apart with sores.

Yeah, that's it. Praise for doing nothing was like that.

The commoners were striding to a re-enactment of the War of Liberation, a timely show a day before the celebration of River Storm's salvation. Danek glanced at the actors moving around on a makeshift stage, performing the same show they'd performed every year since he was a child.

"Oh, King Vaerin," a woman yelled as the actor handed her a doll wrapped in a blanket, a makeshift version of a baby Kienna. "I just had a baby. I can't take another."

"The orphanage only has room for three. I have four. I will entrust you with her life," declared the male actor. Danek rolled his eyes and looked away. The acting never got better, no matter how many times they did it.

The walls of buildings and merchant carts were filled with banners and signs that warned the public of everything beyond the southern lands, including pictures of demonized creatures pressed against the painted images of the magic holding them all within. It read, "Never Forget Who Destroyed the Land."

King Vaerin was the only mortal to wield magic. The gods of the world chose him as the keeper to ensure the world remained safe. This magic caused madness in the realm, and the demonic world rose to steal it, which caused the War of Liberation. Barely any survived beyond the barrier, and now the people within relied heavily on the king's magic to keep them safe. King Vaerin sealed the North from the South to cast out evil. Soldiers recounted this in Danek's history studies, talking about the unnatural ways these creatures walked and smelled like living rot with fur on their backs and scales on their belly. His military instructor, Dren, often held a faraway look in his eye when talking about those days.

Danek didn't know how much he bought into the stories of what lay beyond. He'd been in River Storm for twenty-five years, and there never appeared to be a threat. Yet, fear kept them all within the wall, ready to fight back if needed. People in the city loosened up a bit when King Vaerin chose the Guardians, creating his own magical warriors. He carved pieces of his own power and bound it to him and the others through rituals and spell work, feeding energy into their bodies like a lifeline. Without him, the magic would wither.

"True light needs no lamp," the actor playing King Vaerin declared, jabbing his sword into the depiction of a shadow-beast. In reality, it was Akin in a black sheet.

He'd seen Akin around in the orphanage growing up. He was a little boy desperate to join the armies and show the king he was worthy of being more than a runt without parents. When he couldn't pass his grueling training as a soldier, he found a purpose in the

Actors Guild instead, sharing history through story.

"Trust the Crown and the barrier, and you'll find no trouble here!"

Unless they were a Guardian. Then trouble followed for a single misstep in the training grounds or using the magic they were gifted without permission.

Red lights flickered around the actors. That part was new. Danek glanced around their little stage, searching for any hint of how they managed to pull that off. His eyes fell on Broan, surging a pulse through the ground to mimic the magic they used as a protection spell into the barrier. The crowd lit up, clapping furiously at the display.

Danek approached the towering barbarian of a man standing tall with a flicker of heat behind his blue eyes, which Danek had to look up to meet. Although a deep-rooted panic that the soldiers might report this incident to the king caught in his throat, he made no indication to Broan. "I don't know why you encourage these ridiculous shows."

"Oh, come on, Brother. This show is already depressing enough as it is. Why not add a little flair?" Broan released the magic, and the actors stepped off the stage to prepare for their next act.

Flair stepped out of the natural order of Vaerin's overly laid-out plan that he meticulously approved each detail of, even down to the costumes each actor wore. The makeshift Orb was not part of that.

Kienna hadn't left the castle yet, so Danek didn't plan on hanging around long enough to see the depiction of King Vaerin bestowing magic to the Guardians. The public's understanding of it was sweet and well-intentioned, but they'd never truly see what they had to go through every day to be competent enough to use it. Broan's free display would put him straight back in King Vaerin's crosshairs, as he usually was anyway.

"Let's go before the soldiers find out you had something to do with that."

Broan shrugged. "Whatever you say, pretty boy."

Danek grabbed hold of Broan's arm and pulled him toward the outskirts of the stronghold. He checked over his shoulder once to see the Actors Guild start up again. The stage lit up, and the crowd leaned in like they believed every word. He almost laughed. It was funny how tightly controlled the telling of history was there. How he had to keep playing the part of Guardian. A symbol meant to make people safe. So long as they didn't question the reverence owed to the king, of course.

Danek dreamed of being the one to tell history—not perform it. To write it in its most honest and unfiltered form. Someday…but not today. Today, his job was simpler. Keep Broan from doing something reckless…again.

—Baila—

Baila chewed on her nails as she walked through the rows of noble palaces. They were practically bitten to the stubs, red-edged and torn to shreds.

Next to the castle, the noble palaces were the only homes built on a grand scale. Most River Storm residents lived in smaller villages to the east of the palace, where they could tend to the farmlands. The palaces, however, housed King Vaerin's noblemen—the men who helped the king turn the war around through council when all appeared to be lost. Most men came from the northern lands beyond River Storm before its time and lived here in honor of the greatest, most powerful king that ever existed. She'd been lucky to get such a fate. Born in River Storm, unlike her peers, her noble blood bought her some grace with the king, though his constant disdain for her mistakes still ate at her.

The streets of River Storm had been swept recently, and the faint scent of soap and ash clung to the air. Everything sat neatly in its place. Stalls were locked shut in rows, each of their signs carved to the same dimensions and painted with the same shades of loyal gray and gold. Even the flowers, if they were flowers at all, were trimmed to identical lengths in planters that bore the king's crest—a serpent coiled around a ruby. Baila took a moment to examine them. Try as they may, they'd never grow much taller. The sun could barely make it through the dense clouds, let alone the magical barrier that curved over their heads. She wondered what a true, sunny day would have been like. Dren spoke of it once when she was younger, a soldier reminiscing on the world of old.

King Vaerin had caught wind, and banners went up immediately discouraging any talk of that world. It was a broken pastime left to the demons, and thinking otherwise would only create rifts through the city. Rifts would lead to weaknesses, and King Vaerin required strength to uphold the fragile system he'd put in place to protect everyone.

Baila rolled her shoulders as she crept through the streets, ignoring the hands of the peasants wanting to reach out and touch her. She often felt like King Vaerin in the old world, creatures now fighting to get in and desperate for the magic he held. People of River Storm bowed to them now, but deep down, she could tell they envied her. She had magic, and they didn't.

Her eye caught a glimpse of someone exiting the castle, a faint glimmer of King Vaerin's magic sparkling across her skin. Her eyes flicked upward at the sight of her. Kienna. Always so perfect. Always so loved. Could never do anything wrong. And when she did, King Vaerin would wipe it away. Kienna was weak. Baila knew it, and yet the king pretended like she wasn't, giving her the Starborn title and mentoring her like she would be strong one day. Baila's fists were squeezed tightly. The blood had left her pale skin nearly colorless. She had to flex her fingers a few times to ease the tension. Song broke out on the square from the Actors Guild, praising King Vaerin and praising the Guardians for their sacrifice to the city.

King Vaerin took the southern lands,
And slashed the demons out.
He gave his power to protect,
So, none would dare to doubt.
The King of River Storm is great,
A crown of flame upon his neck.
And with him come five Guardians,
To guard his light and crush the threat.

Baila cringed. The people held such high honor for her and her peers, yet they never quite captured the honor they deserved. Even if the Guardians never did anything to deserve it besides standing at a wall every day. Unless training brutally and bearing the weight of the king's chastisement was worth much to them.

She didn't imagine it was, yet the image of the Guardian's strength held enough importance for the king. So, it was enough for her. It kept enough questions at bay from his subjects. If they saw the world of the gods, they wouldn't realize that they were in chains, too. Everyone stuck to the roles that the king gave them upon birth, never allowed to step outside.

Just peasants.

Baila was sure one day she could be the true Goddess of this realm. She wasn't designed to be anything else, so that was the best ascension for her. Heavens forbid it, but if anything were to happen to the Great King, she knew she would be fit to rise in his place.

The peasants would truly bow to her then, and they would live in harmony. Those were only dreams, though. She'd never be able to create a harmonious world with lush green ivy and trees. Not without the King's magic. With that in mind, she motioned toward the barrier.

As she continued, she noticed Kienna walking near a soldier with a disgruntled woman on the streets. Whatever was about to transpire, Baila didn't dare get caught up in it, so she kept walking. After a few moments, she caught a glance over her shoulder and knew she had made the right choice.

Chapter 4

—Moira—

The sunless city only drained Moira's soul. She shifted uncomfortably at the barrier as she waited for the sunset, greedily collecting even the tiniest sliver of light. It wasn't often that it happened, but judging the formation of the clouds and the tiny openings, she knew she'd be in for a real treat.

Danek and Broan approached from behind her, bantering over who would win in a duel using only compliments. "I don't even have that many nice things to say in my vocabulary," Broan scoffed.

Danek smirked, running his hands through his dark, curly

hair. His skin was light-brown and smooth, like river clay kissed by morning sun. "Exactly! You'd run out after the first jest. I'd annihilate you."

Moira shook her head. Why did they argue about such silly things?

"Only time you would, pretty boy," Broan sneered and bumped Danek's shoulder lightly with a crooked grin.

Moira smiled. The orphanage was rough on all of them, but Danek and Broan stuck together, thick as thieves. Their mischievous upbringing carried with them now in camaraderie.

"Evenin' fellas," she said, tossing them both some bread to chew on before getting started. Though their magical energy came from Vaerin's sources, using so much in the barrier every day wore on them more than sparring physically did. Eating and drinking helped, but naturally, the only medicine for fixing a tired soul was to rest.

"We all set for tomorrow?" Broan stepped closer, lowering his voice to a whisper.

"You sure we won't run into trouble crossing the river?" Moira asked.

She didn't know why she let them talk her into it. King Vaerin persistently discouraged any type of business in the western lands. Though they were technically part of the barrier's wall, those were about as forbidden as the southern lands. He never said why. Just didn't want anyone over there.

Naturally, this only fueled Broan and Danek's curiosity further. How they even had time for curiosity was beyond Moira. With King Vaerin always watching them, putting them through intense training scenarios, and loading their schedules with classes, noble dinners, and public appearances to the point of exhaustion, they had little remaining time for any outside thinking. Though Moira did have her ways of breaking out of the routine.

"Moira, relax," Danek chuckled. "It's not every day that we get to respond to real danger. We might not get another chance until the next Quarter-Century Celebration."

Moira sighed. "Yeah, but do we need to?"

"We've been through this already, Moira. You were on board with it earlier." Danek's brows deepened.

"I know, I know. But some things have changed for me. I just…" she paused. She knew she could trust Danek, but she wasn't so sure about Broan. She held her vulnerability in her palms and squashed it. "I can't afford to go to the dungeons if we get caught."

"Pretty boy has got a diversion already planned with his trail of broken hearts," Broan teased.

Danek rubbed the nape of his neck without attempting to refute. One of his girlfriends tipped Danek off that she had heard of strange things happening over the river, and merchants indicated that it appeared threatening and insecure.

Moira shook her head and took a bite of the bread she'd brought, considering. It bore the scent of sun-dried grain and cracked seed. Its crust flaked, but the inside was soft and speckled with bits of husk. It tasted faintly of earth and smoke, which wasn't particularly delicious, but she was much hungrier than usual.

"Well," Moira said between chews. She covered her mouth to speak through the bread. "I trust you all know the stakes if we get in trouble. So, if you're sure—"

"We're sure." Broan grabbed a hunk of stone the size of a small cart and set it near the barrier wall.

Up close, the Orb of magic pulsed. To most people, the faint glowing didn't appear to the naked eye. It had been designed that way, to hide the city from the outside. Any creature traveling beyond the barrier wouldn't know a whole city stood beyond it, though Moira didn't know the true science of it. She'd never seen it from the outside. Yet, she couldn't figure out how creatures could be so terrible out there. She came from beyond the barrier as a child, and she was fairly normal. Well, normal for River Storm standards, that is.

Whatever happened during the War of Liberation and the gifting of magic to the king must have turned everyone else rabid. That's the only way Moira could make sense of why only demons lived beyond now and no humans.

"Kienna will be late. Again. Got caught in some weird display that I'm not even going to get into," Baila said as she approached.

"Good to see you, too, Baila." Moira cracked a smile in hopes of breaking through her rugged exterior. Her fiery red hair reminded Moira of the warmth of the sun. She could sense the Great Star getting closer now, her skin twitching in anticipation.

"We were in training," Danek explained, pushing Broan's boulder out of the way so they could work. "She lost again."

Broan's lips curled upward. "Who was more upset? Kienna or the king?"

"She stumbled a lot during our duel. I think this magic is hurting her, or something weird is happening. She's still struggling to use it. I don't know if she'll ever get it," explained Danek.

Moira considered this and remembered her training sessions with Kienna. She used magic at the beginning and then avoided it the rest of the time. Come to think of it, she kept using weapons. Even Moira wielded better in Vaerin's battle room, and her magic stemmed from the weather and the energy of the sun. Nothing that could be pulled easily in a room of stone.

"Do we even know what elements she draws magic from?" Baila crossed her arms.

Moira shrugged. "Fire sometimes. But where would you draw from to see the future?"

Broan scoffed. "It's not the future if whatever she sees doesn't happen."

"Hmm," Moira hummed. Kienna used to share her vision with

the Guardians, but since she struggled with magic and they didn't, she'd grown closed off and didn't seem to care as much about the friendships they had formed over the years. They started their journey with magic nearly ten years ago, dabbling in small versions of incantations and barrier work. Only within the last year did the king start feeding them stronger power. Within that year, Kienna was named the Starborn, a weird choice by the king when she was the weakest mage of them all. They all thought it would have been Baila. Since then, Kienna closed herself off. "Why doesn't she ask Vaerin to take it away?"

"It's a gift," Baila reminded them. "One she should take with honor."

Danek tensed. "Not if it's hurting her."

Baila rolled her eyes, pushing his presence to the side, but then glanced softly back at him as she grabbed onto a strand of hair. Curling it between her fingers, she said, "Relax, I'm sure that's why they spend so much one-on-one time together. He's probably helping her."

A grin returned to Broan's face. "I'm sure that's exactly what they're doing." He added a crude gesture with his hands, enough to make Danek sigh and look away.

Moira scoffed at the thought. She didn't like the idea that magic would hurt anyone. Like Baila said, it was an incredible gift that coursed through her body. Feeling the power of the sun was like that: raw, ultimate beauty that could light the world with one single ray. Moira was grateful for her magic. She thought all of them were, regardless of their differences.

They all had varying powers tied to distinct elements of the world. Danek wielded the most abilities out of all of them, and he used them softly with great reverence. He was gentle in that way. Moira looked back at Broan, who was not soft. King Vaerin gave him power over the stones beneath their feet. The earth. He could wield and bend them to his will, and he did so brutally, but also masterfully. Then there was Baila. Moira tried not to let the distaste she felt mirror on her face. Baila commanded nature. She had the power to grow a tree without any sunlight, commanding the ecosystems that went along with it. The city needed Moira and Baila for the crops, as the city so often went without the true sun.

King Vaerin didn't explain why he chose those elements for them aside from the fact that they fed their personalities and where they would thrive. Moira agreed wholeheartedly with her power of the sun. She would need it with the journey she was about to embark on. Soaking up the rays, she brushed her fingers along her stomach and smiled. The bright light coursed through her and gave her warmth in the darkness of the city, but the impending doom of her own unspoken mistakes loomed over her.

She glanced around uncomfortably and dropped her hands to her side.

Chapter 5

—Kienna—

Banners fluttered in the windless silence, an attempt to liven up the muted city for the upcoming celebration—those banners, having once read "Hold the Power. Trust the Power," now bore painted scenes of River Storm and people dancing.

Kienna sighed. No one danced in River Storm.

Aside from the guild's noise in the square, there was no time for joy. Every citizen was assigned a role once they came of age. Children who once ran the streets would soon muck stalls and chase orders until new ones replaced them. Everything under Vaerin's rule moved in cycles. Kienna wouldn't be part of that future. Guardians weren't allowed romance, let alone children. Vaerin's rules ensured their focus.

Already late to the barrier, Kienna pulled up her hood and turned from the castle. Better not to stop for the praying hands, worshiped like Vaerin himself. She bolted past the familiar troupe of street performers but stopped when she saw a soldier approach the opening between the Atelier, River Storm's premier fashion house, and the Gilded Quil, a shop devoted to all things written.

A woman dressed in worn-out silks from the northern lands with fake jewels adorning her hair stepped out of the boutique with a sign in her hand that read "The throne was built on our graves." She tried her best to look the part of nobility, but the deep wrinkles under her eyes said she was tired beyond her years, and her sunken cheeks indicated she ate in rations like everyone else.

Kienna tensed. Her peers would probably say something about her tardiness, but she already sensed the tension around her growing. The woman held a fire in her eyes that only indicated something terrible was about to happen. The soldiers knew it, too, as more appeared outside the Atelier. Attention floated over to them from the square, but the woman only swiped at them with her picket, yelling, "You can't cover this up. My boy is missin', and something tells me your king knows where he is."

More armored suits began to appear from their patrols around each alley, pushing back the common folk in the square. Kienna stepped forward, trying to hear, but the woman's eyes fell on her, and she immediately jutted her sign at her. "You know, don't you?"

"Me?" Kienna pointed a finger at her own chest, already feeling dumb. Of course, the woman meant her. Her eyes were burning straight into her. "Who's your boy? Maybe we can help find him?"

The woman's jaw set. "You bitch. He was last seen with *you* nine days ago."

She had to think. She could barely remember nine days ago, but an image of a boy no more than fourteen, drawing on a stone wall, came to mind. What he was drawing, she couldn't remember either, but it was her duty at the time to stop him. If she'd been called to take him, it meant someone had to be there to calm the public after. As a Guardian, it was *her* duty. Why couldn't she remember this fully? Oh god, did she get the boy killed? She found herself wishing she'd kept going to the barrier now.

King Vaerin's army general, Dren, firmly placed his armored hand on Kienna's shoulder, his face shrouded with cold command. "Duty calls, Starborn. She's riling up the city against the crown. You can't overlook sedition."

Kienna jolted her head to Dren. Named the "Starborn," Kienna stood as the face of the Guardians, not quite as their leader, but as the propaganda of peace. She held the flame that ignited the rest, and with that came her duties of upholding Vaerin's image, escorting people who broke the rules to the castle for punishments, and, of course, public executions if necessary.

They had never been necessary until now. This was the first time she had to step up against sedition. It was such a rare occurrence in River Storm that a public execution would disturb them all, the opposite of peace. King Vaerin had his ways around that, of course. The woman's fate was etched in law now, and she wouldn't be able to get out of it. Kienna wasn't ready. With Dren guiding her forward, she didn't appear to have a choice.

"What did you do with my son?" The woman kept swiping at her. Kienna tried to remain calm, but Dren kept pushing her toward the woman, who was now swinging her sign into the air. "Stay back! This city is lying to us. They're—"

Kienna couldn't hear her screaming above the sound of her heart beating furiously in her ears. It drowned everything out—Dren, the crowd, the woman's voice. There was only the pulsing thump, faster and louder, until it felt like it was in her throat. She forced herself to steady her hands. Any sign of the trembling inside of her would only spark a riot. The people couldn't see that she feared this or disagreed in any way. Even if she was sorry, the woman couldn't see it either.

And the lack of emotion only enraged the woman further. She spat in Kienna's face. It was almost enough to make Kienna eager for what was about to occur, but the weight of it all still held her down. How'd this happen? She was heading for the barrier when this broke out. Was the woman waiting for her? Probably, and now her blood would be on Kienna's hands.

Gasps rippled through the crowd like wind through dry leaves as Kienna ripped the sign from the woman's hand and reached out to grab her. Kienna's magic surged back into her body, unstable and angry. A flame coursed from her hand and onto the woman, burning her arm where she touched. The woman screamed a raw, primal yell, and the stench of charred skin curled into the air. Kienna's stomach turned. The smell was acrid and thick. Human. The scorched flesh bubbled under her hand. If she let her fear radiate, she'd risk incinerating the woman completely, and she had only wanted to send a message for her to stop.

Soldiers apprehended the woman and escorted her into the middle of the square, pushing aside the Actors Guild as if they were nothing more than props. Her feet skidded across the cobblestones, the scorched arm trailing smoke. She pleaded, yelled, and spat angry words that Kienna still couldn't hear. Kienna followed, her legs slow and disconnected from her body.

How on earth was she meant to explain this to the crowd after?

Dren handed her his sword. She stared at it and then at the woman as the soldiers pushed her down and bound her hands behind her back. She was crying now. This all felt like an overreaction to a woman grieving her son, who was probably right about him being missing.

Something was wrong in River Storm, and now the public would see it.

Kienna's breath wavered. Her fingers wouldn't close around the hilt. Her vision flickered. The crowd blurred, then sharpened, then blurred again. The people in front of her dropped to the ground. Then they were standing again. She blinked. She needed to steady her heart rate or her flames would explode.

Dren stared at her for a long time, his jaw tightening. When she couldn't take the sword, he said, "Don't you fucking look away."

He swung.

The sword came down in one brutal arc and severed the woman's head from her body. It hit the stone with a wet sound and rolled across the stage with the mouth still half-open and the eyes wide in shock. Blood spurted from the open neck, spraying across the stage and splattering hot across Kienna's chest and face. She didn't move as it hit her in droplets and streaks, sinking into her clothes.

The crowd was silent. Soldiers moved fast, scooping up the head like debris and carrying it away. They'd be up all night scrubbing the blood off the streets to wipe away her memory, but it would cling to Kienna's hands no matter how hard she tried to wash.

The bile stopped in her throat. She couldn't swallow it.

And then her mind spun.

River Storm was on fire. People were dead. She was walking through a scorched village, her adopted mother lying on the ground with her head chopped clean off, eyes glassy and unblinking. She reeled forward. Moira. Danek. Broan. Baila. All of them. Headless.

She couldn't breathe. The heat built behind her eyes as her mind returned to what lay in front of her. The body at her feet, its blood already pooling toward her boots. She didn't want to be here, but Dren continued to look at her. Kienna had responsibilities. King Vaerin was watching, as he always was, from the top of his terrace. She was designed for this, to keep the people peaceful when the king could not.

Tears stained the faces staring back at her. Everyone curled into one another to hide the ghastly scene in front of them. Kienna closed her eyes for a moment and took a deep breath, allowing her body to shine slightly with fire. Through a trembling voice, she said, "May King Vaerin bring peace to her soul…uh…and may this unfortunate incident remind us that our King…"

"Is gracious," Dren whispered.

"Our King is gracious. This woman took our peace from us… but we should…uh…"

"Rejoice." Dren's voice grew impatient.

Kienna wanted to pass out. She couldn't do this. "We should rejoice in the glories of our mighty King. Our King will provide you all with fresh lamb stew tonight in thanks for your bravery. Please, take his gift, and enjoy your evening. Everyone is relieved from their duties and will be graced with this extra hour for their own free time."

She let go of the fire and turned away immediately, ready for her night to be done. She took solace knowing the way they remembered this day would be muted after they received the king's gifts to them. Not quite forgotten, but a shimmering appreciation for why it happened.

Her eyes landed on a painted mural alongside the cobblestones of the Guardians with halos of light standing between civilians and shadowy monsters. The caption below read "Their lives guard yours."

Kienna tried her best to smile.

Chapter 6

–Kienna–

Kienna wiped her face clean of the tears and the splattered blood before approaching the barrier on the outskirts of the city. Twisting images of the head falling onto the street replayed in her mind in a loop. She had to fight not to vomit all over herself. Her hands were already trembling with the unsteady paces of her breath. More visions flashed in her mind. Bodies were burning around her, making her stomach knot further. She had to pull her shit together now, or it would alarm the others. King Vaerin hated distractions. She intended not to be one, but they'd see the blood on her shirt. She swiped frantically at it, pulling it in ways she thought would hide the deep crimson splattered on the light brown tunic. She saw these visions before. Why did they affect her so much now?

The rest of the Guardians were already hard at work sealing the barrier. From a distance, it was nothing more than a stretch of stone, a modest, towering wall that was old and weather-worn, half swallowed by the gray horizon. But the closer she got, the more the illusion unraveled, revealing itself as a monolith, stretching endlessly upward until it vanished into the clouds.

Magic shimmered like electricity across the surface, warping the air in a rhythmic pulse that beat like a second heart. Without magic to see, it mirrored the world around it, reflecting sky and stone until it looked like nothing was there at all. But through the power of Vaerin, the Guardians could see the truth behind it: an orb-like field of color-shifting light, rippling over the stone in waves of pressure and sound. It vibrated like thunder.

The skyline loomed in the distance, shrouded in the early evening mist, while the Guardians diligently wove an additional layer of shimmering magic into the barrier. Colors of green sparked from the grass as Baila pulled the energy from it. The green shimmered across her hair, turning the copper strands to molten bronze. The glow caught on her pale skin, giving her freckles that looked like scattered moss. Her eyes, already sharp and emerald, glinted like glass. She wove the magic into the barrier like roots taking hold. These roots spiraled upward into the sky, threading deep into the wall around them. The glow dissipated from her body, and her freckles shifted back to specks of brown.

Danek placed his blue aura over Baila's, sealing the roots in place. As they did this, Kienna hoped to slip past them. Her cloak billowed in the wind behind her as the air crackled tightly, sharp in anticipation, before lightning struck. She wanted to be struck by lightning at that moment.

Moira stood beyond the shade of the great stone wall where the pulsing magic hummed against the earth. She basked in the rays of the setting sun, its final light spilling like honey across the gloom. Sunlight kissed her skin, shining a soft gold along the smooth, warm brown of her arms. She seemed to hold the glow within her. Pale orange shimmered from her palms, reflecting the very sky she drew it from. Her ringlets caught the fading light in delicate halos, and her deep brown eyes held its warmth.

As the magic flowed into the barrier, the Orb illuminated with a deep saffron fire, shooting upward and flowing over all of River Storm. Briefly, specks of sunlight kissed the city, a blessing to the farmers who grew their crops in gray. When Kienna passed, Moira gave a weak smile and nod of her head, black ringlets falling out of place over her face.

"Nice of you to fucking join us, princess," Broan scolded, his voice dripping with sarcasm as he loomed over them all. His broad shoulders created a shadow that stretched across the entire group, emphasizing the weight of his disapproval.

"Stop calling me that," Kienna growled.

"When I die."

Heaving his broad chest inward, Broan raised his arms high. With all his strength, he slammed his oversized fists into the ground, sending a tremor through the earth beneath their feet. The land quaked in answer. He dug deep, drawing power from the aftershock. Swiftly turning back to the magical Orb, he hurled the gathered force forward, finishing Baila's roots with stone.

It was too messy, the way he worked. Kienna would have preferred a more elegant manner of drawing from the dirt, but she didn't get to bend the earth, so she figured Broan could do whatever he wanted.

"Is the spectacle necessary?" Danek sighed, passing his magic over the ruined field to heal the devastation of Broan's showmanship.

Small remnants of cracked earth clung to the dirt like jagged scars.

"Where's the fun in that?" Broan spat, continuing to wield his power to protect River Storm. Nearly seven feet of brute strength, Broan looked carved from some frozen northern stone—light-skinned but aged with rugged color that hinted at years under sun and snow alike. Stubble shadowed his jaw in uneven patches, like a beard still trying to decide if it belonged. His pale blue eyes flashed with defiance. His cropped sides bristled with sweat and grit, the short fade catching the glow of his contained magic, while the longer strands tied back in a warrior's knot burned like tarnished copper in the light.

Kienna unclasped her cloak and reached for a water canteen that Moira had brought for everyone. When no one was looking, she tried to dump the water over herself to rid the blood staining her clothes. Then she turned to the barrier and stared into specks of dust floating around inside. She tried to keep her heart from bursting out of her chest, the blood still dripping down her pants. The others hadn't noticed yet. For that, she was thankful.

As soon as Broan finished his show, Kienna went right to work, zooming her vision in and out to identify any breach that would have been left from their seals. Small pockets of air formed within the magical barrier, floating around like a ball bouncing through water. She took a breath and pulled deep within herself, straining to bring anything to the surface. Focusing her mind away from the blood on her hands proved to be a difficult feat as her muscles tensed, and only a faint glimmer rose through her hands. She burned the motes inside the barrier away as quickly as she could, a trembling pain surging in her bones. It was as if the king refused to return the magic to her fully, even in her need for duty. He fed her more when she was younger. It lasted all but a day, and then he told her she was too defiant. She didn't think so, but she kept pushing through anyway.

Each Guardian went through their motions time and time again. It was like shaping a clay vessel by hand. Baila formed the structure, coaxing branches through the barrier like the pot's frame. Broan pulled the clay from the earth, giving it weight. Moira warmed it with sunlight, softening it to be shaped. Kienna ignited and sealed it with fire while Danek brought the wind to cool it, setting the magic in place.

Beads of sweat dripped down her forehead. She'd been working on her third round of pulling magic, struggling to keep her focus. Baila stepped up and closed her section. Her eyes glared idly at her. "Work a little faster so we can get out of here, would you?" She paused and looked at Kienna in closer detail, but she didn't say anything.

"Work faster," Kienna mocked under her breath as her cheeks warmed.

"I heard that," Baila said as she walked away.

Kienna huffed. "This fucking wall can kick rocks."

She stared into the bubbles forming around the Orb as Baila surged a set of vines into another section of the wall. The scent of iron on Kienna's clothes and the memory of burning flesh disoriented her. Kienna caught herself staring into the bubbles blankly for too long as they pulsed with shadows. For a moment, at the edge of her mind, she thought she could see flickers of fire, trees, and strange faces she almost recognized.

Probably tricks of light or her trauma playing to the tune of her exhaustion. Kienna didn't wait to find out as Baila's voice rang in her head, so she zapped them shut as best she could and moved on.

"Kienna, you want some bread?" Danek called.

She turned to face them, and Moira's face dropped. She reached over and smacked Danek's arm. "Did you make her bleed that badly in your training?"

"Of course not!" Danek scrunched his body to avoid another blow from Moira.

Kienna glanced down, too afraid to see herself. Her pants were drenched at the bottom with streaks of dark maroon blood covering her boots. She had tried to pour enough water over them, but it wasn't enough to hide the evidence. Her hands started to tremble.

"It was a public execution," Baila said. She looked at her nails, picking at them for dirt. Her eyes didn't move, as if the words barely phased her.

"Whose?" Broan asked.

Kienna's jaw went tight as heat built up behind her eyes. "I'd rather not talk about it."

"Did *you* do it?" Moira asked, stepping closer to Kienna. She went to grab hold of her, to hug her, or to hold her steady, but Kienna only pulled back.

"I said I don't want to talk about it. So, move on. I'm going to get water."

She went to the river to fill her canteen, hating how they looked at her. She couldn't tell if they were disappointed that she wouldn't tell them about it or the fact that she was involved in it to begin with. This was the first execution in their history of Guardianship. Of course, they wanted to know all about it, but they'd never grasp the weight of what it was truly like. They'd never have to experience how it pulled her down with such an immense force that she could barely breathe.

Kienna sighed and stared across the water, narrowing her eyes until the distance drew closer, sharpening into view. When the miles of distance came into focus, she noticed the grass first. It grew bright green for a few steps before it faded into a dull brown. It never changed, no matter how often she looked. Beyond the shifting grass, the land remained distant and unreachable. She could never see any further.

No one ever crossed to the far side of the river. Only merchants from the northern lands came close, riding in by ship. But they stayed near the docks and never set foot past them. There was no need. The king sealed it on his own, presumably with the stars, and the land across was dead and forgotten, its purpose long gone. To reclaim it would be a waste. "Hey!" Broan yelled, tossing the boulder Kienna had been using for rest to get her attention. "We know you're King Vaerin's favorite, but you still have duties like the rest of us!"

Kienna bounced back as the boulder spun past her face and into the river. Water surged against her, seeping into her close-fitted leathers and thick wool before she was able to dodge out of the way. Her tunic and pants clung to her like a second skin, wet and heavy. At least the blood flowed away, but it didn't stop the heat rising inside her.

"Are you fucking kidding me right now?" Her heart pounded, fists clenching deep into her palms. Her whole body tensed. As the sun began its further descent beyond the ground, the chill of night sent a deep shiver through her bones, but the boiling rage that overcame sent the cold away. "You insufferable ass!" Kienna leapt up from the riverbank with fury smoldering in her eyes.

Power ignited within her veins, propelling her through the air with a force that could rival a thunderstorm. Not fire. She landed in Broan's path with an earth-shattering thud, her presence as formidable and daunting as her adversary's. Her body blazed with a blinding white energy that crackled like lightning across her skin. With a furious grip, she seized Broan's shirt, twisting until a button snapped off.

And then it was gone.

The power ripped out of her as fast as it came, and her legs buckled. She hit the ground hard, lightning vanishing from her veins. She didn't hear Danek shout her name. Didn't feel the earth tilt beneath her. Didn't see the K on her thumb burning into her skin.

The world went black.

Chapter 7

—Kienna—

Kienna's mind traveled across the barrier, slipping through the cracks as if the magical pulses were nothing to her. Leaving her body felt strange, but she'd be back. She wasn't dead; she was projecting.

It was a familiar feeling, not one she had a lot of practice with, but she could tell she'd done it before by how easy it was. As soon as she crossed, she found herself back with her body. That couldn't be real. Her real body would have never survived the electrical surge. It would have disintegrated her the moment she fell into it.

She scanned the forest. Large pines towered over her, flourishing with the open air and lack of magic harboring the light. Was this right outside where they stood? Or did she make this up? Could it be a vision? She wished she knew for certain what was happening, but thoughts left her mind when a man appeared right in front of her.

She locked onto his eyes. His gaze, deep green and unblinking, startled her. His head tilted with a smile as if he'd spotted an old friend. He wore no armor, only a thin tunic of scales. The hide of a wolf crowned him; its head fitted over his own like camouflage.

"Are you okay?" the man asked.

Kienna hesitated to answer. The K on her thumb tingled with a gravitational force, pulling her toward him. She knew him. A deep-rooted connection told her not to be afraid.

"I think so," she answered, her voice an ethereal version of itself. She gasped at the sound. Was this man a god? Is that why being here was so surreal? "Did I die?"

He laughed. "No. You pulled your own magic today. It depleted you faster than you're used to."

She studied him. There was a familiarity to the sound of her *own* magic, like she'd been told this before. She creased her forehead. The man never stepped out of the trees, but his face held a warmth that told her to wait.

"Do you feel the memories coming back?" he asked.

Kienna's body tightened around her mind, a flood of images surging through her. Memories of her sparring lesson with Danek returned, reminding her of how she pulled magic outside of fire before the king could catch her. There were images of King Vaerin slapping her across the face over the years and then healing her, only to wipe the memory every time he did. Then she saw the boy, the one she escorted away days ago. He was dead now. He never stood a chance the moment Kienna handed him over to King Vaerin for questioning. Another mistake she would have to mourn later. Sparks of another boy flashed into her mind, one who escaped before the king could get to him years ago, disappearing through the barrier she sealed every day. Kienna's eyes widened. She wasn't surprised the king siphoned her memories, only hurt that he would. "I can give you more back later," he whispered. "Your friends are calling."

She let her divine form slip back through the barrier and settle into familiar skin. Her bones ached from the shift, but her mind was clear now. She remembered more than she should have…more than the king wanted her to. And that changed everything. She knew his weakness. His softness.

Though he terrified her, he wouldn't hurt her. She couldn't figure out why, but her memories indicated as much as they slowly flowed back in. They were never fully complete, but they did tell her one thing: If he wasn't going to kill her, she would use every breath she had to reach beyond the barrier and keep building toward something new.

She woke up to Broan dumping water on her face. Not the smartest move after she had about annihilated him. Kienna chose not to mention it now, realizing he was only trying to help a frantic Moira calm down and get her back awake.

No one understood magical burnout. Vaerin gave them all enough energy to perform their duties, but no one else could tap into anything other than exactly what the king gave them. Kienna understood it well enough now with the memories coming back, but they didn't know that either, and her passing out must have been a huge shock. All they could see was another moment of failure, a struggle to grasp the weak strings of magic. They all saw her as feeble, despite her physical abilities. They'd never know her. What she could do. What she *just* did.

"What was that?" Danek asked, kneeling beside her with concern etched in his brow.

Kienna studied all of them. They lived in oblivion as she had. To think their world was anything but a lie. She couldn't bring them into it. She refused to put their lives in her hands if she fucked up. She shook her head. "It's nothing you need to worry about. It's Starborn stuff."

"We can talk about it, Kienna," Moira sat next to her on the ground. "You don't need to bear all these tragedies on your own."

"I'm not ready to share," she said, but not as shaken as she was before. Seeing the man outside the barrier grounded her. Kienna was still trying to make sense of who he was and why he could ground her. It would take a few days for her memories to stitch themselves back together in full pictures, assuming the king didn't siphon them again. Until she knew more, she figured she'd hold that secret. They wouldn't get their memories back, so telling them anything would put them on a path of treason. Kienna desperately wanted to keep their heads on their shoulders. "I'm sure I'll process it later and then we can gab about it."

"Not gab." Moira looked almost hurt. "Do I gab?"

"You do like gossip," Danek rubbed the nape of his neck.

"Well, at least I'm not a snob about it."

"Hey!" Baila scolded.

Moira stood up, rubbing the dirt off her pants. She reached out her hands to Kienna and helped her up. She glanced at Baila. "If you got offended by that, that's your problem. I wasn't talking about anyone. I was defending the fact that my inclination for gossip is my intent of care."

Kienna's wet clothes clung to her. A chill sank into her bones, making her shiver. Lucky to be awake right now, she knew she would struggle to finish the day. And she still had one more section of fire to flow into the barrier, meaning Danek couldn't finish either.

"Okay," Moira chirped, her voice ringing out like birdsong in a poorly timed attempt to ease the tension. "Don't forget we have Vaerin's dinner tonight at the castle." She paused. "Also…you're coming with us tomorrow, right?"

"You mean the celebration? We are all required to be there, so yes." Kienna searched her new memories to see if she had made plans outside of that with them. She doubted she would have. She rarely made plans with them anymore. Any time she had to herself now was given to the divine outside the barrier, doing memory work. It was easier being alone than it was having to lead them through it all. It would be too confusing for them, and they wouldn't understand anyway. Baila and Broan already looked at her with such disdain, and Moira and Danek with pity. Kienna only found misunderstanding, so she put an invisible wall between them.

Moira scratched her head. "Oh, I thought Danek was going to tell you—"

Broan grumbled. "What are you doing? The fated Starborn will tell King Vaerin. Then she'll ruin all the fun."

Baila snickered behind him as she ripped at some bread. "Must be nice to be his favorite."

"Like a toy." Broan roared with laughter, and Baila followed suit. Danek and Moira shared a glance and then took a step toward Kienna, one that she met with a backward step away.

Her cheeks warmed again. They thought so little of her since becoming the Starborn, and she only wanted to keep them safe. Being the favorite wasn't all treats and backhanded compliments. None of them had to suffer the fate of sending someone to a bloody death simply because it was her job. This was why she couldn't bear to be around them. They never understood.

"She needs to come with us. Her *and* Baila." Moira's hands drifted to her side as she winced, a motion that only Kienna noticed.

Even basking in the sun earlier, Moira hadn't quite been herself lately. Regardless, she continued, "We're a team, and we need to do these things together."

She was mothering the group again, probably too used to having to do so with Danek and Broan in the orphanage. Kienna usually hated it, but it did have moments that helped pull her back from the outside.

Broan snickered, a mischievous glint flashing in his eyes, but after exchanging a series of pointed glances with his companions, he slumped his head back and groaned, like a child being forced to share.

"Where exactly are you going?" Curiosity got the best of her, even though Kienna was certain she shouldn't go.

Danek glanced around his shoulder. "We are going to the west side over the river."

Oh, they were stupid. Kienna tensed. "That's forbidden."

"Told you!" Broan stated, lips curling.

Danek held his hand to Broan. "Yes," he said to Kienna, blinking slowly. He filled his cheeks with air, blowing outward. "But Aine thinks she heard some soldiers talking about some threat over there."

And they trusted Aine now? Aine was a noble girl, like Baila. She and Baila were good friends, and the poor girl had eyes for Danek, like half the other girls in the city, including Baila, if her own observations held true.

"Why not tell King Vaerin?"

"I don't know, Kienna." Danek flopped his arms to his side. "This could be our chance to do something besides stare at a barrier all day. And if nothing is over there, then we can be somewhere quiet for once, away from all…this."

"Aren't you curious about what's over there?" Moira asked.

"Curiosity and stupidity are two different things," Kienna responded. It'd be stupid for her to continue to entertain this conversation. Heads rolling around her feet perked her vision, a future she hoped wouldn't come true. A slight twitch in her hands caught against her side.

"But you are curious, right?" Danek inched closer.

Kienna's cheeks flushed. She needed to shut it down. Yet she found the words fumbling out of her mouth. "What exactly do you think you're going to find over there?"

"Adventure." Broan crossed his arms, packing up his stuff to leave.

Danek rolled his eyes. "I'm hoping to find out."

"You know, I used to see the barrier falling in visions and found myself wondering what was over there or thinking I'd find adventure or something different. But that's my *curiosity*. If I crossed it, that would be *stupidity*. See the difference?"

Danek coughed while sipping water from his canteen. "I had no idea."

"About my vision?"

"That you thought about what was over the wall."

Kienna shrugged, looking at the rest of the group. "You don't?"

Broan stepped too close, his towering body making her head tilt upward. "Of course we do. But you're Vaerin's fucking puppet."

She sneered at him, but Moira stepped in between them and inched Broan away slowly. Baila crossed her arms, studying them.

"What Broan meant to say is that we had no idea you thought that," Danek said.

Kienna's eyes cut away. "No one does. We're not that close."

Danek blinked, a flicker of hurt crossing his face from Kienna's harsh words. It's not that she didn't want to be their friend. She was tired of worrying about everyone dying, and she couldn't allow herself to care.

She opened her mouth to say something to soften the blow, but Baila's voice cut in before she could. "What about King Vaerin?"

Kienna mustered a laugh, turning back to the barrier. She searched deep within herself to pull any form of magic at all so she could get out of there already, but the energy within her continued to drain. Her chest tightened. It was like the very bubble she had been trying to seal had wrapped around her instead, isolating her from the others. "I don't intend on betraying King Vaerin, if that's what you're asking." It was a lie, but one she had to tell for their sakes.

"Let me help you finish." Danek lit his fingers with blue static.

"No," Kienna scolded. It was her own damn fault that she was so alone, pushing them away like she did. If being alone meant stopping her faint vision of their heads at her feet, she'd do it. Every single time.

Baila kept pushing. "So, what has you thinking of what's beyond if you don't intend on betraying our King? We already know what's out there."

"Baila," Danek said, gently placing his hand on Baila's shoulder. "Let her be. I think we've done enough bantering today, and none of us understands what goes on in Kienna's world."

Kienna met his eyes. She couldn't quite place his statement as pity, and she hated the warmth that flooded her through it. He stood up for her. Would Danek be able to stand with her? Would any of them? She wasn't sure, but she could test the waters to see where they stood, and she wouldn't have to be alone, after all. Her mind flashed to one of the memories slowly stitching itself back together of the boy who escaped River Storm years ago. Before getting her memory back, she knew the incident existed. It was something the king wanted them to remember in some way. It was the birth of the Guardians, their very existence as the king's warriors. King Vaerin wanted them to remember the wrath that consumed the city with his god-like power. Whatever happened to this kid, she needed to see how *they* remembered it. If she could trust them with more.

Kienna steadied herself. "Do you remember that M'Ran kid?"

"The traitor who almost destroyed the barrier, trying to escape River Storm?" Broan kicked the dirt. Not a good start, but the wheels were already turning.

"He did escape," Moira said. "Kienna and I saw him."

Kienna couldn't confirm or deny this account from Moira. Her divine intervener never restored that part in full. Vivid images danced around in her mind of that night, yet she struggled to remember if *she* saw him or if it came to her in a vision. Still, the experience cracked something open in her chest. There was a reason the man beyond the barrier wanted her to have these memories, even if parts remained unseen in her mind.

"What happened to him?" Danek's eyes widened, shifting around quickly. "Do you ever see him in your visions?"

"You know I can't project that well," Kienna lied once more, digging her boot into the ground. She never did see the boy again, but her projections beyond the barrier told her enough about the M'Ran kid. "Sometimes I play it out in my head on what might have happened to him. It's a gut feeling, but I think he made it out all right. And sometimes it has me wondering…maybe there's more out there."

An uneasy silence overcame them, everyone working to comprehend what Kienna said. Kienna herself reeled from the revelation. Her memories came in thickly now, visions of whole worlds beyond River Storm. And she told them about it. She couldn't believe she said it, exhaustion playing on her mind now. They all looked at her with varying expressions of confusion. King Vaerin's Starborn was now speaking about what was beyond River Storm. The words would rain down punishment for years to come, and she kicked herself internally for saying anything at all. So much for keeping their heads off the ground. She was way too tired to be talking about anything of the sort.

Baila stepped forward, her fiery red hair catching in the sun and fuming with the steam of her fury. "So, you're too high and mighty, judging them for wanting to explore across the river, yet here you are thinking about what's beyond the barrier?"

"Hold your tongue," Danek scolded quietly, combing through their surroundings to ensure they were alone. "No one is talking about beyond the wall. We know our limits. But we still need to see what's over there."

Kienna sighed. She couldn't understand why it mattered so much. She needed to steer them back to solid ground. It was a mistake to trust them with any of this. "Listen, we owe King Vaerin everything, and this city depends on us to set the example. If we start crossing rivers because Aine said some shit about a threat, then other people will start crossing rivers. And where do you think that leads us?"

Dead. With their heads on the ground. She couldn't get the image out of her mind. She'd need a bath, or twenty, to forget. "All I'm saying is you should rethink this plan," she pleaded.

They all shared glances. Kienna turned her back to them, searching from within to reignite the spark and finish off the barrier. The flame continued to light and then faded from her palm, like scratching rocks against each other in hopes of finding heat.

She was trying to decipher if she couldn't muster the energy or if she didn't want to. Thoughts bounced across her mind. What if the barrier did fall? Would she care?

Kienna picked up a small rock next to her boots and tossed it into the Orb. The raw energy scorched the stone in one breath. With her lungs rattling, she focused heavily on the magical current swarming around. Her eyes welled with tears. She had to be everything for them, and they didn't even realize it.

The Starborn.

Shocked by the sudden swell of emotion, she quickly wiped the moisture from her cheeks and fixated on the stone built tall above her head, encompassed by years of magic.

Danek's hand settled on her shoulder, steady and warm, his green eyes locking onto hers. Green like the man beyond the barrier. Kienna forced a cough as Danek continued. "I think you need a break more than you know. Say you'll come with us tomorrow."

She thought it was a funny way of phrasing that. It wasn't a break if they thought there was a threat over there. She'd still be working. Kienna shook Danek's hand off. "I think I'm good. I'm too tired to fight off the king's ridicule."

"He'll ridicule us anyway. At least we'll be doing something to deserve it this time," Moira said. She softened. "Danek's right. You need a break."

"Come, or don't come." Broan rolled his eyes, annoyance practically steaming off him like a kettle about to boil.

Kienna looked at Baila, who'd gone suspiciously quiet. "I'll go if she goes."

Baila scoffed. "Only to keep you idiots alive."

She looked between them, a group of misfits all thrown together to protect a city that probably didn't need any protection if what she's been seeing was correct. She rolled her eyes. "I'll think about it. But he better not catch any of you."

"He's not going to catch us," Broan said. "Now let's get out of here."

"The barrier is fine," Danek whispered to Kienna. "We'll help you with the rest after tomorrow."

Kienna glanced over her shoulder at the churning shimmer of particles still floating around in the orb. Danek's words repeated themselves in her head. *The barrier is fine.*

No, she thought to herself. *The barrier isn't fine.*
The barrier was a cage.

Chapter 8

—Kienna—

Gourmet foods from all over the city were prepared and garnished with spices and herbs from the northern lands. Pans of roasted chicken legs sat on the table. The skin was lacquered in gold and mahogany, gleaming where it was soaked in fat and wine. Red grapes clung to their stems, collapsing into the broth with sprigs of thyme. Aside from the chicken was roasted boar, spiced pies, goat cheese, and fresh loaves of bread. Every glass was filled with ruby red wine. On rare occasions, King Vaerin treated the Guardians to such a meal. On most other occasions, they ate the same bland stews as any other commoner in the village.

The king's table stretched the length of the hall, a looming slab of oak, burnished to a dark sheen that caught the firelight like oil. Its edges were carved with ancient runes. At the center, a massive candelabrum rose like twisted iron antlers, and each taper burned with a crimson flame.

A servant stood behind every chair, silent and stiff-backed. Only the Guardians and a few adorned soldiers sat together, staring at the table's head. King Vaerin's chair was elevated slightly, high-backed, and carved with serpents and sunbursts. The upholstery was a deep crimson that swallowed the light at an angle. The seat was empty.

"Do you think he forgot?" Moira whispered over the table to Baila.

Baila scoffed. "King Vaerin doesn't forget anything."

"Yeah, but I'm getting hungry." Moira moved her fork and fiddled with the golden utensil. She sat next to Broan on her right and Dren to her left. The presence of Dren reminded Kienna of the square earlier, the haunting images of the headless corpse and Dren's blade. He had bathed since then, combing his greasy strands of dark hair back and dressing in finer, nobler garments. The everlasting stench of barley filled the room. Kienna shifted to Moira and noticed she looked a little green.

Kienna's heart drummed against her chest, and sweat coated her underarms. The king was late. He was never late. He had to be late because something happened, and it'd be all her fault. Dren chugged his wine, his fingers tapping lazily on the black oak table. Eventually, the grand doors to the dining hall slithered open, and King Vaerin stormed in, face taut and a stillness in his eyes that silenced the room.

He wore black leather, polished and lacquered like obsidian caught in candlelight. His tunic clung to his lean frame, cut high at the collar and clasped at the neck with a single dark ruby. His sleeves were snug to the wrist, bound with gold cuffs shaped like twisting thorns. His dark brown hair, draped smoothly past his shoulders, had the color of deep mahogany. He had it parted cleanly and combed back, half-cusped with another ruby gem. The scar above his lip broke the symmetry of his face, curving him into an ominous masterpiece with his narrow nose, sculpted, high cheekbones, and an elegant shadow casting down his face.

The room stood for him and waited until he took his seat at the table. His deep, gray eyes scanned the Guardians. "None of you thought to change for the occasion?"

Moira cleared her throat. "We came straight from the barrier, Your Grace."

"And how long have you been sitting here, waiting?" Vaerin added. He let the seconds pass in silence while the room shifted. Vaerin sighed and dimmed the flames. "That's better. At least I won't have to look at you sorry shits."

Kienna flinched. She found the courage to look up from the table and meet Danek's gaze. His fists gripped tightly around his fork. If Kienna hadn't known any better, he looked as if he were plotting an assassination right then. Surely not. Danek couldn't even hurt a leechbug if it had latched onto him…unless he had to.

"Don't just stand there," he waved to the servants. "We can't eat without you plating for us." The servants moved vigorously. As they did, Vaerin turned his attention back to the table. "Broan."

The barbarian of a man shrank under the king's scrutiny. He tried to keep his exasperated sigh at bay and then answered. "Yes, Your Grace."

"Reports around the city indicate you used magic today during one of the shows?"

"Yes." Broan didn't try to defend his actions. The entire table knew it'd be pointless.

King Vaerin bared his teeth and lashed out with magic, pulsing a deep red ray of light over Broan's plate and thrashing it against the wall. "You think because you *have it*, you can use it? In the middle of the city?" He rose from his chair, finger stabbing in the air like a blade. "You don't even understand what *control* means. Magic isn't power to wield however you like. It's *permission!* And you did not *have* it."

Vaerin sat back down, flickering the lights up a little to reveal the room. The servants had stepped backward against the wall. The fear kept their faces gaunt, but they were smart and trained well enough to keep their postures prim and perfect. As soon as the lights dimmed back to a normal brilliance, servants continued plating, replacing Broan's shattered dish with a new one.

The king cleared his throat and spoke again with more control. "You will not make me look weak."

His attention turned to Moira. From across the table, she pricked up and appeared to be diverting her eyes to Dren. The king stared at her, studying her through the narrow slits of his eyes. When it grew too awkward to bear, Kienna threw on a smile and stood, holding up her cup. "Congratulations on your reign and River Storm's peace, Your Grace."

"So, it would seem," he replied, but his stare remained taut on Moira. "Tell me, Moira. Have you managed to deal with your old flame?"

If Moira was seeing someone, Kienna missed it. They'd been pressed so hard in training since the day Vaerin gave them magic, it was hard to believe anyone could pull off a relationship outside of the ones that existed in the castle. Not to mention the impending fear that anyone within these walls could die for a misstep. But they didn't have any worry about that. They weren't required to escort people as a symbol. Kienna sat back down.

Moira pressed a napkin gently to her lips. "Yes, My King. I took care of it."

"Good." His stare remained on her, almost as if he was testing

Moira to see if she'd break. "Because relationships are a distraction, and you'd be doing your city a great disservice if you were distracted."

She nodded. Was that why Moira had been acting differently lately? What else didn't Kienna know about the rest of the Guardians at the table? Whatever she didn't know, the king likely did, which only made her worry even more about them wanting to cross the river. Did they think they would get away with it?

The king had eyes everywhere.

"Well," Vaerin said, voice light, as if nothing had happened. "I'm glad we got that out of the way." He raised his golden cup, turning it slowly in his hand. "I asked you here tonight to say thank you. Truly. You've trained hard, and you've earned this praise." He paused. "Each of you." Without waiting for anyone else to follow, Vaerin lifted the cup to his lips and drank, eyes lingering over the rim as if daring them not to believe him.

"Thank you," Baila said. "We are honored to be amongst you in your great home and hope we can continue to make you proud."

King Vaerin didn't smile, but his eyes gleamed. He let another silence fall between them and then said, "Good. Loyalty deserves its place here in River Storm."

Broan and Moira shifted in their seats. Kienna saw the discomfort radiating from them and could only hope that they were rethinking their evening plans. She tried not to let the fear affect her so much, but King Vaerin had a way of making her feel so completely worthless. Only to turn around and tell her she was the most important thing to happen to the city since the beginning of his reign. The constant confliction made her head spend. Maybe that was his intent. She couldn't tell anymore, but she was tired of it.

"Dren," King Vaerin toasted his cup again. "Thank you for joining us tonight."

"I wouldn't miss it, Your Grace." Dren toasted back, quick to drink again.

"Tell me how your trip to the northern lands went."

Dren slurred his way through a description of meeting the merchants at the loading dock, seeing lands that bored him, and people so dull he couldn't imagine any issues with control or pull for power. King Vaerin didn't seem worried either, but the northern lands benefited from King Vaerin's protective wall, too. Clearly, creatures beyond the South would never stop at River Storm if they broke through. They'd devour the world. At least that's what they believed, according to Dren. There's no telling what the world beyond would truly do if the walls came down, but Kienna was beginning to see through the bullshit.

"I thought we valued the northern lands for trade. Surely, they can't *all* be dull," Moira said.

Vaerin smiled and grabbed hold of his cup again. "Good point, Moira. Tell me what you understand about the North."

Kienna tried to will Moira not to answer. It was a trap, after all. Danek and Broan set their silverware down, barely getting started on their meals. Everyone prepared themselves. Moira reached for her cup as well and then pulled her hand back.

"They are our main providers of spice, jewels, and fabric. It's how we get most of our goods that we can't make here in River Storm. In return, we provide meat and leather from our livestock," Moira responded.

"What about you, Kienna?" Vaerin pointed his cup toward her. "Did Moira miss anything?"

Well shit. Now she was trapped.

"Derbent and Kostro are our greatest allies," Kienna's hands grazed her pants, finally dry after her incident at the river. "But the rest of the North would easily rally if needed."

"Why do we need allies in River Storm?" Vaerin prodded. His gaze narrowed as he opened the question to the entire table.

"We don't. We're the greatest city in the world," Baila smiled.

When Vaerin challenged her on this, she fumbled. Kienna would have, too. There was no telling if they were truly the greatest city in the world when they were but a city *hiding* from the rest of the world. So, maybe the greatest city in the North.

Danek decided to take a crack at Vaerin's question. "Allies ensure control."

"Ah! And what do we get out of control?" Vaerin's brows rose with excitement.

"Peace, I suppose," Broan shrugged, biting into the slice of meat that had since gone cold. "Or at least silence."

"Kienna?"

She clung to this question. It was a philosophical debate they'd run around in circles often with King Vaerin. He hadn't ever heard the answer he wanted, which was why he kept pressing them. But she knew what they didn't. "We get security. And survival if we're lucky."

"So, control is what makes people believe they're safe? What if they're not?" King Vaerin drank from his cup again, slowly watching the Guardians squirm under his scrutiny.

Danek placed his fork on the table. "We get loyalty, and with that comes power. Control gives us the comfort of knowing no one moves without your say so."

"If *you* say so." The king toasted the room.

Vaerin let them be, finishing the meal on his plate in stride. Kienna struggled to get any bites of food afterward, grappling inside her head to stay sane. The others sat stoically, picking at their plates.

Desserts flooded in at one point, but Kienna remained oblivious that her meal had been switched for tiny cakes. Sweet sugar and honey wafted around the table, replacing the savory salt. Servants flowed in and out of the room, cleaning and making sure the king and Dren had enough wine to fill their guts. A low chatter between the soldiers of valor buzzed around.

Kienna's exhaustion ate at her. She needed to eat to replace the energy she'd used up throughout the day, but she couldn't quite bring herself to do it. Her stomach coiled with exhaustion, not hunger. "Your Grace," Kienna interrupted the quiet. She was taking a chance, and part of her told her not to, but she'd hoped the king would understand, given what she had to do earlier. "Thank you for the meal tonight, but I wonder if I would be permitted to be excused? I'm tired and I just…I'd like to go home."

"Anyone else feeling tired?" King Vaerin swept the room with a flat stare.

"For fuck's sake," she murmured under her breath. Kienna slumped in her chair and tried her best not to cross her arms.

No one said anything, which was enough of an answer as any. Kienna groaned, tensing her chest to prepare for the next wave of Vaerin's wrath. He stood from the table and crushed his golden cup in his hands. If he'd used magic to do it, it hadn't been obvious. The patrons at the table flinched.

"You are losing focus!" His voice boomed against the stone walls, the fire flickering with the echo. "You were chosen because you were supposed to be more useful."

Vaerin scanned the room, his eyes flicking over each Guardian like a blade. "I look at you now, dressed like peasants, and I see children begging for safety. You don't deserve to be Guardians. You can't even hold your posture under pressure, let alone power. For the sake of the gods, you're all adults. Fucking act like you can hold your own."

He turned back to Kienna and scowled, his eyes glowing red. "Weakness like yours is why cities fall."

Hot tears flooded Kienna's eyes. She held her jaw tightly, biting her lips as she fought to hold them in. That's what Vaerin wanted, for her to let another burst of weakness show. She wouldn't dare do it now. If she did, the king would certainly secure another opportunity to chastise her. Broan's lips were already curling upward from the public display of her humiliation. It didn't happen often, so he took a front row seat when it did.

King Vaerin wiped the wine from his hands and allowed his servants to clean his leather tunic. He softened and sat. "I am harsh, but it's because I have passion. You are the chosen children of River Storm, and I hold you to the same standards I hold myself. Is that understood?"

"Yes, King Vaerin," the table echoed together.

"Good. I scold you like my own. I would die for each of you. I would hope you would do the same." As he said it, little trinkets of gold were placed on the table in front of each of them. Thick golden serpent armillas for each of them to wear the next day. Tiny jewels were carefully crafted inside the bracelet—rubies. The gem of River Storm.

Kienna ran the bracelet through her fingers, testing the weight of it but never putting it on. Baila was quick to try it out, and Moira could never resist something shiny. They perked up quickly. Broan toasted his bracelet to the king, but Danek remained silent, staring at the eyes of the snake. More gifts.

She wondered what gifts she was going to find at home, as the entire city would have been visited by the soldiers by now. The fire under her skin settled in her bones, not quite going away, reminding her that mulling over this would do her no good, and it was time for her to move on. If she didn't, he wouldn't just punish her. She could take that. He'd punish them all. So, she put the snake on her wrist and thanked her King for being so gracious.

His eyes didn't blink. Didn't move. They stayed locked on her, like a blade waiting to fall.

Did he know what she did?

Chapter 9

—Kienna—

The night sky stretched endlessly above, heavy with presence but cloaked with dark clouds. The moon and stars hid behind them, and the natural glows of the night were blocked out. Kienna still felt the sting of Vaerin's harsh words against her face. It had been a slap. Danek summoned the wind and took it upon himself to light the way for them, illuminating the stone paths with fireflies ahead of their feet. As the Guardians took one step after the other, the walkway grew brighter, casting a gentle glow that danced across them as a sweet melody chimed around them. The crisp air faded into a soft breeze and brought the smell of summer rain.

Moira stopped to breathe in the sudden change of season, eyes held blissfully shut as her nose pointed toward the sky. Kienna's face turned into a scowl. "Would you stop altering our minds like that? King Vaerin will kill you."

"As you wish." Danek released his magic. The path faded back to a bleak shadow in the overcast. The melody prancing within their minds halted, and the air grew frigid once more.

"You're quite good at illusions," Moira admitted.

A sly smile played at Danek's mouth as he thanked Moira. She seemed to be the only one receptive to the invasiveness of his magic. Healing required a sense of mind manipulation, mastering the ability of perception. It was blissful if one didn't understand that their mind was being tricked into feeling okay. Almost like swallowing a poppy.

"I'm surprised the *king* doesn't have us all sleeping in the palace by this point," Broan said as they neared the villages. Kienna eyed him. That would be a gift, but one she was happy she didn't have to accept. Living in the villages was their way of keeping control, for the Guardians to serve as King Vaerin's eyes. No one would dare do anything defiant, even at home, with Guardians around.

The cottages sat evenly apart from each other, all the same size. The only way to tell each home apart was purely from memory and location. *Twenty rows down. One house over.*

King Vaerin built River Storm tactfully, carefully designing everything as evenly as possible. It was a way of ensuring all subjects received the same treatment, thus proving more loyalty to him.

"You complain about this every night," Moira said. The evening had taken a toll on her normal mood, and she did nothing to hide it.

"Vaerin is a careful man." Kienna was mindful of her words. "No one will stay there. Not even me."

Broan kicked the dirt, his large feet quaking bits of the ground beneath him. There was no one else in the city who looked like him.

A burly man and torso so solid, people used to say he was chiseled from stone. Though his features were less rigid than a rock, he crumbled things around him with as much strength.

Danek and Broan turned on row five. "Goodnight!"

"Those boys are always up to no good." Moira clutched against Kienna's arm. Her shoulders flinched upward for a moment, but she continued forward. "Now do you want to talk about what happened today?"

Kienna shrugged. "It was an execution. Nothing else to say."

Moira stopped her from moving and turned to look at her. "There's always something to say about death. You've been pale all day."

"Yeah, that surge of magic—"

"Before then, Kienna. You're clearly not handling it well."

Kienna ripped her arm from Moira's grasp and took a step backward. "You handle your business, and I'll handle mine, yeah?"

Moira sighed, her fingers finding the snake trinket alongside her wrist. Her deep brown eyes went to the ground. They were in row eighteen. She looked down the row and said, "Get some sleep, okay?"

Kienna nodded and watched Moira head home, then she walked alone until she reached the last row of her journey. Her house lay closest to the main wall. Vaerin had placed her there in hopes that her visions would sense an attack before it came. It mainly hummed and kept her awake, feeling like another form of control.

She took a minute before going inside, climbing to the roof of the house, and perching herself in the darkness. Her eyes scanned the village homes, looking to see if anyone was out after curfew. Broan and Danek had reached their home, closest to the orphanage and the noble palaces. The streets were bare. Her eyes flicked to the sky. There was nothing left to look at there either, so she climbed back down and went inside. She was greeted with the smell of berries and a freshness of trees that she couldn't quite place through the hints of food boiling from the hearth.

"Oh, good! You're home!" Kienna's mother, Maren, turned from the stove. "I just finished a stew. Some soldiers dropped off a bundle of meat and vegetables from the harvest. They said the king wanted to make sure you ate. That your appetite might be of concern."

Kienna rubbed the nape of her neck, looking at the gifts around her. There was food, of course, as everyone was promised, but to the side was also a chest of jewels. She wondered if the king gave everyone in the city such fine gifts or if it was only her. It had grown extremely late by now, too late for Maren to be cooking. "I honestly just want some sleep."

Maren tsked. "You are overworked, and now you're no longer eating?"

"I'm fine, Mom, really."

"No, not fine. I'm going to talk to Jacob. Maybe we can speak to the high sorcerer." Maren busied herself with the stove, tinkering around with the plates. "We hear you…in your sleep sometimes. It's like you're wandering but not—"

"Rest is all I need." Kienna squeezed Maren around the waist, residing in the shadows of her room for some peace and quiet.

Sinking her body into her bed, Kienna closed her eyes as tightly as possible until her mind drifted. A soft warmth stirred in her branded thumb, the faintest hum threading into her thoughts. She caught herself starting to soar through lands she'd never seen before, wondering what her life could be like if King Vaerin had left her in the burning tree…if she survived, of course.

"Mm." She fell deeper. She was starting to *dream*.

The burning on her thumb pulsed harder. It faded as quickly as it came, but it left behind the impression of someone whispering her name. Her body became dense, and suddenly, she was unable to move. Panic prickled at the edge of her mind.

She had been sure she was falling asleep, but now it was like she was being pulled into something else. She swayed at the whispering of trees and a gentle aroma of pine.

Something pulled harder, and Kienna vanished.

Chapter 10

–Kienna–

"You made it! Welcome back."

Kienna opened her eyes. No longer in her bed, there was a coarse, crunchy layer beneath her. Trees soared above from every angle in the clear sky as stars danced around the moon in gleaming constellations. It left her breathless.

She stood agape, skimming her surroundings, but she turned when she realized she was not alone. A man crouched near a tree behind her as if he wasn't sure whether he should stay hidden or not. Kienna's lips curled upward, and she sat down. "Where are we today, wolf man?"

"The Malintale."

Kienna's hands brushed the dirt, her fingers coating with the brown soot. She tried to make sense of what was going on around her. She'd never been able to sense the things in her projections, and she was grateful that she hadn't experienced the razor-sharp agony of slipping through the barrier. "Where is that exactly?"

"Right outside your home, if you climb high enough."

"Am I actually here?"

"No," came the man's deep reply. "You're still in River Storm."

She took in the deep wind brushing against her hair, whispering secrets on her skin. She couldn't recall her projections feeling so serene. Maybe she was having a vision instead. Her fingers crumpled the leaves beneath her, and then her eyes wove between the stars. "Are *you* real?"

He stepped forward. "You know I am." She did, but she asked every time they met like this to make sure her mind wasn't caving from the pressure and making him up.

Kienna turned away from the sky and met his eyes, the eyes she'd seen in her vision at the barrier. He wore the same animal covering, the head of a fanged beast that rested over his like a hood. The hide clung perfectly to his shoulders. The man's sharply carved face bore regal angularity, features that she never saw in River Storm. His clear green eyes with a rim of deep-rooted forest fixed on something out of reach, like memories. Beneath his hood, windswept hair with dark roots that faded to muddy brown curled back in defiance of order. Expiring youth dancing across the gleam of his round eyes. He had to have been about her age. Looking at him now, her hands began to tremble. Even if he was young, he had a type of commanding force about him, like he had lived more life in his years than she ever had. He was also extremely attractive, and that only made her blush further.

He sat next to her. "You feel off today."

Kienna twiddled her thumbs and looked at the trees around her. "I had to execute someone."

"*You* did?" He seemed shocked.

"Well, not me. Dren, that soldier I told you about—"

"Your 'mentor'?"

"Yeah. He did it, but I had to give a speech and offer gifts. It felt so..." Flames surfaced on the pads of her fingers. "Now that I remember, I'm so angry. And sad that I had to hurt someone for this lie. I hated every second of it, and I can't get it out of my mind."

The man scoffed. "I'm surprised your king didn't erase that memory for you."

Kienna looked at him, unsure if she should continue. She'd already been too vulnerable. He knew way more than he should about River Storm. Yet, every night they found each other, she couldn't help but trust him. Despite all her training against it, he was the first thing that ever called her mind to the outside. And he restored bits of her memories. She didn't know how he could do that, but it kept her grounded in River Storm, and she needed that. So, she stayed.

"What the hell are you even wearing, anyway?" she asked, glancing up to the fanged beast on top of his head, like the creature was eating him, and he looked utterly ridiculous.

"This is a Malintilian wolf." He said it so matter-of-factly, like she was supposed to understand that. Her silence must have answered for her. "It's a creature of the forest. He was my guide until old age took him. I honor his memory by giving his body purpose, and he honors me by helping me stay hidden."

"We don't have wild animals here in River Storm. Only livestock." She studied the wolf atop his head once more and sighed. "So, you're a forest creature, too, then?"

His expression shifted to amusement. "Ouch, Kienna. You think I'm an animal?"

"Are you? Some savage creature, I mean?"

"What do you think? We've been meeting for a few months. Surely you have your own opinion?"

A few months should have been enough to know, but they never spent more than a few minutes together in forms less fluid than this. Kienna could only shrug. "Your wolf hat isn't helping."

The man took the wolf off his head and gently placed it near a tree. He motioned to it and then to himself, as if he was showing himself off for the first time. Color rose to Kienna's cheeks as she tried not to smile. "Will you ever tell me your name?"

For the first time, he looked troubled. He started to drum his hand against his leg. "It's better if I don't."

"Better for whom?"

"Both of us, honestly. For your own safety, should things…you know…" He meant if things went wrong. A pine-sweet breeze swept between them. He paused, watching her expression shift.

Kienna tried to hold in the anger about this, though her skin harbored a flame threatening to break out any moment. She was, in fact, committing treason in her sleep to be here. The least he could do was let her do it fully and reveal who he was. What was so ominous about his name?

His hands brushed hers, and she started to cool. The touch sparked her mind and made her jump, but she didn't pull away. Is this what she resorted to now for connection—to be anything other than angry and confused? Maybe it was.

"Do you want me to show you mountains?" the man asked.

"We have mountains in River Storm."

He smiled. "Not like this." With the flick of his wrist, the forest swirled around them, and they were now standing in front of towering giants that grew higher than the River Storm barrier itself. Hundreds of spires peaked with green trees and snow. Then it faded, and they found themselves by mountains so green that they could have been a forest, too. A waterfall roared from a high cliff. She wanted to run her fingers through the water, jump off the cliff, and see where else it took her. Then her mind drifted toward the barrier, shimmering faintly at the edge of her consciousness. A reminder of her reality.

Their surroundings fell back to the forest, and the man was looking at her now with one perched eyebrow. He reached for her, but she backed away. "What's the point of us meeting?"

"Aside from me fixing your memory every night?"

"That's not the only reason you're here, right?"

He shrugged, voice darkening. "I don't know. Maybe I have a personal vendetta with River Storm being built to control what you remember."

She was too tired for this. It didn't bother her so much that he danced around her questions most nights, but something about seeing a dead body had her already feeling on edge. "If that's the case, then you're here to…do what?"

"Free you. Expose Vaerin," he hesitated, the corner of his mouth twitching. "And to show you the world we started imagining together."

What was she doing? Now was the time to pull away from this. She let the disgust encompass her. She had to. If she encouraged any more of this, King Vaerin would strip the people she loved bare and cast them into the coursing magic to burn. There were always heads rolling around her, and she couldn't outrun it, no matter how much she wanted to.

Kienna recoiled. Her voice cracked. "I don't belong here. Time to wake up, Kienna."

The man folded his arms and leaned against a tree. Kienna started to pace. When pacing didn't work, she slapped her hand against her face. He tilted his head and cocked a smile. "What are you doing?"

"I need to go back to River Storm. Being here with you is—"

"Relax," the man said, closing the distance between them. "You're *in* River Storm. This. Between us," he motioned his hand in the air between their heads, "is not magic. At least not anymore. Your king won't even know you've wandered."

Kienna scoffed. "Release me, then."

The man rolled his eyes and shrugged his shoulders. "We've done this before. Can we skip this part for once and get back to envisioning the world you wanted?"

"I have a responsibility inside those walls," she whispered as she listened to the crickets chirping around her. "I'm supposed to protect people from this. I can't keep meeting you."

"Whatever you say, Kienna. I'll see you tomorrow."

Kienna jolted upright in bed, chest heaving as if she'd fallen from a cliff. The thick silence pressed in around her, amplifying her inner turmoil. Alone, she rubbed her eyes, struggling to grasp the fading threads of the vision.

She had to tell King Vaerin, but something stopped her. He'd been shifting her memories. She went through this every day, trying to grasp her reality versus what the King told her. And this man…he wanted to tear it all down. She *wanted* him to.

Too alert to sleep, Kienna threw on a robe and went to the window. The barrier was quiet except for a faint orange flicker to the east. As she leaned closer, a cool, pine-scented breeze slipped through the sealed window. Her breath caught. River Storm's air never smelled like that. Kienna narrowed her eyes. The ember vanished in a pulse of haze. She reached for the magic again, trying to call him, but he slipped further into the shadows of her mind.

Groaning, she pulled dyes from beneath the bed, swirling them into thick paint. She was out of wood for carving and needed to find something else to calm her. Kienna clipped strands of her hair, twisted them into a brush, and began to paint.

With strokes of colorful hues, she recreated the world she

dreamed of. Forests. Mountains. Falling water. A young man with the greenest eyes she'd ever seen, wearing a wolf on top of his head. The storm inside her stilled as she worked into the night. Surer of herself, Kienna believed in her soul these were no longer dreams. She wanted something, a surprise even to herself, but fighting against the control of River Storm proved difficult. What would she be willing to do to get out? It was a question that haunted her as she brushed against the canvas.

Chapter 11

—Kienna—

Kienna woke abruptly, face down on the table, and her hair splattered in the dried-up paint concocted the night before. In a battle between a quick bath and being late for Vaerin's morning briefing, Kienna knew she would be embarrassingly dirty on a day meant to celebrate her king.

She threw on some pants and boots, still tying the tight corset laces she wore around her tunic as she threw open her bedroom door. She yelled a quick goodbye to her mother, an echo of Maren's voice yelling after her to eat breakfast before going. Kienna was already out the door and bolting for the citadel to give her address to the public.

The humid air hit her like a warm breath. It smelled like sunbaked stone mixed with the iron of magic. Clouds hung lowly, smudging the sky in shades of dull gray and bruised white. Kienna sprinted past the village homes as early risers stepped out to clean their front porch.

Once the village was out of sight, Kienna's stride slowed to a brisk walk to not alert the River Storm nobles gathered in the city square. The streets were swarmed with people practicing their march for a parade later. Men and their horses clopped through the cobblestones, carrying large jousting sticks. King Vaerin loved a good joust. People had already gathered by the stage that had been built overnight, where she would stand in front of the castle and tell the public about how great this city was and how blessed they were by the grace of their king. They were waiting for *her,* and she was late. And dirty.

He had already convened his briefing before the speech without her. She barged inside the citadel next to the castle, interrupting him mid-sentence. Everyone sat in chairs around a large table with gold cups and a breakfast feast laid out for the noblemen. Cold silence overtook the room, and the eyes of generals and city advisors alike fell on her. Kienna found little comfort even as she sat next to Moira, cheeks inflamed.

"What happened to you?" she whispered.

"You couldn't have bothered to clean?" Vaerin peered at her, a light chuckle echoing from the crowd.

She'd been a fool to stay up too late when she was dead tired, not bathing before retreating to her room to paint, of all things. King Vaerin pinched the bridge of his nose between his eyes and spoke slowly, his eyes cutting toward Kienna. "This display is abysmal."

"I know. I'm so sorry. It's not my intention to embarrass—"

"Enough!" Vaerin flicked his hand off his face and summoned

Kienna forward until her body was no longer in her seat. She stood face to face with Vaerin, the weight of his narrow gray eyes pressing against her. The sudden transfer of her body from one place to the other spun her mind around in a disoriented web. He picked and prodded at her hair, grabbing her hands to examine the dye that stained her flesh. "Painting again?"

"I couldn't sleep." Kienna could barely look at him.

"I would have preferred you not be here at all than to show up like this."

Kienna lowered her head to the floor, but in no time, Vaerin had already pulled the paint off her body and brightened the dark circles around her eyes. Her clothes shifted into something that matched his, a regal burgundy dress that fit too tightly in areas she preferred to keep modest. Her hair shifted from her untamed mess into carefully crafted curls.

"Appearances are important, my child." When he called her "my child," a part of her still carried a flicker of pride, even if she knew better. "At least it wasn't that pesky wood carving. Now, get out there. The public needs you now more than ever after yesterday's… incident."

"That's it?" Broan stood from his seat, his voice laced with contempt. His fists slammed into the large table, knocking over the wine that had been provided to the men in the room. The noblemen stepped backward, soldiers reaching for their hilts. "If any of us showed up like *her*, we'd be punished. But I suppose some of us are above the rules now?"

Vaerin turned swiftly to Broan, eyes beaming red. "You will not speak out of turn again." The two stared at each other intensely until Broan finally caved, diverting his eyes with a clenched jaw elsewhere. The king stared at them all like they were specks stuck on his boots. One corner of his mouth lifted. Then he blinked and smiled warmly. "You all look much better than last night. I'm pleased to have you here with me on stage. Now, let's go before the public thinks something is wrong."

The king walked toward the entrance, allowing his soldiers to open the doors and guide them back out onto the square. A larger crowd had gathered by now, surrounded by soldiers who had no doubt *encouraged* them to attend. The king allowed the Guardians to leave and then turned away.

He wouldn't be on the streets like them. He was the king, of course. No, he would be on the terrace above them for everyone to look up at. This would create the illusion he wanted. The king above all, and his trusted Guardians among *them*.

Everyone bunched together inside the walls around the castle. Its normal spacious cobblestone paths were now filled. Kienna's eyes shifted to the Atelier, the woman's head bouncing through the streets flashing in her mind. She tried to shake it off, but her eyes met a commoner's— someone she knew had been there—and it all came rushing back.

The streets were more silent than they had been in previous years. If she didn't say the right things, River Storm's unrest could grow. The king's voice rang inside her head, telling her not to fuck up.

As she stepped onto the stage, Danek, Moira, Broan, and Baila trailed her and took their spots standing in the back to face the crowd. Kienna stood slightly in front of them to elevate her position as speaker and face of the Guardians. She hated it. They hated it. The entire thing came off too rehearsed.

Sweat bubbled under Kienna's dress. She wanted to pull on it, adjust it to fit her properly, but she resisted the urge to show she was completely out of her skin. A few coughs rang out in the stone enclosure.

King Vaerin appeared at the high terrace above the square, hands folded, his voice projecting across the city through his magic. "People of River Storm." He paused. Kienna could only imagine he was staring at every commoner who dared to look directly at him. "Today, we mark another year beneath the steadfast sky. Another year held aloft by our strength and our unity. And of course, the walls that have never failed us. You, my trusted people, are the reason River Storm endures."

Kienna glanced at their faces. All of them were locked on the king, awestruck by his glow. It's why he hated it when they used magic out of turn. His magic commanded their attention regardless of any situation, set to always enthrall them.

"Without you, there is no city. Without your discipline, your devotion, your daily acts of service and sacrifice, everything about us would falter. I present to you my Guardians, the ones who carry the burdens of the barrier for you. Without them, the barrier falls. Along with all that lies behind it."

No one dared to speak. The heat started to boil around them. People wiped their brows, adjusted their shirts from their arms, but they kept their gaze on their king, even through his pauses.

"You are the bedrock. The breath of the storm. The soul of our order."

Another pause. So many fancy words that meant nothing. But they didn't know that. All they knew was they had a god for a king who protected them from the cruel world outside.

"And yet, as with all great legacies, we are tested. Yesterday held such a test. A moment of sorrow, yes, but also one of clarity." Yes, Kienna had a clear understanding about the situation. "We lost a voice to disobedience. We lost a life to grief turned outward, to fire turned against the very hands that once fed it. And though punishment is never our aim, peace demands its Guardians. Justice, though painful, must sometimes burn."

She commended the king. She didn't think he would address it. His executions were usually private. Facing the situation head-on bought him enough points with the crowds, and a few people started to clap. Kienna wondered if they understood anything he said.

"My people, you did not falter. You watched with strength and grace. And through it all, she stood among you." The king motioned his hand down to Kienna. She straightened but Danek's hand steadied her. "Kienna, our Starborn, did what had to be done. For you and for River Storm. In her, I have placed the flame. She is the hope of our future, alongside your trusted Guardians. Through them, the wall is sealed, and our safety is assured."

King Vaerin lifted his hand to the sky. "Let us raise our eyes to the barrier that kisses the clouds and remember. It is not stone that holds back the dark. It is us. Our unity. Our trust."

That got the crowd cheering. They completely forgot about the woman yesterday and whistled for their king. He paused, waiting for it to die down.

"Today, we celebrate not only the city, but all who serve it. Now, with pride, I turn this platform over to the light of River Storm. The flame made flesh. Your Starborn, Kienna."

Her body tensed. Moira handed her cards, Danek patted her on the back, and Baila told her not to choke. Encouraging words. Kienna stepped forward. Her vocal cords laced with magic—King Vaerin's doing, of course. She looked out to the crowd and wondered what it was they could have her say that King Vaerin hadn't said already. There were five cards filled with words. It was yet another long speech in blistering heat with restless people who watched her stand there and let a woman die.

She glanced down at the cards and read the first line. *We guard the city in your honor.* The words held no truth. Kienna didn't guard the city in their honor. Kienna guarded the city in the king's honor— *for* his honor. If King Vaerin cared about any of them, she'd missed it. Maybe it was somewhere in her stolen memories.

"Gotta say something, princess," Broan sneered behind, crossing his arms. Moira gave an encouraging nod. Kienna looked up from them to lock eyes with the king. She could almost hear his voice ringing in her ear to smile. Her body turned back to the crowd, where she found Maren standing close to the stage, curving her fingers around her mouth to mimic a smile.

Kienna exhaled and obliged, reading through the senseless letters on the cards. She couldn't remember what she said, only that words came out of her mouth. By that point, they were Vaerin's words as well, being spoken through her with the magic he laced into her throat. When he was done with her, he wisped it away, and he disappeared into his castle. The crowd applauded and then dispersed.

"That could have been worse," Danek said, cautious to approach her. He wiped sweat from his forehead.

Kienna finally pulled on the dress, ready to escape back home to burn it in a hole and change into her regular attire. She pushed her silver threads back and turned to Moira. "If I wasn't already, I'm in for tonight."

"Yay," Moira beamed, grabbing hold of her hand.

"We have a boat to take us across," Danek smiled. "Aine said she could leave it by the docks for us."

"Any other ladies helping us tonight, pretty boy?" Broan teased.

"Are you sure this is a good idea?" Baila whispered.

"We'll be fine!" Broan bumped his shoulder ferociously into her. "Enjoy *your* party. I'm going to joust."

Chapter 12

—Baila—

Broan stood out among the knights, dressed in wool and leather. He would have been a laughingstock to the crowd, but they already knew he didn't need armor to protect the stone wall of his body. King Vaerin only allowed Broan one round of jousting every year—the finale. It wouldn't be fair for him to pummel every soldier off their horse. It took away from the spirit of watching someone rise and take on the challenge of fighting the giant.

Horses whinnied frantically in their stalls. The crowd spilled across the viewing seats, and nobles sat high in the Crown Tier.

Banners fluttered in the wind. Below, commoners packed the stone benches along the tilt, faces flushed with the humid heat in anticipation. Baila sat amongst the nobles with Aine. The king watched from the Flamecrest, his box of royalty, his silhouette etched in crimson light. Knights below thundered down the King's Field.

Each soldier who fell from their horse received a mocking laugh from Baila. If they couldn't even manage to hold a lance properly, they were unfit to protect King Vaerin.

"Where's Danek?" Aine asked, peering around the crowd.

Baila's expression deepened into a foul sneer. She'd asked Danek if he wanted to come to the joust with her earlier. When he turned her down, she brushed it off, but it stung. He had a long trail of women following him around, so he didn't need Baila. Just Aine, apparently.

The crowd roared as a young soldier slammed his lance into the final opponent before Broan's time of glory came up. Baila knew that the young boy didn't stand a chance against the Guardian, but allowing him to try drove the people wild in the city. It's the closest they would ever get to taking down the magically gifted. Like a fun game they could never win, but they had to try anyway to kiss the same sky as the gods.

King Vaerin stood to address the arena. His voice amplified like thunder, a spark of magic shimmering over the veil of his box. "Today, two warriors stand before you as proof of our strength. Let them show you how strong we are." The crowd applauded.

Aine clapped her hands. "He's so eloquent."

"Of course he is. He's the king."

Vaerin's eyes fell on Broan. "Glory belongs to those who are loyal. Let this clash echo beyond our barrier!" Baila's lips curved upward. She stood and clapped, inciting the crowd to follow suit. "Begin."

Broan and the soldier lined up on opposite sides of the field, the long line of poles separating them down the middle. Baila crossed her arms. The barbarian barely held his lance in his hands.

"He's a buffoon. Can't he take this seriously?" Baila asked, sitting back down.

"He's fun to watch." Aine clapped again.

Baila peered at her round, elegant face. Her blonde hair was braided back to show off her collarbone. "This is meant to bring honor to our king. Not to have fun."

"Okay, Miss Priss. Just enjoy the show!"

The flag dropped, and the horse beneath him stumbled forward, nearly buckling with the weight. The soldier on the other side sprinted forward and moved his lance in front of him, but Broan pushed with mighty force and blew the soldier back off his steed. Predictable. But Vaerin liked it that way. He'd never let a Guardian lose in front of his subjects. Otherwise, the commoners would think they could defy the gods.

Baila understood that. The king didn't even have to lift a sword to show his power. It reflected through her. And Broan. And the others. They existed as his standing power.

Broan jumped off his horse and bowed to his king. The crowd roared. Baila tensed her jaw. Some of the other Guardians didn't see what she saw. If they saw their king as the visionary she did, then Broan would have bowed deeper to him. They'd been getting restless with their talk of uncovering secrets and doing things they shouldn't. Baila would need to watch them. If King Vaerin wasn't careful with them, they could crumble his regime. She wouldn't allow that to happen.

—Kienna—

King Vaerin had called Kienna to the castle after the jousting match. She didn't even have time to change her clothes, so she found herself still tugging at the same, thick red dress as before, the fabric drenched with sweat underneath. She sat stiff, hands clasped in her lap, rehearsing half a dozen apologies in her head. For the sweat, the speech, for existing too loudly today. The silence before he entered stretched thin and sharp like wire.

The king stormed into his council room, throwing off his cape and draping it over his throne. Kienna stood from her chair, ready for him to scold her, yet again, for fucking up the speech. What did he expect? She was no public speaker; she was a trained warrior.

"You did well today," he said.

It was so far from what she was prepared to hear that she found herself stumbling a moment, picking her own jaw up off the floor. The king turned to her again as he sat down on his seat of jewels. "I'm not sure what you mean, Your Grace. You spoke for me."

The king waved her off. "That was the plan all along, my child. But you held your composure after yesterday's atrocities, and for that, I am grateful."

"Okay..." Kienna's brow rose.

"I have a gift for you," the king said, rising again. He reached behind his throne and withdrew a bundle wrapped in embroidered linen, offering it to Kienna. She hesitated before unwrapping it, her fingers moving carefully over the linen. The fabric inside shimmered even in the dim light of the council chamber. Inside lay sleek leather trousers that were smooth and cool to the touch, a light wool tunic lined with silver stitching, and polished boots too fine for the battlefield. "You should wear them."

"From the North?" she asked, unable to stop herself.

"Of course," he said, smiling. "Nothing from River Storm would suit your worth."

She hated that it warmed her. That she wanted to believe him, despite what she knew. "Oh, wow," she said. She couldn't remember having garments so nice, aside from the random wardrobe changes like today, where the king decreed she wear a gown to address the crowd. "Thank you."

She bowed down, her tension drifting in his presence. Kienna was fully aware that he had bought her favor, but she didn't quite care too much. She wanted to, but she'd have to save everything she made and then some of Maren's stipend to be able to afford such fine shoes alone.

"My child, I care deeply for you. My harsh words, my strict rules, they're designed to make you strong. You know this, I hope."

"Yes, Your Grace." Kienna's mind unraveled to her voluntary treason with her man of the forest and found herself wanting to scream at herself. His hands had held her steady in the woods, but Vaerin clothed her. Fed her. Saved her. Didn't he?

The guilt came fast and ugly, wrapping around her chest like a steel band. She had betrayed the man who made her into something real. Regardless of his flaws and transgressions against her, he did try to help her. Perhaps she was the reason he had to buy her favor, siphon her memories, and hit her when she talked back. She had no other good explanation for it. The king loved her in his own way. Why couldn't that be enough?

Vaerin placed a hand on her shoulder, not roughly this time, but steadily. "I know your heart, my child. Even when you doubt yourself. You are strong."

Kienna's eyes fell to the floor.

—Moira—

Moira focused on her reflection, painting gold and teal specks along her face. Outside, faint music drifted from the distant village square. The scent of roasting fruit and sweet wine wafted through the window, but Moira stayed where she was, draped in candlelight and gold.

"Rhior!" Moira called out. He looked up with a pause and a soft expression that didn't quite meet his eyes. "Do you think I painted too much on my face?"

Rhior stepped closer, his expression unreadable. "You look fine."

His soft brown skin with hints of copper caught the candlelight, casting a golden hue over the edges of his northern features. His arms slipped around her waist with practiced ease. "You're beautiful," he added, almost as if it were a duty to say it. Wiry and lean, his body held the story of hunger and hardship, a past that hadn't entirely let him go. The years had hardened him in places Moira still remembered as soft.

"Be careful, love," she said, easing herself out of his hold. Her hands drifted to her abdomen, an unspoken reminder. Rhior pulled her close again, slower this time. His lips skimmed her neck with the same urgency as always, familiar and unchanging. She knew that touch. It had nothing to do with her. It was only about what he wanted. She jolted away again. "I need to go soon."

"Right," he said, the edge in his voice not fully hidden. "But we never finish anything. We're supposed to be together. Isn't that what *you* wanted?"

Moira took a step back and studied Rhior. His stubble was beginning to grow stubbornly. It was the boyishness that had first drawn her in. Her first. Her only. Even now, pregnant and unsure, she clung to that version of him.

Rhior kept his hair short and neatly combed and his clothing practical but well-tailored. He looked the part of a merchant. Moira knew his success had more to do with his looks than his skill—how easily people gave him what he asked for—but that had always been part of his charm. Rhior was the closest thing she had to family now, even if it was forced.

She sighed, still holding his gaze. "I'm sorry that this is the life we have."

"Don't be." His voice was flat, but he reached out and touched her cheek anyway.

"I never want to lose you," she whispered. "Or our family."

Rhior's hand lingered on her cheek, but his jaw was tight. "I doubt the king will care if he ever finds out."

Moira's stomach turned slightly at that. The words reminded her of the king's warning, his assumption that she'd discarded Rhior entirely. But she hadn't. She married him instead. Impulsively. Foolishly. Perhaps the baby clouded her judgment. Moira wore the ring he gave her on her pinky, a gold band that no one paid attention to. It was easier that way.

She told herself this was enough. It had to be.

Chapter 13

—Kienna—

The weight of the clothes was armor tailored to her soul. They hugged her in all the right places. For the first time in a long while, she felt like she belonged in her own skin. How clothes could do that was beyond her, but they gave her a beauty that she couldn't deny.

Vaerin dismissed her shortly after she let the noble girls see her. They giggled and made a fuss for a moment, but it appeased them, and they promised to bring more garments when their fathers traveled for business again.

Kienna left the castle, trying to move slowly as darkness began to take hold of the city. She slunk into the shadows behind the market stalls to get out of the castle borders unseen. That proved to be the most difficult with soldiers on heavy duty, patrolling the streets as more people were out than usual during the celebration of River Storm. Once she cleared the storm hold walls, she inched her way along the back until she found herself behind Moira at the aquarian markets. Moira greeted Danek, Broan, and Baila as she asked, "Kienna?"

"Probably getting fucked by the king," Broan chuckled.

Kienna rolled her eyes and appeared out of the shadows. "If the king had time for that, I imagine you'd be first in line."

Broan folded his arms and leaned back, mimicking her stance with a smug little smirk. His mouth pulled to one side in a twisted parody of her seriousness, mocking her without sound. Her eyes squinted, but she only laughed while he continued to act like a child.

Baila's stare held firm on her, dipping to Kienna's boots before climbing slowly upward until she paused on her silver-threaded tunic. Her lips pressed into a thin line, and then she looked away to the river.

"Shall we?" Kienna asked.

"After you, princess." Broan stepped aside for Kienna to lead.

She scoffed but moved ahead anyway, stepping into the riverfront market. Empty stalls cast long shadows in the quiet. Goods were left sitting out in the open in each stall, guarded by fear. Fear of the king, or, depending on who was asked, fear of things that moved after dark. Behind her, Moira ran her fingers over a rack of furs, the scent of woven fabric and woodsmoke curling through the air.

Danek stepped in beside Kienna, the soft shuffle of his boots barely audible over the river's rushing. He offered her a warm smile and greeted her with a hushed voice, "Looking good, Kienna."

She glanced at him, catching his reflection in the river glass, moonlight skimming the gold in his green eyes. His brown skin, usually sun-warmed and steady, looked cooler in the dark. Always so polished, so infuriatingly composed, like someone who belonged in a painting, not among the rest of them.

"How's Aine?" she asked flatly.

Danek kept his smile but pressed a hand to his chest like she'd struck something vital. "I'm sure Aine is cozy by a fire, thinking about me walking next to you."

"Sounds like Aine needs to get a life."

They moved on in silence, winding past shuttered vendors toward the edge of the merchant shipyard, where northern traders docked their small boats. The river stretched nearly two miles wide here, but the current was rapid and cold. At the end of the dock, a single weather-worn boat bobbed gently in the river.

Kienna tried not to laugh, pressing her lips together and gazing up into the dark clouds. No wonder Aine was able to get it so easily and tuck it away to avoid detection. The boat was made of old planks and sealed with patchwork tar. But it was quiet and would have to do.

Danek didn't even try to defend it. He and Broan untied the rope, each taking an oar while everyone climbed in. The boat groaned under their weight, especially once Broan stepped in, and then they pushed it out into the waters. The men sat in the middle to paddle, and Baila took the front while Kienna and Moira took the back. The city lights blurred behind them, swallowed by fog and distance. As they moved ahead, the oars lit up with magic to fight against the small current of the water moving south.

Kienna pulled at the fabric of her shirt to ease the bumps rising on her arms. A strange smell of pungent earth and smoke arose as they neared the western bank. The river was wide, nearly four miles in certain areas. The Guardians found the shortest path forward, but two miles was grueling work regardless. If it wasn't for the magic they seeped into the oars, they would have rowed for nearly thirty minutes, but their advantages cut that time in half.

Broan pulled the oar through the water with ease. "No turning back now."

When the boat thudded gently against the shore, they stepped out into the water to drag it the rest of the way. Kienna was careful not to kick any of the loose pebbles from their stone path. It didn't feel right being there. A strange tremor rose in her bones, and it wasn't because she was now disobeying her king after he showed her kindness. She stopped as dry land approached their feet. "Something's wrong."

Danek peered across the land. "Everything looks fine."

Kienna's eyes fell on the barrier. The towering stone wall stood a couple of hundred feet high with glowing pulses, but then the light simply stopped. To the untrained eye, it would be invisible. No one could tell from that far away. Kienna's eyes could only see distance up to a mile, barely over the river, but the closer they got, only truth was revealed. The stone wall itself continued for who knows how long, creating the illusion of protection, yet the lack of magic left the wall bare.

"Where's the star's fire?" Baila asked, peering around the wall.

Broan laughed. "You didn't truly believe King Vaerin sealed the western barrier with actual star's fire, did you?"

Danek dug his elbow into Broan's side. "Of course not."

Kienna kept looking at the barrier, trying to see if maybe it was supposed to pulse differently than the magic they used from the elements of the earth. Maybe magic from the stars would be different.

When they were teenagers, starting their journey in Guardianship, Dren would tell them about the West and how King Vaerin had to sacrifice the land's vitality to spark the magic of the Orb that rested over the entire city. He said the king sealed it with the fire of the stars and left a part of his strength there to hold it, and now, the West sleeps because he demanded it.

"I don't understand," Moira said. "Was there a breach?"

"I think they didn't seal it," Kienna said.

Maybe this was the threat Aine told Danek about. Kienna guessed that some nobles got brave and came to the western bank and noticed it, but they couldn't see the magic. How would they know there was a threat?

"Explains why we weren't allowed over here," Danek scoffed. "Our life is starting to feel more like a prison."

"How can you say that?" Kienna and Baila simultaneously scolded.

Broan rolled his eyes. "Here we go."

"Kienna, are you kidding?" Danek turned to her, brows dipped with a scowl. "You were talking yesterday about this. We are stuck behind this wall in a foreign land—"

"It's not foreign, Danek." Kienna crossed her arms. She didn't sound so sure, but she stuck to her grit, the weight of her new boots caressing her feet. "We grew up our whole lives here. Baila was born here. It's our home."

"I didn't," Moira said. She was five when she got here, much older than the others.

Baila tsked and stepped into Moira's path. "You don't even remember that world, so stop trying to claim you had a home before getting here."

Moira blinked back tears. "Danek and I are the only ones out of place, then? The only ones who think our life is meaningless?"

Danek threw up his hands and backed away. "Whoa, I didn't say that, Moira. Are you okay?"

Silence overtook the group as Moira started pulsing with an orange glow. As soon as she was aware of it, she let her magic fade and ran her hand over a ring on her pinky finger. "Let's go already."

Kienna was glad to drop the argument and followed Moira out onto the soil. The coarse dirt cracked for a few steps before hardening. The sour, burned earth grew thick in the warm air. Ash clung to the back of her throat like smoke from an old fire. The clouds thickened with unusual ferocity compared to the stable, light gray clouds of River Storm. Vegetation faded to a sickly brown. The trees leaned inward, their bark darkened and slick as if rot had soaked through from the inside out.

Without the barrier, Kienna stood conflicted. She knew so much about the king that she wasn't supposed to, like the harvesting of her memories, but realized that, maybe, she still didn't know enough. She wondered if maybe he wasn't aware it wasn't sealed. It would have been best to tell him, but how would she explain they were over here to find it? She had to rehearse more answers in her mind.

She could only tell him that she had gone over. Perhaps the thought of the threat surged her into action, and she went immediately to keep the city safe. She would have to leave the others behind, of course. He would ask why. She would say there was no time to get them, and he would give her some more boots for being a hero. The thoughts were vain, ones Kienna tried to fight, but her mind muddled.

In the distance, shadows flickered between trunks too quickly and shapeless to catch immediately. Creeping thoughts of danger pricked at her neck, and she fought the urge to leave Broan behind as deadweight if they had to fight ghosts.

"Kienna," Baila broke the silence. "You mentioned yesterday you saw Connak M'Ran leave the barrier?"

"I did," Kienna scanned the wall, wondering if this could have been how he managed to get out. But that couldn't be true either. She swore she saw it from the villages, not from here.

Broan nudged her. "Elaborate, princess."

Kienna flicked a glare at him. "I was reading outside when it happened."

"Remind me when this happened again? I don't remember it." Baila pressed.

Kienna resisted the urge to tell her she wasn't surprised. No one would remember. She barely did, but tiny bits came back to her when the forest-dwelling man would help her with her memory. Plus, it happened so long ago that it wasn't like she would have kept the perfect picture in her mind. She scratched her head. "It happened ten years ago. So, I must have been about fourteen. Moira was nineteen."

What Kienna could recall was that she told Moira about the incident. She was too scared that King Vaerin would punish her, so Moira stepped up and reported it for her. The king relentlessly questioned them for hours. Kienna could remember the fear, but not all the words, as River Storm scraped bits of her mind clean day after day.

Vaerin told the public that Kienna was mistaken in what she saw—that she'd been in training the whole day when he left, not watching someone escape. The whole situation was confusing. Even now, with some of her memory intact again, Kienna couldn't keep it all straight. The only clear thing was that the incident sparked the birth of their magic. They started in small spurts to test the waters. It wasn't until recently that he fed them more power to begin their real training.

"I've never seen anyone walk through magic," Kienna continued. "But he did, I think. Climbed the stone. Jumped over. I have no idea how. I touched the Orb once with my hand, and it shocked me. It's hard to explain."

Broan's mouth curved upward. "Yeah, I touched that bitch once, too. I learned not to do that again."

"Had he gone mad?" Danek asked.

"He looked lucid to me," Kienna shrugged.

Broan yawned and tossed a rock into the river. He grunted and pulled out a flask before he wandered deeper into the deadlands. Danek followed.

Kienna glanced back to where Moira and Baila still stood, the three of them locked in a silence that said more than words ever could. Whatever thread had tied them together was strained, frayed by the many questions of who belonged where and why.

They all turned from each other, Moira and Baila veering toward the ancient ruins. Kienna watched them go over her shoulder, then walked toward the barrier wall alone.

Chapter 14

—Kienna—

Kienna didn't know why the others cared so much about the ruins. Small stone towers and boarded-up homes were scattered about the land with holes and burnt wood. It did not take a lot of power to deduce that there wouldn't be anything of interest unless they were looking for silence.

She grew closer to the stone wall and the void that followed. The desolate wasteland continued for as far as she could see. Kienna pushed her vision forward, hoping there was enough magic inside her to zoom for miles. She locked onto a strange figure that she couldn't quite identify, but before she could figure out what it was, her vision stalled and slammed her back to where she stood.

She shrugged it off and diverted her attention back to the barrier. What was over there, right on the other side? Nothing. It had to be nothing because then the king would have sealed it. So, why was he so concerned about people going across the river?

A growl arose behind a crumbled wall of stone next to her. She had thought these ruins were barren. Kienna never bothered to ensure she was truly alone. She didn't think she had to. Now, she was kicking herself for being so careless. She turned her head ever so slightly to find a wolf as tall as her chest overwhelming her. She jumped back in haste, tripping over the root of a tree surfacing from the ground.

Landing hard on her back, Kienna braced herself for impact only to be left waiting as the creature stood in place, shackled in chains. She stood slowly, the ache in her bones cracking with every move. Her breath grew shaky.

Malnourishment faded the animal's coat, its skin sinking into its ribs. Its soft, silver eyes blinked sadly at Kienna, indicating she was not in danger. Kienna's heart slowed. She took a step forward, matched with a snarl and a step back from the overbearing wolf. Its size alone should have been enough to deter Kienna, but the proud feeling that washed over her fear magnetized her and pulled her in with a wave of energy.

The wolf's face reminded her of her forest dweller. With the thought, her mind shifted, and her vision blurred. The ruined trees stretched and healed before her, air lightening with the scent of pine. Kienna could smell the freshness as the full force of the sun illuminated her face. She knew she stood in the same spot, though her surroundings were full of life.

"This used to be part of the Malintale Forest." The man stood behind her, crouching in the rich soil.

She turned to face him. "What happened?"

"Vaerin happened. He destroyed half of it and then trapped the rest of its creatures over here to die."

"This animal I see," Kienna pointed, wiping the forest paradise away and bringing the man with her to the ruins that stood in her reality. She paused for a moment, realizing the magnitude of what she had done with her magic. That wasn't Vaerin's power. It couldn't have been. She bent his mind along with hers, something she'd never done. He'd done it, though… Was she feeding off his magic?

The man pointed to the wolf on his shoulders, confirming her suspicions. "A Malintilian Wolf. Smaller than she's supposed to be. They're usually the size of horses."

"Dangerous?"

"Not if you give a reason otherwise."

"How?"

The man shrugged. "Set her free."

Kienna glanced at the wolf, studying it. "How do you know it's a she?"

It was a stupid question. She should have been trying to get his name or trying to understand more about what his life was like on the outside. Not worrying about something she could have checked for eventually on her own…though she wasn't volunteering to peer that far underneath.

"Her eyes are wide and round. Males tend to have narrow, beady eyes," he paused. His expression grew solemn in admiration. "There aren't many of their kind left, sadly."

"Is that Vaerin's fault, too?"

"Yes, this was the home of their species. Some were able to get out and reside on the eastern border, but not many."

A familiar discomfort overtook her. Through the silence, the facade of the past surrounded them once again. The forest grew tall, the stone piecing itself back together within the small village.

Towering wolves roamed the land, living harmoniously with the natives. The restoration of peace around her put a glimmer on the edge of her mind. It was like a dream; one she'd soon forget as the glimmer pressed in. She reached for the hand of her visitor, but he pulled back sternly.

"You look nice," he said.

Kienna looked down at the silver threads and black pants and boots now stained with mud from the river. Her cheeks flushed. "They were made up north. Too nice for what I'm used to wearing, but they were a gift."

"How much do you remember today?" He bit his lip and folded his arms.

"He is in a good enough mood. I don't think he wiped it."

The man flung his arms in the air, his eyes now piercing with anger as they drifted down to her arm, catching a hint of the golden snake around her wrist. She'd put that on for extra flair. "And you still wear his gifts?"

"Am I supposed to wear rags?" Kienna scoffed. Her chest tensed as she huffed for air.

"What do the people of River Storm wear?" He asked it like he knew the answer. When Kienna's attention darted to her boots, he shook his head. "You're not better than them because you have magic, Kienna. You shouldn't act like you are."

"Because of what I'm wearing?" Suddenly, the clothes fit too tightly and felt like they wouldn't be able to withstand the heat of her flames bubbling through her blood. "You don't understand anything about what we go through here. You live out there. Don't try to judge me because of what I put on."

They weren't arguing about her clothes. It was an easy topic to start a fight. They were arguing because she panicked the other night and told him she had to stay in River Storm to protect the people. She tried to push him away after months, and she could see now that she might have hurt him.

She stepped forward as a makeshift wolf passed between them. She smiled. "Listen, we're okay, you and me. I need to refocus on how we interact, that's all."

"I can't stay," he told her. Kienna's smile dropped, her fantasy world fading swiftly. Her world came back to broken stones and darkness. "But I *am* coming for you."

She shook her head. Did he even hear her? "What does that mean?"

"Kienna, the barrier is coming down tonight."

He reached for her hand, but she pulled back. "What?"

"I have a small army on the outside, and we're ready to attack. You only have to tell us how."

A raging fire began to bubble inside of her. "We didn't agree on that. We weren't there yet…we were…we were talking."

"No, we weren't, and you know it. His gifts have clouded your mind."

Her throat grew heavy. "What could you want from River Storm anyway? You clearly don't need his magic."

His brows furrowed, his chest sinking with a small, adoring sigh. "*You*, Kienna."

Kienna let out a short, uncertain laugh. She tried to find the joke within his words. When she couldn't, she replied, "I'm unremarkable. And not worth a war."

The man loosened his grip and cocked his head. "I have to go."

"Wait!" Kienna pleaded. There was so much happening, too much to process. She couldn't be responsible for this. King Vaerin would never forgive her. "I don't know what to do."

"Do you want to see the world you imagined?"

"I do. But—"

"Then tell us how to get in."

She hesitated, studying the way his green eyes stared at her intently. He didn't look like he wanted to hurt anyone. This was the man who honored a wolf on his head after its death, who gave her memories back, and kicked dirt when she told him all the things Vaerin had said to her. She should be kicking dirt, too. Instead, she wore his fancy clothes and bowed to him. She was in a stalemate between the two.

"It's not sealed over here," she heard herself saying. "But you'll be seen before you even cross the river."

"I only need to get one soldier in. Then I can take it down."

"How?"

"Stay clear of the wall. Once it blows, climb over the far east side and run into the trees. I'll find you."

Kienna's surroundings faded. She stood alone with the wolf once again. A strong resolve kept her steady as she looked around her. It struck her as the right thing, her heart set on leaving River Storm and escaping whatever the king was doing to her. The only thing that kept her from fully committing was the lives around her. Could she live with herself if others died because of it? She wanted to reach back out to him and tell him to stop, that they needed a better plan, but the whimper of the wolf caught her attention.

She stared into its large eyes, admiring how astounding the creature looked in detail. She needed to set her free before anything else happened. At least she could try to avoid her life being a casualty in a fight she didn't even know she had asked for.

A buzzing of energy shimmered through her. Before she could lose it, Kienna reached her mind over to the wolf. A calm wave rushed over them both, followed by the wolf turning to reveal her chains. Kienna only hesitated a moment before reaching toward the metal links. Her fingers tingled with raw power. A single touch was all it took for the iron to crumble like dust.

She looked down at her hands. She'd never been able to use power like this, a power she didn't even realize she had until now.

Did Vaerin accidentally give her too much, and now he siphoned her because he was scared? She didn't get that hint from him, but how else could she do this?

The wolf took a cautious step back, shaking its body to rid itself of the final remnants of its captivity. Then, slowly, it turned its silver eyes on her. Kienna had given the beast freedom. There was nothing left to say or do except to admire the creature, patterns forming in her mind that could easily fit into a wood carving at home. With a powerful leap, the wolf bounded into the ruins.

Before vanishing completely, it paused to look back at Kienna one last time. Their eyes locked, and the moment held a promise to always remember this kindness. She almost thought she heard a *thanks* ringing out in her mind, but figured she'd made it up. Then, it disappeared. Kienna's eyes followed its path, her vision sharpening beyond what should have been possible. At first, she saw only the empty ruins stretching before her, but then something moved. A shadow, right at the edge of her enhanced sight. It watched her, waiting. A wrongness radiated from it, and ice flooded her veins where fire used to be.

She must have stared too long because the shadow blinked out of view before it reappeared, closer. Gone again, then closer still. Then, it stood right in front of her. Kienna didn't get a chance to see its face. The shape exploded into smoke, curling around her, pressing in without weight or form.

The air bent. The world fell off balance, and the part of her brain meant to keep her safe lit up like a fire line. A deep-rooted panic highlighted her raw instinct that everything about everything was wrong. Her breath caught with fear, her pulse thundering. Without thinking, she turned on her heel and ran.

Chapter 15

—Beyond the Barrier—

Far beyond the barrier, across the burning edge of Sarton where desert winds met the chill breath of the river, the man stood cloaked in sand and silence.

Though his eyes could not reach Kienna directly, his mind could sense her. Her pulse flickered like a flame behind fogged glass. She had reached for him again, but she'd pulled away. The man didn't blame her. What he asked of her would shake the foundation of everything she knew. But she had summoned him. She wouldn't have if she weren't ready to be free of her own chains.

She was nearing the edge, struggling like a bowstring pulled taut, one tug from snapping as she wavered in front of the king. He bared his teeth.

"Are we ready, Commander?" a voice asked behind him.

He turned to face his second, a sharp-eyed figure clad in dark, scale-woven cloth. Around them stood their small legion of warriors, sculpted by moonlight and shadow. The Hollow Blades, they were called, trained for silence and secrets.

The commander's forest green eyes lifted toward the glowing dome. The barrier shimmered in layered hues of blue and red, hiding the city within. From here, the wall was a radiant lie. Peace woven in light. He knew better.

He had studied it for over a year: the way it pulsed, its rhythms, its weaknesses. Then, one day, Kienna had opened a door, not physically, but mentally. It was a dream she probably didn't mean to share. He tried not to enter uninvited, but when she left the gate open, he wandered with her, floating along the streams of her subconscious. He saw what she feared, what she hoped for, what she carved and painted in the dark.

The man never showed himself in *those* dreams. He only suggested pieces to go with them, landscapes she hadn't seen, and colors that probably didn't exist behind their walls. He'd watched her imagine the world, then waited until she figured out what she wanted. Only then did he appear.

It had taken some time to get her to come around, but when he held her stolen memories and gave them back, she'd caved quickly enough. She could see the king for what he was: A scared sorcerer, fighting to hold onto the control he stole. Maybe this would have been easier for her if she knew everything, but he had to dance carefully around the truth. If he went too deep too quickly, she'd shut him out. From her perspective, everything about the world beyond would have sounded absurd. Even the truth would sound like lies.

Now, he stood at the edge of the truth. He knew how to bring it down.

But still…he hesitated. "Hold off," he ordered.

"I thought you were sure she'd come," his second said, voice dry.

"I was. I still am."

"We've exhausted our resources, Commander. We cannot wait much longer."

He stared once more into the wall of light. "Give me two hours," he said. "I'll get to her."

—Kienna—

Kienna's heart pounded as she wove between the dead trees, her breath coming in short gasps. She barely noticed when she nearly ran straight into the other Guardians who were studying the scattered skeletons among the ruins. Danek was right. There was a threat, and the others already looked like they had forgotten all about it.

"Whoa, Kienna!" Danek said, grabbing hold of her arm.

Her body trembled, but she couldn't find the words. Whatever that shadow did inside of her shut down any part that could have explained what she saw.

"What's wrong?" Moira's eyes grew wide with concern.

Kienna didn't answer. She tried so desperately, but she couldn't. The fear wrapped itself around her throat like a vice, and all she could do was pull her arms away and keep moving, hoping the others would follow and that whatever had grabbed hold of her in the shadows wouldn't follow her back into the village.

The boat was still tied, bobbing gently in the water. She almost reached for it but stopped. Taking the boat meant leaving the others stranded, and even if she was shaken, she couldn't do that. Instead, she sprinted along the riverbank, boots thudding against the damp earth as she made her way back to River Storm. The trees thinned as the land curved, and faint moonlight struck a shallow bend in the water.

Her lungs burned, her mind raced, and then she saw a spot where the current slowed, the stones visible beneath the surface. Without hesitating, Kienna waded in, boots slipping over slick stones as the cold water soaked her to the waist. Half swimming, half wading, she pushed through with frantic urgency, finally dragging herself onto the merchant square's bank, wet and trembling.

When she crossed the dock, her pace finally slowed, but her hands shook as she caught her breath. She scanned the empty market stalls. The wooden planks creaked beneath her feet, the sound of the rushing river the only noise in the unnerving silence.

A short while later, the boat creaked into its dock on the square's far side, and her group climbed out one by one. Danek reached her first, his breath slightly ragged from running. "Kienna, what happened?"

Broan, Moira, and Baila appeared behind him, each wearing varying expressions of concern and frustration. Kienna still couldn't speak. She shook her head and dropped onto a bench against an abandoned stall. It was all too much. The barrier missing. The threat beyond the wall. Whatever monster watched her. The others joined her, settling in the stillness of the deserted square, watching the last traces of clouded moonlight fade into the dark sky.

She sat there for what felt like hours but could only have been minutes, letting the wind dry the water from her clothes. She shivered. Her heart still pounded from the sprint, from the shadow, from whatever it was she left behind.

The river continued its steady course, oblivious to the weight pressing on Kienna's chest. She closed her eyes, trying to shake the lingering terror of the shadow she had seen alongside the imminent threat at the barrier. She'd told the man with ease how to get into River Storm. She didn't even think it through—just said it—and now what?

River Storm was in danger.

Everything remained eerily still. No music or laughter. Only the sound of the water. The tension between the Guardians built slowly—Kienna's silence, Broan's scowl, Moira's side glances. A wave of dread passed between them all before the heavy thud of boots broke the quiet, and the world returned to Kienna at a regular pace.

The soldiers' presence was immediate and commanding, armor glinting in the dying light. "King Vaerin requests your presence," Dren said, leaving no room for argument. The Guardians exchanged uneasy glances before following the line of soldiers toward the castle.

Night had fully descended, but River Storm did not sleep. The city rushed back like a roaring river. Lanterns glowed on every street. Laughter echoed from distant parties. The city still celebrated, unaware of what could be coming. Up the hill, the castle loomed with unnatural brightness, torches and braziers flaring against the sky. Inside, the halls buzzed with tension and more guards than usual. Footsteps were sharper, and faces were drawn tightly with urgency. Something had changed. Kienna's stomach turned.

"This isn't normal." Moira hugged her arms around her waist.

"Obviously not," Broan replied. "You think Vaerin called us in for evening tea?"

Danek scanned the soldiers. "They're on edge. Do you think he knows where we were?"

"No shit. But that's not it. It has to be the barrier," Baila whispered. "This is why we shouldn't have days off, but you all wanted to go off and have your little adventure."

"You came, too, so get off your high horse," Moira said.

Kienna didn't speak. Her heart was still racing. A familiar presence pressed at the edge of her thoughts like an insistent leechbug.

It was *him*. Somewhere nearby. Close enough to sense her and pull at her mind. Then, without warning, a hand caught her wrist and pulled her into a side stairwell meant only for the servants. If any of them had been roaming, they were certainly quiet and didn't make themselves known.

Kienna gasped. It *was* him. The man from her visions. How did he get over and through so fast? Did she spend that long at the market before the soldiers found her? Did she care? His grip calmed her through the strain she'd encountered, and she wanted to fall into him for a minute. But she couldn't.

"You." Her voice trembled.

"I need to know you're coming with me when we blow the wall," he said.

The castle stairs echoed, and they quieted themselves, pushing closer to the damp stone. His breath brushed against her, and her eyes trailed to his lips for a moment. It was not the time for that, but she didn't think she'd be seeing him or smelling his pine scent.

He scanned her, brows furrowing. "You're hesitating."

"I—"

"We don't have time for doubts, Kienna. I need to know you're with me before I take the wall down."

She snapped out of her trance over him and considered what he was asking of her. She wanted to go—needed to go. Kienna knew it in her heart, but this would be the start of her visions of rolling heads. Her stomach ached. "You want me to abandon River Storm?"

"I want you to be free," he insisted, though uncertainty flickered in his eyes.

Kienna's voice cracked. "And the city? Everyone inside?"

"I don't want to see it burn, but I can't promise it won't."

"Then why ask me?" Kienna backed away, breath unsteady. Her

voice grew too loud, and he had to move closer to shush her.

His demeanor shifted to both urgent and pleading. "Because you don't *belong* here. You know it. Vaerin will never let you go, and he'll break you."

"How do you know so much?"

His expression tightened for a moment, the calm beginning to unravel. "Because I've seen it." His jaw clenched. There was pain there. The sound of footsteps growing louder and more distinct reverberated through the narrow hallway. He looked over his shoulder, muscles taut with anticipation. "We don't have time," he said.

Soldiers rounded the corner into the stairwell with weapons drawn. The man let out a sigh, his shoulders rolling back as he straightened. His resignation in the way he stood faded. He perked at the sight of them. "Well, well." His eyes flickered toward the guards. "I suppose this was inevitable."

The soldiers hesitated for a mere second before closing in. Kienna barely had time to react before their hands were on her, too, cold metal clamped around her wrists. The man, however, did not resist. Instead, he smirked, tilting his head at the nearest guard. "Careful. I'm worth more *alive* to your king."

Kienna jolted. Why would Vaerin care if he were alive?

They were dragged through the castle halls. Kienna's pulse thundered, but the man moved with careless ease, his body relaxed as though this were nothing more than a midnight stroll. It unnerved her. As the massive doors to Vaerin's council chamber creaked open, a palpable shift in the air washed over her. The atmosphere became charged with tension, a thick, tangible presence that enveloped the room.

Vaerin was waiting. His sharp eyes settled on them. When they fell on the stranger, his mask cracked. "So, you return."

The man smiled. "Miss me?"

"You should have stayed gone." Vaerin sneered.

"And yet, here I am."

The glimmer of rage settled in Vaerin's sneer. He studied the man, considering him, then turned to the room. Baila, Moira, Danek, and Broan stood near a crowd of soldiers, cusped in their grasp. Kienna's eyes darted back and forth, trying to figure out why these two were talking so casually. Who was he?

Voice dry and unamused, the king said, "Tell me, Connak, how *did* you get in?"

The tension thickened at the sound of Connak's name. Loud, audible gasps filled the room's air as they murmured of the return of the one who defeated the walls before. The name echoed in Kienna's ears: the boy who had left River Storm.

Connak grinned. "I found your weakness."

Vaerin spun around, his movements sharp and deliberate. He locked eyes with Kienna, the silence between them crashing like a tidal wave. "Of course," Vaerin's voice came with a venomous whisper that cut through the air. His piercing stare bore deeply into Kienna. "It was *you*. I should have known."

His words punched her in the chest. Everything she worked for now lay crumbled in front of her. She'd given the king her life. Had that not meant anything to him? A surge of rage stirred beneath the panic.

Kienna staggered backward. "Let me explain—"

"You let him use you." The boom of Vaerin's voice shook the core of the castle.

Heart pounding, anger rose to meet it. Kienna turned toward Connak, searching his face for anything, any type of denial or support to pull her out of this bind. He knew what King Vaerin was like, more than anyone. But Connak simply stood there with one hand resting at his side and his chin tilted like he was already preparing for the fallout. His expression was unreadable, but his silence said enough.

"Do something," she hissed, voice tight with disbelief. Connak said nothing. Her fists curled at her sides. "You spineless bastard."

Vaerin stepped closer now, voice sharp. "You see now? He doesn't care for *you*. He never did. You are nothing more than a tool." He turned toward the soldiers, his anger sharpening his words. "Take him. *Now*."

The guards surged forward, reaching for Connak, but their hands grasped at empty air as his form flickered. The smirk remained even as his body began to dissolve like mist in the wind.

Kienna's stomach dropped. A conjured image. He had never *truly* been there.

She stared at the space where he had stood, disbelief flooding into something heavier. Her breath hitched, and her limbs locked in place. He was a ghost playing a trick. She'd believed in him, trusted him enough to question everything, and now she was left with nothing. Shame wrapped around her chest, but beneath it, a deeper ache took root.

She felt alone.

But how did he touch her? His fingers had wrapped around her wrist with real weight. His breath had touched her, and the heat from his skin. It wasn't a common projection of light. It curled around her senses with real presence. That form of magic shouldn't have been possible outside of their king.

And yet...it was as it had been in her dreams. Kienna's mind reeled, trying to separate the memory from magic, the illusion from intimacy. Her skin still tingled where his hand had been. The mind manipulation made her think of Danek, how he used touch and light to heal, and how he could create projections and sounds. Did Connak have that magic, too? If he did, King Vaerin had lied to them. Of course, he did. He lied to them about everything. Kienna saw the same reflection register on Danek's face. His brows twitched as he tried to hide it.

Vaerin turned back to Kienna, face hard as stone. "Traitor." He flung a ray of magic into her gut, and she curled to the ground, the intense shock of his power seizing her muscles. It was pure agony. "You betrayed your people, your home, your own Guardians. All for a ghost."

Her voice failed her. She hadn't meant to.

"Take her to the dungeons," Vaerin said.

"No!" Danek gasped. As the doors closed between them, he met her eyes.

Too late.

The last thing Kienna saw was Danek's face, shocked and full of helpless rage, as the doors slammed shut and the firelight disappeared. They dragged her as far down as they could, leaving her in nothing but the cold hush of stone.

Chapter 16

—Danek—

Danek moved swiftly through the winding corridors of the castle, his footsteps light and senses sharpened. The air in the lower halls grew thick with dampness, and a faint, putrid scent rose from the depths of the dungeons. He had to see her.

Reaching the entrance, he found a lone soldier standing guard. Danek pulled a small, heavy pouch from his cloak and pressed it into the man's palm. The soldier glanced at him. He looked around nervously and licked his lips. "Go. But be warned, it won't be a pretty sight."

Danek descended the slick stone steps, each footfall echoing off the damp walls. The smell worsened as he went deeper, a mixture of rot, mildew, and stagnant water. Puddles covered the uneven ground, their surfaces rippling with the occasional scurry of rats. The sound of dripping water was unrelenting, a slow, torturous rhythm that set his teeth on edge.

His eyes caught her body, barely rising in the dark. What the hell was Vaerin doing to her in there?

Kienna lay on the cold floor, shackled at her wrists and ankles. Her clothes were soaked, clinging to her skin, and smeared with grime. Her body bore fresh bruises, deepening shades of purple blooming along her arms. Hair clung to her face, half covering her hollowed eyes.

Danek knelt beside her, his voice laced with urgency. A soft flicker of light pulsed at his fingertips, blue threads twisting with every beat of his heart. "Kienna." She stirred, barely. Her eyelids fluttered open, revealing a wave of exhaustion. "Let me heal you," he pleaded, already reaching toward her.

She jerked away, as much as her chains would allow. "No," she whispered, her voice raw and weak. "Let me rot."

"Never." Danek's jaw tensed. "The king is punishing you for something you didn't understand."

"You don't know what I did and didn't understand."

It was like a knife in his heart. He wanted to know her, if she'd only open up enough to see him. "I want to help you."

She exhaled shakily, turning away. "I knew about him, Danek. He told me exactly what he wanted to do, and I didn't say anything. I'm a traitor."

Danek shook his head. "Vaerin is lying to us."

She let out a bitter laugh. "Does that make it better?"

He wanted to argue, but the weight of her pain silenced him. He summoned a dim light. It flickered, casting a fleeting glow on the damp walls before fading into the darkness. He reached for her hand, but she withdrew again.

"Danek, go. Before they find you here."

Why did she have to be so damn stubborn? "We need to get you out of here. Jacob's back from the trade routes, and I'm talking to him—"

Kienna sat up, clawing at him. "Don't bring him into this mess."

"They're worried about you. We all are."

"Just go!"

Danek hesitated and then stood, reluctant to leave her in this state. But she was right. If he were caught, it would only make things worse. For them both. Before he left, he turned back once more. "I'll fix this," he promised.

She didn't respond.

As he ascended the steps, he clenched his fists, his anger growing. A faint tremor passed through the stone beneath him, reacting to the turmoil brewing inside. King Vaerin never addressed them after the incident. They were all too scared to ask about it now—about the magic that existed outside of him. Danek spent the days wondering how Connak had that magic. Did the king give it to him? Or did he always have it?

He walked along the back of the castle, weaving into the small, pathetic garden between the noble palaces. He made his way through the path with renewed purpose, finding his way to Kienna's brother. Jacob was ranked high enough now in the King's Guard to have some influence.

Danek barely gave him time to react. "She won't last long in there. You have to convince Vaerin to show her mercy. He won't listen to me."

Jacob's face darkened. He stared ahead at the castle, his jaw twitching. He had always been protective of Kienna, but now, as a soldier under Vaerin's command, his position was precarious. He had some pull with the ranking leaders, but defying Vaerin was another matter entirely.

"I don't know if that's possible."

"Make it possible." Danek's voice was steel. "Or you'll be mourning her before long."

—Kienna—

Danek's presence was fleeting. The dungeon walls closed in around Kienna, pressing against her mind like a living force. She barely moved. Her body was heavy with exhaustion, and her mind was fractured and raw. The small cracks in the walls above barely let in any light, but she kept her eyes fixed on it, watching the last traces of the sun slip below.

When night came, the cold took hold.

It wasn't only the chill of the damp dungeon that disturbed her in the dark. It was the shadows that lengthened, twisting unnaturally. They writhed toward her, whispering things she couldn't understand.

Then came the water.

A sharp inhale caught in her throat as it rushed in, flooding the stone floor within seconds. Ice cold, it climbed her arms, her legs, her chest. She gasped as it surged over her head, cutting off her air, filling every crevice of the cell. She thrashed, but the chains held her down. Her lungs screamed; her vision blurred. When she was sure she would drown, the water drained, leaving her gasping, coughing, and shivering on the cold ground.

It happened again.

And again. Night after night.

Each time, the water stole more of her strength, the shadows grew darker, and the whispers clawed deeper into her mind. The cycle of suffocation and clawing for breath left her broken and on the verge of losing herself entirely.

Then, silence.

The shadows retreated, and she was left alone once more, trembling in the frayed edges of her mind. Death would be better than this. Time barely moved. She tried to keep track of the days by counting the number of times she drowned, but it happened too often now to remember. She sat in her filth with shame chained to her wrists.

Some days, she pulled debris out of the water and shakily etched images into the hard walls. She spent the hours carving into the stone with whatever tools she could find. Often, her fingers traced a single curved line, like the arc of a mountain or the curl of the wolf's eye she'd seen across the river. Other times, she etched an outline of the barrier's shimmer, cracked and incomplete. These drawings became her talismans, reminders of who she was. When her fingers bled, she lay in the grime and sang the same song until her voice gave out.

"Round and round, the silence spins,
The dark has teeth and grins and grins."

The guards would open the doors now and then to provide her with a meal. That was a good enough indication of how long she'd been there, but she soon realized meals came in weird patterns. They'd throw one down, and minutes later, throw another, and then it would go still for a long time. "Round and round, the silence spins."

She thought she was going mad. Every second ticked away until the light faded, and when it did, she went through her routine with the shadows. "The dark has teeth and grins and grins."

Then one day, she stopped fighting back, and the shadows

grew tired of playing. When that happened, footsteps echoed down the corridor. She barely had the strength to react as the heavy iron door creaked open. Soldiers entered, and they hauled her up by the arms. Her legs barely held her weight as they dragged her from the dungeon. They moved quickly, guiding her through the twisting halls of the castle, further into its cold heart. When they finally stopped, she found herself standing before the other Guardians.

They were waiting for her.

"The dark has teeth—"

Every face bore a different reaction. Horror. Pity. Contempt.

Even Broan, who rarely hid his disdain for her, looked disturbed by what he saw. Kienna stood, shoulders slumped, trying to suppress the unbearable shame twisting through her chest. "The silence spins."

Her clothes clung to her frail frame, still damp and stained. Strands of her hair hung in heavy, matted clumps around her face, and her cheeks had grown slightly hollow, the curve of her jaw more pronounced. She looked tired and worn.

King Vaerin stepped forward, his presence suffocating. "This," he said, gesturing toward her broken form, "is what happens when you wander from the crown. It poisons your ranks."

The dark has teeth...

Baila's eyes never left Kienna, locked onto her with a steadiness that revealed nothing but strength. Moira flinched, her hands balling into small fists at her sides. Danek's jaw clenched, blue sparks flickering briefly at his fingertips before he forced them away.

"Damn." Broan shifted his weight uncomfortably and muttered under his breath. It was a rare crack in his otherwise hardened demeanor.

"You will all report any hints of treason to me immediately. If Connak ever reaches for you again," he turned to Kienna, "I expect to know it." The king looked them over with a blade-thin stare before he gave a dismissive wave. "Leave."

One by one, they turned away, their expressions burning into Kienna's mind as they walked past her. When they were gone, the weight of exhaustion was too much. Her knees gave from the weight of it all.

"And grins and grins."

Kienna awoke in a room unlike any other she had seen in River Storm. Light flooded every corner, an unnatural brightness compared to the dim, torch-lit halls she was used to.

Magic hung thickly in the air. It was a humming energy that wrapped around her like a cocoon, knitting together the bruises on her skin and soothing the aches in her bones. She still hurt, but the overwhelming agony dulled to something distant and manageable. For the first time since the dungeon, she could breathe.

But she wasn't *free.*

King Vaerin's voice broke the silence. "You look better." There was no warmth in his tone. He stood near the doorway, arms crossed, watching her with that calculated expression she had come to dread. "Healing magic works wonders, doesn't it?"

Kienna pushed herself upright, wincing at the stiffness in her muscles. She met his eyes cautiously. "What do you need me to do?"

Vaerin's lips curved into a scowl. "To make amends."

She swallowed hard, her throat dry. "I—"

"You don't have to explain," he cut in. "We both know what you did."

Kienna lowered her head. "I made a mistake."

"A mistake?" Vaerin stepped closer. "You let an enemy in. Even if it was mentally, he gathered more intel from you because you couldn't control your own mind. You compromised everything we've worked for." His eyes darkened. "You'll have to work harder to prove you even deserve a place here in this realm."

The words hit hard. Would he kill her? She never expected him to make such a threat, but would that be the punishment worthy of endangering the barrier?

Kienna struggled to keep her mind from unraveling. If the *Great King* had trained her to use her visions and strengthen her defenses, she could have avoided this altogether. He left her in a cryptic tomb, fumbling around to find any breath of light. She wondered if the king truly cared about any of them or if he only wanted to control them. *Round and round, the silence spins.*

He exhaled sharply and straightened. "Fortunately, I have a solution."

Kienna's skin prickled as a purple haze crept over her limbs, settling into her veins. A heavy sensation followed, like a damp cloth smothering a flame. She inhaled sharply, unsure whether it was meant to help or restrain her.

Vaerin carefully watched her. "I'll be removing your magic," he said, as if this were kindness. Maybe it was, and he didn't know it. The pain of magic's existence inside of her would finally go away., but he thought he was taking away what made her special in River Storm.

Kienna stiffened but nodded, swallowing hard. This was her way forward. Her chance to atone. She couldn't afford to question any of it anymore if she valued her life. She inhaled again, trying to settle the uneasy churn in her chest.

That haze wasn't entirely unfamiliar. There had been times in training, even in rest, when her magic was muted, when her spells fizzled before they reached their full form, or when her instincts slowed, like she was reaching for something out of grasp. She had truly begun to think she was the one who was broken.

But now…she wasn't so sure.

Then it was gone. She noted the subtle shift. This power had always burned inside her, however quietly. Now it barely pulsed, like embers buried deep in ash.

"You will not be joining the Guardians in reinforcing the city barriers anymore," Vaerin continued, his tone clipped. "You've lost that privilege."

Kienna clenched her jaw, her fists tightening in the sheets. Was it ever a privilege to stand at the wall day after day? She didn't think so anymore, but she wouldn't tell him that.

The king paced. "You'll continue your battle training, of course. You will fight all four of the Guardians every day. They will be instructed to use their magic with magnitude."

What did the rest of them have to go through after all this— while Kienna was locked away? She assumed King Vaerin was not ignorant of the fact that they had come back from the west side of the river before she got caught with Connak. Was his wrath worse because of what she did?

Thinking about facing them again brought phantom bruises that she knew would follow and images of the looks she would endure. The silent judgments.

The dark has teeth and grins and grins.

They wouldn't go easy on her after what happened. Each blow would be their vow of allegiance to the king. She wouldn't be fighting to endure their power. They would have something to prove, too.

Kienna could almost predict resentment boiling in their upcoming matches: jealousy of Vaerin handing her extra gifts as a child. She suffered the anger of his healing hand time after time, while they had to lick their wounds clean. He gave her a family as a baby while they scraped by in the orphanage. The scales were tipping, and there would be no defense for the stain on her soul.

Vaerin tilted his head. "You want to be strong, don't you? This is how you learn. Until you prove yourself, you will remain under punishment."

Her nails dug into her palms. "And if I can't do it?"

His smile was chilling. "Then you'll stay exactly where you are. Useless and disappointing." The air in the room thinned. "Not to mention your life hanging in the balance."

Kienna glared at him. She had no real choice.

"And," he stepped toward the door, "when you're not training, you'll be on the farms, mucking the shit off the ground like a commoner. Then we'll see if you earn the right to be more." Kienna gritted her teeth. She didn't trust her voice, so she said nothing. "Oh, child." He softened as his hand waved over Kienna's mind. She resisted the urge to slap him away, shadows of the dungeon still haunting her every move. Another wave of his magic flowed through her now, a lighter haze tickling her brain until her thoughts softened. Only a little.

He'd have to try a lot harder now to erase what she suspected. She clung to as many memories as she could while they fled her mind. Still, any reservations she might have had were replaced with gratitude. How gracious of her king to give her another chance. To not kill her on the spot. He'd only been taking care of her when he threw her in the dungeons. She was more at ease internally, but her body recoiled slightly, fighting against what truly happened and what she felt now.

Vaerin lingered for a moment longer. His eyes gleamed, a small smile tugging at one corner of his mouth like he was tasting something savory. Then, he turned and left, the door clicking shut behind him.

Darkness spins, and it grins. She couldn't remember the song.

The hum of healing magic still filled the air, but Kienna barely heard it now. She felt nothing at all.

Chapter 17

—Broan—

The sparring room stank with sweat, and burnt magic scorched the air. Broan prepared himself in the center, his breath steady but tense as he faced Kienna. The other Guardians lined the walls. King Vaerin stood to the side, arms crossed, watching intently as he always did. Sparring wasn't as fun now with an unworthy opponent. Kienna's tunic barely clung to her body the way it used to. She was a ghost-limbed girl struggling to keep up.

A week passed before King Vaerin summoned her. Broan was disgusted by the sight, uncomfortable in the wake of a skeleton.

She'd put some meat back on after the king healed her, but damn, the images were etched deep into his mind now.

"Hit her harder," Vaerin demanded.

Broan glanced up once. He'd break her. "It's not as rewarding when she doesn't fight back!"

"Now, you imbecile."

Broan wavered, his eyes darting between the king and Kienna. King Vaerin slammed his magic through Broan's body and pushed him into Kienna's. They both tumbled to the ground, aching and rubbing their bones. "Fuck if I deserve this," he said under his breath as he rose.

Vaerin's voice sharpened. "Was I unclear?"

With a grunt, Broan sent a blast of magic toward her, but it was half-hearted with a hint of restraint. Kienna fell back.

"You brought this on yourself," Broan muttered. A rare twinge of guilt hit him after he said it, though. It's not something he'd say to the dead.

Vaerin scoffed. "Pathetic. All of you. I should have put each of you in the dungeons." He turned his attention to the others. "She could have killed you all. So, I suggest you join him."

—Baila—

Baila jumped in quickly. She rolled her sleeves and went right to work, unleashing green lights through the room and into Kienna's body. Kienna grabbed hold of a shield and deflected, but Baila saw the limp in her gait. A smile cocked on her face, and she pulled her magic to her feet.

A plant sat on the shelves against the wall near the enchanted weapons. Vaerin didn't usually give them artifacts of their elements, but Baila appreciated the new battle tactics available to them.

She surged forward, pushing past Broan, who stopped moving, and latched her core magic into the vines of the plant, pushing her power into it. The leaves grew, vines pummeling out uncontrollably until they grabbed Kienna's feet and knocked her to the ground.

Her head slammed onto the stone, but Vaerin caught it with his own magic. "Keep going."

"With pleasure."

—Moira—

"Baila, stop!" Moira reeled at the horror.

King Vaerin thrust his powers onto her, pushing her into the sparring ring. "Either fight her, or you'll be fought."

She resisted the urge to hold her stomach, her fingers trembling. Yes, Kienna messed up, but Moira couldn't rationalize the brutal torture. She was barely out of the dungeons. This was overboard.

A lazy surge of rays scorched Kienna's arm. Tears formed in Moira's eyes as she sobbed, "I'm so sorry."

Weapons clashed to the ground when Baila's plant grew bigger than expected. Broan sent a quake of earth up, and it flung Kienna back into the walls, the statues crashing into pieces.

Moira shook.

"Blow your fucking magic, or you can suffer the same fate in the dungeon."

Face growing pale, Moira lit the orange embers in her palm and hit Kienna as hard as she could. Another tear rolled down her face.

—Danek—

Danek didn't need coaxing when Moira received her threat. He coursed the wind in from the halls and spun Kienna around in a twister and then displayed images that weren't quite so friendly.

In the midst, he threw in his healing magic, hoping Vaerin wouldn't see him. The king's eyes were locked on Baila, so he figured there'd be times he could be more helpful than harmful.

Still, seeing the fear in her eyes while the others pushed their full force of magic, tugged on him. This needed to end.

—Kienna—

Kienna fought back, dodging and countering when she could, but the lack of any magic at all slowed her down and made her vulnerable.

The ground beneath her trembled, cracked, and then split, an earthquake from Broan rippling through the room. Kienna lost her balance and crashed hard onto the stone floor. Vaerin didn't catch her this time as her head slammed into the ground.

Dizziness called, and blood coated her tongue.

Vaerin raised a hand. "Enough."

Danek rushed forward, kneeling beside her. "Let me heal you."

"No," she rasped, curling away as he reached to touch her. She could see the shadows lengthening from his hand, and the thought of being touched made her body shake.

The king surged his unfiltered power into Danek, knocking him out of the way. "Stubborn. But you'll learn. All of you." He crouched beside Kienna, pressing his palm to her skin. Magic surged through her with unwelcome force. Her wounds faded, but the humiliation remained.

Danek crossed his arms and looked away.

"Get up," he ordered. "Go shovel shit."

Kienna clenched her fists. "I've been on farm duty for a week—"

"And you'll continue," Vaerin slapped her face, "until I say otherwise."

Her cheeks pulsed with heat. She didn't bother bowing when she stood, which she'd pay for later. Kienna left on heavy steps. She sulked out of the castle halls and into the city, weaving her way through the villages and to the stables and farms north of the homes.

The cows were giddy to see her, and the goats bleated loudly with their hooves, prancing around the stone paths. Kienna's hand grazed one of the horses standing in the yard. Its rough hair bristled in her fingers, the fine muscles of its body bulging firmly and confidently. If she could ride them away, she could slip through the northern lands and escape this hell.

There was no way into the northern lands, though, unless she planned on finding a ship to take her. Or she could climb the mountains. A sigh escaped and she took to the stalls, shoveling the dirty scraps, replacing them with clean hay, and making sure the animals had fresh water for the evening to come. As she did, she could feel small pricks in her mind, knocking to come in. It was probably *him*. The man beyond the wall—Connak. Sweet with his words and sharp with his silence. He hadn't even bothered during her weeks of suffering. What could he want after all that? She wasn't stupid enough to fall for it again. But still, the presence lingered, tapping at her thoughts like a pebble on glass.

You don't get to use me, asshole. She slammed a stall door harder than necessary, hoping the force resonated in her mind. This had been a game for him, a weird pissing match with Vaerin to get under his skin. Where he was now and what the king intended to do about it, she never heard. The wall never came down, and there was no breach to the Orb. That had to be a good sign. The other four were spending way more time sealing every inch of it ever since, so it had to be stronger.

Kienna tossed some fresh hay onto the path to lead the goats back into their stalls for safekeeping at night. The animals wouldn't be hunted by anything wild, but rumors circulated from time to time that older kids from the orphanage would sneak through the farms looking for anything to fill their bellies.

She closed the barn door. Farmhands were turning in for the night as the cold set in. They all laughed and joked as they headed toward the villages, their banter echoing through the night. They sounded so simple with the things they worried about.

Kienna left alone, weaving through the uniform streets of villages. She counted each home as she passed until she reached the end of the line, closest to the barrier. A slap in the face to remind her. Her fingers rubbed together achingly, but she turned her back and went inside. Maren looked up from the table and let out a breath like it had been caged behind her ribs. "Thank the Mother."

She jumped up and ran to Kienna. Too tired to push away, Kienna fell into the comforting resolve of her mother's dainty arms and exhaled. Not long after, Jacob came through the door, another similar sigh of relief escaping into Kienna's ear.

Jacob had been in Vaerin's army for five years. Though they had never seen a threat big enough to incite a soldier's action, he had gone north of River Storm many times to accompany trade routes and help keep the peace in restless wards. Maren held the impossible task of having two children in the service of their king, one that must have been noble but utterly terrifying at the same time.

"How was it today?" Jacob asked Kienna cautiously, scanning her body for any bruises. He wouldn't find any. The king made sure of it, but he hadn't healed her cheek. A small welt already formed underneath her eye, and Jacob fixated on it.

"I think I like farm duty," she lied, hoping to pull his attention away.

Jacob smiled. "I always thought you belonged with the goats."

Kienna pulled away from her mother. "I'm going to bed."

"Oh, please stay," Maren pleaded. "I've barely had you both home at the same time this year."

Kienna and Jacob shared a glance and agreed to sit at the table to appease their mother. Silence filled the room like a wave while Maren busied herself in the kitchen preparing a late meal, nervously fumbling with plates and cups. Kienna's eyes landed on Jacob's coarse hands lined with scrapes and deeper cuts as he thumped the table gently. They were the same age, Kienna and Jacob. Maren had Jacob early; a tough labor, she had admitted, since her husband had died in Vaerin's War of Liberation.

Resolved to raise her baby alone, she didn't expect to be given another one. But when soldiers entered the gates with children in hand, Maren couldn't resist the coos of the baby girl whose eyes glowed with the night moon. It was Jacob who got her out of the dungeons. He admitted that much to her. What he promised the king, she didn't know, but the lightness of his heart slipped day by day.

The sound of shattering glass startled them all out of their thoughts. Kienna jumped, pulling out of her chair and scanning the room for danger, heart thrashing in her chest. *Grins and grins.*

Jacob placed his hand on Kienna's shoulder. "Mom dropped a

cup."

The shards of glass lay splattered on the ground, Maren clumsily picking them up. Kienna found her breath and knelt to help, her own hands shaking as wildly as her mother's.

"You shouldn't be here," Maren cried.

Kienna smiled faintly. "It's okay. It's only glass. We can clean it up."

Maren turned her body swiftly to Kienna's, grabbing her hands and knocking the glass back down. Her eyes scanned Kienna, a twinge of guilt wrapping tightly around her lips. "This isn't your home."

"Uh, Mom," Jacob stepped forward.

"Hush, child," Maren demanded, a confidence in her voice that neither of them was used to hearing from her. "And sit."

Maren took Kienna back to their wooden table, an intricate carving of wood that Kienna had built for them years ago. It was a beautiful round table, large enough for the three of them, but carved so intricately with florals along the edges and sturdy enough to handle a crash.

"When the soldiers handed you to me, I swore I would protect you," Maren's voice shook. "But I've cowered to our king, and your heart has suffered enough."

"I think you're tired, Mom." Jacob reached for her.

"We let them think you're nothing, but surely, you know there's something special about you." Maren searched deep in Kienna's eyes.

Jacob knelt in front of his mom, gazing sternly at her. "It's time to stop."

"We can't be scared anymore, Jacob. We can't let them ruin what she is. You've seen it. You know."

"Is someone going to explain to me what's going on?" Kienna shoved her chair to the ground.

Maren and Jacob shared a prolonged glance until Jacob slumped his shoulders. "Kienna, do you remember when we were children and climbed the pine trees near the barrier?" He looked to his mother for guidance.

She nodded. Those trees had since been torn from the ground.

"I do," Kienna said. "You fell, and Vaerin had to heal you. It was awful."

"Jacob was badly hurt when he fell. We couldn't move him, and no one would come that far out to see what happened. You wrapped your body around him, yelling for help, but there weren't any people around who could be of use," Maren said.

"*You* healed me," Jacob echoed.

Kienna rolled her eyes. "No, I can't do that. Vaerin healed you."

"The light that came out of you was so bright, I thought I had died." Jacob's voice was serious, but the gleam in his eye said he thought fondly of this incident. "Vaerin was nervous about your magic."

"Why did he give it to me, then?"

"He hadn't given you anything yet," Maren said quietly.

Kienna crossed her arms. "No one has magic here unless Vaerin gives it."

Jacob and Maren shared another knowing glance that only annoyed Kienna further. It was like they were in their own troupe while she sat on the outside.

Her shoulders went rigid. "What is it?"

"Right after you healed Jacob's body, Vaerin took a strong liking to you and some others who shared these unknown abilities. Sure, he gave out some magic, but you already had it before you joined him."

"Why has no one in the villages said anything?"

"They're dead. Anyone who has ever seen your magic before the king's gift…They're all gone."

Jacob nodded. "I've seen him assassinate enough people."

What they were speaking of…that was treason. Not that it

mattered. She already had her own record of it. But what would King Vaerin do to her family? He already indicated he had no problem killing her. This teetered beyond her now. "You're lying," she said, standing quickly to walk away.

Jacob reached for her hand. "Why would we lie about this?"

She pulled away, her breath catching. "Because if it's true, then everything I've done in the name of the crown, everything I believed...was evil. *I'm* evil."

"Kienna," Maren started gently.

"No," she said, shaking her head. "No, I can't. I can't do this right now." The room held a thick silence. "I need to go to bed," she said, voice thinner as she slipped away before they could stop her.

Her bedroom welcomed her with a familiarity that wrapped around her like a blanket, but even that warmth couldn't shield her from the storm. Paintings—scenes of forests and stars—lined the wooden walls. Wood carvings she had shaped with her own blade littered the shelves, little animals and abstract shapes she had made to calm her nerves in the quiet of the night. A new carving sat closest to her bed.

The wolf she freed.

Kienna sat on the edge of her bed and stared at her hands, recalling the golden light Jacob had described. Her fingers trembled. Could it be true? Had something always been inside her?

If so, how much more of her life had been built on these lies that Vaerin crafted? The barrier. Connak. Magic.

She pressed her palm to her chest where the warmth of that magic once lived. Only a hollow echo remained. Kienna searched her memories, wishing she'd clutched onto more, but everything swirled into a confusing storm. Who the hell was she if she wasn't meant to be there? Her head spun and reeled from the information. If she wanted to, she could call Connak. He'd clarify it for her. Kienna swallowed hard. She couldn't make that mistake again. He messed with her head. He got her thrown in the dungeons. Now, she was fighting alone when all she wanted was to be held.

Kienna wrapped her arms around her legs and lowered her head.

—Connak—

Connak watched outside the barrier, as he did every night. His forces were growing weary, tired of sitting in the unforgiving plains between Sarton and Northpass.

As creatures of the forest, the blazing sun drained their energy quickly, but Connak did not waver. He stood at the edge of the shadow line, the place where the unnatural barrier glow met the dust of the dead grass. He could still see the shimmer of Kienna's spirit inside the city.

Pain tugged him, regret threading through the steady pulse of strategy in his mind. He hadn't meant for her to suffer. He only wanted to pull her free. Now, that damage was his to fix.

He knocked again in Kienna's mind. A slight opening nudged him away with the gentlest "Go away."

The corner of his mouth lifted like a crooked truth. He turned to his second in command. "Prepare your forces. She's ready."

Chapter 18

—Broan—

Broan and Danek lived comfortably near the orphanage on the outskirts of the palaces. They didn't need nor want anything bigger. Broan had his tools for stone masonry and Danek his quill and paper.

Broan slid a pebble into place on his makeshift model of the castle. "You scheduled for the butcher today?"

Danek bit against his quill, eyes trailing the light trickling into their common room. "Not today." He paused. "Do you think the king assigned me to the butchers to torture me?"

Broan chortled, his laugh smoldering deep within. "He sure as hell doesn't do anything to make us feel fuzzy inside."

The stones of the castle crumbled onto the floor.

Figures, Broan thought. *It was a weak structure anyway.*

He bundled the stones and put them in a metal can, then turned to Danek. He'd been sulking since getting back from the river. Today was no different. "What's got you down, pretty boy?"

"Hm?" Danek stopped chewing on his quill. "Oh…nothing."

Broan poked his elbow into his side. Danek yowled and moved away, his palms surging with magic. A bright glow sparked and lit the room with blue and gold. It was hard not to sneer. Broan respected Danek. It was Danek who strengthened them in the orphanage, pulling Broan out of more than enough fights to last a lifetime. He found them a house, but he also cared too much, and it made Broan want to puke.

"Spill your guts, Brother, or I'll spill them for you."

"Why do you think King Vaerin didn't seal the barrier over the river?"

"Fuck if I know."

Broan didn't care to spend much time worrying about what their king did and didn't do. It was odd. He admitted that much. But who was he to question how Vaerin did things? The kingdom belonged to him, not Broan.

"And what about Connak's magic? None of this bothers you?"

Broan shrugged. "Is this how you spend your energy?"

Danek's eyes lowered.

Broan wouldn't get around this one without going headfirst. He rolled his head back to look at the ceiling. "I get my power from the king, and I'm having a damn good time with it. I thought you were, too."

"Yeah…yeah, it's useful—"

"Useful?" Broan cocked his head. "It's fucking invigorating!"

Danek sighed and propped back down. "Some things don't add

up anymore."

"Like what?"

"Well…maybe beyond our barrier isn't dangerous."

"Be careful with your conspiracies, Brother. People have died for a lot less."

"That's what I'm talking about!" Danek shot out of his chair again. "People dying!"

"Easy, it was a figure of speech."

Broan's fists tightened. He didn't have luxuries like Kienna or Baila when it came to thinking outside of their lanes. Thinking about what the king did would not serve him at all, and it wouldn't change anything. They were still in River Storm, still bound to Vaerin's command. If they fought against that service, they'd be mucking cow shit like Kienna was right now.

"You need a woman in your bed."

Danek's eyes fell on the door, a dull glaze forming. "If I ever tried to leave, would I have your support?"

Broan's body tensed, his jaw feathering. Rarely did he find himself so speechless. "Danek." He hardly ever said Danek's name either. "You're not going anywhere."

"I don't like it here, Broan. It's the same torture every day, being called worthless and then watching our friend rot in dungeons."

"Not *my* friend." Broan said it with confidence, but his teeth clenched all the same. If Danek were in the same position, Broan would be up in arms, too.

"I'm serious. I'm tired of this place. I'd rather take my chances beyond."

"Maybe keep that to yourself, yeah?"

"Yeah. Whatever. I'm going to go climb something."

"Brother," Broan sighed as Danek motioned for the door. "I'll have to follow you wherever you go to keep your ass alive. Don't get us killed."

Danek slammed the door off the hinges behind him.

Broan stood and adjusted it back on. Clumps of dirt rose from the ground to meet his hand, a bronze glow flowing with ease from the tips of his fingers. He welded the clumps into strong clay, manipulating each grain until it clung to the hinges. The door stood strong.

"So dramatic. And he thinks I'm theatric."

—Kienna—

Rain and smoke filled the air as Kienna moved like a shadow through the alleys of River Storm with her cloak wrapped tightly against her body. Boots stepping lightly on the cobbled path, she slipped past lantern-lit homes and vigilant guards. Each step closer to the castle slammed her heart against her chest. She didn't know what she was looking for exactly, but everything in her bones told her the truth was hidden. The castle's library was a maze of knowledge, endless shelves climbing so high they disappeared into the ceiling's gloom. The air shifted to that of ink and old leather.

Kienna lit a small lantern, its flame barely more than a flicker, and began pulling books from the shelves. She needed to be quick as she omitted farm duty to be there.

History of River Storm, one cover read. Another, *The Age of Conquest.* She'd seen these titles before, displayed in study rooms and etched into the wall of the Guardian barracks. At first, the pages said exactly what she expected: A brave king rose from chaos, and a city was born of his mercy. But as she climbed the jagged ladders to the highest shelves with books coated in dust and rarely touched, the stories began to change.

They didn't contradict each other exactly, but tiny details were off. One praised Vaerin for founding River Storm atop the ruins of a forgotten land. Another claimed the city was built where an ancient kingdom had fallen. Some spoke of him slaying a great evil; others hinted he arrived only after the chaos ended.

The *War of Liberation* was worse. One text described Vaerin with his body bloodied, carrying children on his back. Another book said nothing of him at all, only "faceless soldiers." And Maren...*Maren said it was the soldiers.*

She pulled another book filled with diagrams and rituals. It claimed Vaerin was *born* with power. The next said he was *gifted* it by the gods. Another? That he *took* it, though the details were hazy and carefully crafted. Kienna flipped through each book, searching for who wrote it and when. Most were written by Vaerin's scribes, all within the time of River Storm's founding. Nothing added up. Her fingers trembled.

"Reading, are you?"

Kienna jumped. Her lantern nearly fell from her fingers. Vaerin stood in the aisle, his face carved from stone, eyes like still water. There was something off about him, something more than his presence. His movements were too smooth, too quiet, as though he glided rather than walked. His eyes didn't blink as he spoke, and Kienna noticed the faintest shimmer in the air around him, like heat on stone, as if the magic within him couldn't quite stay hidden. Was he using it right now?

"Sorry, Your Grace," she said quickly, masking her fear. "I must have gotten lost in the stories."

He stepped forward. "About the War of Liberation?"

"I was hoping to sharpen my mind. So, I could remind myself of your greatness and learn to be more like you."

A small, cold smile flickered across his lips. He said nothing more, turning and leaving without a sound. The moment he vanished behind the rows of books, Kienna's lungs remembered how to breathe. She fled the library in a panic.

The streets were nearly empty now. How long had she been in there? Lamps burned faintly, casting long shadows on the walls. Kienna's stride was brisk as she checked over her shoulder with every step. That was too calm an encounter with the king. Was someone following her? She scoffed at herself. Why would they? She didn't have anything! Kienna reached home and slipped inside only to find absence. Maren was always home before sundown.

"Mom?"

Nothing. She sat on the edge of the table, removing her boots while she waited. When the door creaked open, she sprang up. "Where were you?" Her voice trembled.

Maren blinked at her, clutching a bag of rice. "At the market. I thought we needed more."

"You're never late."

"There was a long line at the herb stall and—what's wrong?"

Kienna's face was pale, her hands shaking. "I've been doing research. and I… Do you think Vaerin is a good king?"

Maren hesitated, eyes narrowing. "Why do you ask that?"

That felt like a resounding no to her.

"I read things. Things that don't match. About the war. About… magic."

Maren slowly set her goods down. She moved to the side cabinet, pulling a cloth pack from beneath it. She began placing items inside: a small loaf of bread, a pouch of water, and a flint stone. Why the hell did she have a flint stone?

Her motions were careful, but her face was clouded with emotion. "You were special, always. Different. You had a way of seeing in the dark and slipping through crowds unnoticed. There were whispers, even then, that you didn't look like the rest of us. Something about your ears…" Maren trailed off.

Kienna had no clue what she was even talking about. Her ears were fine.

A rumble shook the ground beneath them. A sudden wave of wind blew through the cracks, rattling the walls. Kienna turned to Maren. "Where's Jacob?"

BOOM!

A light unlike any they'd ever seen cracked across the sky. They stepped outside. Above the barrier, sparks of pent-up magic burst upward like fireworks, then fizzled into nothingness. The wall shimmered. Parts of it cracked. For a heartbeat, Kienna could see beyond. There were trees and a sky not made of bruised stone. The light was different out there, though nightfall had taken over. A distant humming called to Kienna, similar to the vibrating she had heard in River Storm when she had magic, but stronger and far more curious.

This is what the Guardians were meant for, she thought as Danek and Broan sprinted alongside soldiers.

Maren gripped her shoulder. "Don't go to that wall, Kienna. This is not your battle. You go up and out."

"That's ridiculous," Kienna urged back. "I'm not going anywhere."

Maren handed her the bag, almost as if she had been planning for this. "Some things to get you through the night."

"Mom, no. I couldn't even begin to imagine what King Vaerin would do to me. Or to you."

"I can't leave Jacob, so you'll do this alone. You understand, of course."

Kienna thought about Jacob, probably standing in the front lines of the wall, ready to fight the battle no one understood. The carefree smile of the child he used to be flashed in her mind, and she longed to see him. "My duty is to the king. I have to go. I must—"

"This is not your story anymore. Go. Find who you are." Maren trembled. Her eyes held Kienna's, as if pleading for her to understand. "There *are* people out there." Her voice came softly under the quaking. "People who will look at you and see what I see. They will know how to help, and they can keep you safe."

Kienna was *supposed* to be safe *here*.

She blinked hard, and when the moment passed, her features stiffened again. "The world beyond that wall…it's not what he told you. Find the woodcarver. He has a letter for you."

Kienna's heart tore in two. She wanted to run. She wanted to stay. Running could kill her family. Betray her king. There was no telling what was out there. Staying, though, would kill her. She didn't have time to ask who the woodcarver was or how to even find this person.

"Tell Jacob—" Another blast ruptured. The world shook again as the sky burned white. Kienna looked at her mother one last time while the Orb crumbled.

"We'll be fine. Now go!"

Kienna turned and ran toward the farthest east wall of River Storm. When she reached it, she let herself grab hold of the crevices, climbing as fast as she could while the world quaked around her. Freedom cracked through the stone.

Chapter 19

—Moira—

Moira slept peacefully until the explosion. She startled awake in Rhior's arms to see the bright glow of red and blue fly through their windows. Her hand went immediately to her stomach, a protection spell waving instinctively over herself. "I have to go."

Rhior passed her a look of disdain, but he knew better than to interfere with Moira's duties. She told him all about Kienna's punishments, mainly to warn him that they needed to be more careful. He helped her out of bed, and she pulled her tunic on and tied her hair back. Her fingers moved with the precision of habit, even as her heart raced. In her mind, she ran through the Guardian drills. *Feet planted, shoulders squared. Energy from the core. Shape the barrier. Then summon the blade.* Tonight, the motions were heavier. It was like the magic resisted being drawn. Her hand lingered a moment over her belly.

As she moved for the door, Rhior gently caught her arm. She dropped her face. "You know better."

"Isn't that your friend running away?"

Moira paused. Outside, she caught a glimpse of Kienna, her cloak a streak in the chaos, sprinting toward the wall. "Where is she going?"

Rhior's eyes didn't leave the figure. "Do you think this has something to do with that Connak fellow?"

"I think…" Moira exhaled. "I think she's leaving."

"Why would she do that? Aren't we in danger?"

"Yes, you should get somewhere safe. We're too close to the wall."

Rhior stiffened, gripping her hand tightly. "You should go with her."

Moira laughed, nervous and sharp. "That is not what we are trained to do."

"Do you even know what it is you're going to fight at the barrier? Whatever it is just blew it down, and you have a baby now, Moira."

"Rhior—"

He lowered his voice as the soldiers rushed toward the wall. "I'm serious. If we have a choice…take it."

Moira looked back at Kienna, who had started to scale the wall. She raised her eyes upward to the wall itself, the energy crumbling. Something in her body recoiled at the idea of fighting near it. Heaviness dragged at her limbs and tightened her chest as though every fiber of her being was urging her not to step into the fray. Her eyes followed Kienna, a part of her already moving with her friend, even if her feet had not.

"You're coming with me," she told him.

"I won't survive out there. Not with those demons…"

"We don't know if they exist."

"Exactly."

"Oh, Rhior…"

He kissed her hand as the thunderous quake ruptured the ground. "Go now, Moira."

She faltered. "If I leave, I can't come back when the battle is done."

A harsh truth and one she could tell Rhior had anticipated carefully. He swallowed hard, fighting to hold her gaze, then he pushed her from him and walked away.

—Danek—

Danek stood at the wall, the wave of the barrier blasting him and the soldiers backward with violent force. He clenched his feet deep into the earth to stay upright, muscles bracing against the wind. Baila, glowing green with magic, rushed to his side and gripped his arms. With a surge of focus, he extended his palms outward, redirecting the gust away from their line.

"I can guarantee that wall is coming down next," Broan shouted over the roar. The dust coated over him. He sneered. "I fucking cleaned my boots yesterday."

"I guess this is what we've been training for our whole lives!" Danek rolled his sleeves. But he would gladly take any sign that it was time to go.

"Where's Moira?" he asked, straightening and scanning the

scattered formation of soldiers. She always preached that they were a team and had to show up for each other. If she wasn't there yet, something was wrong. Perhaps something got in and snagged her. He searched the crowd, half-expecting to see Kienna, too. Vaerin forbade her from being a protector of the barrier, but she was a warrior at heart. Either instinct or her simple curiosity would have pulled her there.

Neither of them was in sight.

"Hold on." Broan pushed his hand into Danek's chest.

The sound of armor locking into place and weapons being drawn sent a chill down Danek's spine. The tension in the air was unlike anything they'd truly trained for.

Broan suddenly snapped his head toward the east wall, pointing. "What does she think she's doing?"

Danek followed his line of sight, and there she was. Kienna, scaling the broken wall, barefoot with a tiny pack of all things. Behind her, unmistakable even through the haze of magic and smoke, was Moira. The golden glow in his palms faded. *Maybe this was the sign.*

"We need to follow her," Danek said, panic seizing him. His voice cracked louder than he meant. "If Vaerin gets his hands on her after this, he won't be forgiving."

Without waiting for a reply, Danek broke formation and ran. He didn't know if he could stop them or even if he should. He was only certain that this was not where he needed to be.

—Broan—

The wall shook, and a sound like thunder cracking from inside the earth caused great stones to topple, sending debris flying in every direction. Broan stood shoulder-to-shoulder with Baila, both rooted in place as dust and disbelief settled over the line of soldiers.

He watched Danek take off like a wildfire, disappearing after Kienna and Moira. Around them, the troops wavered. Some backed up; others stood stunned. The top of the wall groaned as chunks of rock rained down into the city.

"Well," Broan muttered, tossing a glance at Baila. "I'm not about to fight whatever is out there on my own."

He glanced again toward the east wall, where Danek had vanished. Danek always ran headfirst into fire—and damn it! Broan said he'd have to follow, didn't he? The call to act tugged at him, but his boots stayed planted.

Beside him, Baila shifted her grip, green light still circling her fingertips. "They abandoned formation," she whispered, more to herself than to him. Her knuckles tightened on her spear, as did the set of her jaw.

Broan shook his head. He needed a reason. "You ever think all those drills, all that talk of 'the threat beyond the wall' was just…talk? Legends to keep us afraid?" He was starting to sound like Danek. "Now we're here, and the wall's falling, and no one knows what's on the other side."

Baila didn't answer, but the silence between them said enough. He adjusted his stance, his sword humming with the tension of drawn magic.

Broan sheathed his weapon with a dramatic sigh, gave Baila an exaggerated, mocking bow, and muttered, "Guess we're dead men walking now," before striding off after Danek.

—Baila—

Baila stood alone, cool and composed as the dust settled. Her green eyes were sharp, almost unnervingly calm. She didn't move immediately to follow the others. Instead, she lifted her head to the towering terrace of the castle. There, like a statue of judgment, stood Vaerin, his cloak billowing in the rising wind, and his gaze was fixed on her. Their eyes met across the distance.

Why was he letting them go?

He nodded once.

Baila gave no expression in return, only turned toward the crumbling east wall where Broan had gone. She dropped the spear as she stepped forward. Not hurriedly. Not out of fear, but with purpose as she climbed the wall.

Chapter 20

—Kienna—

Climbing the wall was every bit of a challenge Kienna thought it would be, but getting back down proved to be even more difficult. She got lucky when half the wall crumbled at the top and fell backwards, giving her less to climb. As soon as she started her descent from the crumbled bits, the rest of the wall began to shake, and Kienna found herself having to jump and pray she landed without breaking anything.

Dropping fifty feet didn't give her good odds, and even she shocked herself when she blew out a faint burst of magic before hitting the ground. Her body slowed and then rolled to a thud in a pile of leaves. How she even used magic at all was beyond her. There's no way Vaerin gave it back, but she couldn't spend much time questioning it.

Kienna stood and glanced around, finding some familiarity with the trees around her as her eyes found the old hide of a wolf. This was where she spent time with Connak when she traveled to him in her mind. That gave her enough courage to push forward, but she had to be fast. If she spent too much time looking around, surely the king would send one of the Guardians after her, and she couldn't bear to fight them when she only wanted to get out of there and figure out where the hell Maren even wanted her to go.

She looked down at her feet before running, realizing that she never had enough time to strap her boots back on. Climbing over jagged stone had already shredded her soles. Now, she faced the thick underbrush of the forest barefoot. It would be worse.

Kienna groaned and stared forward, leaving the barrier behind as she pushed into the wall of endless trees. The forest swallowed her quickly with dense trunks rising in every direction, their shadows stretching long over the uneven ground. The sharp terrain bit into her skin with every step. She stumbled toward the nearest tree and let her shoulder catch its rough bark. Slowly, she slid down, pressing her back against the trunk as she tried to catch her breath. Her lungs burned, and her legs screamed.

She perked at the sudden crack of branches snapping behind her. Kienna lifted her head as her fingers slid toward the hidden dagger at her hip, heart pounding and aches forgotten. She didn't give whatever was out there time to react. She lunged upward with immense speed.

"Whoa!" Danek yelled, barely dodging the blade.

Kienna's body flew past Danek's and heaved into the ground. She scrambled up, ripping her dagger in the air. If this was who King

Vaerin sent to get her, it would be an easy fight.

"What are you doing here?" she growled.

"I could ask you the same question. We saw you scaling the wall, so we came to get you." Danek crossed his arms.

"We?"

"Hey, princess." Broan approached slowly with Moira behind.

Three against one could prove a little more difficult. Kienna inched backwards, but the others didn't draw any of their weapons. In fact, Moira looked too tired to even be there, her deep chestnut eyes searching for the nearest place to rest her head. Kienna scoffed, her eyes rolling back to the sky.

Danek held his hand out to her cautiously. "We're not here to fight. I just...wanted to make sure you were okay."

"You shouldn't have followed me," she said, placing her blade back in its holster.

"What did you expect us to do? Let you come out here on your own?" Moira stepped forward, her voice sharper than usual. "We're a team."

Kienna snorted at the thought. This was far from what a team should be doing together. "Well, Baila didn't have any issues staying put. Maybe be more like her for once."

"Ha!" Broan leaned his back against a tree across from her. "Trust me, I think we'd all rather be asleep right now, but pretty boy here got all glassy-eyed and wandered off, so here we are."

Danek shot him a glare. "I didn't ask you to come."

"Oh, yes, you fucking did. Don't even pretend you wouldn't have held it against me," Broan said, crossing his arms. "Now, we're in the damn forest."

Kienna looked between them, her jaw tight. "This isn't some spontaneous getaway. I'm not going back, and you have no idea what's out here."

"Do *you* even know what's out here?" Moira snapped. "Either way, we're all here now. None of us is clean in this anymore."

Danek stepped between them, raising a hand. "Can we not do this right now?"

"Oh, I'm sorry," Broan said. "Didn't realize the forest came with rules."

"Stop talking about the forest," Moira hissed. "Start talking about why we're even here."

Frustration nipped at Kienna. She was ready to shoot back another argument when a deep vibration rolled through the earth, cutting clean through the noise. The forest around them stilled, and the branded K on Kienna's thumb pulsed in a way she'd never experienced before. It synced with the soil like a heartbeat buried in the roots, lingering in her bones with the familiarity of her magic being restored.

"What is this place?"

The four stood together, backs against each other, staring at the arcane forest that unfolded before them. Gentle paths flowed between the trees. Towering pines stretched endlessly upward. Their thick trunks coiled with timeworn roots that clawed into moss-carpeted ground. A cold mist clung to the air, curling through the undergrowth and pooling in hollows, softening the already dim light that filtered through high branches like sacred fire.

"I had no idea this was here," Moira gasped.

"We have to go back," Broan instructed, turning to the group.

"No," Danek said calmly.

"What do you mean, no?" Broan's voice rose, raspy and out of place in the still fog around them.

Moira straightened, putting her hand on her hip. "Do you think Vaerin's going to understand when we return that we left his city to fend for itself when that barrier came down? Do you think he's going to forgive us for allowing it to fall in the first place?"

Broan started to say something but paused. He faltered for a moment and then huffed. "So, what then? We all followed the traitor out to our doom? We're all traitors by default."

Kienna flinched, though no one noticed between their bickering. She stepped away, her skin prying from Danek's arm. The coolness of the forest in the night settled deep, bumps forming across her flesh. She pulled her cloak around her further, the icy chill in her toes climbing through her muscles.

The snap of another branch jolted Kienna's attention in Broan's direction. It was subtle but unnerving.

Her eyes locked with something crouched in the trees, eyes like scorched embers. "I think we need to run." She could have sworn she saw teeth, not bared, but in a grin. The group continued to bicker. "Now!"

Snarls rang around them. A smell, sweet and almost floral at first, then sharp and foul, followed them. Kienna kept her eyes trained, scanning every path she could. She weaved through the trees, the others close behind. She didn't know where they were anymore, only that they had to keep moving.

Her breath burned in her throat, the cold air like glass in her lungs. Her steps faltered, raw feet catching on roots and debris. She gripped a nearby trunk, and its bark bit into her palms, encouraging her to stay upright.

Spins and Spins.

Her vision blurred at the edges. The forest twisted in all directions now. Nothing was familiar, and there was no sense of where they'd come from. She couldn't tell if they were gaining ground or going in circles.

Silence spins.

Kienna stopped abruptly, the others nearly colliding with her. Danek, Broan, and Moira stood in silence, wide-eyed and waiting. She swayed slightly, her hands braced against another tree, fingers trembling. The wounds on her feet throbbed in rhythm with her heartbeat, each step since River Storm cutting deeper. She found herself to be vastly unprepared for this.

She should have found Connak first, reached out to him to come and get her. Maybe he would know more about the woodcarver. He'd know how to keep them alive in this forest. She couldn't get herself to cross that barrier, even if it were the smartest move for survival. At this point, regardless of what Maren had told her, leaving River Storm was like a death sentence in its own right.

Maybe they could go back. She could find a way to explain to Vaerin what happened. Perhaps he would understand. His punishment would be harsh, but... No. She barely survived the last one. She tried to breathe and think. The tree's rough bark dug red into her skin.

Grins and grins.

"Oh, fuck," she cried, heaving in small sobs and clinging to the tree again as if it were the only thing left in the entire world. The temptation to reach for Connak hit her again, but she waved it away.

Kienna hacked out a cough, searching for a fresh source of oxygen. Instead, her stomach turned and expelled everything in it. She bent her back over, and her throat filled with sour bile, evacuating all over her feet. The warm vomit seeped into her deep wounds, causing Kienna to wince and cry out in pain.

"Have some fucking composure," Broan scolded, but his voice cracked halfway through. He turned away quickly, pretending to tighten the strap on his gauntlet as the contents of her stomach splattered near his feet.

She wiped her mouth clean and slid down into the dirt, back against the tree. Her tangled strands of ashy hair blended into the crease of the wood.

"Are you okay?" Danek asked.

Kienna shook her head. Exhausted, she closed her eyes and took in as much air as possible. "Do you think everyone in River Storm is okay?"

Broan scoffed, kicking dirt over her. "Now you're remorseful? Fuck me."

Danek waved his hands over Kienna's feet. A bright light illuminated her for a moment, and the raw flesh mended itself. Kienna's skin crawled as tissue stitched itself back together, but she didn't fight. "I think River Storm has the mighty Vaerin to protect it."

As if Danek had spoken the words into existence, a deep and powerful wind cascaded through the forest. The canopies swayed with the blast and then resumed their stillness. The group looked up quickly and could see the subtle, luminescent glow to the west.

"He put it back up!" Moira's hand flew to her mouth as her eyes went wide.

"Nice going, pretty boy. Now we're never getting back." Broan slammed his fist into a tree, leaving a hole in the trunk where solid bark had been. He glared at Danek.

"We need to keep moving, then." Kienna struggled to her feet. She toed around her vomit and composed herself. "Whatever I heard back there is still among us, and we're sitting ducks if we stay right here."

Broan bowed menacingly, placing his arm out to his side for Kienna to walk ahead. She glared at him from the side of her eyes but didn't hesitate to move forward. Scanning the forest trails, the only thing she knew was not to go west. The barrier of River Storm now stood as her compass.

East it is.

Chapter 21

—Kienna—

"Over here!" Danek called after they had been walking for hours.

The group followed quickly, climbing a slope of slippery moss to see what Danek had uncovered. In front of them were a few small buildings, smashed down and nearly swallowed by the forest. Though it didn't replace the safety of walls, it was the best they could get if they wanted a sliver of rest.

"We should scope it out before we settle." Broan grabbed the loose rubble and tested the stability.

They split up, checking the ruins and even the trees surrounding them, and then they picked the corner with the tallest pillars and finally rested. Kienna tore strands of her sleeves off as best as she could, wrapping the strips around her blistering feet.

Danek moved to heal again, but she waved him away. "Save your energy."

"I'm so thirsty," Moira's voice was hoarse. "Have we even seen a creek or any food since we've been walking?"

"I haven't seen a creek." Danek looked at the muck on his boots with a sigh.

Broan flopped his arms. "And now she's gotten us killed, too."

Kienna rested her head against a stone and watched the trees above her. The forest floor appeared to be getting darker, with no hint of moonlight or stars above.

"We should sleep in waves," Broan said. He sneered at Kienna. "At least then we won't have to worry about dying from something wild. Just thirst and starvation."

Kienna glanced up, daggers forming in her eyes. "Please let the forest kill you first."

"You get the first shift." Broan turned away and closed his eyes.

Everyone settled in, shifting and adjusting until stillness took hold. Kienna stood. If she sat too long, she'd give in. Sleep clawed at her like a sweet-smelling trap, and she couldn't afford to fall into it. She paced the edge of the clearing, scanning the trees. Shadows flickered across the bark, fast, darting shapes that pulled her focus in too many directions.

She pressed a hand on her temple. Grins and... Silence. Her jaw clenched. "What are the fucking words?"

Kienna's eyelids drooped, but a twig snapped and wrenched her back to the trees. She shook Danek and Moira and motioned for them to wake Broan, reaching for her blade as she inched closer out of the ruins. It was the brushing of a feather against her thoughts that fueled her with enough fury to lunge forward.

She and Connak tumbled to the ground with brute force, but it didn't stop her from pinning him before the others could react. She pressed her blade tightly against his throat. "The fact that you would even dare!"

"Get off, and I'll explain," Connak said.

Pale blue glyphs flickered to life along the roots and stones around them. Kienna didn't budge. Her thumb glowed orange and violet and burned. Connak grabbed her hand, gently but firmly. The twitching in her muscles eased.

"Let's get up," he said.

She began to move but then froze. "Get out of my head!"

Kienna roughly shoved him back. He hit the ground but pushed her off smoothly, catching her wrist in time to keep her skull from striking a stone. He pulled her dagger from her hand before she could even react. "You can calm yourself on your own, or I can do it in your mind. Your choice."

"I won't let you back in there," Kienna snarled. "Ever again."

"I'm not here to fight you, but my mind is stronger than yours, and I won't let you hurt yourself."

She crouched near him, her wrist still in his hands as she shook. For a moment, she imagined driving the blade through his chest. It would be easy. Fast. But then what? Murder wouldn't fix the ache in her head.

Connak let go of her. "If you let me in, I can give you the memories he took from you."

Kienna's breath caught. The glyphs around her brightened, reacting to the tension in her blood. Her mind spun as Broan cleared his throat from the clearing. "What did you mean by that? About the memories?"

"Your king siphons them," he said freely.

"Our memories?" Moira gasped.

Connak looked at the rest of the group for the first time. He held Kienna's blade carefully as if he was preparing for her to lunge over and grab it. She thought about it but decided he was now going to be their best bet at getting away from whatever hunted them. She huffed instead.

"Kienna has told you nothing?" he asked.

The group all shared glances and shook their heads no. Kienna thought that question was hardly fair. "Even if I had, he would've wiped it clean."

Connak nodded slowly. "That's what he does best."

Broan puffed his chest. "I'm still lost."

"They're saying the king wiped our memories," Danek explained.

Connak stood from the ground, wiping the leaves from his clothes. "Not all of them. Just the convenient things that kept you loyal to him."

"Loyal how? I'm pretty sure most of us hate him," Moira said, finding a seat against the stone walls to rest.

Connak tapped his finger to his chin. "Yes, well, your king is messing with ancient magic he's had no training in. I'm pretty sure twenty-five years of experience over centuries of power is not enough to master *everything.* My guess is that he only managed to jumble things around, but never quite erased them fully. That's why I've been able to give Kienna hers back."

The pressure in Kienna's thumb eased. Though she struggled to trust him completely in this moment, she couldn't find the threat. She, too, rose from the ground but inched closer to Danek. "Can I have my blade back?"

"After you move past the urge to kill me, maybe."

She hated the way his eyes sparkled with warmth, like he couldn't help the crooked half-smile that tugged at his lips. It was too soon, the weight of the dungeons still clinging to her. "And tell me why I shouldn't kill you?"

All she could remember now was that Connak threw her to

Vaerin, and she rotted because of it. Even if she knew that the king could have altered the way she remembered it, it didn't matter.

"Listen, I can explain that," Connak said, shifting on his feet.

She crossed her arms. "Yeah, please do."

"You should all rest first."

"No chance."

Moira glanced from the wall she'd been resting against. "I'd like more clarity on that night, too. First off, you were there, and then you weren't. What was that?"

Broan kicked his foot against the ruins. "Well, we're waiting, barrier boy."

"That was projection magic. It's a fickle thing, so I don't recommend trying it unless you've mastered the illusions. Secondly," he glanced at Kienna. "I shouldn't have come in for you. I should have stuck to the plan to blow the wall. I could have pulled you out after. It would have been more effective."

Danek frowned. "Why would you want to pull her out?"

Connak motioned toward their resting place again. "Let's get out of the open. Please. I'll start a fire, then we can talk."

Chapter 22

—Connak—

Connak crouched near the ruins, coaxing a fire to life with practiced ease. Embers danced high in the mist. It would have been easier if Kienna had sparked the fire alive for him, but she didn't trust herself as much as she didn't trust him. He tried to stand near her, but she moved away, squeezing between Danek and Moira instead. Broan remained standing, with arms crossed. He'd be a tough one to crack. Not because he believed in his king behind the barrier, but because he was built of stone. Blue symbols around the trees floated lower, letting the night sky take over.

Connak sat across from the group and stared at them over the orange glow. He didn't know what to say. Not really. He didn't expect he'd be harboring all four of the Alistile children. He wasn't even supposed to be harboring Kienna yet, but as soon as they linked minds, he couldn't stand by anymore and watch her.

He drummed his hands on his lap, deep in thought. So much history had happened, and none of it was shared with them. At least, not in the way that was helpful for his case. King Vaerin's indoctrination and memory theft ran deeper than any truths he could share. Like with Kienna, exposing them too fast would make them run for the trees. They'd have to learn naturally to trust him and to trust his world. "Do you all know where you came from?"

"Out here somewhere." Danek waved his hand around, not sure where to point.

"Yes. Each of you was born with magic from the Crown Eternal—"

"The what?" Broan interrupted.

Connak sighed. "The Eternal Mother. She who breathed the world?" He looked at their confused faces. Of course, the king wouldn't hold onto sacred traditions of the realm. "None of this makes sense to you?"

"None of us really had mothers," Danek shrugged.

"That's not what that…" Connak paused to steady his tone. It wasn't their fault. "Forget it. That part doesn't matter right now." He exhaled and adjusted the strap across his chest, eyes sweeping over the group. "They didn't send me to explain, only to extract. But it doesn't look like you're going to let me get away from that." He looked at Kienna a moment longer, then added as an afterthought, "Which means I'm improvising."

Moira narrowed her eyes. "Let's start there. Who are *they?*"

Connak blew air forcefully. "I can take you to our people, and they can explain. This conversation will take time…and…trust."

"So, you don't trust us?" Danek straightened against the wall, suddenly tense.

"Do you expect me to?" He stoked the fire again to keep the flames going, brushing his sweaty palms against his pants to get a better grip on his stick. Kienna stared, an intensity burning into him.

If she'd let him back in her mind, he could make this right. He could talk to her away from the group, explain everything, and give her back the bits of memories that might be gone. He could gauge if she trusted the others enough for him to trust them, too, but she kept herself sealed. That didn't stop him from locking onto her face and holding it in his memory. Seeing her with the shadows of fire dancing along her face grabbed him and entranced him.

"Here's an easier question," Moira said, pushing leaves out of her path as she scooted a little and stretched out her legs. "You're clearly from out here, but you've lived in River Storm. Were you one of us?"

The question wasn't shocking, but he was surprised that they even remembered his existence within the wall. "No, I wasn't. We never crossed paths. I was a shadow in the corner back then. Easy to miss."

Moira tilted her head. "But you were inside the barrier."

"King Vaerin wouldn't let anyone in without a reason. So, how'd you get past the wall?" Danek asked, steady but weary.

These weren't easy questions. He'd been trying to dance around these topics, but his history with his people and with the King of River Storm was far more complicated than a child defying the electrical pulses of the barrier. He was selected the minute Vaerin took them from their lands. "It was easy to place a wandering child near the barrier to get picked up. The king wanted magic. He would have taken all the children to find which ones had it."

"They just...left you there?" Danek asked.

"Like bait?" Broan said.

Kienna shifted, her eyes studying Connak. He'd never shared

this with her, but he could tell she was searching her mind for any memory of it. He only shook his head. This conversation was getting too vulnerable for him.

He had no words to describe what he went through as a child. His people put him in front of River Storm, sealed his magic, and hoped it would incite the right series of events to kickstart prophecies he had no interest in knowing at the time. Without his magic, the king tossed him out into the streets and called him worthless. His throat bobbed. King Vaerin had stripped his memories and didn't even bother to place him in the orphanage. Connak had to wander the streets in the shadows, picking through trash to eat and sneaking to the river to drink the dirty water.

It would have been a mercy for the king to have killed him instead.

"Look," Connak sighed. "I know you all want answers. Real ones. But I can't do it here. We're too exposed, and there are things still out there hunting you." He pointed south through the trees. "Dove Port is where it starts. The rest…that'll be up to you."

He glanced toward the dark edges of the trunks, his posture tightening. He turned back to Kienna, the firelight flickering in her expression. She chewed her nails. "What's Dove Port?"

"It's a trader's town outside of the Elvish clan. It's covered by winding hills and a much larger army that can hold us until we're granted passage elsewhere."

"Did you say Elvish?" Moira gasped.

Connak's nervous tick returned, the drumming of his hands, fingers twiddling. "Oh, I forgot you didn't know about us."

"Us?" Kienna turned in shock. She leaned in even closer, trying to pick apart his more prominent features.

He tried to stay cloaked in shadow, wear a hood, and he even used the wolf for a time to keep himself a mystery, one he had since left behind. But now, the firelight carved soft lines across his face.

He knew his appearance well and that it stood out amongst the human form. Connak's cheeks were angular, but not unnaturally so. His ears tapered to a point, barely noticeable when hiding behind his wind-tousled hair, the color of auburn bark. His eyes were still forest green, flecked with bits of warm brown that shimmered when the fire caught them right. He spent many months seeing himself through Kienna's eyes. He knew what she saw now.

"I thought Elves were folklore," Broan laughed.

"We don't go by the term *Elves,*" Connak said. He threw a branch into the fire. "We are Elvish, but most of us in these parts are not pureblood, so we only claim it by descent."

Kienna remained close by the fire, still looking at him. "My mother told me before leaving that she wanted me to find out who I was. Am *I* Elvish?"

Moira and Danek looked at each other with questioning gazes while Broan quietly chuckled to himself. She was so close, but Connak couldn't tell her who she was or who she was supposed to be. He simply shrugged. "Partly yes."

The flicker in her brows indicated that wasn't quite what she wanted to hear, but he found comfort in the fact that she wanted to know in the first place.

"She also said something about a woodcarver."

Connak jerked. How did Maren, a woman of River Storm, know about the woodcarver? Kienna wasn't ready for that truth yet, so he bit his lip. "Then we need to go to Dove Port."

"You'll get me to the truth, right?" she asked. Her eyes flicked around, to Moira, Danek, then to Broan. Connak nodded. He would do everything he could to get her wherever she needed to be. Kienna's chest released, and then she said, "I'll go to Dove Port."

"And the rest of you?" Connak asked.

"I'll go, too," Danek nodded.

Moira shifted her body, her hand briefly floating to her stomach, and then she nodded also. "Me, too."

"Well, I'm not going back by myself, so you've got me, too." Broan diverted his attention elsewhere and crossed his arms. Danek shook his head with a subtle smile.

Connak tossed his stick into the fire. "Get some rest, all of you. I'll keep watch for a bit."

The others didn't put up a fight. It meant they could find blissful sleep for even a few hours. They settled onto the hard ground and closed their eyes. Kienna scooted away, but Connak saw her staring at his ears again. He smiled at her, offering peace.

She lingered on it but then turned her body away and tightly shut her eyes.

Chapter 23

—Kienna—

A deep humming startled Kienna awake. She scanned the forest around her, dim light fighting through the canopies. Birds chirped, but not in the way she had heard them in River Storm. They were dull back then, sickly almost. The birds here sang songs with rich, deep melodies that greeted Kienna's heart. She was beginning to feel it—the quiet pulse of belonging threading through the world around her. It was foreign, almost frightening, because she could not recall a time in her life when the ground itself had welcomed her. Connak's words from the night before snagged at her thoughts: *partly yes.*

Partly Elvish. Partly…what? If she was not whole, then what was she? A fracture? Her hands drifted to her perfectly normal ears.

The fire dwindled. Kienna shivered and loosened her body for a stretch. Her muscles ached, a sudden reminder of what it had been like to lie on a prison floor with no comfort or warmth. A yawn escaped her before she could stop it when her eyes fell on a visitor sitting on the edge of the ruins, who had not been there before.

"Oh, fuck!" Kienna jumped from where she lay. "What are you doing?"

"I've been trying to keep your trail all night." Baila's legs swung from the jagged stone wall. "It took me forever, but I finally caught up."

Kienna stood, eyeing Baila. Her red hair shimmered in the forest light, body radiated a subtle glow of sparkling green. Baila's features stood more prominent now than in the overcast gray of their city. It was clear that she belonged in the forest, her connection to the foliage only strengthening. Kienna kicked her foot into Connak's boot. He flinched, pulling his blade swiftly.

"I thought you were keeping watch."

"I've only been out for a minute," Connak said. "What happened?"

Baila jumped down from the wall. "He's been out for much longer than that. I kept a good eye out for you."

By now, the others began to stir.

"Look who made it," Broan said, voice coming in rough and slow.

"Did you at least bring water?" Moira's lips cracked with flecks of white at the corners.

"Don't you live here?" Baila turned to Connak, blinking fervently as she cocked her head. "I figured you'd have had them well taken care of already."

Connak shuffled his feet. "It never came up."

"Hm. Perhaps you could get them something now?"

He squinted his eyes, studying Baila for a moment before agreeing. "I'll only be a moment."

They watched Connak run into the trees, his body a blur of motion between the trunks. He jumped, caught a branch mid-stride, and vaulted upward, weaving through the canopy with a predator's ease.

"He's…interesting." Without turning back to the rest of the group, Baila clasped her hands. "So, does anyone want to explain to me what's going on?"

Danek shifted his weight and kicked at the dirt. The group glanced at each other, but no one spoke. Broan broke the silence with a grunt. "Why don't you go first, flower girl?"

Baila turned slowly, a single brow lifting. "Well," she said, arms folding now, "after you all kindly left me behind in front of a falling wall, I saw the trees outside. Men were pouring in. I was expecting those god-awful slithery things but didn't see a single one. Only men. So, I left."

She paced a few slow steps, brushing dried leaves from her sleeve. "Now I'm not sure I made the right choice since, apparently, there *are* demon creatures out here."

Danek raised his head. "How do you know?"

"I saw one. While sitting in a tree. It was horrendous." She flicked her finger toward them. "Now your turn."

"Connak is taking us to Dove Port," Kienna replied.

Baila stopped pacing. "So, we're not going back home?"

"I don't think that was ever the plan when we left," Moira said. "I'm sure the king's already plotting our murder."

"But he *loved* us," Baila whined, her voice tight with despair.

Danek turned toward her. "Baila, he *kidnapped* us."

"So, you trust this man from beyond the barrier?"

"I don't know," Kienna dug her boot into the ground. "He's already caused enough trouble for us in River Storm, but he might be a better bet now than trying to crawl back to Vaerin. Do you think he'll receive you with open arms for stepping away? Or do you want to spend the night in the dungeons? I can tell you firsthand, you'll never stop seeing the shadows, even when he wipes your memories."

"My memories?" Baila jerked her head to Kienna, her brow dipping into a deep crease. She scanned the group slowly, eyes lingering on each of them. Her gaze was cool, like early frost on green leaves, but it thawed the moment Connak stepped into view.

He handed over a skin of water. Moira's eyes grew wild. She reached for it immediately and chugged it in ragged gulps, the liquid spilling down her chin like rain before she handed it over to the others.

As Broan reached for it, the forest stilled, and the guiding blue glyphs shifted to a deep maroon. That color already spoke so many layers of danger to Kienna. She wondered if the glyphs represented the color or River Storm. Connak pulled out a sword from his belt, the steel whispering through the air with a hiss, cutting the silence before a clicking gurgle jolted everyone into position.

Kienna reached over, ripped her own dagger from Connak's belt, and glanced to her left through the darkness of the trees. A rotting smell hit her first, foul and wet like meat left out in the sun. It clung to the back of her throat. Danek, Baila, and Broan were already pulling out their own weapons, but Moira was unarmed, barely even dressed for battle.

Moira shot a pleading look around. Kienna stepped backward to push Moira behind her, motioning for the others to follow. They'd barely covered her when a beast lunged out at them. Kienna pushed her blade upward, but not before claws ripped into her shoulder. She yelped out and dropped to her knees, scrambling to find her footing. Then she sliced the air again, inching the creature backward.

Broan charged forward and slammed his body into the creature, causing Kienna to trip over its distorted figure. She tried to get a good look, but it moved quickly between the trees, weaving through and knocking them over. Baila stepped forward and thrust her hand in the air, reaching for the vines above. They slithered around the trees and caught the snarling mass.

Kienna's eyes grew wide, looking at the long body. It was slick with scaling patches on its underbelly, but matted, wet fur covered it everywhere else. It was almost as if a wolf had been meshed with a lizard of sorts. A huge lizard. She looked at Connak. He stood there, amused, and then he grabbed his own sword and went to slice the creature. Before he could, it raked through the vines and surged forward with speed, knocking everyone down.

The beast snarled and inched toward Moira, jumping on her and surging its teeth forward. Her eyes were shut tightly, waiting for it to sink its spikes into her, but Connak grabbed hold of it and slammed it into the ground, driving his blade deep into its chest.

Kienna reached for her shoulder, jagged streaks seeping with blood. She tried not to shake too visibly, but Danek had already seen and was rushing to her. Another creature emerged from the forest, grabbing hold of him with a hooked hand before he could make it to her. Danek kicked his boot up, wrestling himself free. One more emerged and slithered toward Kienna. She gripped her blade tighter.

What followed was a blur of chaos. Steel flashing, snarls clashing against cries, limbs twisting as friend and foe collided in tangled motion. After a few slices in the air, Connak, Broan, and Danek ended up near Kienna while the other beast stalked toward Baila and Moira. Baila pushed for the leaves to help, but they were constantly rejected by sharp claws and teeth.

Connak drove his blade upward, cleaving the slick underbelly open. Black blood hissed as it spilled onto the ground before them. Kienna hopped back quickly to avoid it pooling into her bare feet. Across the clearing, the beast knocked Baila down and scratched at Moira. Before it could make its mark, a man dressed in black with light, ashy hair fell from the trees and wrestled the abomination away from her, and in one fell swoop, he snapped its neck.

He and Connak shared a nod toward each other, and then the mysterious man jumped back into the trees and disappeared. Connak motioned to the rest of the group, reaching for Kienna to help her forward. "We should get out of here before more of them show up."

—Connak—

Connak flowed through the forest like water. He had spent the past year slipping between the trees, a shadow among the roots. But moving alone was different. Now, he had five others to protect. No matter how competent they were, one was injured and shoeless, and the others wouldn't quit bitching. It was like listening to a flock of baby wyverns fighting over a single roasted hare.

"I could have taken that creature out on my own if Broan hadn't gotten in the way," Kienna said, limping forward in the dirt.

"Yeah, whatever, princess. You still look like a skeleton," Broan fired back.

"I'm trying not to get killed out here," Moira gasped.

"Let's not forget you all dragged me into this," Baila added.

If looks could kill, Baila would be dead in the spot where Kienna stared at her. "Why are you even here, then? You can go home."

"Yeah, whatever. They all followed you, and I wasn't going to be alone."

Broan scoffed, kicking the leaves out of his path as they pushed through some foliage. "I followed pretty boy. He followed Kienna. But technically, I'm blaming Danek."

"Oh, please. You followed because you couldn't live without me."

"Don't flatter yourself, Brother."

He didn't know how much he could take of them all pointing fingers at each other, bickering, but it made the long journey even worse. He turned to the blue glyphs, following their path. As markings of the Hollow Blades, Connak used their trails a hundred times, threading through the forest from his camp to Vaerin's wall and back. They pulsed faintly now, as if the bickering gnawed at the trees, too.

Kienna tugged on her shoulder. She wouldn't let him or Danek heal her. She'd said it was because she'd been healed by the king her whole life, and she wanted to be left alone, but he knew she didn't trust him enough yet.

—Kienna—

"May I offer you some boots?" Connak asked, sliding closer to Kienna as they walked. She glanced at his empty hands, a confused sneer pulling at her brows.

Then a pair of boots dropped from the trees.

Connak motioned to them, his chest puffing proudly. Though Kienna wasn't impressed, she was grateful. She picked them up and ran a thumb along the stitching before pulling them on, her feet screaming through the pain as she did.

"A Shadowmaster. He's handy to have around," Connak pointed to the canopy. "The Captain of the Blades, I mean."

"What's a Blade?" Kienna asked, tightening the laces and

adjusting the boots to her legs.

"Mainly *heathens* but stealthy," Connak shrugged with a gleam in his eye that indicated he thought fondly of these *Blades*. "They're my army."

Kienna let out a breath of laughter, unintentional but real. He had to have been her age. "In River Storm, they didn't give armies to just anyone."

Connak knelt as she tugged at a stubborn strap, then rasped near her ear. "This isn't River Storm, and I'm not just anyone."

She glanced up, catching the gleam in his eye before he stood and continued forward into yet another twisting turn of trees. He was frustrating; so sure of himself. Yet, somehow, his presence was lighter than the burdens she carried. The sting of his betrayal still sat raw in her chest, but he made it hard to stay angry.

She smirked, shaking her head. A vine from the underbrush curled gently around her boot as she stood, brushing against the leather. She paused to stare at it, turning to find Baila to see if she'd been messing with her. Baila was sipping water near Danek, staring idly off into the trees. The vine lingered before recoiling into the forest floor. Kienna drank in the sight, so connected yet distanced at the same time. Magic buzzed like a swarm of bees around her, but the looming threat of their attack weighed on her. There were demonic creatures, as King Vaerin warned.

She thought back to him…the king. Her mind wandered to the clothes he'd given her, how the fine leather had warmed her. How his voice, when it wasn't cruel, had almost sounded like comfort. She hated that she missed that version of him, the one that let her see long enough to believe in him.

The thought sickened her. She scoffed and shook it off, nose wrinkling. But the ache in her chest didn't go away either, and despite everything, she turned and looked back to see if she could see the shimmering magic of the Orb.

Chapter 24

—Kienna—

"We can stop here," Connak said.

They stumbled upon a cabin made of fine oak. Its natural beauty was a welcome sight to the visitors. The trees had grown around this cabin, roots stopping short of where it stood. Connak opened the door. Inside was not much, not nearly a testament to the beauty of what was on the outside, but Connak seemed proud, a gleam in his eye when he looked around. In the far-right corner of the cabin was a cot. Adjacent to that, a modest fireplace already burned brightly.

"It's a place we use when coming and going," he said, his voice tinged with distance. "I built it for the Blades for when the council would send us out on missions."

Baila strolled into the cabin freely. "What sort of missions?"

"The secret kind," he winked, stepping aside so Broan could fit through the smaller framed door.

Kienna studied the finely cut logs inside the cabin walls. The intricacy of each slice and peel to make such a fine oak vibrantly stood out against the wild forest. Carvings of stags and bears were etched deeply into some logs; others bore no image. There was no pattern to indicate why some areas had etchings and others did not, only that it appeared men grew bored in the night, waiting for sleep.

She longed for the calm allure of carving, the feeling of being so safe that one could chisel their mind onto a log. "Did you build the cabin by yourself?" Kienna asked.

"Mostly. The roof was a bit tricky, so I had some of my men help from the trees, but the wind helped me carry the rest of it." Connak sifted the fire and placed a pot into a rack over it. "Anyone care to eat?"

Broan grumbled out a husky snort. "You plan on scorching berries tonight?"

"Of course not," Connak said. "I plan on hunting in the forest now that we have some shelter."

Connak stepped into the corner behind the bed and retrieved a large bow. Its wood was a rich mahogany polished to a soft sheen, limbs inlaid with silver filigree that curled like vines. Bracing the lower limb of his bow behind his boot, he stepped through with ease. He leaned into the curve, flexing the wood with his thigh until it arched enough for him to slip the upper string into place. With a soft *thwick*, the string locked into the notch. It shimmered faintly, taut and impossibly thin as if spun from spider silk.

Selecting a single arrow, he nocked it with calm precision. Kienna rolled her eyes. He had quite a bit of confidence for one arrow.

"Danek. Kienna. Care to join me?"

"And why not any of us? If you want someone who can carry a stag, I imagine you'd want someone a little less dainty," Broan quipped.

"She looks like she's about to pass out." Connak pointed to Moira. His eyes flicked to Baila, smiling sweetly back at him. "I don't like her, and I need your strength here to protect them if anything goes wrong."

Broan couldn't help his boastful smile. He wrapped his arm tightly around Baila like he was ready to take on the task of protector. Baila pushed hard against his towering body. Kienna and Danek followed Connak outside, shifting back into mysticism. A static clung to their bodies, hair rising from Kienna's arms.

The forest thinned, and the sky finally broke through the clearing. Kienna glanced at Danek as he studied the clear glimmer of the sun moving to the horizon. Hues of pink and orange illuminated the cabin. Though Kienna caught glimpses of these while she wandered with Connak's mind, Danek probably never had. He stood, mouth open, staring directly into the sun. Moira stepped outside, falling in next to them. A tiny cry escaped her lips as her skin began to glow.

"Let's go," Connak pointed back into the forest.

Kienna, Danek, and Moira drifted back from their daze. Moira smiled at them as Kienna and Danek followed after Connak. They stalked cautiously through the undergrowth of trees, careful not to step on the twigs and leaves that would alert the animals of the woods. They passed multiple stags, rich in meat that would have fed the group nicely, with the potential of drying the rest for a fine jerky.

Eyes followed them, but the animals never moved. What was he waiting for? Connak held his bow steadily while he picked up his feet in a strategic dance around the brush. Steering further into the forest, he raised his hand. "Wait."

Ahead, a creature appeared with matted black fur and jagged

limbs that bent the wrong way. Its eyes glowed crimson, and its snarl revealed rows of teeth that matched the beasts that had attacked them before. It loomed over a stag as it writhed in its last moments. The creature hadn't yet struck fully. It savored the kill, watching the life of the animal drain slowly. Kienna wrestled between wanting to take her eyes off the ghastly creature and trying to force bravery into her heart. She picked the ridges of her nails, her thoughts starting to spiral. *Grins. Grins. Spins. Oh, fuck that stupid melody.*

Connak raised his bow, pulling the string with ease. He released, and the arrow soared through the air, piercing the demon creature straight in the chest. It let out a yowl before falling lifeless to the ground.

"Surely we aren't eating the leftovers of the stag that thing killed," Kienna said as Connak crept forward.

"And hopefully we aren't eating whatever *that* is," Danek expressed, pointing to the unnatural creature.

"It's a Shadowmaw. One of Vaerin's creatures," Connak said.

"Those do not live in River Storm," Kienna said. "King Vaerin is a lot of things, but he was not a master of the demons we worked hard to keep out." Kienna studied the Shadowmaw's horrid, gray skin. Dead before Connak even pierced its heart.

"Sure, Kienna," he said, his lips pressing tightly. "I'll let you pretend for now."

Connak leaned over the stag, observing the animal's frame. The maw had barely snagged it but hit it with enough force to begin the first stages of death. Covered with muscle, this stag appeared much larger than the ones they had passed. Its coat glimmered like copper beneath the dusk light, antlers wide and elegant like a crown.

Hands brushing gently over the wound of the animal, Connak closed his eyes, a gentle wind picking up pace between the branches of the trees. A faint crease formed between his brows. His shoulders tightened for a moment, as though the spell demanded more from him than he let on.

Kienna's long hair followed the breeze, waving peacefully over her face. She could hear Connak whispering something but couldn't quite make out the words. She leaned forward, hoping to get a clearer view, but he was done before she could see. The breeze slowed to a stop. Kienna held the breath she meant to take as the stag stirred.

Against all odds, it rose tall like a king.

"That's impossible," Danek straightened, wide-eyed as the stag shook off the remnants of the maw. "That thing was dead. How did you—"

"Teetering," Connak said. "There was just enough soul left to save."

Connak and the stag held each other's gaze. The stag lowered its head to Connak, and his hand brushed lovingly on its antlers. A gentle pat on his head was enough confirmation. The stag turned to walk away. With a nod, Connak signaled for them to stay near to him. Danek and Kienna trailed closely, trying not to startle the majestic being as they strode through the forest ground. They entered a hidden encampment bustling with wildlife.

The songs of the birds bellowed loudly. Squirrels played and chittered with each other in the trees, erratically scrambling around in a playful chase. Stags and does pranced along in large waves. There were the wolves that towered like the stags above mortal men. Their massive forms were cloaked in thick, dark fur that shimmered with silver streams beneath the forest's pale light. Their eyes burned with an ancient, ember-glow.

"Keep moving," Connak whispered. "The animals don't like it when we stare."

"The wolves. Are they the same as the one I freed?"

Danek reached for Kienna, gently tugging her arm for attention. "You've seen one before?"

Kienna nodded, taking her wrist back and moving forward

with the stag. The wolves remained in the corner of her eye as they continued. "Vaerin had one chained across the river. It was smaller, though."

"Is that why you were so disturbed when you found us?"

"I'm curious, too," Connak peered over his shoulder. "I knew you were irritated, but—" Heat rose in Kienna's cheeks. Did he watch her when she wasn't aware? "I don't, unless you leave your mind open and call for me," Connak responded.

Kienna recoiled inward, folding her thoughts tightly and pulling the shutters of her mind closed until no trace of him could seep through. She huffed.

Danek looked between them, his brows scrunched and lips parted. The poor fool, so unaware of Connak's link to her mind. He exhaled. "Seriously, though. Why were you so terrified?"

She waved her hand to brush him off, but they both stared, so she caved. "There was something else there. I never got a good look, but it didn't feel right. It twisted inside of me and sparked another level of fear." She shook her head. "I can't see why Vaerin would need these creatures."

"You keep giving your king more credit than he deserves," Connak said lowly.

"I do not." Kienna's thoughts spiraled. She hadn't meant to. He was a vile man who took things from them and tortured her in a dungeon. And still, she stumbled through her mind, trying to make all the pieces fit together, for everything to make sense. King Vaerin hurt her, something she knew he did, but never quite understood in the moment. At the time, he felt like a man who had a twisted way of caring, only wanting for her and the others to be stronger. He called her "my child" and gave her gifts. Then he threw her in the cell and took her to the brink of death.

He gave her a home, but he had taken her from her own to do so. The same man who handed her fine boots and told her she was worthy conjured monsters in the dark. It shouldn't have made sense.

But it did. And perhaps both stories held some truth.

Her heart twisted with the weight of it. She hated how her memories tried to defend him. She didn't' want to believe he was a villain. That word was sharp-edged and too final. It felt like betraying the person who gave her a life in the first place. He raised her to survive. She was strong because of it. The ache in her chest wasn't for a king or for River Storm. It was for the illusion of a father figure who had built a cage with a smile, and now, she saw the cost of it all. She wasn't sure if surviving him had ever been the same as living. Kienna bit her lip, her thoughts wild in the darkness.

The stag stopped and turned to Connak, bowing its head to him and moving aside to reveal a small doe, lying peacefully on the cold ground. Dead.

"Did he bring you here to bring her back?" Danek asked.

"No, she's been dead for a little while, at least an hour." Connak sadly studied her. "He's giving her to us to take for meat."

"Just like that?" Kienna said, taken aback.

"Well, I did save his life," he said, offering a small shrug. "Us forest dwellers work in unison most of the time. For protection, we feed and sacrifice for the other. It's why the forest remains so harmonious to us…most of the time. She's small," Connak brushed her fur. "She should be easy to carry, and we can let Broan cut it for us."

"You'd better let me do it. I've had experience with butcher work before," said Danek. "And Broan is not gentle."

"Good," Connak grunted as he dragged the doe over to Danek. "You get to carry it back."

They heaved the creature over Danek's shoulder while Kienna took in the forest. She was in awe of the harmony around her—how easy it was for nature to work together to keep flowing. It was like one big family that trusted each other enough to survive together.

She didn't get that chance in River Storm. The Guardians were a family forced on her, a group of people she couldn't trust with much regarding her own struggles. It was all about power and control inside the Orb. Out here, there was no control. It was belonging. Belonging to something bigger than fear, something beautiful. Different. She nearly mocked the realization, then softened.

Maybe Connak was right.

There was a world out here waiting to be explored, full of mystery and—dare she admit it—magic. Even now, the faint pulsing beneath her skin told her that River Storm was a lie. Now, she could learn about everything the world had to offer her. It was a growing hunger, gripping her now. She shouldn't have wanted this, knowing she left a family behind with a king who lied and siphoned memories. They'd probably never remember her after the king cleaned the mess of the wall falling. And still, as she glanced behind her one last time, she could see the world she wanted.

Chapter 25

—Kienna—

"Dove Port is a day's journey south from here," Connak explained after they had finished eating and cleaning up. He set the bones in a pot of water for fresh broth. "This cabin is pretty secure, but our current circumstances still warrant someone to stay on guard."

"I can take the first shift," Kienna said. The forest rejuvenated her spirits. The humming of magic and elusive creatures sparked her mind with inspiration.

When the others fell asleep, Kienna grabbed a log. Using a small knife to cut away at the bark, she dragged the tip across the softer bits of wood until it started to look more like the magical creatures of the forest—stags and wolves hovering with majestic royalty, protectors of the tiny animals. The antlers gave her an additional challenge as she tried to weave her blade carefully in some spots to stack each groove in different directions.

Lost in her craft, Kienna missed waking Danek for his shift to keep watch. She would have missed waking Baila, too, but she awoke on her own. She approached Kienna, picking up one of the stags and studying the carefully crafted beauty. Unamused, she set it back down. "Not tired?"

"Inspired." Kienna kept carving.

"Hm." Baila glanced out the window, eyes resting on the stillness of the moon. "When did you know that you were going to leave River Storm?"

"Same day you did." Kienna stopped carving, placing the wood down gently in front of her.

Baila sat down beside her, rubbing her arms and glancing toward the door. Her voice was soft, almost childlike. "Do you think we can go home now?"

Kienna didn't look at her. "We're not going back, Baila. You know that."

Baila's head dropped to the floor. "I…I miss my family. Don't you miss your mom? They must be so worried. Mine, too. My father—" she cut herself off with a small laugh. "Well, he worries in his own way."

Kienna bit against her tongue. "Maren told me to leave."

"Really?" Baila blinked. She waited a breath, then picked up another carving Kienna had crafted. "So…aren't you afraid for *her* now? What the king might do, I mean?"

"I am."

There was another pause. as Baila tilted her head. "It's just…I can see now that the king has lied to us. All of us. But what if this," she motioned vaguely to the cabin, "isn't what you expect either? What if we're walking into another cage?"

"I've already lived in a cage."

Baila gave a soft, sympathetic smile. "That's fair. I just know I was safe behind those walls. I know they were all lies now, but at least I understood them. Out here, everything feels…crazy."

She leaned in slightly, lowering her voice so as to not wake the others. "I'm scared. I want to trust this path, I do, but don't you ever wonder if we've made a mistake?"

"Yeah." Kienna looked at Connak, sleeping near the cot. "But I can't turn back now. My mother told me to find someone. Apparently, they have something for me, and…"

"I get it," Baila reached through the silence, her fingers brushing Kienna's wrist. It lingered for a moment. "It's like an adventurous quest if you ask me." She stood from the ground and brushed off her legs. "Listen, I know we didn't get along in River Storm, but I always knew we were like sisters, you know? So, I'm glad I'm with you."

Kienna smiled. Her heart warmed from the sudden affection from Baila. It finally felt like she'd done something right when the one born in River Storm agreed with what she was doing. Even if she struggled with it herself sometimes, Baila's buy-in meant more to her than she thought it would. "You feel connected here, don't you?" Kienna motioned toward Baila's glowing palms. "You're responding to the forest."

"It's been fun being able to use my power, that's for sure."

Baila stirred the pot of bones and water, smelling the steam as it continued to bubble. She reached over to some herbs lying on the ground and crumbled them into the broth. Kienna carved, and they sat in peace for a while, enjoying the moment.

"I'm going to take a walk," Baila whispered after some time. "There's this amazing clearing down the path that gives way to the river and a lake! I found it while you were out hunting. It helped me clear my head. And the moon; I've never seen anything like it."

"Can't be as radiant as the sun was when we went hunting," Kienna said, setting down her blade. She stretched her fingers to relieve the tension.

Baila grabbed her arm and smiled. "No, it's huge. Especially reflected on the water. Want to come?"

"It's not far, right? We probably shouldn't leave the others."

"Oh, not far at all. Around a five-minute walk. We'll go see it and come right back."

Kienna looked around at the others sleeping. Technically, Baila was supposed to be on watch. What if they left and then something attacked the others? It wasn't a good idea. "Baila…"

"Oh," Baila's face fell. "You still don't trust me."

"That's not what I said."

"No, it's fine. We can stay. I get it."

The way she looked, so helpless and sad, made Kienna's heart tug. Baila finally warmed to this world and to her, and she'd turned her down. She stood and motioned for the door. "Come on, then. Let's see this moon."

The walk was indeed short, and the moon was as big and as glorious as Baila had said. It shimmered against the lake like a pale sun dancing with the stars. It had certainly been the most glorious thing next to the sun that Kienna had ever seen. Her expression softened toward Baila with relief that she had decided to go.

"I'm glad we did this," Baila said, placing her hand around Kienna's arm.

There was a faint throbbing beginning to build through her palms now. Kienna figured the forest was calling her, but then the throbbing started to hurt. Kienna tried to respond, but Baila was too quick. She wrapped a sleeve of magic around Kienna's wrists and bound her mouth. Before she could react to that, a sack went over her head, and she was immobilized.

She tried to thrash and fling herself back. Whatever Baila had put around her kept her from screaming. She opened the doors of her mind, hoping that whatever was happening didn't dampen her ability to reach Connak. He'd told her that whatever linked their minds didn't require magic…it just was.

Kienna didn't know how true that was, but she had to try.

Chapter 26

—Connak—

Connak shot from his sleep, desperate to come back to reality. He heard Kienna screaming in his mind, grasping at him for help, but this time it felt different. Her fear pressed against him like a cold breath on glass. He saw an image of a rolling hill under a full moon, shadowy figures in motion, and a glint of silver steel flashing in the dark. He couldn't make sense of it, but the helplessness buried in that cry rooted itself deep. Sweat pooled over the line of his hair. Instinctively, he scanned the room. It didn't take him long to realize Kienna was not there. "Damn it!"

He hopped around to pull on his boots and tighten the strings of his shirt. The others startled awake, but Connak didn't give them enough time to react before he darted out of the cabin with enough force to nearly tear the door right off the hinges. Trees whistled loudly in anguish, rain drumming heavily into the ground, and soaking their tunics. The forest mourned. Echoes of the wildlife bellowed.

Connak studied the path, the brutal swaying of the trees. Where the fuck was his Captain? Even from afar, he would have been able to catch this. His vision blurred through the darting water, slapping his face. None of the glyphs lit his vision. The only clear direction was south, into the hills of Dove Port. The heavy footsteps of the Guardian clan followed quickly behind. Yet another presence lurked and took their path alongside their disheveled formation.

It was a Malintilian Wolf, a creature born in the Malintale Forest. Connak was grateful for her presence now, a clear indication that fate had chosen Kienna's soul to be bound with a guide. The wolf would hold Kienna's life in her hands. She was a protector, one Kienna needed now more than ever. Connak paused when he reached the hills, his eyes ebbing and flowing as he scanned the terrace. Rain lightened outside of the Malintale, the magical presence dissipating into a steady state of normalcy.

"What the hell is going on?" Broan crossed his arms.

His eyes fell on the wolf. She was much smaller in stature compared to the wolves Danek and Kienna witnessed in the forest, but she still managed to reach the average man's chest in height alone. She bared her teeth at Broan instantly.

"Fuck, what is that?"

"Easy." Connak held his hand out, pushing Broan behind him. "Kienna's been taken. She's here to help us."

"Taken?" Moira and Danek shared a glance.

"We were all there in the cabin. How did they get in?" Moira asked. Her black coils fell sloppily in clumps down her head from the deep slumber. The rain took kindly to her locks now.

Connak studied the river, their first sense of a deep flowing water source since being in River Storm. "I can't tell if they went to Northpass or Alverton, and I can't sense her."

He spent minutes analyzing. Going to Northpass meant having to find a direct passage around the river. The water flowed subtly in parts, but he knew there were areas of deepness that could not be walked nor swum by normal beings. None of the present company would have been considered normal by any means, he knew that, but they were not raised to be anything but—aside from the magic Vaerin trained them in. Out here, that made them normal.

Now, going to Alverton meant running through Dove Port to cross the bridge. The captors wouldn't risk that, with Dove Port standing as allies to the Elvish. It was likely whoever snagged Kienna—and possibly Baila—had a boat, something they lacked at this moment. That, or they had magic.

When Connak glanced at the remaining group, he only felt further conflicted. Moira was in a constant daze of exhaustion, as if something were sucking the life out of her. He had his suspicions before, but he was certain as he looked at her. She would not be going with them on this journey. Though Danek and Broan were fine warriors, both held so little knowledge about the world around them. None of them had been able to conjure much magic in this new realm. *Baila did.* Curious thing to remember. Connak knew they needed to find where their magic truly came from.

"Moira, I'm going to send one of my commanding officers from the forest to take you to Dove Port." Connak turned to Broan. "You can manipulate the earth?"

"Mainly earthquakes and a few quips of moving the dirt," Broan said proudly.

"I need you to pull the earth from the river so we can walk across."

"You're bloody dreaming."

"Well, unless you can swim seven miles in one go, and I'm guessing you can't, then I would prefer you give it a try." Connak clenched his fists and then released. They still thought their magic was Vaerin's. "Sense the hum of the magic in this land and let it flow through you. Focus on the energy of the earth and follow it to the bottom of the river and pull."

Broan sneered as he rolled his sleeves and placed his hand directly in the dirt, taking a deep breath. The earth connected to his hand instantly, a faint bronze glow linking him to his magic. The earth rumbled, and his eyes widened in surprise at the surge. The quaking was too subtle. It wasn't enough. With a firm grip on Broan's shoulder, Connak sent a pulse of his own magic through him. The ground trembled in answer as if it recognized its true wielder at last. Danek stepped backward, holding out a steady hand for Moira. They both watched in awe.

Broan's eyes caught fire with sudden light. A spark crackled from his temple, weaving a glowing trail through his hair. It was an elemental sigil born from the earth, claiming its own. A gift from the Eternal Mother. The river raged uncontrollably, waves of water crashing into the shore. The rain, fueled by the angry waters, heightened its intensity, drumming heavily. At last, the earth under the water arose, a small pathway leading them across.

As if summoned by the quake, a tall Elvish man from the Hollow Blades appeared amongst them from the shadows. Connak's second in command moved like mist over moonlit roots. Tall and unnervingly still, his frame was all wiry strength, built for the shadows. His long, ashy blond hair fell like smoke across his shoulders, catching a glint of silver in the twilight. Gray-brown eyes, like clouds brushed with earth, flickered. Dressed in all black, the rain sauntered down his leather tunic, rolling over his features.

"What happened?" Connak asked quietly.

His Shadowmaster shook his head. "Someone placed a dead zone. I couldn't slip in."

Connak grunted. Who would even know how to place a dead zone? They were specific runes meant for one thing only: blocking Shadowmasters. It severed the tether to shadow, flattening space around it.

He sighed. It didn't matter anymore. He turned to Moira. "Moira, this is Tilsin," he yelled over the drumming of magic in the river. "Go with him to Dove Port."

"What use am I in Dove Port?" Moira echoed back.

Connak edged closer to her, careful to stay out of earshot of the men behind him. "You're of no use to your child dead, Moira. Go to Dove Port. That's how you fight now."

Moira's eyes fell on him, her brow scrunching for answers. For anything that would indicate how he could have known that.

"Go!"

Moira did not hesitate and went with Tislin through the storm. Danek and Broan steadied themselves as the path finished its ascent. The Malintilian Wolf stepped forward with them. Her silver eyes scanned the darkness beyond the river as if seeing through realms. She walked with Connak now, as a vow of a Guardian finding her true bond.

"Care to explain a little more about what exactly we're missing here?" Danek looked ahead.

"All I can see is Baila and Kienna walking near the river, and then a scream ripped through my head." Connak rubbed the back of his neck, eyes narrowing as he knelt to study the ground. "I can't see her now, but I can hear what's around her. It's faint…but there…dry wind, shifting sand, and a dragging foot. I can't tell much else, but I do know she didn't choose to go, so we're going after her."

Broan kicked the dirt. "Why is all the trouble we keep getting into because of that fucking girl?"

"Would you like to go with Moira?"

"I said it would be trouble." Broan ran his hands over his new sigil, a lightning spine carved in flesh across his temple to the back of his neck. "I didn't say it wouldn't be fun."

"Then let's go." Connak ran onto the new bridge.

Chapter 27

—Kienna—

Someone ripped the cover from Kienna's head, and Baila released the seal of magic over her wrists. She looked around frantically, trying to gather enough intel to send to Connak. Maybe he'd know where she was.

Parts of the river were still visible, but they were deeper into the desert now. She could tell by the number of trees and the lack of clearing from the east that they'd traveled quite a distance into the night. How they got there so quickly was a blur, almost like stepping across distances in huge leaps. She had heard Baila panting as they moved, and at some point, their feet were in sand. Then she heard the soldiers, and she was being carried the rest of the way on a wooden cart with the bag over her head.

Now that it was off, a soldier reached over and dragged her body out of their vessel and shoved her forward. Kienna pushed her feet into the dirt. "Unhand me!"

"Relax," Dren said, stepping away from another wave of men.

Her heart nearly stopped at Vaerin's Commanding Officer standing in front of her. She should have smelled him first, the stale stench of a drunk, but apparently, the desert had hardened him. He was dressed in full armor, and she wondered how he could have managed such heavy clothing in the heat. They had to have been days away from River Storm.

"No one is trying to hurt you," he said as Kienna tried to pull away.

"If you didn't want to hurt me," Kienna gritted her teeth, "then why would you put a bag over my head?" All she could see now was Dren, swinging his sword through the air and slicing a woman's head off. Would she be next?

"The king needed assurance that your Elvish man couldn't follow our trail."

He would be on their trail now, but Kienna didn't tell him that. She only squinted her eyes and peered at Baila for betraying her. She should have expected it. Baila was so loyal in River Storm despite the cutting words and magical manipulation.

Dren pulled her further into the camp that rested in a dry clearing where the forest gave way to sand and scrub. The encampment stood in uneasy stillness while soldiers waited for their next order. Only one tent rose from the desert floor, its fabric snapping quietly in the wind. It was large, more ornate than the regular desert tent, clearly belonging to someone of importance.

Kienna shifted her attention back to Dren, who approached

another soldier guarding the entrance. "Are we ready?"

"Yes, the king requests her presence," said the soldier.

Kienna recognized him as a castle guard from River Storm, who had always lingered near the throne room. He was one of Jacob's friends. "Thom, is Jacob—"

"Is he here yet?" Baila flicked her damp auburn braid over her shoulders.

Rain clung to the tips of her hair, remnants of their passage, only further disorienting Kienna from how quickly they must have traveled to cover this much distance into the desert after the downpour at the river. Now, they stood in dry terrain, and though the desert air was cool beneath the stars, the heat of the buried sun radiated through the sand.

"He's on his way," Dren said. "Wait in the tent."

That may have been her only chance to ask about Jacob. Kienna glared at Baila as they entered through the flaps. The interior was dim, the only light coming from a single gold lantern swaying on its hook. Its glow caught on the seams of the tent and shimmered faintly in Kienna's eyes as she stood in silence.

"Are you going to explain anything?" she asked, voice quiet but with a growl.

"I do my king's bidding, Kienna. I don't have anything to apologize for," Baila shrugged.

Kienna scoffed and stared at the lantern. "This was my chance at a normal life."

"Spare me the victim act. You never appreciated what he gave you. He made you a god, and you spit it back in his face." Baila stood now, her eyes glowing ethereal green.

Kienna pinched the bridge of her nose. She was so tired of everyone lying to her. She couldn't keep it all straight anymore. She sighed. "How did you get us here so fast?"

"Oh, that? That's god magic, Kienna. Stepping through wind as space contorts to your whim. That's what you could have, but you want to play rebel."

She went to ask more, but voices echoed from outside, and then the flap rustled.

"Your Grace." Baila stood straight as the king entered.

He filled the space like a storm spilling into a valley. In River Storm, he was unreachable, a towering symbol of power to an entire people. Here, on the edge of the Malintale Forest, he was a little more ordinary.

His steely eyes softened. Gone was the cold sovereign. In his place stood a man, worn but relieved. A man who would hand Kienna gifts and tell her she was perfect. "I'm glad you're alright, Baila. You've done well getting back here safely."

Baila smirked.

Vaerin turned back to Kienna and stepped forward, lowering his voice. "I know you're frightened. I know the world beyond River Storm feels…vast and chaotic."

Kienna blinked, caught off guard by his gentleness. She expected him to kill her, but his worry was so genuine. Maybe he did care about her. "It is," she said, but tried her best to maintain a careful distance in her heart. "But it's also alive. There are so many things I can't explain."

Vaerin nodded. "That is why we worry. When magic stirs, it does not always awaken what is good."

The way he said it carried an unexpected weight. For a moment, Kienna believed him. She lowered her guard. "Yeah, but there's so much out here." Her body began to shimmer with a white glow. Vaerin stiffened, but Kienna continued. "I've been told there are places that can help me learn who I am."

Vaerin cocked his head. "You wish not to return to River Storm? Have I not been a fair and just king to you?"

"Oh…" Kienna faltered. A sudden, familiar tug pinched her

skull. Pain lanced through her temples, a small push for control. She winced. "Forgive me. I only meant there's more to learn. Out here."

"The only thing you need to learn is that Connak speaks in riddles and half-truths. You place your faith in him and forget he threw you in chains."

Kienna opened her mouth to argue. It was Vaerin who threw her in the dungeon, not Connak. It just happened to be Connak's fault… sort of. She struggled to keep it straight, only wishing she'd let go of her pride and let Connak restore her memory. She tried to recall why she'd run. The beatings, the mind games, the manipulation, but her thoughts only tangled further.

The king continued. "What do you think they gain by taking you away from River Storm?"

"I…I don't know." Her eyes fell to the sand-dusted ground.

"River Storm's demise," Baila answered coldly.

Vaerin took Kienna's chin gently between his fingers, lifting her eyes to his. His touch was soft. The heat in his skin cooled. "My child. You are not *my* prisoner. You are one of my most trusted warriors. My Starborn. I'm sorry if I've made you think otherwise." His gray eyes searched hers, calm and calculating. "A king must protect his people. That burden darkens the heart. Come home, Kienna. Let me give you the truths you seek. I can make you powerful."

Kienna blinked. Why now? Why not before? Why not the others?

Weariness dragged behind her eyes. Running from shadows. Running with no clear answers. Connak told her some things, but not enough to know if she was truly heading for what she sought. And the bond between them only confused her more. Did she leave because she wanted to? Or because someone convinced her to? On and on, her thoughts went. As her mind softened to the king once more, she had to wonder if her memories were being manipulated again. Did King Vaerin have such quick control that she'd flipped so easily? Her heart stopped in her chest, her throat tightening.

"Maybe..." she swallowed, her mouth suddenly so dry. "Maybe I could bring the others back...from the forest?"

Vaerin's expression cracked, his lips twitching. His hand slapped her across the face, swift and controlled, before he took a step back. Kienna reached for the raw skin, hands trembling. Then, as if it never happened, he straightened his cuffs. His voice returned, smoother than silk, "Your heart lies elsewhere. I see that now."

"No, I just—"

"It's fine," he said, nodding to himself. "I can see this will take time. I'm patient enough to wait with you. I understand more than anyone how fragile family can be."

Her breath hitched before she could stop it. "Can you tell me if Maren and Jacob are okay?"

Vaerin's lips curved upward. "They're fine. For now. Everyone is. The army that took down our wall left as soon as you did."

Baila huffed a loud breath of air. "So not all is lost, then?"

"What's important now is that we rescue you and show our people we are stronger."

Kienna's stomach curled. Could she live with herself if she went back? Would Vaerin kill her family if she didn't? Maren was so sure when she pushed Kienna away. She even gave her a mission: find the woodcarver. There was something out here for her, and even Maren knew it. But did Maren know her own life would be on the line now?

Outside, a shout broke them from the calming allure of the tent. A chaotic rustling engulfed the camp, sounds of metal unsheathing while soldiers clanked around clumsily.

"What now?" Vaerin scolded. He stepped out of the tent, Kienna and Baila on his heels. On the edge of the camp stood three figures— Connak, Danek, and Broan. And beside them, a towering wolf larger than anything River Storm soldiers had read about. Kienna's heart fluttered to see the creature had made it out of the barrier. A faint twitch caressed her mind. Vaerin took them in calmly.

From across the way, the soldiers charged forward against the three. Kienna watched Connak move with ferocious and swift speed she'd never seen before. His blade collided with the soldier's sword in a jarring clash that echoed through the trees. The soldier fell off balance and went sprawling backward. Kienna flinched. Even from where she stood, she saw Connak's arms recoil slightly, his muscles tightening as the shock of the impact reverberated through his shoulders. The wolf snapped at anyone who dared to get close as she weaved through the army.

Fear encompassed what little men stood before the camp to protect Vaerin. The king watched, amused. He didn't seem threatened, standing there at the tent's opening while the Elvish man and two of his own Guardians pushed forward with seamless ease. He turned to Kienna instead and shrouded them with an orb that buzzed with familiarity. "Forcing you back to River Storm now may be too messy. I could explain their deaths easily enough, but…you're smarter than I give you credit for."

"What are you talking about?" Kienna asked.

"I need something from you."

Outside, Connak hurled a streak of magic at the barrier. It only flickered. "What could I give you?" Aside from the life that she'd already given, of course.

"Information, my child. The only way to stop this foolish attack for my power is to find their base." Vaerin brushed her face so gently and so quickly she almost missed it. "I never could find it. It's hidden, and they're going to lead you right to it. I need to know where their magic lives, so we can destroy it before it destroys our kingdom."

Baila crossed her arms. "Connak doesn't trust me."

"So, it seems." Vaerin considered this. "Well, let's change that, shall we?"

The king struck his hand so hard across Baila's face that her lip split. Before Kienna could react, he shoved a burst of searing magic into them both. Their bodies flew into the Orb, electricity snapping at their skin.

Vaerin smoothed his tunic and combed his fingers through his hair. "You'll take my daughter with you. If you stray too far from the task...well, I'll keep a close eye on Maren and Jacob." He lifted his palm again, then locked eyes with her. "Try not to let them misguide you. I've learned quickly that they only wish to control you all." He turned to Baila. "Daughter."

Baila stiffened but nodded. "Father." Her voice came out flat, uncertain.

Kienna froze, eyes wide. She turned to Baila, stunned. Baila returned the look, discomfort breaking through her usual composure. She glanced away quickly.

Vaerin raised his hand. A swirl of smoke billowed around him. Within seconds, with soldiers in tow, he disappeared behind the cloud. The Orb dissipated, and they were gone.

Kienna coughed from the thick smoke filling her lungs. The dense fog consuming them made it hard to see, almost as if a sandstorm had picked up and flung grains into their line of vision. An eerie calm engulfed them at the edge of the desert.

Let's go! The words rang in her head, warped and muddled, like sound carried through water. It wasn't Connak's voice. Kienna's gaze darted around, searching, but no one else was there. Stress pressed in, her pulse thrumming from the magical blast. Her mind had to be fracturing. Perhaps the voice was a sign she was slipping into madness.

"Kienna!" Connak yelled. She snapped her head toward him, seeing his hand outstretched waiting for her to take it as Broan dragged Baila from the empty clearing they stood in. Kienna instinctively opened her mind. She had to warn Connak, but the words caught, a heavy weight sinking her heart into the abyss. Fear bound her silence, sealing her fate as Baila glanced back at her from the corner of her eye. Kienna closed her mind, but she grabbed Connak's hand anyway.

"We should go," Danek suggested, wrapping his arm around her and helping her through the sand. Her ribs ached from the surge of magic the king flung into her, the buzzing of electricity from the Orb still pricking at the hairs in her arm. She wanted to rest and process, but she knew Danek was right. There was no telling if King Vaerin would be back. He disappeared into nothing, taking a handful of soldiers with him. That level of power was surreal. Seeing it solidified her decision to keep silent. They were running from a man more lethal than they previously knew, and his *daughter* walked among them.

Swallowing hard, Kienna unlatched herself from Danek. The wolf padded to her, stopping Kienna from her path. Her lungs locked at the sight of the animal, her stature reaching Kienna's shoulders. Deep silver eyes bore into her soul. It was like the wolf could see every piece of her. The thought made her shudder. Every piece of her was dirtied by the king's request and the secrets they forced her to hold.

She dropped her eyes but kept walking as Connak pulled her forward. He had secrets, and now, so did she. Glancing back at the wolf, she wondered how it came about finding them and why it stuck around now. *Go,* she pleaded. *You can be free from all of this.*

The wolf snorted through its snout but looked away. Kienna couldn't tell if the creature heard her.

Chapter 28

—Moira—

Moira stumbled wearily over the hills, Tislin taking great caution to hold her steadily on their descent. They stopped for water often and rested so Moira could regain the energy she so lovingly donated to her womb. Her hair, matted from the wind and rain, clung to her cheeks in thick strands. Though the forest's showers had helped cleanse the grime of travel, she desired a proper bath, one with oils and warm water to rinse the wild from her skin.

She could admit the forest was beautiful, but Moira wasn't one to romanticize the trees. She preferred open spaces with the sun brushing her shoulders and the breeze shifting gently across wide skies. Out here, in the hills with the golden sun overhead, she felt a version of herself she had almost forgotten. Seated beside a lake with her face tilted to the light. She let her body rest. The sun touched her skin and, slowly, she responded. A faint glow shimmered along her arms.

Tislin watched from nearby. "You connect with the weather," he said, settling beside her at the foot of Lake Lysiria. Its surface sparkled endlessly, like the sky made liquid. Waves lapped gently at their feet.

"Mainly the sun," Moira said. "Though I've summoned a cloud or two in my day."

Tislin's eyes remained locked on the lake. "Tell me about your husband."

"How do you know that?" Moira tensed and stood up.

He didn't move. "The gold you wear as armor," he gestured to the bands around her arms. "You take them off whenever we stop to rest. But the ring. That stays."

"Perhaps it was my mother's." Moira's hand drifted to the band on her right hand.

"Perhaps. But your mother didn't give you a child."

Silence.

She'd worn looser clothes to hide the changes. No one among the Guardians had said anything. Had she been so obvious in the forest that Connak and Tislin could tell, or were they better at observing? Above them, a single dark cloud marred the sky.

"We're trained in secrets." Tislin's voice was kind. "Your secret is safe with us."

Moira let out a shaky breath. Her hand dropped to her side, and the cloud moved on. "His name is Rhior. He's… My husband is a coward." After she said it, shock overcame her. She'd been holding in these feelings this whole time with no one to talk to about them. Now that she said it, she felt guilty…but relieved.

Rhior pushed her away, told her to leave, and then refused to go with her. It was a funny thing. She almost had to laugh about it. He thought going into the arcane forest was safer for Moira, but not him. He thought he could survive the king's tyranny but didn't trust her enough to keep him alive. She didn't know it then, but he had severed the part of her that thought he was perfect and that they would have lasted forever.

Either way, she knew he would have died in the forest when they were attacked by those creatures. Moira turned to Tislin. "It was you in the forest, right? The one who killed the creature that attacked me?"

"It was."

"I can never repay that debt, but I'll certainly try."

Tislin shook his head and pursed his lips. "There's never a debt to repay when doing the right thing."

It was such a raw and honest thing to say; something Moira was not used to hearing. King Vaerin always had a way of making everything into a debt. Having a debt wiped free dug a pit into her stomach, but then the hole filled itself, and Moira relaxed. "Connak's going to find Kienna and Baila, right?"

"Yes."

Moira looked at Tislin for more. He didn't give it, so she asked, "You're his second in command? Meaning he does have his own army?"

"He's had the Blades for four years. He's a formidable commander."

"But he's so young. You trust him, then? Because you both asked me to trust him with my friends' lives, and I didn't come this far for them to all die in this land for—"

Moira was cut off by a kick in her womb. It was far too early for that, but she felt it nonetheless. Her hand immediately went to her stomach, her eyes growing wide. She looked at Tislin, not expecting him to understand her fear—that she might be miscarrying, but the heat of his gaze indicated maybe he did.

His hand brushed over hers to help calm her nerves, a sudden spark shooting into her knuckles, and then Moira's mind folded into itself. The lake fell away, and she found herself standing at the edge of a dune under an inverted sky. Stars trickled downward like sand. Connak stood, cast in gold, even younger than he was now, leading a group of Blades across shifting ground.

A voice rang out in her head, like a child's whisper barely above the wind. "He'll burn for her at the end of the world to keep her safe."

Moira turned to see a cradle of thorned vines. Inside was a glowing, flickering light. She gasped, then her vision adjusted back to the lake, staring at the bright reflection of the sun dancing along the ripples of the waves.

"What did you show me?" she asked Tislin.

"*I* did not show you anything. What happened?"

Moira replayed the baby's kick, his touch, the spark igniting an image of Connak, and a reassurance that he would hold Kienna's life in his hands to Tislin. That magic had to be his. She didn't see visions. She played with the weather. The visions belonged to Kienna, and Kienna wasn't in the vision, so surely, she hadn't summoned Moira's mind.

"You know, there are tales of a time when a baby born with magic can fuel a mother's abilities," Tislin said. Moira felt her stomach again, but the kicking stopped. He removed his hand from hers and stood up. "We should get going. Dove Port is over that ridge."

Nestled between the glistening Lake Lysiria to the south and the winding Goldmere River to the north, Dove Port emerged like a dream on the horizon. The Silver Span Bridge was long and sweeping as it stretched across the river to the northern mainland, carved with ancient runes of peace and trade. To the west, a luminous forest pulsed gently with silver light, less ominous than the Malintale but equally alive.

Moira's breath caught. Stone buildings arched in elegant curves, crowned with domes and spiraling towers. Ivy wove through every level, courtyards blooming with gardens suspended in the air. Artists and scholars walked alongside sailors and merchants, and laughter echoed from every open window. The city was a celebration of the world.

"It's more than I could have imagined." Moira's eyes widened, staring in wonder at the open city. It greeted her with a bright burst of sun.

Tislin's focus stayed on her. His gaze burned against her as the golden rays of the sun clung to her skin, warming her rich brown complexion. She wasn't tired anymore. Tislin's lip curved upward as he said, almost to himself, "You are from here."

Moira shot him a glance. Her home was destroyed. That's what she'd been told. Yet she was told so many other things that were lies twisted with memories she couldn't quite find anymore. The way this city made her feel, she had no problem believing it could be her home.

As they walked, narrow beams of sunlight trailed her movements, slipping through the canopies and alley arches to find her shoulders. The light, warm and reverent, followed her with quiet curiosity. Tislin smiled, hands behind his back, as he strolled. The people around them paid him no mind. His pointed ears set him apart, but his presence barely rippled through the crowd. He would have stuck out amongst the people in River Storm, but not here.

"Dove Port is our strongest human ally," Tislin said as they crossed the stone path. "The last among men still willing to stand beside the Elvish clans. There are others, but our ranks thin with each moon's passing. Even *this* alliance is fickle, but they're used to my presence here."

"I see." Moira acknowledged the city thoughtfully, but his words from before lingered. "Why do you think I'm from here?"

"You are named in the old tales."

As if she was supposed to know the stories of the folklore he had meant. She tipped her head to indicate she did not. Tislin guided her to a weather-worn tablet in the city's heart. It depicted war full of ships, fire, and chaos about as well as any stone-carved tablet could. At its center, soldiers were holding a child and crossing the bridge. Moira leaned in, fingers tracing the etched child.

Tislin pointed his hand over the images. "Dove Port fell first in the Great War. A slaughter, by all accounts. Vaerin could not resist the tale of a human child *born* with magic."

"Born with it?" Moira furrowed her brow.

Tislin nodded. "No one knew, of course, for a while. But when Vaerin's army broke through, the soldiers found a child in the Lysiria cradled in a bubble of protection. Did you know that 'Moira' means child of the sea in Edranic?" Moira tilted her head. Tislin continued. "Edranic was the tongue of old empires."

"So, the child…me. I…was born with magic?"

"This is what the folklore says."

"And found *in* water?"

"It would appear so."

"And named as such? A child of the sea found in the sea." Moira cocked an eyebrow. She could buy into bits of Tislin's story, but folklore always managed to be weird prophecies of the future that might or might not mean anything, written by old men and women who spent time predicting futures and not forging them. "What are your thoughts on these stories?"

Tislin's eyes drifted toward a troupe of street musicians weaving through the alley, their mandolins lifting with a ballad of forbidden lovers. The song was oddly timed, but Moira found herself lingering on its softness. When the tune faded, the quiet between them deepened.

"The Great War was not so long ago," Tislin said. "We are all aware of the four children he took from this realm. An Elvish, a half-blood, a human, and a barbarian. *You* are still the only human outside of the King of River Storm with natural magic in this realm."

She wondered why the king cared so much about her and the others as children. If he had his own magic, why wouldn't he leave everyone be and siphon himself into his own bubble? He could create whatever life he wanted. He had it in River Storm. What did he gain from stealing children and destroying her home?

"In River Storm, Vaerin calls the war his *War of Liberation*. Like he freed people," Moira said, looking at an image on the tablet of soldiers carrying the child away over the long bridge.

"You lived there. What do you think?"

Moira paused. "My husband is a coward. The king is a coward. Tell me, are you a coward, Tislin?" It wasn't fair for her to turn her disdain for cowards on him, but the thought of Rhior abandoning her and the king imprisoning her made it hard to hold it in.

Tislin considered this, his eyes softening. "Cowardice may be a subjective observation."

"But it was a yes or no question."

"I'm standing before a woman whose fire has outlasted grief. Whether I claim bravery or not would do little to soothe you."

"But?"

"No *but*. I simply try each day to be the sort of man who does not run."

Despite Tislin's belief, this answer did soothe her. She needed a world full of bravery with less cowardice when it came to doing what was right. She wanted to believe that Rhior exemplified some bravery when he pushed her to leave him in River Storm, but it was not the sort of bravery she needed.

Moira took in the Elvish man with his pale skin, tall stature, and the way the light hit his shadows and made him glow. He had the most wonderful specks of orange sunlight in his eyes. His composure, dare she say, was incredibly sexy, and she found herself wondering what an Elvish man would be like. Her body glowed at the thought. She had to divert her eyes quickly, ashamed for having any thoughts at all about it. She was a married woman, after all.

"Come," Tislin smiled. "The Elarent House has agreed to host us for the evening while we wait for your friends."

Moira's cheeks burned red as she followed him from the city to the elegant wayhouse. Her mind wandered back to the vision that plagued her at the lake. Not only was she still worried about her friends' safety, but she was unsure what the vision meant. The words were clear enough, though ominous and dark. Connak would burn for Kienna. Moira would sort through the meaning of it all later. What she wanted to understand was what the vision meant for her. Was Tislin right? Could her baby be fueling magic into her body and sending prophetic visions?

Moira detested prophecies. Her hand floated to her abdomen again, a reaction she did when she was overwhelmed. Her possessing visions added to the city's lore as a child of water, and that made Moira feel muddled. The salted breeze caressed her face as if trying to soothe her through her unwavering thoughts. She curled into the smell.

"Onward," she mumbled to herself.

Tislin opened the door for her into the wayhouse. For once, despite lacking her past and recent memories, Moira knew she saw the future ahead of her clearly.

Chapter 29

—Connak—

The desert was unforgiving during the day. As soon as Connak retrieved Kienna and Baila from Vaerin's camp, he took them west to avoid the sandwraith pirates who scoured the eastern bank of the river for travelers. The journey was much longer this way, but fighting the wraiths in the heat wasn't a risk Connak was willing to take. Plus, there were rumors of a sand beast that—if awoken—would end their journey immediately.

He led them through the western dunes through towering sand where the air shimmered with heat, turning the horizon into an endless mirage. Everyone was encouraged to use their water sparingly, but they were all running low by the time they stumbled into the ancient desert ruins.

"This fucking heat is going to kill us if we don't stop," Broan said as Kienna stumbled in the sand. He moved past her and let Danek pick her up while the wolf whimpered.

Connak agreed. He'd grown accustomed to the desert for a time after he escaped River Storm since it was the only land that existed between the Elvish clan and Vaerin. If he didn't have the Elvish healing abilities, he, too, would have grown scales with the lizards and the desert people.

"We can stop here," he said to everyone.

He brushed his feet through the sand, searching for the partially buried stone structures until he found the opening he'd used as a child. Connak pulled the lip of the stone and stepped aside for everyone to enter. The tunnels were dark with ribbons of light shining through areas the sand didn't cover as tightly. The darkness was a comforting escape from the blinding sun above.

Danek set Kienna down gently against a cooler area of stone, her wolf pancaking closer to her. They rested together, her head falling onto Danek's shoulder. Their lips were cracked, and Connak knew they'd all run out of water by now. He'd have to go into Holbeck to get them more; otherwise, he'd put them at risk for heat stroke and dehydration. They'd be desert food for the thornhorn jackals in no time.

"There's an oasis about two miles from here. I can get us water there," he told them, pulling the lip of the hidden ruins closed.

"I can't walk another two miles." Baila rubbed her feet and sighed. Her skin burned a fiery flame that matched the color of her hair. Connak reached out and washed his hand over her, the red lightening to a bright pink, sealing the cut on her lip as well. Her brows furrowed as she studied him. "Oh, that was…thank you."

Connak nodded. "I'll be back. Give me one hour."

He pushed the lid open again and reacclimated to the scorching heat and blinding sun. This was no place for anyone to stay, let alone those with little experience between the extremes of the weather. King Vaerin was smart to camp where he did, right between the sandwraiths and Holbeck. Both were treacherous. He'd have to fight his way out of Holbeck if he ran into the wrong crowds. If they were playing a game of old scholars' pastime, King Vaerin had made a deadly move that put them in a dire situation.

Connak loosened his grip and stretched his fingers. His only goal now was to find them water before the glassmaw snakes could slip their way through the opening.

—Kienna—

Kienna's lips cracked, and she desperately wanted the burn to leave her skin, but Connak only healed Baila. She clearly needed it more with her pale complexion. Connak was a good person, but Kienna wondered if he would have healed her if he knew what she did. That Baila was a downright traitor who lied to everyone and slithered her way in to manipulate them like her father.

It's the first thing she prepared herself to tell the group, but Vaerin had her family, and she wasn't ready to feel their blood on her hands. So, she'd give up the hidden city to the king and prayed that he'd let Jacob and Maren go.

Kienna brought her fingers to her mouth, her nails going raw from how much she'd been picking and gnawing at them. The wolf next to her whined as she did it. Kienna regarded her, intrigued by the instant reactions the wolf gave to everything she did. It took her some time to get used to her presence with them, but she had to admit she was happy to see the wolf again, looking healthier than she did in River Storm. Danek placed his searing hand on hers. She was sure he meant to gently help her stop ripping her cuticles to shreds, but it only sent a flare of pain.

"Stop that!" Kienna snapped.

Danek twitched and then removed his hand. "If I had water, I could heal you."

"Don't die for me, Danek," she said.

"For you?" Broan spat. "Ha! Lover boy wouldn't do anything of the sort."

Danek sat up and punched Broan in the shoulder, his eyes piercing through him. Kienna didn't have enough strength to ask what he meant, though she suspected it deep down. Danek sat back against the stone, jaw tight as he began picking his own fingers. "Anyone want to talk about why the king let us all go again?"

"Or we could sit in silence and rest before we have to go back to the desert to burn," Baila said, shifting around in the cave.

Tiny scuttles echoed throughout, glass-like beetles reflecting light like tiny prisms as they scurried along the walls. At least they weren't leechbugs. Kienna had never directly been attacked by a leechbug, but most merchants complained about them during their mating season. They were vile bugs that attacked any unsuspecting person stupid enough to get close to their nests along the bank of the river.

"I second resting," Kienna said and lay her head against the wall. Her hand drifted to the wolf's back, her black fur a comfort in the unknown. Her body leaned into the creature's presence. Kienna could almost feel a spark of connection, but a pinch to her neck jolted her away from the wolf. She slapped at a beetle on her skin as another climbed onto her shoulder and over her neck. She slapped at it again, but it bit her first. The wolf next to her growled. "Ouch!"

The glass refractions of the bug sent shards into her fingers, which she immediately went to pluck out, but her skin tingled and started going numb. Out of the corner of her eye, she could see more beetles climbing out from a crevice and into the cave.

"Not to alarm anyone," Kienna stood from the floor and inched toward the rock that closed them in. "I think we need to leave now."

"No," Baila whined. Broan simply grunted in agreement.

"Yes." She was already pushing at the top but struggled to get it to budge. "We are going to be absolutely covered in beetles in a minute if you don't all move now."

Danek opened his eyes and jumped to the center of the room with her and the wolf. "Yeah, I would get up if I were you."

Broan followed suit when he noticed the swarm of beetles. He grabbed Baila's wrist and yanked her up, too. Meanwhile, Kienna kept pushing the lid with no luck. Connak had sealed them in tightly. Try as she might, she only found her blisters opening from the burns.

"Don't just stand there," Broan said, the group huddling into a circle. "Open it already."

"It's stuck," Kienna grunted.

Beetles crawled along their feet now, an overwhelming clicking of their legs reverberating along the room. A high-pitched, hollow hum escaped from the beetles, a sound that would haunt Kienna's nightmares. She slammed her fists upward to make it budge. Broan pushed Danek and started to help her. "If you don't want to suffocate by beetle, I suggest you all fucking help!"

Danek jumped in, swiping beetles off his pants, and pushed with them. The lid started inching forward, but it wouldn't be enough time. Baila was busy dancing around the room, smooshing the bugs, which only made their hum turn into a screech, like an instrument that fell out of tune.

"Baila!" Kienna scolded. Her heart pounded, tiny bug bites

leaving her body numb. Her strength failed, but she wasn't prepared to die in an underground temple by desert beetles. "Leave the bugs alone and help us push!"

Baila jerked and let Broan help her up until she summoned a great spark. Succulents curled into the stones and opened like mouths, prying the top open and revealing the harsh desert sun. Broan thrust Baila out of the opening. She reached her hand out for Kienna to grab it, but Kienna slapped it away and leaned on Danek instead to climb. Danek studied the interaction for the briefest of moments and then pulled with all his might.

Broan and Danek helped the wolf out of the temple, something she clearly did not enjoy. Then the men followed afterward, and they pushed the lid closed as a few beetles scurried out. Kienna fell into the sand, her body aching and pulsing with numbness. Her legs were too sore to move, but she knew they had to get up before the sun completely baked them.

"Come on," she said, heaving her body.

Everyone followed, running in awkward strides to find new muscles to use that hadn't been affected by whatever beetle that was. They were thirsty and tired and had no idea where they were running, but they figured it would be better than the bugs whose bites had now started to make Kienna's skin blister and pop with golden pus.

A large gust of wind picked up from the east, propelling them forward but slapping their bodies with grains of sand that burned. When it felt like they had completely lost their vision altogether, Kienna collapsed as the sand covered her. Still, it was a better way to die than to be covered by those beetles, so she closed her eyes and let her body relax. At least now she wouldn't have to sell out Connak's people and find their hidden source of magic.

Kienna awoke with water splashing her face. She gasped, searching for the shadows that would creep in next to torment her. Only Connak's shadow loomed over her. Her heart settled, but the threat of the dungeons still pricked at her skin.

Connak must have healed them in their sleep because the blisters and burns were all gone. They sat near large rock arches that were the color of dried blood, looming like ancient gates. Kienna's wolf lay near her, licking her paws and gnawing on a bone. Connak said it was the remains of a jackal she caught after he'd healed her, too. She was relieved to see the wolf had made it out unscathed. Her hand brushed against the creature's massive paw, fingers trailing along the soft pads for comfort as she steadied herself.

"You're lucky you made it as far as you did in that sandstorm," Connak told them. "I was leaving Holbeck when the storm relented, and I tripped over Broan. I'd be upset that you didn't listen to me, but it looks like you got bit by glass beetles."

Danek rubbed his face, pushing his fingers into the bridge of his nose. "The whole place swarmed with them. We would have died."

"That's unusual behavior for the beetle." Connak looked around. "They're great creatures in dark caves to help reflect the light."

Kienna looked at Baila from the corner of her eyes. She hadn't thought anything of it then, just that maybe the bugs were swarming at the smell of fresh blood, but now, it did seem like they came in unusual waves. Baila looked away uncomfortably. Whatever she did, there's no way she intended to kill them. King Vaerin still needed Kienna alive. Regardless, she was playing with magic in a world she didn't understand, and they all suffered.

Connak stood and studied the sky, an endless and cloudless

void of blue and bright white. "Our water sources have been stocked enough to get us to Alverton. We should get there by high noon if you're okay to move."

Broan picked up a handful of sand and tossed it aside. "Are there any more beetles on the way?"

"No beetles," Connak said. "Only a bridge to Dove Port."

Moira would be waiting for them in Dove Port. How disappointed she would be if she knew what Baila had done to them all. How disappointed she would be to know Kienna harbored this secret inside of her. She dreaded going to Dove Port now. It was only one step closer to helping King Vaerin win whatever war he started twenty-five years ago.

Connak stared at her as she glared at Baila. Kienna had to force her jaw loose, but she wondered how much he could see in her head, even as she worked to keep the pages tightly closed.

The wind kicked up, brushing sand over her boots. "Then let's cross it." Her voice was a little too calm.

Every step toward Dove Port felt like walking into a trap of her own making. Connak still watched while Baila said nothing. No matter which way she played this, Kienna knew the secret twisting in her gut would break someone.

The only question was: Who?

Chapter 30

—Connak—

Alverton was the only thing left between the group and Dove Port. The gray industrial city was only good for forging weapons and battle armor. They found themselves rallying closer to King Vaerin's cause as opposed to the Elvish. The Silver Span Bridge, built years ago as a sign of peace and unity, connected both Alverton and Dove Port, but when King Vaerin took over, the bridge lost its use. It became heavily guarded on both sides to ensure spies didn't cross to collect intel.

Connak led them through the shadows and to the river to drink. The Goldmere, restless and wide, shimmered under the light. He crouched beside the bank, eyeing the narrow stone bridge in the distance. Three guards. All River Storm. Spears upright with helmets glinting. They hadn't noticed them yet, which was a good sign.

He motioned for the others to huddle low. "There's no chance we'll cross that bridge by force. Not without raising an alarm that calls for more soldiers. I doubt any of you are up for another fight."

Broan scratched his jaw. "We could send the wolf ahead to draw them out."

"No," Connak said flatly. "The wolf is not expendable and not for us to command."

Danek frowned. "I could use an illusion."

"Or we swim?" Kienna's eyes narrowed toward the water.

Swimming would not be ideal, even if they were in the best shape. None of them were water benders, and asking Broan to lift another makeshift bridge would only cause too much attention. "Not with the wolf," Connak shook his head. "Even if she could make it, we'd be spotted."

A pause stretched. Then Baila spoke from behind him, her voice clipped but calm. "We don't need to fight. Or flee."

Connak glanced back. "What are you suggesting?"

"I can forge an order if you get me paper," she said. "One from Vaerin's inner guard. Royal mandate for prisoner retrieval. We say we're taking her back for questioning and that we are headed to Dove Port to intercept a rebel contact."

"Disguises?"

"You'll have to find those, too, but I don't see any other way that gets us across the bridge. You'll have to act like one of Vaerin's."

Connak drummed his fingers. He had no idea if this would work, but he didn't see any other option. Danek and Broan were on board, but getting Broan across was another challenge as he towered over them. "You'll have to be the Guardians truly. I can't hide you. It'll just be me."

"We can improvise," Baila said.

By mid-afternoon, they were walking up the bridge. Connak and Baila led the rest while they held Kienna bound loosely between them with a makeshift shackle around her wrists, hidden enough to slip. Broan and Danek followed with scowls, and the wolf, doused in ash to mask its gleam, padded beside him like a war hound.

Connak squared his shoulders and clenched his jaw. It was Baila's plan, but the others looked to him to keep the facade going. One misstep and they'd be fully improvising a fight they didn't want to have.

The guards stiffened as they approached. "State your business."

Baila handed over the parchment without a word. The soldier squinted at the seal. The ink had barely dried. "She's the Starborn," she said smoothly, gesturing to Kienna. "The king wants her back before the scum in the forest vanish with her. There's a bounty tied to her blood, and he demands passage to Dove Port to retrieve another."

Connak watched the guard's expression flicker, eyes moving from the paper to Kienna's dirt-streaked face.

"She looks too calm to be a prisoner of the king," the soldier said.

"Wouldn't you be?" Connak said coldly. "If you knew the king would be the one to cut your throat himself? There's no use running when the king condemns it."

The soldier eyed them. "The Starborn left the king with quite a mess to clean up. I could slit her throat right now and do him a favor." He stepped up and grabbed Kienna by the jaw. Connak was quite impressed with how well she held her composure, considering he pulled his blade and set it against her throat.

"You could," Baila sighed. "It'd do us all a favor, honestly. But the king has orders, you see." She tapped her finger against the papers she had handed him. "Unless you'd like for him to slit your throat afterwards, too."

The man with the blade studied Kienna for a moment too long. Connak could see Danek tensing beside Broan, fighting every urge he could not to lash out and rip the soldier away. "She's right," said the other. "Let them go." Finally, the guard dropped his sword and motioned for his companions to step aside and let them through.

Though relief flooded Connak at the sight of Kienna's freedom once again, his mind speculated those around him. He expected more tension, especially with the wolf in tow, but the soldiers trusted Baila so quickly—too quickly.

"Anything you want to tell me?" Connak whispered to Kienna as they stepped onto the bridge.

"No," she said, but the quiver in her lip told him everything.

He focused on Baila, then back to Kienna. He couldn't be too sure, but his suspicions were rising. It wasn't enough to stop his path, but the nervous tick of his hands returned to the side of his leg.

Chapter 31

—Kienna—

Baila hovered over Kienna. They ditched the fake shackles after about a mile and walked with ease when the soldiers were out of sight. When Baila got so close that Kienna could smell the flowers on her skin, she turned and growled, "Give me space."

The wolf snapped her teeth toward Baila as well, and she quickly stepped backward out of arm's reach. Kienna thanked the stars for the wolf in that moment, and every moment since they connected in River Storm.

Baila was gauging Kienna's position. She could tell every step of the way when Baila would watch her and listen to everything she would say. For that reason, she said little. There was no point now in trying to connect to the world around her. Her mission was clear.

"Oh, thank the heavens!" Moira ran up the bridge as they cleared into Dove Port.

They smelled of sweat and iron, hints of blood staining their bodies from the battle at the camp. Kienna's skin pulsed slightly with the desert heat still seeping into her pores, but Connak tried his best to heal everyone. Even Danek, who had run out of his own energy reserves.

An Elvish man, cloaked in shadows with ash blond hair, greeted Connak with a firm clasp of hands. Their grips locked, strong and sure, pulling each other in until their shoulders bumped and their arms wrapped briefly in a half-embrace. Then came the backslap with the lopsided grins.

Moira wrapped her arms around Danek first, but not without telling him how horrible he looked and smelled, which was impossible because Danek never looked terrible a day in his life. Then she turned to Kienna, relief flooding her dark eyes. She motioned for a hug, but the wolf stepped forward and turned her away quickly.

"Ha!" Baila said, and then her face reddened beyond the slight burn on her cheeks. "Sorry, it's just that creature has been snapping at me the whole journey across the bridge."

"She's probably hungry," Kienna said, but the tension between her and Baila didn't dissipate.

"Tislin, can you send word to your brother?" Connak asked. "They should know to expect us before we surprise them with…" he motioned to the Guardians, "them."

Tislin nodded and vanished through the shadows of Dove Port.

The Elarent House bustled with the comings and goings of shipmasters and merchants who closed for the night. The wayhouse sat near Dove Port's lakefront, a modest bar and inn where people gathered to drink, rest, and forget the world. Laughter spilled from its crooked shutters, carrying the scent of salt, smoke, and someone always on the verge of song.

Kienna sat with the rest of the group at the last table in the corner before the wayhouse filled to capacity. She hugged herself tightly, watching the shadows in the room and wondering if King Vaerin would show up out of nowhere and kill them all. He had enough motive to do it now, especially with Broan and Danek. They actively chose against the king. There was no telling when their lives would fall into the hands of a River Storm death. Hiding the tremor in her hand, Kienna would rather have been sitting with the wolf outside. She needed time to gather her thoughts and to take in this new, strange world. Plus, there was a weird connection forming between them. It was faint, but she realized the wolf would not be going away anytime soon.

Tislin entered the wayhouse and caught the group in the corner. Moira waved him over with a warm smile, grabbing him a chair to sit next to her. A clinking of mugs and jovial laughter cheered as the Elvish man sauntered into the corner with them. Broan had filled yet another pint of beer, roaring with the other men as he chugged it down.

The others feasted on roots and vegetables plucked near the forest's edge. Their veal was cooked to perfection; a craft the innkeeper must have spent her life mastering.

"Did you hear the Elvish are back?" a man asked behind them and pointed to Broan in the center of the room. "Apparently, the Vikings, too." He was stained with oil and grime from the shipyards, belly swollen with ale, and his voice boomed with drunken bravado. His companions hooted and jeered in kind.

Kienna eyed them warily, studying her surroundings. She'd just learned about the existence of Elvish folk. Hearing about the existence of Vikings only confused her. Though most were in good spirits, others cast equally weary glances toward Connak and Tislin as well as Broan. Then Broan bought them all another round on Connak's dime, and they all perked up.

Broan stumbled his way back to the table, flopping down in his chair and leaning into the group. Kienna stared at his head, realizing she hadn't noticed the red marking on his temple until now, too consumed with surviving. She wanted to ask Connak about it later but wondered if she'd get the chance now that she had Baila breathing down her neck. She'd have to open her mind for him, and she feared that would spill everything out onto the table.

"When I tell you the sand about had us covered all the way over our heads." Broan slurred his words. He'd started back in on his story of how they valiantly crossed the desert. "If it hadn't been for that fucking wolf, we'd probably still be under it."

"Well, Connak did get to us soon after," Danek said, reaching for Broan's cup.

"Oh, yes," Baila agreed. "Connak saved our lives. I thought the king was going to kill me and Kienna when they showed up. He's *my* hero."

Connak flushed and glanced at Kienna. She tried to hide the scowl on her face and play along, especially once Baila's foot tapped hers under the table.

"Yeah, it was something alright." She said it with as much enthusiasm as she could find, but found she did not have much in her. When she looked back at Connak, she couldn't tell if his brows had furrowed because she'd hurt his feelings or because he was onto her.

She looked down at the wooden table, but Tislin lingered on her. There was no telling how long *he'd* been watching. He sat silently observing everyone since he'd sat down, and now the discomfort of his archaic eyes on hers made the hair on her arms stand.

She shifted in her seat and cleared her throat. "How long have you been in the Blades?"

"We are born into our roles," Tislin said, a faint smile tugging at the corner of his lips. He relaxed in his seat. "Though some of us do choose other routes."

"So, which is it?" Kienna crossed her arms. Riddles and half-truths.

"I joined the Blades when they gave the army to Connak. Though my brother would have preferred I command my own army under his brigade."

"You didn't want your own?" Kienna leaned forward, struggling to hear him over the growing din.

Tislin shrugged. "Some of us aren't destined to be as great as others."

"Maybe not," she replied, pursing her lips together.

Kienna leaned back, fingers grazing over the K branded on her hand. She didn't think she was destined to be great either. Maren thought she was. She gave her hope, but King Vaerin ripped it away, making it hard to enjoy anything about this moment in this carefully constructed city with views more beautiful than she'd ever imagined she'd see in person.

Broan stood and stumbled into the table. His mug spilled to the floor, and everyone scrambled to avoid the stench of beer soaking their clothes.

"I should take him upstairs," Danek offered. He tried stabilizing Broan, who leaned heavily against him. Before they could fall, Connak stepped in, taking Broan's other side and guiding him up the stairs.

Moira bowed her head gently. "I'd like to rest as well." She placed her hand on the table and smiled at the women. "I'm so glad you're both okay." Then her eyes cut to Tislin. "See you tomorrow."

Kienna looked at Tislin, too. He'd returned Moira's warmth, and she wondered what that was all about. Had Moira caught the eye of a mysterious Elvish man? A smile tugged on her lips, but then Moira retreated, and Baila stood to go outside. Frowning, she followed.

Baila pulled her hood up and disappeared into an alleyway between the wayhouse and Tarn's Markethouse, where crates lined the back like forgotten soldiers. She stopped where the lake unveiled itself, the moon mirrored larger in its waters than in the sky. The wolf trailed behind, keeping close to shadows and side streets. The wolf's wildness drew too many eyes. She most certainly did not appreciate it when Connak requested that she stay hidden. She circled once with her hackles raised before finally slinking into the alleyways. Even now, her silver eyes glinted from the dark, ears twitching and tail flicking in irritation. Regardless, Kienna would need her if things turned ugly. She nodded in the wolf's direction as she reached Baila.

The two women stood in silence, the lake breathing moonlight around them. "Daughter, huh?" Kienna's fists tightened.

Baila lifted her ethereal green eyes skyward. "King Vaerin never wished to claim that title, honestly." She ran her fingers through the ivy draping down from the terraces above, the vines growing longer beneath her touch. "But yes, he is my father." Baila dismissed the confession with a flippant shrug.

"No one else knows?"

"It's not relevant to my story," Baila rolled her eyes.

Kienna scoffed. What the fuck was she talking about? She lived in a noble palace in River Storm with strangers, then? They thought her father was an advisor who had migrated from the North into River Storm. Why did it have to be a lie? The only motive for lying about it was to use it against them because none of them would have trusted her from the get-go if they knew this.

"Not relevant? You tricked me, Baila. I fell for your lies when you told me you believed in what we were doing. Him being your father is more than relevant."

Baila's laugh came out with a suppressed, dull hum. "I can't help you're stupid, Kienna. If you believed me, then you haven't been paying attention, and that's your fault."

Kienna pushed her focus to the boxes in the corner. She was livid. She wanted to put her hands around Baila's throat and burn her to ashes, but she now found herself held captive by her, and all she could allow herself to feel now was sadness. "Do you care so little about us that you would do this?"

"All I care about now is making sure you deliver on what King Vaerin has asked of you. My feelings toward you or any of the others mean nothing." Baila's lips tugged into a sneer, her freckles pushing upward. "Though I will tell you that I *do* detest you."

Kienna snuffed, and for a second, she felt like her wolf. "I pity you, Baila. I can't tell if you're this desperate for his approval or if you enjoy being his pawn."

Baila slapped her hard across the cheek, her hands glowing a sickly chartreuse. "Let there be no mistake that I am not his pawn. I serve a *just* king."

Kienna shook her head, her mind flashing to the dungeons. The gasping. The drowning. *That* was not just. The tremor in her hands returned when her memory fought against her body. Now and then, she'd see a sparkle over everything that happened, and it grew confusing to think about. *Grins and spins.*

"It's not too late to change your mind. You and I, we don't have to do this." She said it with a plea in her voice.

"He's made it clear that you do."

Footsteps echoed behind them. They turned to see Tislin emerging from the shadows, hands guarded carefully behind him. "Didn't mean to startle you. Only meant to ensure you both got your rest."

They shared another glance amongst themselves. Baila turned toward the wayhouse and disappeared. Kienna lingered for a moment, her eyes meeting Tislin's across the darkened path. His expression was unreadable. There was no kindness nor accusation. It was still, like a soldier waiting to be sure the threat was over. She couldn't tell exactly what he could have heard.

She assumed it was everything.

—Connak—

The water calmed Connak. He admired the lake with a sense of ease, aware that the shadows and night weren't always as sinister as his leaders once claimed. There was something sacred in the quiet between the waves. Men in the shipyard retired from their work, their elegant boats creaking in the harbor with each ebb and flow. Every ship lapping up and down shared similarities, built long ago by the prized woodcarver of Dove Port. His hands had shaped more than planks. They'd stirred currents far deeper than the harbor.

"Any word from Trinity?"

Tislin stepped out of the shadows, his presence shifting with the weight of secrets. "We can ride through tomorrow."

"Thank you, Captain." Connak turned to his friend with relief. "It's been a long year."

"Commander." Tislin moved closer with practiced caution. He didn't abandon formality. Instead, he placed his shoulder against Connak's, guarding his back. "We may have an issue with the girl."

"I know." Connak could sense her. Even though Kienna kept her mind tightly sealed, he lingered at its edges.

Hints were revealing themselves in a sort of confusion that radiated in her core. Not quite here, not quite there. Doubt, maybe a flicker of grief, bled through.

The others had taken to the environment easily, their call home beckoning. They were thriving. But Kienna had not tapped into her power even once. She hesitated in Northpass, a bystander in her own awakening. Connak could see the unnerving look in her eyes when they arrived, like she wasn't sure whether to run to them or from them.

"Do you think she's going to turn on us?" Tislin's eyes remained trained on the shadows behind Connak.

"I don't think so, but Vaerin won't be kind to our efforts."

"You trust the girl that much?"

"I have to. Or your brother will hang me when it's all said and done."

Connak drifted back to Lake Lysiria. The rhythmic crash of water lulled his thoughts into focus. Kienna wasn't evil. He could feel the truth of that as much as he felt the night air on his skin. Vaerin, on the other hand, had stared through him with rage at the camp. There would be no forgiveness now. No way to put it all back into the fragile bottle it had sat in.

The ground was already stirring, armies assembling. The weight of death. "We may have started the war sooner than intended."

And in his bones, he knew it was true.

Chapter 32

—Kienna—

Kienna and Danek were up before the sun to watch it rise above the Lysiria and breathe life into the world again. The rays shimmered on Kienna's golden skin. She had to squint to let the glaciers of blue adjust to the sudden burst of brightness. Danek sat near her at the docks. "Sometimes I'm still shocked that you were crazy enough to climb the barrier. I've wanted to do it for so long. Now I wish we had all done it sooner."

Kienna flashed him an empty smile. "Perhaps we can go back and do it again."

"Ha," Danek nudged her. "I wonder what this Elvish city holds. It's odd that they had to ask for permission yesterday."

"They are a little cryptic, right?" Kienna's gut turned, knowing this was the hidden city they were going to, and she'd have to be a traitor for the second time in her life.

Danek rubbed the nape of his neck. "I don't know. They might have secrets, but so does Vaerin."

Behind them, the city of Dove Port started to come alive. Merchants took to the streets to open their shops, artists and musicians working to capture the mood of the morning in their own special ways. A flute whistled in the air. Sailors hoisted the sails, bright white canvas sailing through the high seas. Pink clouds greeted their ships on the horizon. Danek's eyes fell back on Kienna, resting on her warmly, but she never knew how to address him or what to say when it felt like he was constantly reading her soul.

She avoided the weight of it. "Do you miss training?"

Danek raised his brow. "I think we've had better practice out here if that's what you mean."

"I mean the routine of it all. It made it easier to pretend we were doing something right."

He laughed heartily, a laugh that sounded good drumming against her ears. He wiped a tear from his eye and said, "I'm more than happy to grapple with you every day if you want to get your ass kicked."

Her eyes rolled to the back of her head. She cocked her face toward him, unamused, and pushed him off the ledge. Danek chuckled again, pulling to his feet alongside her. The joyful whinnies of horses echoed. Danek and Kienna turned to see Connak being greeted by a few soldiers, handing their steeds over to him. Connak bowed gracefully to each as they relinquished the reins.

When the group met by the forest line, there were horses for everyone. Connak hoisted Moira onto her horse carefully and then turned and lent his hand to Kienna to mount her steed. She mounted the horse on the other side instead. He bit down on the edge of a smile, that gentle playfulness still dancing around his eyes. The wolf stood still next to them, clearly shaken by Kienna's ascent onto another creature.

"I'm sorry," Kienna whispered in her direction. "It feels disrespectful to ride you." The wolf appeared to acknowledge Kienna's statement by turning her head. She reached her hand over, but pulled it back. "It's just...I don't think you're meant to walk beneath me."

"You should give her a name, you know," Connak said.

Kienna glanced down. "What?"

"The wolf. She's waiting for you to name her."

"How do you know?" Kienna shifted in the saddle, pulling the reins as the horse sidestepped.

"I had one, remember?" Connak pointed to his head, reminding her of the ridiculous hood he wore in the Malintale while he waited to break her out of River Storm. "Admittedly, he wasn't my guide for long. Only a month or so, but he led me where I needed to be, so it was long enough."

Kienna considered this, her gaze drifting back to the wolf. "What does her species call her?"

Connak grinned. "You could ask her yourself."

Kienna waved her hand. "I can't speak to animals, present company excluded."

Broan roared with laughter behind them. He slapped Kienna on the back as he edged his larger horse forward. The city was hesitant to give up its largest stallion, but the other mares could not fit the overpowering frame of the giant man. "This new world has made you funny. Bitter. Still annoying," he added, "but funny."

"*Try* speaking to her," Connak said and then mounted his own steed, a little chuckle escaping his breath. He turned to the people of Dove Port, watching and waiting. Their eyes were on the trees, a mystical awe lingering. Connak thanked them for their hospitality and then charged his clan to move forward.

"They think we're the answer to their prayers," Tislin whispered to Kienna.

She startled, as he wasn't previously there. "Why? They seem to be thriving."

"Yes, but the King of River Storm still lives. And he tore through this city to get his magic."

She cocked her head. "I thought he already had magic."

"You've got a lot more to learn." Tislin pointed toward the city. "They're scared, so our presence serves as a beacon to them."

"How exactly do they expect us to help?"

"There's this old saying through these parts. 'When the lost flame reunites with the god of light, the forest will breathe again, and the tyrant's crown shall turn to ash.'"

Kienna shook her head. "Moira mentioned you liked your folklore."

"I may have read it in a children's book." A gleam sparkled in his eye as Tislin's lip curled up. "But the forests have been alive as of late. So, perhaps…" He trailed off, letting his horse move forward without her.

He's odd, Kienna thought. Her eyes fell to the wolf walking next to her. *But so is having a wolf nearly as big as a horse trailing me.* Kienna studied the creature, watching her stride through the forest as if she owned the trees. And why shouldn't she? She was a magnificent being. Her black coat was splattered with gray specks as if the gods decided to flick a paintbrush at her in the middle of creation. It reminded Kienna of her own hair, laden with a mixture of dark brown and ash highlights. "Okay," she said out loud. "What's your name?" She waited, feeling silly for expecting an animal to talk to her. "I can't continue to call you wolf now, can I?" She sighed. *What's your name?* Kienna asked again through her mind with a little more desperation. The wolf simply blinked. She rolled her eyes. Of course, Connak had her do something that didn't work. Grinning, she pushed forward.

As they continued into the forest, the trees began to change. Still towering like those of the Malintale, their trunks gleamed with silvery undertones, and their bark shimmered faintly with light. Flowers burst in quiet clusters at the bases with violets and golds and iridescent blues, not like the wild chaos of growth, but a harmony only the forest could compose. Sunlight pierced the canopy in broader, brighter beams, casting pools of warmth on the moss-carpeted ground. Connak lifted his head. "This is the Sister Forest."

Kienna's heart caught. They were getting closer to what Vaerin wanted her to find. She tugged her horse to stop walking while the others moved ahead. The wolf stalked closely to her. Her chest tightened at the pull, like a tuning of her bones. The magic here was deeply old, not new like the history of River Storm recounted. The feeling of home rushed over her, and it called her to find it. Hands trembling, the challenge reverberated inside of her and lit her up. It wasn't quite like a fire, but more like the rising sun casting warmth. Danek paused, too. His hand flexed near his side, fingers glowing faintly with forest light and subtle veins of blue spiraling up his wrist. He didn't speak but stared at the overwhelming pulses flowing through his body.

Kienna shivered. The pull toward the Elvish city burned sweetly. The tug toward River Storm echoed bitterly. The two halves of her began to war in silence. This *was* the place. The place her family would die for if she didn't give it up. She looked around the trees with a swelling of emotion. The forest whispered desperate pleas to remain hidden and sacred.

She got off her horse as the wind danced through her hair playfully, acknowledging her. The sweet melodies of the birds chirped to each other. Crickets buzzed lazily. The sun dappled against her skin. It was the quiet press of solitude with deep stillness. She exhaled a trembling breath.

The others had stopped by now, all looking at her as dread began to rise. It started in the pits of her stomach and clutched her chest. Her hands were shaking uncontrollably with the weight of what she was experiencing. She knew in her bones this forest was her home. And Vaerin wanted her to destroy it. Or Maren and Jacob die.

Everything started to spin. She couldn't do this. Her eyes met the wolf's, its presence a shock as she began to panic. "I—I can't—" The wolf started to respond, reaching its snout to Kienna's hand. The thought of touch against her skin sent a flame spiraling into her soul. Fear and guilt overtook her. Kienna ran off the path and into the deep forest. Another crushing weight hit her chest. It didn't quite feel like the prison River Storm did, but the expectations of random prophecies and trying to decipher everything around her resembled that. The anxiety sent her running until her lungs burned and her legs flamed.

She shook, desperate for clarity, but the panic ravaged her.

Tears fell from her eyes, like ice against the fire inside of her. She spit, hoping to rid herself of this sudden display of raw emotion. She spit again, her mouth growing unusually dry. The trees started to spin faster. Kienna couldn't stop it, so she glued her eyes to one tree to keep her steady.

"What's wrong?" Moira asked behind her.

The sound of her voice broke her trance, grounding her back to the stillness of the forest. She realized she had been staring at an intricate carving in the oak. Glyphs, not quite like the blue carvings from the Malintale Forest, remained etched into the trees all over the forest. This tree, however, only had a simple "A + G" engraved.

"Can we trust them?" Kienna's voice was hoarse. *Silence spins.*

Moira stepped closer. "I trust them because you did. But if you have doubts, tell me why."

"It's weird," she said as Danek stepped out from behind a tree. "Just a few months ago, my only concerns were my faulty visions and holding a barrier on a wall." Her fingers traced around the rough bark of the tree, pinky grabbling on the initials. Her head hung, hair covering her eyes through the choked tears. "I'm struggling to wrap my mind around this world."

Moira eased forward, and the wolf bared her teeth. She stopped, watching the creature wearily, and then continued. "I get it. I don't think anyone could have imagined this magnitude of change."

"How are you all adapting so well? This isn't messing with your heads?"

"Should it?"

Kienna wanted so badly to tell Moira she had made a mistake. That they were wrong to follow her into the forest. She had been so confident then, and now she wanted to go back and keep Maren and Jacob safe. "This place feels a lot like my visions. More like a dream that's not fully there... I... Maybe Vaerin was right."

"Don't be a fool," Danek scoffed, tensing his fists by his side. "Vaerin has done nothing for us."

Kienna turned swiftly, her body growing fiercely close to Danek's, and heat radiated from her skin. "He gave you magic and taught you everything you know." She knew Danek was right, that Vaerin had twisted everything, but sometimes her mind still sparked with fragments that were too tender to be false. The boots. The brush of fingers against her cheek. The lie of love dressed in kindness.

"Everything we *think* we know," Moira said, still as soft as a bird. "Open your eyes, Kienna. He took us from this place. He did *not* rescue us."

"He raised us. Maybe we owe him more than we gave him." Kienna hated saying it. She was so close now, but if she could go back, she wouldn't have to reveal something she didn't understand to the king.

"What did he say to you in the camp?" Danek's eyes were wild and confused. "How can you not know that this is where we belong?"

She wanted to tell them everything. He had her family; a statement she didn't even know was true, either. They could be dead already. She didn't know any of it. All she knew was the forest called her with a whispering of the wind in her ear.

More heat surged through Kienna's body, rising from the impossible pressure of it all. Her blood boiled. She pressed her hand hard against the tree, trying to steady herself, but the fire was already crawling beneath her skin. From the branded K on her thumb, a thin trail of smoke curled into the air.

Connak and Tislin approached them, Broan and Baila following carefully behind. The stirring in the forest served as a warning for them to tread cautiously. Clouds shifted overhead, an angry flood threatening the once pleasant weather. Growling echoed, the wolf foaming desperately to keep Kienna safe. Tislin waded around the forest as the blue in her eyes grappled with the gray storm. He placed his thin, long fingers on her shoulder.

As he did, the ground shifted beneath Kienna. The forest blurred past, the trees smearing into shadow and light, until she stood in front of another man. He was Elvish, but not exactly. His face reminded her of Tislin's: round eyes speckled with green and hints of blue, cheekbones that tried to be otherworldly but didn't quite succeed. He had a pale scar near the collarbone. His core was etched in light gold, something she could have missed if she weren't looking so closely. He didn't see her, but as he turned, she wondered if he could *feel* her.

The world tugged again. Smoke coiled around her like a summons, dragging her through the dark. Time unraveled. Maren appeared before her, curled in bed. She was safe in River Storm, but thinner now, tears streaking across her grimy face. Her cheeks were hollow and her breath uneven. Still, she was alive.

A whisper brushed Kienna's skin. It was Maren's distant voice. *Don't forget the woodcarver. We'll be fine. Now go.*

Her mind reeled from the shift when she found herself barreling through the trees at a great speed until she landed near another Elvish man, hovering over a woman. She had soft features, and her hair was dyed from the ash of trees. They devoted themselves to a baby, and then a knock came to their door. *Vaerin.*

The very image of him sent a pang through Kienna's head. She recoiled, and then a haze slammed her body back. She flung into the tree, where the initials carved in the wood glowed briefly before fading.

"Interesting," Connak said.

Flames erupted beneath Kienna's feet, blasting her upright before Danek or Moira could reach her. The ground scorched as she rose, fury snapping through her like a whip of heat. She jabbed her finger into Connak's chest. "What was that?"

The shock of the power still surging in her body should have been enough to push him off his feet had he not defended it with his own magical shield. Connak's magic, more controlled, blasted the flames away from Kienna. "*That* was magic. Surely, you've experienced it before."

"I know what magic is, asshole," Kienna growled. Her mind raced. "That was out of control. Too many things… I couldn't keep it straight. And then the fire… Maybe because we're so far from Vaerin's power."

"You're mistaken if you think that magic is from Vaerin," Tislin said.

She knew it wasn't. Even Maren told her, but breaking the years of his influence proved harder than she thought, and she was frightened by what it could mean.

"What are you saying?" Danek perked up. He and Moira had been stomping on flames that had sparked when Kienna flung herself into the air.

"I think it's time you start sharing some more truth," Broan said, arms crossed.

Baila glanced around nervously, shifting briefly behind a tree. Kienna saw her in the corner of her eye, and it only infuriated her more.

Connak thumped his fingers against his hip. "We're already so close. Can we keep going, so you can see it for yourselves?"

Riddles and half-truths. Vaerin's voice echoed in Kienna's mind. Her eyes grew wild. She begged for the words to leave, backing away. Connak and Tislin shared a glance. The forest itself grew visibly distressed, the sky dropping rain to extinguish the fire blazing around Kienna's hands.

Calm down, Kienna heard in her mind.

Kienna's eyes widened, and then Connak reached her, first by mind, and then by body, grabbing her by the cheeks and pressing his forehead onto hers. He barreled his way in, calming the flames in her palms.

—Connak—

Fire covered her mind, engulfing the forest trees in heat Connak had yet to feel in his life. She held a wild panic in her eyes, searching for a way out of the flame. Her fear radiated around her. Connak stepped through, ignoring the mental pain it took to get through the fiery branches in his path. He shushed her, grabbed her, and heaved her into his arms.

Flames flickered, almost as if they were being temporarily stalled from their path of destruction. Connak felt an urgent gratitude that this had only started in her mind. "I wouldn't have taken you from River Storm if I didn't think you could handle this," he told her.

"He has my family, Connak," she sobbed. "And Vaerin says you're lying to me."

Connak looked at the damaged trees smoking in her mind. They were in the same forest, but now, it was fractured. He couldn't understand how quickly she turned since he had last visited her mind. She held wonder before, and now, doubt jaded and pulsed through every inch. Everything the king had done to her since the dungeons had created a jarring shift.

"I have never been and will never be your enemy," Connak said.

"How do I know?"

"Let me show you."

Connak unveiled a land in tiny waves, nature and magic flowing in harmony. Elvish children danced along the forest floors, their melodic laughter echoing out through the swaying of trees. Peace rushed over Kienna's mind.

—Kienna—

This place, where she stood with Connak, felt like home. An ache encompassed her soul; or was that yearning? A desperate need for something. She could see her whole life laid before her, memories that had been stolen and jumbled.

It flashed in waves. She was a child, healing Jacob. Then the king was bringing her to the castle and telling her he'd like to give her magic. Then she was watching a boy escape from the barrier. She remembered it all—the incessant beatings and manipulation, too. Everything she'd been forced to forget sat heavily on her chest now.

Connak's soul burst through hers as he dived deeper into her mind. He gave her *his* pain and sorrow, *his* joy, too. There were so many things about him she didn't realize. Like the fact that he struggled in the desert, alone, as a kid. Or that he left behind a love to take on the Hollow Blades, dedicated to watching and guiding Kienna. Things that could never be spoken into words, she could see. It was the first time he truly let her into his own mind with every vulnerability, everything he had to go through to keep her from becoming Vaerin.

Connak gave her everything from the moment their mental connection sparked to life. It was something that had always been there, growing quietly beneath the surface, and once it had, they were woven together. Even now, she still didn't understand how it worked or why it was there, but he lived in her mind, and she lived in his. It was something she knew he carried with careful, unwavering purpose.

"He wants me to give up the city." Her voice trembled, but she was safe here with Connak. No Baila. No Vaerin. Just them. "He'll kill them, Connak."

"He won't, Kienna. I don't know why, but I know he won't. Otherwise, he would have done it a long time ago when Maren helped me get out." He flashed another image to her of her mother doing just that.

Kienna searched his face for answers. Was Maren a whole different person than she thought? Her mother worked in the mills. Until she told Kienna to go, she'd never hinted at any other type of life. "Can't we get them out?"

"I have Blades staying close. They're working on it. All I ask of you now is to trust me."

"Okay," Kienna whispered out loud for all to hear, but her eyes were still shut while she clung to the tranquility of Connak. "Let's see what's here."

Chapter 33

—Kienna—

Connak led them for a few more miles into the forest and then left them standing amongst the trees. He said he had to call the Eternal Mother to guide him the rest of the way home and didn't explain more than that. Kienna saw Baila glance at her. She knew she'd be expecting Kienna to tap into Connak's mind and follow him.

She should have. Maren and Jacob were on the line, but the thought of finding the woodcarver here also tugged at her. In the end, even if she'd tried to tap into Connak's mind, he was much smarter than that. He wouldn't have let her in, and she wouldn't have seen what it took to unveil the glowing mist that appeared right in front of their eyes. Like a curtain being pulled back, the shimmering veil appeared. The world beyond it shifted, and an entire city unfolded from the forest as if the trees themselves had made room.

Kienna's heart stopped in her chest. The sheer scale of the towering trees was immaculate. With trunks as wide as castles and canopies that stretched so high, they seemed to brush the very stars.

"Welcome to Trinity," Connak said as he stepped into their view.

"This is just hiding here in plain sight?" Danek asked.

"Our leadership takes guarding the Eternal Mother seriously."

Broan folded his arms. " 'Crown Above. Eternal Mother.' You don't make sense."

"They're the same thing," Connak laughed. "The Eternal Mother is the goddess of our magic, and the Crown Above are the islands that harbor it." He pointed to the bridges of woven, golden vines that arched gracefully between the great trunks. They led to sprawling platforms of polished wood and smooth stone. "Those islands feed the elemental powers of our people. They grow through the deeper roots of Elvish magic. Some say She who breathed the world sleeps within the floating isle, her breath still humming beneath its stone."

Broan grumbled but couldn't find a stone out of place to kick. "Too fancy for me."

Connak grinned, motioning forward. "Let's keep going. The queen will need to know we're here."

Around each island were great halls, courtyards, and towering spires crowned with glowing crystal orbs that danced with lightning, fire, water, and wind. Each orb glowed with its own hue of white-blue lightning that split the dark like a storm. Ruby fire burned as if molten within, and sapphire water rolled in endless waves as pale emerald wind swirled in ribbons of light. They strobed uncontrollably, as if reacting to their presence. The city breathed, alive with magic.

Beneath their feet, the bridges were as sturdy as the ground yet light as air, swaying in the soft winds carrying the scent of flowers. A distant roar of waterfalls sounded throughout the entire city. Further below the bridges, deep down, was the forest floor. Kienna tried to determine how far it was, but she couldn't imagine the barrier at River Storm being any taller.

She wondered if the elusive woodcarver Maren mentioned was here in Trinity and if he had a role in building these ethereal bridges. Broan nudged her to keep moving and motioned for her to close her mouth, but not without mocking her first. She rolled her eyes but obliged and hurried along, brushing against her wolf to ground her in a city that was far from being grounded. As they marched through, the group caught their first glimpse of agile warriors. Tall and graceful, the Elvish guards moved in perfect precision. Their eyes shifted to the Guardians as they passed, heads turning and mumbling in silence.

"What was he thinking?" Kienna heard one of them say.

She turned to catch more, but Baila was right behind her. Kienna sneered and fell in closer to Moira as they were led up a winding path in the center of the largest tree in the forest. Tislin held the line in the back, but a visible change had overtaken him. The unwavering confidence he wore like armor was now cracked as his shoulders tensed and movements stiffened.

"You okay?" Moira asked.

"Of course." Tislin shifted his eyes. "Only searching for the shadows that I can slip into."

His hands lingered near his belt, instincts coiling tightly like a spring as if he expected danger behind every light-drenched corner. It did nothing to help Kienna's weariness as she watched him jolt his head to the distant chamber in the path. Danek trailed closely to Connak, eyes full of wonder, asking him questions about everything they passed.

"Should we be worried about something?" Kienna asked, her

eyes sliding to her wolf. The animal looked utterly at ease, tongue hanging in an easy, carefree grin. Her tail wagged loosely behind her.

"Oh, no. This is my own personal quarrel. Though I can't imagine anyone will be happy to see any of us, honestly." Tislin's face dulled. "I'll be reuniting with my brother today. We've been…estranged."

"About you joining the Blades?" Kienna recounted.

Tislin nodded.

Up the path, Kienna saw the dominion of Elvish rule. It was not a palace. There were no golden thrones nor marble floors polished with pride. It was only a tree with a vast, cathedral-like chamber carved inside. Its bark-formed walls curled up into towering archways, braided with ivy and glowing moss.

"This is the Heart of Trinity. It grew from the forest, connected to the Crown Above," Connak explained.

Kienna blinked in awe. The lack of ornamentation struck her deeper than opulence ever could. She braced herself for cold grandeur or symbols of dominance like King Vaerin's palace, but this space unraveled the tight knots in her chest. The moss shimmered with a pulse that mirrored her own heartbeat. High above, branches intertwined, forming a canopy laced with hanging crystals that shifted softly with elemental light.

"What's that smell?" Moira tipped her head to the sky and exhaled like she'd been wrapped in a cozy blanket.

"Ancient rain." Connak shrugged again.

He had to be playing with them now. The Crown Above? Ancient rain? What the hell did he mean by all of it?

They walked across long, elegant walkways of root-polished stone curving along the chamber's edge, leading to the alcove where council members gathered in quiet dignity. The queen's throneless palace was a raised platform encircled by a shallow ring of water.

"Your Majesty," Connak bowed immediately as an elegant and regal Elvish woman appeared from the door. She was followed shortly by a group of men and women, some Elvish, but some that appeared to be of other descent.

One man towered above them all, similar in kind to Broan, who stood tall at the sight of him. Tislin's eyes fell on another in the council and he quickly bowed his head as they regarded one another. He looked familiar to Kienna. His skin was a sun-kissed tan, and his hair was a dark blond, cropped similarly in fashion to Connak's, which contrasted the flowing locks of others around them. But no one could stand in comparison to the queen. She had an archaic nature to her youthful, almost luminous skin, like moonlight on marble. Her pale blue eyes studied the group before her, reflecting like glass that had seen too many winters. Ice-blonde tendrils, neatly spun in gentle braids and curls, wove with silver strands that cascaded down her back. Her garments were layered with flowing gossamer and leaf-threaded silk, though there were hints of armor beneath.

Connak turned to the familiar man and placed his hands behind his back in some sort of formal, militaristic formation she'd never seen him in before. "High Commander."

Silence deafened them. The only sound pulsing from the deep-rooted palace was the hum drumming from the floor. It pulsed through Kienna's feet and into her.

"High Commander?" a smaller-framed man asked behind him. Human.

The man flicked his eyes on Connak, jaw tight. "You idiot. Our armies were not ready to retrieve them."

This was not the greeting that Kienna had expected. Connak was so eager to get them here that she assumed they were prepared for this moment, but the High Commander's cold face didn't carve much contrast between her experience in River Storm.

"Ours were," Connak argued, standing tall in defense. "We waited in the Malintale for years."

The queen lifted her chin at this but didn't motion to speak. She watched her officers quietly with a curious gaze on her stoic face.

The High Commander tilted his head and shot daggers through Connak with his eyes. "You're a *fucking* idiot."

Connak sighed unapologetically. "We have them now, so let's get them briefed."

"You mean to say you didn't do this on your long journey home?" He folded his hands into themselves and blinked once in disbelief. Kienna almost cringed for Connak. She wasn't sure whose side she would have taken in this argument. She was still frustrated at the things left unsaid, edging tensions higher. She understood, though, with her memories intact now, that they had to see it to believe it.

"It's the High Commander's duty to indulge our secrets, is it not? We are just your army," Connak said and shrugged, like his public scolding barely touched him.

"I figured since you were so keen on breaking command, you wouldn't worry too much about what *my* duty is against your own."

The queen eyed the ratted and torn group standing behind Connak. Her eyes landed on Kienna, resting longer than expected. "I am Queen Elira." She motioned to them all, her face warming a little. "We welcome you to our city. Truly. But it appears this will have to wait."

The great wolf padded silently alongside Kienna, tail low but alert. Elira's eyes fell on the beast, narrowing ever so slightly in curiosity. Then her focus slid sideways to Connak, one brow raised. He only shrugged with a sly smile, pride flickering in his eyes despite the reprimand.

"We have a war to prepare for, thanks to Connak," she said, weaving her fingers together. "All I need to know is, are you with us?"

Connak turned to the group, imploring for their answer.

Kienna darted her eyes to Baila. "Perhaps a little explanation—"

"Tristian," Elira sighed, snapping her fingers.

The High Commander stepped forward. Kienna's chest stilled as the memories of him flashed behind her eyes. She realized she had seen him in her fleeting vision back in the forest. Why? She had no clue.

His ears were slightly more rounded than the queen's, and his face was set in a perpetual mask of seriousness. He was a complementary contrast to Tislin. That had to be the brother Tislin mentioned. His eyes, a piercing blend of green and blue, shimmered like the sea under a stormy sky. There was no trace of the ethereal frailty the queen had displayed.

The queen spoke again, "Our High Commander of the Trinity army will escort you to your safekeeping until we have a clear view of Vaerin's troops."

"Troops?" Danek asked, back stiffening.

"You didn't think Vaerin's finest would be taken from him without a fight, did you? He will come for what's his."

Kienna's shoulders tightened, the blood in her face draining and paling her. How could Vaerin find them so quickly? She'd never sent any messages. She hadn't even thought past what was right in front of her.

As if she could read her mind, Baila stepped forward. "He's coming? Here?"

"Not him and not here. This is just a taste of what's to come." Elira spoke with coldness, an emotionless grace to her face. She waved her hand. "Commander, please."

Tristian stepped forward, ushering the group to move with a quick pause between him and Tislin as their presence neared each other.

Kienna pushed past him. "You can't hold us here without even telling us why. Are we your prisoners?"

Elira kept walking, as cold as the icy blue of her robes.

She searched Connak's face for an answer, but he was equally shocked. Kienna pushed forward, but Tristian grabbed her arm. The moment their skin touched, a faint shimmer of golden light sparked between them, crackling softly like a whisper of magic, visible and pulsing only for a heartbeat. She rocked on her heels as her vision threatened to blur.

With eyes wide, Tristian's hands tighten around hers for a moment longer than necessary. His expression cracked, lips parting slightly as though her touch echoed within him, too. For a breath, they paused in a vibrating silence. Kienna's heart desperately pounded against her chest. She didn't know this man—yet every part of her seemed to.

Was *he* the woodcarver?

Just as quickly, Tristian blinked, and the mask fell back into place. He looked away, jaw tightening, and without a word, he pulled her arm forward after the others.

"Who are you?" Kienna demanded, her voice nearly trembling. The pulse from his touch lingered beneath her skin as she tried to free herself from his grip. "Why did you shock me? And why is everyone so cryptic around here? You can't keep us without telling us what we're doing? Connak!"

Riddles. Spinning. Grinning.

Despite her protests, it made no difference.

Moira slid to Kienna's shoulder to anchor her, despite Baila's presence. Kienna needed answers, proof this place was worth saving. Now, she wasn't so sure.

Broan let out a whistle. "Well, fuck, this got complicated fast."

Chapter 34

—Broan—

The High Commander brought them to a tiny treehouse to sit and wait. Broan wanted to sneer. The curved wooden steps and dangling lanterns weren't deadly at all. It was merely a play structure and leafy curtains. Broan did have to hand it to the Elvish people though; every crevice of the forest was built with immaculate skill.

He'd dreamt of building castles one day with stone, but he'd never imagined that the craftsmanship of the forest would knock him off his own feet. Even a treehouse, though not nearly as intimidating as stone, said something special about the creatures who refused to tear down the world that was already here to live.

Kienna sat coiled up in a corner biting her nails. The damn woman had been anxious ever since leaving the desert, and Broan figured it'd be best for her to suck it up and enjoy the fucking place. Though he was willing to admit that he was glad she wasn't gloating.

After all, she'd been right to leave River Storm. Broan knew the moment the Elvish man pushed his magic into his own to spark it to life that he was not a River Storm warrior by any means. Where else could he erect a bridge out of nowhere? He was never this strong in River Storm, under the direct control of the king. Broan would never give it up now, and he had Connak to thank for that. And maybe Kienna. But fuck her. He'd never tell her that.

He turned to Baila, figuring he'd given Kienna enough praise in his mind. "That was a good move at the bridge. How'd you seal the king's decree so easily?"

"I've seen him do it once." She shrugged, looking over her shoulder out the window of the house. She, too, had been antsy since leaving the desert. Broan squinted at her and then back to Kienna. What weren't they telling them?

Danek reached for a bowl of berries sitting on a table. He tossed it into the air, catching it in his mouth. "When? I don't think anyone's allowed into Vaerin's council room when he's working through such matters."

Baila shifted, but Moira placed her hand on her shoulder and said, "Well, however you did it, it got you all back." She wrapped her cloak around her body and sat up to look into the city. "I hated the Malintale, but this place is so beautiful."

Women and their beauty. Give Broan a city forged in strength, and that would be enough for him. He shook his head and glanced at Danek. His hands were lit in a faint blue. He probably didn't realize it, but even his features were shifting slightly. He looked less like Danek of River Storm and more like…Connak. It was not directly in appearance, but Broan couldn't put his finger on it, and damn it, he was already pissed he'd noticed.

Looking away, he huffed. Then he closed his eyes and waited. It would be a shame if this forest made him soft.

The council eventually agreed to meet with them after Connak had apparently pushed relentlessly. Tislin had to deliver the news to take them back to the Heart of Trinity. The High Commander, previously wrapped up in war prep, found enough time to send his Blades Commander to scout for the war as punishment for acting like a glory-drunk fool and disobeying command. Now, standing before the High Council, Broan figured he didn't owe them any allegiance.

"Step forward, please," Queen Elira said softly.

Broan stepped out of the shadows of the trunks and up to the stone disc. Elira and three others stood amongst him near the throne, glaring down harshly. The red sigil pulsed along his face. He had never stood before a council so cold and domineering before, and he'd been in front of King Vaerin.

"State your name."

"Broan."

The queen looked at him for more. When he did not give it, she sighed and turned to the larger man on her right. "He's yours to question, Kaelthar."

Kaelthar, a large, burly man who towered over the Elvish as Broan had towered over the people of River Storm, stepped up. In comparison, Broan was not nearly as large as his counterpart, though the age difference appeared to be substantial.

Broan stood tall in his presence, ready to undertake any questions the council threw his way. Baila went before him and Moira before her. The questioning was brutal, an interrogation that had Baila faltering and stumbling over her words. He shifted uncomfortably before they called him, watching as both Baila and Moira had been turned away and escorted back to the treehouse without many answers, though there wasn't much they could have given Baila.

It had made sense, Broan thought, for them to exercise caution when speaking to her. She was shifting the moment they came into Trinity, and it even made Broan nervous. Their caution granted a little respect from Broan at that moment. Moira, on the other hand, already knew where she came from. Her excitement radiated the moment she told them after they returned from the desert. She whispered good luck to Broan before being escorted away.

"Who gave you your name?" Kaelthar began.

"Danek and I were orphans," Broan started, folding his arms. It was a boring question they should have already known, so why waste the breath? "It was a name I chose for myself when I got older."

Kaelthar nodded, sharing a murmur with the queen. "Tell me about your king."

"What about him?" Broan yawned.

The queen was pleased with this. "How close were you to any of his ranks?"

Broan shrugged. "The king was a controlling asshole who lent us his magic. There's not much else to tell from my point of view."

Kaelthar regarded this. "Would you die for River Storm?"

Broan shifted his weight. This was not a question he heard them give to Moira or Baila. He cleared his throat. "There was a time when I might have." He paused, taking a moment to think back to the harsh winters in River Storm, the black clouds. He had strength back in the city that no one could match. He'd even told Danek that living as powerfully as he did in River Storm was invigorating, and he'd never thought to question their king outside of that—other than his kinder treatment of Kienna at times. But his sigil was proof that he was far more powerful out here, and the king could kiss his ass. He raised his chin high. "I'm certain that time has passed."

"I've heard enough," Kaelthar determined.

"Three questions?" Broan prepared himself to fight them as he did the king. He wouldn't let them determine his worth based solely on three questions. "The girls had way more questions before you decided they weren't fit for more."

"Silence, Broan Darsen."

The name rang out, and the crimson on his head glowed as if it were connected to the roots feeding the room they stood in. Pride danced through his veins, but he couldn't tell why.

"You come from the Vikings of Clan Darsen," Elira stepped forward, the melodies of her voice instilling a fierce commanding of attention. "You are the son of mountain storms and council steel, the first Viking of magical descent."

"A lot of fancy words," Broan grumbled.

"Your blood is Viking, and the Eternal Mother saw you fit as a babe for magic. You belong here," Kaelthar clarified.

He heard of Vikings in fairy tales also, but it was starting to sound like the king's scribes wrote the world as it was and pretended it had been made up. Maybe some of it was because the Vikings were written as smaller men, not nearly as burly or barbaric. Probably not as handsome either, but Broan didn't think it was the time to share those thoughts.

Regardless, he wanted to know more about Clan Darsen. If Kaelthar was his path to doing so, he had no problem staying. He had a clan, not a tragic orphanage story, but a group of men and women just like him. He couldn't help the confident arrogance waving over him. Not only did he have this clan now. He was chosen from this elusive *Mother* to harbor magic.

"Well, seeing as I belong here, you wouldn't mind if I stayed for the remainder of the questioning, would you?" Broan asked, placing his hands on his belt to puff his chest out a little more.

The council was visibly taken aback when he asked this, but Kaelthar only smirked, and it bought him enough favor. Broan stepped back into the corner by Danek and waited.

—Danek—

Danek's heart raced. He didn't need to hear that he belonged here from a bunch of council members to know that he did. He was confident about it the minute they stepped into the forest's path. His body was agile, full of luster and life. He knew it.

Stepping forward, Danek dropped to his knees, bowing with pride. Behind him, Broan let out a subtle breath of air and mumbled, "Kiss ass."

"You may rise," Elira said.

Her blue eyes of crystalized snow pierced him. Was *she* the Eternal Mother? She was exactly what he had pictured a goddess would look like. The thought made him want to shine even more.

"Thank you, Your Majesty," Danek replied, trying to mimic that same body stature that Broan did. He found it difficult to look as tall and mighty as Broan, but he desperately wanted his heart to show them he was no pawn of River Storm.

Elira smiled, a look that did not fit her features well. Warmth attempted to melt the ice that had become a part of her. "Connak put up quite a fight to try and be here for this discussion. He spoke many kind things about you, and he wanted me to apologize for his absence."

"Oh, that's okay," Danek rubbed the back of his neck. "I trust

Connak is out doing important work."

"He is." Elira nodded. "I don't have any questions for you, son of M'Ran."

"Not even one?" Broan's voice boomed from behind. He stepped back when Elira's piercing gaze fell on him. Danek saw her share a similar glance with Kaelthar at one point, hinting at a strain between the Viking and Elvish clans.

"His heart is true," Elira said, waving her hand. "He wears it proudly and on his sleeve, I might add. I have no concerns that he will fight with his proud Elvish blood."

"I'm eager to learn everything I can," Danek said. "What does it mean to be a son of M'Ran? Isn't Connak also of M'Ran?"

The man of human descent, Alister, stepped forward. He had questioned Moira, proving to be quite the interrogative foe in litigation. "M'Ran is an Elvish city north of here. You were born there. So was he. He wanted to tell you about it himself, but he has an act for making light of situations that have more severity to them."

"I would love to go there. Possibly see the people I come from."

The ice in Elira's eyes melted for a glimmer of a second, a wash of sadness flooding the room. "M'Ran was destroyed in the war, along with its people. Connak was the only one left. And now you."

Danek sat with her words longer than he should have. His brows tightened, and he found himself staring at his boots. He wanted to stay neutral about it. He didn't know how to mourn a people he never met, but he was grateful for at least one person left to learn from. Connak was a formidable ally—confident and agile, like all the things he knew he could become as well. But Danek knew that the loss of the city of M'Ran meant that he truly was an orphan, inside and out of River Storm. His muscles remained stiff, bracing for a blow that had already come.

He glanced at Kienna. For a moment, when she looked at him, he could see a hint of Elira through the coldness of her blue eyes, but it faded through the warmth still radiating on her skin. Her face brought him comfort, though she was as pitiful as him at that moment. She was off, constantly questioning her path. At times, she wanted to go back to River Storm, and that mindset would not fare well in this room.

They aimed to discern alliances. To make sure that the five Guardians of their enemy in River Storm were there to help. Baila didn't convince them, though she was trying, perhaps, a little too hard. Danek gave a half-hearted smile to Kienna and turned back to the council.

"Connak and I, are we—"

"You are not brothers," Elira confirmed. "Distant cousins, maybe, but no way of telling anymore."

"Fascinating," Danek riveted.

"You may stand with Broan if you'd like," Alister stated, indicating it was time for Danek to move on. He bowed again and retreated.

He fell back to Kienna. She was searching the room, eyes sharing panic. He wished he knew how to do what Connak did in the forest, if only to know what went through her mind.

To help her, he thought, *would be the greatest honor of all.*

Chapter 35

—Kienna—

"Step forward, miss," Alister said. He was a short man with a slicked ponytail tied neatly down his back. His small, narrow eyes beaded, and a permanent furrow in his brow pulled at his face.

Kienna studied the room, taking her time to step into the ring of questions. Her hands shook, breath labored. She dug her nails into her palms in hopes of stopping the sense of dread washing over her. Danek may have been okay with Connak's absence, but Kienna yearned for him.

She had nearly burned down a forest down in panic, and she

didn't understand the chaos that overtook her then. Fear raged through her, worrying she might take down this council as well. Danek gave her a soft nudge. His touch grounded her just enough. For that, she was thankful.

"State your name," Kaelthar requested.

"Kienna." She stuttered and hoped they wouldn't notice.

The Viking nodded to his council members and stepped back. "All yours."

"You came face to face with the King of River Storm in the desert." Queen Elira commanded the room. She stared at Kienna with a precision that indicated they didn't quite trust her. They had every right. Kienna knew it.

"I did," she responded. It wouldn't do her any good to lie about it, though she'd have to dance around any questions on the interaction itself.

The silence was deafening, the humming of the trees around her hitting like a drum. The queen was studying her, eyes picking apart the bits of her that she disapproved of. "Care to share how you are here, then? And not in his grasp?"

What was she supposed to say? Connak and the others were so convincing in their battle that the king decided to let them all go? That he didn't even bother to obliterate them? They didn't ask Baila about this when she had gone. Now she found herself trying to channel her inner Baila, something that absolutely disgusted her, but she didn't see any way around this. She trusted Connak enough to tell him, but her first encounter with the queen had been rocky at best.

"He thinks I'll come back to him after I see the world for what it truly is." It wasn't exactly a lie. He did say that she would discover that the Elvish people spoke in riddles and half-truths.

"Is he right?" Alister asked, peering down at her.

Kienna dug her boot into the wood beneath her feet. "I wouldn't say this has been the warmest welcome, but I do try to avoid the king when I can. I hope you prove him wrong."

It didn't feel right when she said it, and she could see Danek and Broan shift to her side. She pledged absolutely no allegiance, but neither did Broan. He had been sure of his shift away from Vaerin. She only danced around it.

This was not going well. The queen's face stayed stoically still, but the council behind her also stirred and murmured in the background in faint whispers. The internal chamber of the tree was hollow, and sound bounced around easily.

"Let me be clear," the queen said. "We are here right now to determine if *you* are trustworthy. Not the other way around. Do we understand?"

Kienna's hands started to shake. She wasn't trustworthy, and she wondered if the queen sensed the same energy. They went hard after Baila, too. They'd both been with the king and got out free. It would never matter how hard the king hit them in front of everyone. His letting them go was never going to look right.

Alister sighed and continued. "What are your powers?"

"I see visions."

"What about the fire?" Broan said.

Though his interruption was not appreciated by the room, Alister's lips pursed. "Yes, tell us about the fire. In the forest on your way here."

"I've never done that before," Kienna said, her voice sharper than intended as she shot daggers in Broan's direction. "It was an accident. But yes, the king decided I'd be good at wielding fire."

"So, he did give you all magic then?" Elira's brows rose slowly.

Kienna shook her head and started picking her fingers. They would have been completely raw and gnawed to the bone if they hadn't been healed in the desert with her glass beetle blisters. She hated the fire within her. It was the part of her that did feel like

Vaerin's. It was the only magic that he let her use in River Storm, so she hated that they kept circling that fire like it defined her.

Elira sighed, expression still unchanged. "And Connak? When did he start entering your mind?"

"A few months ago."

"And your king found out about him when?"

"Two weeks before the barrier came down...or..." The memories were still healing themselves together. The dungeons were the hardest to put back together for Connak. Not because they weren't there, but she'd tried to forget them on purpose. Her song emerged at the tip of her tongue now, and she only wanted to avoid the nightmares that would follow. But she truly didn't know how long she'd been down there. Two weeks struck her as a fair assessment. Danek confirmed behind her.

The queen let another wave of silence pass. Now that the memories of the dungeon resurfaced, Kienna resisted the urge to back herself into a corner and hide. Where was Connak? She tried to open her mind to find him, but the static in the open air felt lonely until it didn't. A small prick at her mind eased her, but it wasn't him.

The wolf whimpered from behind. She looked back to see the silver eyes resting on her as she panted next to Danek. Surely there was no way, but the council latched on to the whimper and Elira asked, "Where did you find the wolf?"

"In chains in River Storm."

"And she bound herself to you?"

"I'm not sure." Beads of sweat formed around Kienna's hairline. The forest was miraculously even-tempered, but Kienna heated standing there in front of everyone.

A barage of queries hit her at once as Elira and Alister delivered rapid challenges, noting the answers and moving on before Kienna could even think of additional information to add. They asked for a direct recount of what she and Connak talked about, how the wolf etched onto her, and her thoughts about her peers. She responded with great caution to their questions, trying hard to keep up. Each answer was like walking a tightrope over a chasm, and her composure slipped with every step.

The interrogation lasted for much longer than Baila and Moira, though the council must have had many reservations about each of them. *Wise*, Kienna had thought when they sent Baila out of the room, but Moira came as a shock. Moira held back many answers to questions about her family and why she split from the group to go to Dove Port. She wondered if there were things she was holding back, even from the team of Guardians.

"Does the brand on your thumb mean anything to you?" Elira stepped forward.

Kienna glanced at the K etched into her hand, the only scar in her flawless skin—yet another reminder of the king's doing. Once, as a child, she'd asked her mother in River Storm about it only to be met with a wary glance and a hurried change of subject. The mark had always ached more during storms, pulsing faintly beneath the skin like a secret waiting to be spoken. "It's been there my whole life, but it mostly hurts when I use magic."

"Does the name Kalyra spark anything?"

"No," she responded flatly. "Should it?"

"It's never been spoken to you in visions before?" Alister asked.

"My visions have never been strong. I only saw things that were relevant to the king until I found that tree in the forest."

"What tree?" Elira jolted her head for the first time, the expression on her face changing ever so slightly. Most probably wouldn't have caught it, but the whole room moved in slow motion for Kienna as she tried to keep herself from spinning with the shadows.

Kienna didn't realize it, but she never answered. Elira grew closer to Kienna. A coldness commanded her attention now. Kienna looked up from the floor, her eyes meeting Elira's as they were now face to face.

"Do you still owe your allegiance to Vaerin, King of River Storm?"

"No," Kienna said, though she couldn't tell if she was telling the truth or not. Allegiance was a fickle thing to her right now. She'd been forced into this impossible task by the king, one she didn't even think she could complete anymore. She wasn't any more loyal to him than she could have found herself loyal to the glass beetles in the desert.

But the queen wanted to know more. She wanted to know if Kienna was willing to shift her allegiance to the Elvish army. She didn't have to say as much. She indicated it with Broan and Danek, two fine warriors with strong magic who were willing to serve their cause to belong somewhere. But Kienna wasn't an orphan growing up like them.

They had *nothing* in River Storm. Kienna had Maren and Jacob. Yes, allegiance proved to be more complicated than the queen would understand.

Elira narrowed her eyes.

Kienna could smell the alluring sweetness of the queen's presence. She smelled of the forest's first rain, cool moss, silver dew, and a whisper of blooming night-flowers. It paired well with her cold demeanor, a scent both grounding and unreachable.

The queen motioned to speak when Connak entered the premises, hidden and quietly at first, but he stepped up, and a sense of urgency caught his voice. The queen moved her attention to him as he said, "An army just passed over the mountains through Dalelry. Tristian has asked for your presence."

The queen nodded, her eyes falling on Kienna once again. "Tame your wolf, Kalyra. She should not be snarling at our people."

"It's Kienna, Your Majesty," Kienna said modestly, her voice a whisper in the ancient council room.

Elira snuffed her nose up and floated past Kienna without another word. She stopped briefly to share a look of disdain with Connak—a glare that hinted at something deeper. As if she blamed him for bringing Kienna here at all, for the need for a war in the first place. And then she was gone.

"I suppose you're dismissed for the time being," Alister waved his hand at them.

Kienna did not take long to turn on her heels and march out of the tree, the alluring and graceful light shining on her as she exited. Connak fell in behind her.

"How was it?" he asked.

"Terrible." Kienna ran her hands over her face to try and recompose herself. The sweat remained, and her eyes burned from tears that had been suppressed behind her eyes for far too long. "I do not think your queen likes me."

"Queen Elira is a guarded soul," Connak said quickly. "You two have that in common."

"Fuck off."

Connak chuckled. "What did she tell you?"

"Absolutely nothing," Kienna complained. "She asked me about my name and my powers and then questioned my loyalty to Vaerin. She did ask me if the name Kalyra meant anything to me, and then she called me that name when she left, which was odd."

Connak held Kienna's gaze. It looked like he had been thinking hard, but then he turned to start down the bridge. He kindly put his arm out for Kienna. She eyed it, studying the breadth of his arm through his tight-fitting shirt. He had a quiet strength to him, one that didn't need to announce itself. She wanted to take his arm, but she couldn't move through the frustration of her interrogation. When she didn't reach out, he put his arm down. "Elira lost a grandchild a long time ago. Her name was Kalyra. I suspect she thinks that child is you."

She chewed the inside of her cheek a moment, considering this. She forgot, in her few hours of being in this new place, that these people were riddled with rich history, most recently involving the Great War. She couldn't imagine the insurmountable loss they would all still be feeling. But she wasn't that child. She couldn't be. She didn't want to be. If she were, she'd have hoped the queen would have greeted her with more warmth.

"I could have used an ally in that room," she said with a hushed voice. She had to push past the song of spinning and grinning a few times and wished that the shadows would shut up already and let her breathe.

"Open your mind a little more, and I'll be your ally wherever you need me."

"It doesn't help if no one can hear you but me," Kienna scoffed, but she resided and reached for Connak's arm at his side. His body was warm and firm, something she realized she didn't mind being so close to. Her eyes drifted to his face, and she couldn't help but smile a little, thinking that she had his favor.

He guided her gently through the trees and down to the forest floor. The cool air wafted from the shadows. Suited in light armor, the army collected under the canopies. Some battalions bore long, recurved bows carved from wood that glistened like starlight, and their quivers filled with arrows fletched in silver-tipped feathers. Others were armed with slender blades forged with emerald stone and curved daggers.

Along one edge of the forest, a handful of warriors practiced defensive spells with brief flashes of shimmering light forming shields around their bodies before fading just as quickly. Their magic flared efficiently. Kienna took in the natural conservation of energy, each mage tactfully weaving power through them.

"Vaerin's army is expected to get to the Goldmere River by nightfall," Connak whispered. "We'd like to stop them from getting across."

Kienna glanced around at the large number of men and women preparing for battle. She hadn't seen an army this big in her lifetime, including River Storm's. Did they need this many people to take down the king?

"There are a lot of soldiers. Is his army truly that big?" Kienna inquired. "I didn't think we had nearly this many soldiers in River Storm."

"I am sure they are not all from River Storm if the legends are true," Connak explained. "We should be leaving now to meet them."

"When will you be back?" Kienna asked, a hint of dread flowing through her as she thought about being in this ancient forest city alone. Sure, she had the Guardians, but she disliked two of them, and the others were so overly optimistic that it made her want to lash out.

"I know you'll miss me," he teased, but his soft expression hardened when Tristian paused near them. He stood straight and placed his hands behind his back. "High Commander."

"Is your battalion ready?" Tristian inquired, a ferocity to his tone.

"Already weaving through the trees for intel," Connak replied.

"And those in the Malintale?"

"Eyes heavy on River Storm. They'll send word if they spot another army. It's only the one on the west side at this time."

Tristian nodded firmly, and then his eyes met Kienna's. She stared at him with curiosity, the closest she'd ever been to talks of battle. A strange tightness coiled in her stomach, part intrigue, part unease. There was something in Tristian's rigid posture, and the flicker of annoyance in his eyes made her feel both watched and dismissed. She couldn't tell if he saw her as a threat, a burden, or something else.

He blinked slowly, jaw tight, and then looked back to Connak. "Ensure the newcomers remain behind. They are not to join." He began to turn but hesitated. "On second thought, bring the Viking.

His strength may be of use."

Kienna stepped forward, emboldened by his pause. "How can I help?"

Tristian turned his head slightly, narrowing his eyes. The light caught the silver thread woven into his dark armor, accentuating the sharp cut of his cheekbones and the grim set of his jaw. The edge of a scar peeked from beneath his collar, as though it had been left there by a blade that meant to remind, not kill. His posture remained rigid, but his eyes flicked toward her hand, the one he'd touched in Trinity's Heart.

"What has Queen Elira told you?" he asked, voice as clipped as a blade strike.

"To train my wolf," Kienna said, grasping for levity, though her voice wavered. She'd be lying to herself if she didn't admit that her skin still tingled faintly from that spark they shared, as if his presence stirred some dormant ember inside her. It wasn't a romantic feeling, she noted to herself, but the spark felt otherworldly at the time. As if *he*, perhaps, was otherworldly. She reminded herself that she once thought Connak, too, was godlike. She gripped her hands to push away the tremor.

Connak remained in his commanding position. His deep green eyes rested on Kienna with slight amusement, but he quickly turned back to a blank slate.

"Do that," Tristian commanded, his tone final. Yet as he walked away, there was a stiffness in his stride, a tension coiled tightly between duty and being someone that he wasn't. Kienna noted this as well, realizing that she stared a little too long.

Connak eased his body, letting out a long, theatrical sigh as if he'd survived a formal banquet instead of a battlefield briefing. "That was embarrassing," he cast a sly glance at Kienna. "I've stood before sandwraiths with less tension."

He stretched his shoulders with exaggerated flair, then added with a wink, "I must find Broan before he starts pressing fallen trees for fun. When I get back, I'll be expecting a flower parade with banners, dancing wyverns, the whole thing."

Kienna smiled, but a sudden surge of dread rushed through her. As he retreated, she found herself questioning: *What the hell is a wyvern?* There was so much she didn't understand in this world. It was so normal to her, yet she still managed to stand in front of a wolf that towered over all the other creatures at nearly shoulder height. And now, Elvish men and women were going to battle against a king she used to believe was the only force of magic in the world.

The thought of war frightened her, especially because people would die because of her. She could have avoided this if only she had gone back to River Storm. Now, she was forced to make a decision: either give up this city and betray Connak and his people, or let the war continue. People would die regardless. Kienna's decision would be solely based on which version of the story she could live with in the end.

Chapter 36

—Moira—

Moira was shocked when they let her wander the forest after her intense interrogation. That queen was not one to be trifled with, but Moira respected the composure the Elvish ruler showed. She was a woman who'd lived through some things, and she wouldn't be knocked down. *That* was something Moira could relate to.

As she stood between the silver-threaded trees, she watched Elvish soldiers sheath their weapons and scurry to pack food and supplies. She couldn't stop herself from feeling helpless. They were riding off to war to fight her king. Except, no, he was not her king.

Pride flickered through her at the thought of being on the other side of the war. Her heart never settled with Vaerin, but she did have to wonder about Rhior.

She was furious with him. She didn't think she'd ever find it within herself to forgive him, but he was still her husband, and their baby was still growing inside of her. It reminded her as it kicked her. Another jarring experience, as now she couldn't tell if it was going to send her through time or send her unraveling at yet another loss of a baby.

The answer came to her when her eyes lost focus on the sprawling forest and soldiers preparing for war. It started slowly, with a haze, like her mind was twirling through space. Moira found herself next to a giant tree split open like a womb. A flickering flame cradled itself in the roots. It pulsed like a heartbeat, but as Moira approached, it blazed violently. A child appeared next to her and grabbed her hand. The touch shocked her, an unexpected experience from a vision.

"Follow me, Mama," she said.

Moira's heart nearly stopped. This couldn't be her child, but the sound of "Mama" echoed so deeply in her soul. She leaned and looked into the deep-set eyes colored brown like Rhior's, and she knew then that her baby was talking to her.

"Follow me, Mama," she said again.

Moira let the child weave her through the trees back to the forest they had been in before coming to Trinity. The tree Kienna found earlier was now in flames as well. Was she seeing a version of the past from what could have happened if they hadn't put the fire out fast enough that Kienna started?

"What is it, child? What do you mean to tell me?"

The little girl, with hair coiled as tightly as hers, only pointed. Moira couldn't figure out what she wanted. The tree continued to burn, but the flames didn't jump across to other foliage. Just a steady flame without smoke. There was a baby in it. Moira's breath hitched, and she moved to grab it, but the little girl tugged on her.

"The Ashborn."

"The what?" Moira asked.

She never got to find out. The vision faded, and she looked up to find Tislin standing in front of her. He was dressed in dragon scales and looked extremely uncomfortable in the armor. The shimmering silvers did nothing to suit his complexion.

"How long have you been standing there?" Moira asked.

"A few minutes. I tried not to disturb you." He rested his hand on her elbow as she clutched her womb. "Are you in pain?"

Moira shook her head, acclimating to the changes. "What is the Ashborn?"

His eyes drifted to the soldiers around him and then back to Moira. It was a sudden shift that she hadn't expected. Did she see something she wasn't supposed to? "I have to go to war, Moira. Do not ask that question to anyone else."

"I won't." She trusted him enough to know he was serious. "Did I do something wrong?"

He softened, the rigidness of his muscles sinking. "No, Sunbeam."

The name caught her attention. She didn't hate it, but it sounded so unnaturally sweet to her ears that she had to shake away the shivers that crawled up her spine. "Sunbeam?"

"You are the first light that has made the shadows move."

Moira blushed. Tislin's face remained still as usual, no indication of emotion. Was he flirting with her? Perhaps she was misreading, and he was being nice. Part of her hoped he was flirting, but the married part scolded her for it. "Well, promise you'll be safe?" Before he could respond, she caught Broan walking with a wave of soldiers. She called to him, "Where do you think you're going?"

"To war." Broan shrugged, like the idea of war with a new clan of people was a good idea. Moira's face must have indicated as much because Broan followed it up with, "Relax, Mom, I'll be fine."

She slapped his arm. "Don't be hateful to me. And that scaled armor is ridiculous."

She gave him a once-over and saw the light silver scales draped down his tunic. The armor barely looked like it would protect him from anything at all. The River Storm soldiers wore full metal, even when they were in the safety of their barrier. Now that she looked back at it, she wondered why the king needed so much protection around the city with fully armored soldiers if he was so confident in his own power.

She didn't question that he was powerful. She'd seen it and felt it, but was he also scared of something they never saw? Oh, what did it matter anymore? She pressed Broan to be careful, and if he didn't come back safely, she'd be sure to kill him a second time. Broan waved her off and followed behind the rest of the soldiers.

"They'll appreciate how much you care one day," Tislin said. He tipped his head to bow to her, and then he jumped through the trees with immaculate speed and height. A small trail of shadows followed him at the tip of his boots. She lost sight of him after the second tree and wondered what being a Shadowmaster entailed.

When he was gone and the Elvish soldiers cleared out, a woman retrieved her and escorted her through the trees to the small villages at the bottom of the forest. Above her, the floating islands pulsed quietly with light. The woman told her they would be firing soon enough when battle began, an indication of the use of magic. Moira assumed the city remained hidden to hide those islands.

"What would happen if someone managed to destroy the islands?" Moira asked as they wove between the paths. They approached a large tree with village homes built around it in layers. Some rose high along the trunks, constructed directly onto the bark with wooden platforms that spiraled upward like a helix. These homes were stacked across levels, each connected by rope bridges and wooden walkways as a woven network above the forest floor.

The home the woman brought her to was wooden, made from rich, honey-toned timber. Floating crystals hovered near doorways and windows, casting soft, warm light that pulsed gently. Their beams were hand-carved with etched runes.

Moira was motioned to go inside. She realized the woman never answered her question as she disappeared. Kienna, Danek, and Baila were already there eating, and the wolf snuggled by the fire. She'd never get used to seeing such a massive creature sitting inside a home.

She stared at Kienna. The silver strands of her hair faded into deep brown. Moira never considered how unique it was, but it reminded her of half burnt bark.

Moira's mouth fell open. *Ash Born.*

Chapter 37

—Kienna—

"I can't believe Broan just went off to war," Moira whispered to Danek. They sat around a smooth table, eating berries and keeping warm by the fire.

The home where Kienna and the others rested sat near one of the tree roots. It was simple, but in no way modest, with intricate carvings of different elements in the frames. Floating crystals gave them light in the darkness of the trees. Inside, a gorgeous stone firepit glowed with controlled flame, its heat radiating into the woven tapestries. The scent of herbs clung to the walls: lavender, pine, and other unfamiliar, calming scents.

Two soldiers were stationed outside the tree, a clear indication that they were still not trusted. That made sense. Kienna and Baila had enough secrets alone to take down the whole city. At least Kienna was struggling with her secrets. Baila remained calm at every turn, watching her.

"I think Broan is trying to find a way to cope with all the things being thrown at us," Danek said, popping another berry into his mouth. "Before we left River Storm, he didn't see a need to get out. He thought Vaerin's magic was 'invigorating,' but now that he knows he doesn't need Vaerin, I think he'd rather kill the king himself."

Kienna listened intently while she sat in the corner, glancing at Baila when Danek mentioned killing Vaerin. A small twitch in her jaw gave her away, but Danek and Moira weren't focused on Baila. They were too busy focusing on Broan and his new warpath.

Flames danced across Kienna's face as she carved her knife deep into a log she found. The motions soothed her from her thoughts as she continued to wrestle with Vaerin's request. Yet, she still wanted to know more about the woodcarver. Who was he? Had she already met him and didn't know? Did he build this intricate city? If he was worthy enough for even Maren to know about him, surely, he'd have to be important. Possibly important enough to build an Elvish city literally into the trees and be powerful enough to also hide it.

Baila inched closer and sat on the rug, stitched and woven meticulously by the family graceful enough to shelter them. Danek and Moira were too busy talking about the floating islands to notice the sudden shift between her and Kienna. "Did the council ask about me?" she whispered.

"No," Kienna responded tautly. Even now, Baila's self-preservation sent flames down Kienna's skin. She desperately wanted to be done with this already, but she knew revealing Baila's secret now would only put Maren and Jacob in danger. Connak's assurances about their safety helped a little, but she knew the king. His vile instability flared in all directions. Maren and Jacob would mean nothing to him if he couldn't have his way.

Her wolf sat near the fire, nipping a bone with such ravenous energy, it was as if she had managed her first fresh kill after a long winter of scarcity. Kienna studied her. *What's your name?* she thought. She'd asked it in the forest before, but now she really needed to know. The wolf deserved a name if she was going to attach herself to Kienna.

The wolf didn't budge. She continued to gnaw, her large ivory teeth scraping against her prey. Her paws appeared to be the size of Kienna's face, though she wasn't going to pick them up to compare. Disappointment radiated in her core. It didn't matter how Kienna asked for the wolf's name or how many times she asked it. So why would Connak tell her to speak to it? She chewed the side of her cheek. *Should I name you, then? Is that what you're waiting for? For me to claim you?*

"We should be doing something," Baila whispered.

"We are doing something." Kienna rolled her eyes, a stone wall slowly building around her. "I am carving a cup. And *you* are sitting in my space."

Baila scoffed, her shoulders tensing. "We're just going to let this city slaughter my people out there?"

"We shouldn't meddle in wars we don't understand," Kienna said lowly, her eyes flicking away to the fire.

"Vaerin would be disappointed," Baila stated. "Don't forget what's at stake here."

She wanted to lash out and wrap her hands around Baila's throat. To tell her to go fuck herself and her father. She deserved it. Kienna never forgot what was at stake. She almost burnt a whole fucking forest down because of what was at stake. How dare she?

Kienna glanced up from her blade, hands gripping tightly

around the hilt. Her eyes peered at Baila, and a sudden, guttural growl escaped from the wolf. Baila straightened and scooted away, sitting near Danek and Moira while they gossiped about all the things they'd seen so far in the forest.

She realized then that she didn't want this. She didn't want to help Vaerin, and she doubted that she would. It would cost her Maren and Jacob, but it was unlikely she was ever going to see them again. The thought that they might not be alive anyway crossed her mind. She had no reason to trust the king and take him at his word. What she did have was every reason to trust Connak.

That was it, then. Her mind was made up.

The wolf looked at Kienna. Kienna jolted at the sudden acknowledgement and observed the wolf. They both tilted their heads to one side. And then the other. Their breath heaved inward together and then back out. This explosive spark of understanding fluttered in her chest. Her hands shook, but she raised them anyway, slowly inching them forward until they met the rough coat of hair blazing over her beast.

What's your name? she thought again.

Ruva, the wolf whispered back.

The name entered Kienna's mind with a radiant warmth, like someone had poured sunlight down her spine. A soft hum echoed in her ears as if the air around her pulsed with shared breath.

Kienna gasped loudly, falling backward. She didn't expect such an abrupt explosion in her mind. The wolf had come in so clearly, like her thoughts were Kienna's thoughts. She stood, a wave of excitement passing through her. "I did it!"

The others turned quickly, standing and on guard.

"Did what?" Danek questioned, hands gently caressing his blade. When he realized there was no threat aside from the uncharacteristic change in Kienna's demeanor, he loosened and ensured it was sheathed correctly.

"The wolf," she laughed. "She spoke to me!"

"I didn't hear anything." Baila folded her arms.

Kienna didn't press, but she held a sparkle in her eyes that poured down to her soul like a warm bath after a grueling day's work. She sat back down on the floor and crossed her legs out in front of her, more comfortable than when she had arrived.

It's nice to meet you, Ruva, Kienna said.

Ruva grumbled out loud as she placed her paw over Kienna's lap. *I am glad you have made a choice.* Then she nestled her head over, her large body filling Kienna's void and warming her blood. Warmth collected behind Kienna's eyes as well, though she fought to pull the tears back. It was an odd feeling—the sense of connection—but the further she came on this journey, the more she realized she *could* have another family.

Chapter 38

—Kienna—

Three days had passed since the armies left for battle. Kienna tried to reach out to Connak a few times to check on him and make sure he was okay. He never answered, which was understandable, all things considered. But she could feel him faintly in her mind. Knowing he was well still didn't calm the pangs of worry crashing against her chest.

He'll be fine, Ruva told her.

She had to get used to having a wolf in her head. It wasn't quite like Connak's voice, where she grew to expect it and had to invite him to have a conversation. Ruva's came with no warning in a voice that sounded like it was meshed with two or three layers. It echoed and blended, sounding friendly, stern, and biting all together.

They stood near the top of one of the finely crafted bridges toward the elemental islands. Each island had a temple built on it, a sacred ground specifically for the Eternal Mother. Some of the women took a trip to pray for the armies to return safely, and Kienna knew this would be one of her only opportunities to be so close to such sacred land again. Naturally, she drew closer to the island of fire. It pulsed with red and orange flame so deep that it felt like a ritual, not an out-of-control disease.

Fire flickered in controlled waves around the sanctuary. It danced outside on the path to the structure with elegant grace. The grass was green, which came as a shock because fire should have charred it. Kienna would have charred it.

I wish Vaerin had surfaced a better power. It's so destructive.

Ruva panted next to her. *Fire is not always dangerous. Give yourself some credit.*

Kienna examined her hands. *Through me, I think it's meant to be destructive. I have never used fire for anything useful like a campfire. It apparently doesn't work that way for me.*

You have other powers, too. Fire doesn't have to define you.

Whatever is supposed to be in there is not. I sense it sometimes, but it's got to be buried deep because I can't do anything else.

Ruva huffed, leaning her large head against Kienna's shoulder. Kienna tilted her own head to rest on the wolf's, and they stood together watching the pulsing flames shoot into the sky.

Would you like to talk about that vile king? Ruva asked. *What he wants you to do.*

How much do you know?

Everything.

Kienna had to wonder how deep this bond with the wolf went.

Could Ruva see her thoughts and memories even when they weren't connected? She searched the wolf for an answer, but everything indicated yes. She wasn't going to be able to hide anything from Ruva. It brought a hint of dread to her stomach, knowing that someone in this world knew all the dreadful bits of herself. At least with Connak, she had the opportunity to shut and fold parts of her mind.

I'm not going to do it, she admitted, looking down at her boots. The glow of the fire island shimmered across the black leather.

Ruva licked her cheek. *I know, Little Flame.*

"The army is back," Danek said, running up the bridges. His voice carried in a way that sounded disrespectful to the islands. They pulsed violently for a moment before returning to a calmer flicker. Danek's lips curved upward. "You were glowing again, by the way."

Kienna's brows knitted faintly as she looked down at her body and then to Ruva. "Glowing?"

He offered a small, lopsided smile. "Only a little. Around the edges. Like…starlight. You do that sometimes when you're thinking."

She didn't respond, only brushed her sleeve, eyes darting away. A faint warmth colored her cheeks, visible in the dim firelight.

He likes you, Ruva said.

Kienna placed her hand on Ruva's head. *No, he's just nice.*

Okay, Little Flame. We shall see.

Kienna attempted to close her mind, but she knew getting Ruva out of her head now would be a waste of energy. She tried not to think about any of that—how men felt about her. She was a pawn to the king her whole life. She didn't want to set herself up for heartbreak later if she did allow herself to love, so she chose to ignore them all. Danek was no different.

Danek's smile softened. "You know, I used to wonder if I'd ever belong anywhere. River Storm never fit. And this place…it's beautiful but strange." He hesitated, then added more gently, "But walking through it with you…it's not so strange anymore."

Ruva stood tall. *I like him.*

Kienna glanced toward him. She didn't speak, but she didn't pull away either. Danek always threw in more fluff when he spoke to her in private. She'd be the first to admit that she barely noticed before. Now she noticed. Ruva didn't help. She parted her lips, but words escaped her, unsure how to even navigate the possibilities.

Danek tilted his head. "You don't have to say anything. I just thought you should know. You're doing better than you think."

A beat passed, more comfortably than expected. Kienna started down the bridge into the forest, Danek at her side and Ruva close enough to her heel to give her and Danek space side by side. The path beyond the elemental islands swirled gently downward to the heart of the village, where lanterns swayed from high, vine-draped arches and magic glimmered faintly in the air like dust motes.

But the light dimmed this night.

From between the trees, the returning soldiers emerged. They were not in lines or formation as they were when they left, but in scattered, stumbling clusters. Their movements were slow, their shoulders slumped as their armor dulled with ash and blood. Their eyes were cast down with a haunting that only war could bring.

Groups of men carried dead or injured comrades in streams of summoned water, shaped by Elvish menders. The water shimmered like liquid glass, floating gently above the forest floor and cradling the wounded as it moved. It wept softly, drops raining to the floor like grief itself had taken form for each body that it bore.

Cries of the injured pierced the hush. The agonizing groans of pain. The whispered names. The grief. One man collapsed upon crossing the threshold into the village, and his partner dropped to their knees beside him, clutching his tunic and repeatedly muttering something—words that didn't reach anyone but the roots beneath them.

The scent of fire and blood rode the air.

Danek slowed his pace. His jaw set, and a blue shimmer pulsed beneath the surface of his skin, as though some inner current stirred to life. He gave Kienna a small nod, then rushed forward toward the injured. As if he had been waiting for this moment, Danek's quick attention caught hold of one of the waves, and he rode it to a clearing. His body luminated, and he took to healing those in anguish.

Kienna stepped forward and watched him work, draining his own energy to heal one after the other. Some made strong recoveries. Others were not so lucky; a fate that tore the Elvish in two. Those who did not go into battle stood and watched in anguish when the news would break of yet another soldier who did not cross the line. The trees would howl in sorrow, an echoing melody harmonizing with Ruva as she mourned for them. Kienna stroked her neck, bowing her head each time a soldier was pronounced lost.

Moira scrambled through the forest, trying her hardest to keep up with bandages and filling flasks of water. If Baila was there, she did not make it known, though there were doubts that she would continue her journey in Trinity. Kienna tried to keep Danek well preserved, handing him water when he began to tire. She hoped he didn't overdo it and find himself passed out in the dirt with the rest of them.

"Help," a man moaned on the ground near Kienna.

She stopped following Danek and glanced down. She knelt to him, and he grabbed her hand tightly. His hands were charred. "I can try," she said as he winced in pain. "What do you need?"

"Water," he moaned.

Kienna reached for Moira, who had been rushing behind her with a new flask. They handed it to the man, whose lips cracked and bled.

"What happened out there?" Kienna asked.

"The army was small," he wheezed. Through broken breaths, he continued. "We didn't expect... a Vorthakai. It took...a lot of us down before we could…stop it." He winced again, grabbing at his ribs. A shadow flickered behind his eyes, and his breath caught. "It didn't move…like anything natural," he whispered. "It was too fast... like it bent the air around it. Like the forest didn't…even know it was there until it was…too late."

"Is Danek free?" Kienna asked Moira.

Moira shook her head, eyes grave.

"You can do it," the Elvish man whispered, his hand trembling against hers. "It's there…like a current beneath your skin. I can hear it."

Kienna stiffened. A strange pressure tingled along her palm through his hand. It was hot, then cold, then both at once as if the man's touch had stirred something raw and untapped. Her fingers twitched. She tried to summon something, a spark or anything that could be useful, but Kienna wasn't a healer. She didn't even know what she needed to be looking for. Still, the air between them crackled faintly.

"I—I can try," she muttered.

What should I do? she asked Ruva.

I don't understand magic. Maybe just try your best?

Kienna closed her eyes, focused on the pulsing in her hand, and let the energy rise. For a moment, the warmth surged, wild and hungry. A flicker of light flashed through her fingertips—then snapped. A spark jolted through her wrist, and she gasped, yanking her hand away.

Why did that hurt? she yelped in her mind. Ruva reacted as well, whimpering next to her.

"Are you okay?" Moira exclaimed, stumbling to her side.

Kienna cradled her hand, her breath uneven.

"I… I thought it was there. It was. But something shocked my bones."

Tristian strode by, dirtied by the grime of war. His eyes were worn with slight burn marks across his cheek. He'd been walking along another wave of soldiers encased in water, a solemn expression indicating more were probably dead than alive. He set his gaze on Kienna as she massaged her hand. "Of course," he scoffed. "Your magic is as weak as your character."

Let it go, Ruva pleaded.

"Hey," she said, her voice almost growling as she turned after him. Moira stayed behind with the man, cradling his body through the aches in hopes that Danek would show or another healer would relieve her. Kienna continued. "You don't have to like me, but don't talk to me like I'm not here trying to help!"

"You're dismissed," Tristian sighed impatiently. His eyes grew tired, the sleepless night of war weighing heavily on his shoulders.

"You can't dismiss me," she argued back. "I'm not your soldier."

"No, but my soldiers were out there dying for your cause."

It was the way he said it, like he had time to calculate these responses, that had Kienna bubbling over. Her eyes glowed brightly like the raging ocean waves crashing against the rocky shores in a storm. "I never asked for a war. I just wanted to get out." Her jaw clenched, fists clinging so tightly the white in her knuckles protruded through her normal warmth.

Tristian nodded his head backward, almost as if he were praying for the heavens to save him from this. He exhaled. "A princess never asks for war, and yet the world always goes to war."

"Don't call me that," Kienna demanded.

He's just being mean now, Ruva huffed her snout like a sneeze, growling toward Tristian.

Tristian tilted his head, voice dripping with disdain. "Look around you. People are dying, and you act like you've already earned your place. Like all of this is about *you.*"

Ruva stepped back, like Tristian had slapped the wolf in the face with it. *He is not wrong, Little Flame.*

Kienna's breath came faster now, chest rising and falling in sharp, uneven bursts. The edges of her vision blurred. Power danced on her skin like an untamed flame. Ruva growled beside her, the fur along her spine bristling in sync with Kienna's rage.

For a heartbeat, everything was still.

"You wear your *attitude* like a crown, too." Tristian's eyes narrowed, his voice cutting like a blade. "People are here dying, and you're worried about a bruised ego. It's time to grow up."

Connak's back, Ruva said, trying to tame Kienna, but she couldn't push past her feelings. She'd decided to join them, and now they were deflating her. Kienna took a step forward, fists trembling. "Stop treating me like a child, then."

"I said what I meant," he replied, voice like stone.

The air between them rippled as Connak stopped walking. He placed his hand on Kienna's shoulder, and the fire dissipated. All that remained was the smoke sizzling in her veins. "We're all tired and possibly feeding off each other's emotions." He gave Tristian a pointed look, as if that were supposed to mean more. "It may be time to take a step back."

"You overstep, Hollow Blade," Tristian snapped, voice sharp. "Or has your time in the shadows made you forget your place?"

Connak firmly stepped forward and calmly said, "With respect, if the Ael'ven Accord holds, it is my place."

Tristian's eyes grew cold, speckles of gray clouding the once beautiful blue and green of emotion. "What do you know of the Accords?" he asked boldly.

"Should the High Commander falter, the next officer may claim authority by the right of the Accords until reason is restored."

The High Commander tensed, his jaw tightening. "You're quoting the Accords now?"

"They were written for a reason," Connak responded, level.

"She doesn't even know why she's here," Tristian continued.

"Why are we losing good people to this cause if she's not ready to fight?"

Connak's expression faltered. Kienna saw him look at her, at the pain now flickering across her face, at the shimmer still fading from her hands. Then he turned his eyes on the wounded scattered across the village grounds, the still bodies being carried past them. Danek was on his knees now, shaking from exhaustion as he tried to heal one more soldier, his light diminishing.

"Everything we're doing is for her. You know that, but…" Connak growled, voice sharp beneath the surface. "We're following orders, and we're staying quiet like you asked us to. But you're debating her place already, so what are we really protecting? I don't know if we can stay quiet anymore, Tristian."

Stay quiet about what?

I don't know, Little Flame. I know what you know.

Tristian's eyes darted around the forest floor. He looked even more tense than he had when he arrived. "Don't do that, Connak. You stick to the plan. Start with getting her to the truth." With that, he turned and walked away.

What the fuck, Ruva? They're not helping me move past the half-truths.

Just don't start singing that song, please.

I'm serious.

Connak shifted as Elira approached, her council trailing behind. She was dressed in her own set of army gear, silver-trimmed armor dulled by battle, her braids wound back like a crown of steel. Regal. Commanding. But Connak's eyes did not soften at the sight.

He stepped forward. "Your Majesty, please," he said. "I understand a lot is going on right now, but Kienna needs to know who she is. We can't leave her in the dark after all this. People are dying, and she needs to know why the king is doing this."

"Not now, Commander," Elira was clearly irritated, her eyes

Samantha Vargas

growing restless. "We have much to do to prepare for whatever comes next in the North." Queen Elira continued, waving Connak behind.

Connak didn't move.

The queen's attention was already shifting to another aide, but his jaw locked, breath shallow with the weight of words unsaid. The silence stretched thin, sharp as glass.

Kienna caught the change in him first. The quiet storm behind his eyes. Ruva let out an uneasy growl beside her, ears twitching. Kienna glanced at the wolf, placing her hands on her back to ease the tension growing between them.

"Elira," he said again, not a plea this time, but a warning.

Still, she walked.

She doesn't like you, Connak admitted in Kienna's mind, *but I won't let her continue to pretend you don't exist. It's a terrible time for it, but if we don't do this now, she'll discard you.* His fists clenched harder at his sides. His voice rose clearer, more forceful, crackling at the edge of command. "Elira!" he shouted. His shout echoed with anger that Kienna most certainly hadn't heard before. The Elvish soldiers halted, turning to see who dared to speak so out of turn to their queen.

"Fine," the queen sighed, turning nonchalantly to Kienna, though she could tell through the dullness that Connak was not going to escape that moment so easily. "You are Kalyra, of the royal Belok tribe. It is an ancient tribe of the Elvish that has ruled over Alistile for centuries. King Vaerin is the enemy of your tribe as a murderer and a thief. If you want to know why we're burying soldiers tonight, hold onto that."

So many questions flooded Kienna's brain. Elira's words didn't make any sense. It didn't spark a sense of pride or belonging. It existed as another confusing piece of information. She wanted to have a conversation. Why did they dance around information like it would burn them all?

They are all bad at communication, Ruva affirmed.

Riddles and half-truths, Vaerin's words echoed, though they had driven her and Ruva mad by now. Everything was blurred by unanswered pieces, like trying to read a map with half the ink smeared away.

"I'm sorry if you think that child is me." She said it without thinking it through. She didn't know if she was that child or if she wanted to be that child. The queen's brows rose in surprise. "Connak mentioned you lost her, so I can imagine if our likeness is causing some grief."

"You told her Kalyra died?" Elira snapped at Connak, her voice laced with a fury that didn't match the calm she had carried before. Her piercing gaze stabbed him like a spear. Connak shifted his weight, suddenly unsure of the ground beneath him.

I'm sorry. I need to tread cautiously with the things I share, and some things are not my place to reveal, he whispered through Kienna's barriers. She shoved him out, cheeks flushing with embarrassment as she realized how publicly exposed she'd become by *his* half-truth. She was aware of herself in this moment as soldiers were crying out in anguish from a war they didn't have to fight if it weren't for her and Connak breaking the River Storm barrier.

"I'm not some mourning shrew seeing dead faces wherever I go," the queen continued, voice cold and poised like a knife at rest.

Connak placed his hands together, though he did not look nearly as sorry as he should have been, with a gleam in his eye. "My Queen, I—"

"Enough," Elira demanded. "Get out of my sight."

Connak bowed and walked away, joining Danek to give him relief in his healing efforts. *Be careful,* he said, pushing back into Kienna's mind. *She will give you answers you need, but the truth is more complicated than what you might see.*

Elira turned to Kienna, her expression unreadable. "Walk with me, please."

Kienna's lips parted as if to say something, but she simply nodded. To Ruva, she said, *Stay here.*

Chapter 39

—Kienna—

They walked through Trinity to the edge of the city, where the plants grew wild and reckless, through the trail for miles until they stopped at a familiar tree. The smell of burnt wood remained as a reminder of Kienna's recent outburst.

"This is where they died." Elira drifted toward the engravings. A + G. The corners of her mouth faltered, her eyes dropping for the first time. The steel in her spine didn't bend, but something cracked behind her eyes that indicated she could have been experiencing a human emotion.

"Who?" Kienna asked.

"Your parents," she responded. Kienna's heart shot into her throat, thoughts swarming her head like bees of an angry hive. Elira continued, "They were protecting this sacred city."

"From what?" Kienna feared the answer.

"Your king."

Her heart was racing. The queen was testing her, of course, by calling him Kienna's king. Would she turn away from that? When Kienna didn't move, Elira motioned to the tree, her regal hands resting on the initials. Kienna studied them, the soft strokes and intricacy that they placed in etching such simple letters into the bark. Masters of wood, they carved it so deeply, the grooves shimmered faintly as if the tree still remembered the touch. The lettering was both art and memory, and a slight tinge of jealousy overcame her at the way love had been so permanently marked.

"Go ahead," Elira urged. "Touch them."

Kienna hesitated but rubbed her hands on the tree as she did the day before. As her fingers touched the engraving, a faint warmth pulsed beneath the skin of her thumb right where the old scar lived. It tingled, as if the tree recognized her. She didn't expect much to happen, but a strong pull yanked at her mind. She could see Elira's face fading until she stood on the other side of the tree alone. Her heart raced. The forest lightened and darkened at the same time. She could smell burnt ash, contrasting with the tiny forest fire she had started. This was a burning of cities far off in the distance.

There was a pinch in her head, almost to pull her back, but something else grounded Kienna in place. The headache, at times, felt unbearable, but she couldn't let go now.

A faint shift in the air came first with a pulsating hum, like a string being plucked in the roots of the forest. Then, crumbled leaves startled her. Kienna jumped backward, two figures walking in the distance toward her. She gasped and hid behind the tree. They were huddled closely together over a small baby.

"She's perfect, Gal," the woman sighed melodically.

The man—Gal—stopped in front of where Kienna had been hiding and turned to the woman, hands stroking the baby's soft hair. The hair was a perfect blend between the man and woman in front of her, light threads interwoven with colors of pure wooden ash.

Kienna studied the people in front of her, cautious not to make any sound. Gal had hair of moonlight that regally fell down his shoulders, unmistakably Elvish in its austerity and pride. His skin held marks of a warrior, but also the suppleness of a man in high command. His eyes were the same pale blue as Elira's, cut from ice, but they melted around the edges, softened by emotion, full of love. He stared gently at the woman in front of him, a softness Kienna yearned for.

"We must be quick," Gal said to her.

She nodded, stepping further into the light, revealing a soft face that was more human than Gal's. Where he commanded with high cheekbones and strength, she danced with a round face and grace. Her hair, woven with deep oak and ash, stopped at her shoulders and curled around strings of gold and silver twigs. Her eyes were speckled with browns and greens, and her smile was so warm she could have made the sun herself.

Kienna stepped closer, the sound of twigs snapping echoing through the forest. The woman looked up. "What was that?"

The twigs, of course, were Kienna's doing. The woman's reaction to her presence unsettled Kienna and made her wonder if she was actually there.

"They're almost here. Hurry, Avenna," Gal commanded. "Give me the baby."

Avenna handed the baby over gently, a soft whimper on her lips. Gal shushed the tiny cries that came from the warm blanket, and magic escaped from his hands. He clouded the baby with bright white, lullabies enchanting the forest as he sang alongside a subtle breeze.

The sound of Gal's voice wafting through the air like the wind on a sunny day drew Kienna near. She moved closer with each word the Elvish man sang until she was upon them. They didn't see her.

When Gal ended the song, his eyes met Avenna. "Kalyra has been blessed with the roots of Trinity now."

"We should go back. I think I hear—"

Large blasts of red magic flew through the forest. Gal and Avenna deflected with their own shields, but the opponent held a stronger resolve. The magic streamed out without any concern for the amount of energy they must have been consuming.

Kienna ducked, her heart pounding against her chest as if it could explode. She covered her head when branches and dirt flung through the air and stayed like that for minutes. When she realized the blasts of magic weren't touching her, she looked up, eyes following the source of red.

Gal screamed for Avenna to run, to take the baby out of the forest to the queen, but Avenna refused to leave. She blasted a hole into the trunk of a tree, one that Kienna hadn't seen before until that moment. She panted frantically, placing her baby gently into the bark, trying her best to shush the aching cries wailing from the baby's lungs.

"It's okay, little one." She kissed the top of the small head and stood side by side with Gal.

Their bodies filled with the core of magic, and they engaged their attacker. Kienna rushed to the tree. She had to fight the external tug out of the vision, but she feared the baby would be hurt by the extreme power slamming into the forest. She reached in and grabbed the infant, shocked by how light she had been. As if grasping for air, she held her for a moment, only for the shadows to waft back into the tree. She wanted to protect the child, a fleeting emotion as she realized she couldn't. Kienna stood.

The man in red was upon the two parents now. He barreled down, slamming Gal into the ground while Avenna pounded on his back. He threw her across the forest, and then it was over. He walked to the tree, the magical glow dissipating from him as he walked through Kienna. The sudden connection nearly made her vomit. It was like two souls merging and becoming aware of the other.

He stopped and turned. His beady eyes fell on her like the eyes of a serpent. He stared into her soul, but then he continued to the baby. Kienna's heart sank into the pit of her stomach when she realized she had been looking at Vaerin. He was much younger then, but it was unmistakably him.

A soldier appeared, dressed in full armor from head to toe. The silver metal on his back held a luminescent glow, as if he had been enchanted with protection.

"Take Kienna to River Storm and tell the troops to retreat," he peered back into the forest, his eyes resting where Kienna had been. "We have what we need."

Kienna's mind yanked back hard, her body flying backward as she had with Danek and Moira. This time, she didn't surge or spark flames. She let herself lay on the ground, eyes wide and chest panting in and out. Her body drained of energy, and the searing ache in her head prevented her from doing anything else aside from feeling the pain of Vaerin's lies and betrayal.

He killed them to take her. She'd already known she was taken, but it had never been confirmed that her parents' death was a result. He took them from her, too, like he took everything else.

"Do you have any questions?" Elira asked calmly.

"Yeah," she heaved. "Too many."

Chapter 40

—Kienna—

"Those were my parents?" Kienna asked, standing amongst the council in their great hall. The vibrant green canopy of their first gathering had shifted, and the chamber shimmered with tranquil blues and radiant whites as light filtered through veined leaves like stained glass.

The council, now complete due to the returned army, stood behind the queen. Connak and Tristian stood to Elira's left as her trusted advisors of war. Connak was calm and shadowed, Tristian rigid and battle-worn. Kaelthar towered near the right, arms crossed, his presence like a fortress of steel, while Alister leaned forward slightly, ever the inquisitor. Beside them stood a regal human man from Dove Port, draped in ocean-colored silk, and a woman whose skin was laden in ash. A man from across the river stood silent, his cloak dusted with soil and his hands calloused and strong. Lastly, an Elvish woman stood apart from the rest, her garments unfamiliar.

Elira nodded.

"Why did Vaerin come for me?" Kienna wanted to know.

"He is a madman hungry for power. You are the link to the ancient and new power forged by your parents, Avenna of Dove Port and Galric of Belok," Elira explained.

I wouldn't bet on that, Kienna thought to herself, regarding her being anything other than a confused girl outside her element. "What is Belok?"

The unfamiliar Elvish woman, silent until now, lifted her head and met Kienna's eyes. "It is the royal line of Alistile."

"You are still saying things that require further questions," Kienna muttered.

Elira grew weary. "Has he taught this group nothing of history?"

Alistile is the realm you live in. It is not Trinity. It is not Dove Port or River Storm. It's everything, Connak brushed into her mind. Kienna met his gaze, a softening "thank you" falling over her body in relief.

Is she indicating that Belok is the true ruling line of all the land? Including River Storm?

She is.

"I understand now," Kienna said. It was no wonder Vaerin saw them as a threat as Kienna joined their forces. He had his own stake in the war aside from power. She shifted her thoughts to something more pressing, staring at the similarities she saw in her father and Elira before her. "You and I—"

"Yes," Elira cut in, annoyed as she tried to wave the question away. "I, too, am of Belok."

Kienna sighed, studying the council of the room. They all looked restless, waiting for more questions. Kienna wondered if, until now, they even had to worry about Vaerin or if they lived a comfortable life. Perhaps Queen Elira chastised Connak because he pulled them out of a life of ruling in peace. Of course, she knew nothing about the logistics of this world and realized she was projecting evil onto them without any evidence. Regardless, it still posed the question as to why they had been hesitant to share these truths with her. Surely it had to be more than the fact that she spent time with Vaerin as his captive.

"Does this have anything to do with a woodcarver?" Kienna asked.

Elira's face became unreadable, though that wasn't much of a change, but she had to take a step back and lean toward the other Elvish woman who mentioned Alistile. No answer was given. Elira only continued to stare at Kienna until she deduced it was time to move on.

They won't be helping you with the woodcarver, Connak whispered.

"I have one more question," she said, almost as a question itself. At this point, she couldn't guarantee she would even get an answer.

"Yes," Elira sighed.

"Why did he call me Kienna if my parents called me Kalyra?"

"You were born Kalyra, a name that was a gift from our Eternal Mother. When Vaerin took you, he severed the power your parents forged through you from the Crown Above. I cannot say for sure why he would call you Kienna, but Kienna is what he wanted you to be. Kalyra is what you were meant to be. You are both."

Kienna's voice trembled. "I don't understand why that's so important."

"Until you choose who you wish to become, neither name will

hold its full truth. Your allegiance is severed until you do."

Kienna stood quietly. The words weighed heavier than she expected. They sounded like names to her, but to the Elvish, they were rooted in her identity and the future she wanted for herself. One rooted in her blood, another forged in fire. She didn't know which to believe in yet.

Kienna pushed her mind to Ruva. They didn't allow the wolf to come into the chambers, but Kienna felt her nearby. *I don't know why what I call myself matters so much. And I doubt I can give that up without understanding more about it.*

The wolf panted in her head. *You don't have to, Little Flame. Just do your best.*

And Vaerin?

Trust Connak.

For the first time, the not-knowing didn't feel like weakness. It felt like a beginning. No one could tell her who to become. She would learn who that was, and it felt like the choice could be hers to make, Vaerin be damned. Ruva tickled her mind at the thought.

"I would like to fight for you," Kienna said boldly to Tristian.

Tristian shared a glance with Connak and then the queen. His eyes lingered on Kienna, weariness etching every line of his face. She had chosen action but not quite an identity. With caution, and perhaps a flicker of reluctant hope, he nodded.

Chapter 41

—Kienna—

Kienna stared at the stars through a clearing in the trees, her arms resting calmly on Ruva. The wolf slept, huffing a grumble in between dreams. Glimmering balls of fire sparkled in the deep night sky, playing tag as one shone and died out for the other to light up. River Storm didn't have stars, at least not in the vibrant colors that cast across Trinity. There was no other sky like the one she looked at that evening.

She mumbled the name *Kalyra* a few times, playing with it in her head. *Hi, I'm Kalyra of Belok*, she said to herself. *No, that doesn't sound right.* She sighed, resolved to the fact that she wouldn't be solving that conundrum right then and there.

Who do you *think I am?* Her voice rang out to Ruva, but the wolf only grumbled again in her sleep, snorting her snout and nudging Kienna to let her know she had heard her.

Behind her, the others rested inside the village homes. Broan returned with the last battalion, unscathed and elated by the war. Though he was not the one to take down the Vorthakai that the injured man had told Kienna about, he had come close, slamming the earth into the beast's belly. It was then swiftly taken out by Tislin with a single arrow from up high.

The story echoed throughout the night. By the time Kienna had returned from the council meeting, Broan was on his third retelling and was eager to start another. He finally talked himself to sleep, to which Moira and Danek slumped their shoulders and breathed a sigh of relief. Danek looked far more tired than usual. He had mentioned that Connak forced him to take a break to rest after Kienna left with the queen. He refueled with as much water from the village fountains as possible and the finest meats and vegetables the city had to offer. By the time Kienna returned, the army had cleared, and the injured were sent to the Trinity healers toward the islands. He didn't hesitate when Broan finally shut up, and he realized he could sleep.

Kienna had watched them all succumb to slumber before she took to the stars. By now, the morning sun threatened the horizon, the night's fire fading at the sight of the first light. A shiver vibrated through Kienna's bones as she stifled a yawn.

In the distance, Tristian's voice echoed. Kienna turned and could see him striding down the path with Tislin, opposites to the same puzzle. Where Tislin stood in light features, kissed by the moon in the shadows, Tristian appeared dark, loved by the sun in the daylight. They both held a seriousness about them.

"And please tell Connak I'd like for the Blades to scope Holbeck,"

Tristian suggested.

"Connak does not take orders from me," Tislin reminded him. "In case you forgot our ranking orders."

A flash of tension passed between them, one not easily brushed aside. There was history in the way they held each other's stares with wounds that hadn't fully scarred, softened only by the familiarity of shared blood. The silence stretched for a heartbeat too long.

"Connak is high off of his incitement of the Accords. He and I need another ranking officer between us at this time." Tristian folded his arms.

Tislin nodded gently, a flicker of the unspoken in his eyes. "Yes, High Commander."

They paused in the early light, admiring the gentle specks flushing through the leaves. Tristian loosened his body and placed his hand on Tislin's shoulder. His voice dropped, more tender this time. "It's good to see you well, Brother."

Tislin bowed his head and retreated through the forest. Tristian turned to Kienna. She straightened slightly, surprised to see his eyes already fixed on her.

"Eavesdropping is rude," he said, approaching her, though his tone lacked true irritation. Kienna averted her eyes, focusing on Ruva. She reached out to scratch the wolf behind the ear, suddenly uncertain under the High Commander's stare. "May I?" he asked, motioning to sit with her. He didn't wait for a response but sat down across from her. His brows furrowed, permanently plastered in the grooves of his skin. His lips pursed tightly against his jaw. Kienna wondered if the tension from his face could be felt through his shoulders and neck permanently.

He is handsome, though, she admitted to herself. A rumbling howl of laughter echoed internally, one that could have only belonged to Ruva. She squeezed her hand warmly around the flesh of her pup.

"Tell me," Tristian began, his voice gruff with exhaustion. "Why do you want to fight?"

She didn't expect another round of questioning. She went through so many series of questions since arriving that answering every detail exhausted her. Kienna stared at him blankly. "I saw enough in the forest."

"Have you ever had to face a battlefield?"

"No," she admitted, unashamed. "But we have been trained extensively on advanced battle tactics."

"Vaerin's battle tactics," Tristian reminded her. "Not ours."

"Yes," she agreed. "I suppose you'd be right."

"You can see why that still concerns me."

"Yes, but our knowledge could help you, too."

Tristian considered this and moved on. "Would you hesitate if it were someone you knew on the other end of your blade?"

Kienna chewed on the side of her cheek until she could taste a slight pang of iron. "I have a brother in Vaerin's army." She turned to him. Her voice cracked slightly, a flicker of vulnerability slipping through. "I would if it were him."

At her side, Ruva let out a restless sound—half growl, half sigh—as if stirred by the tension in her partner's voice.

Tristian nodded slowly, his expression shifting. The tightness in his posture eased, if only a fraction. "I would, too," he said quietly. "For Tislin. Even if I had to grit my teeth through it." Tristian exhaled slowly, his eyes drifting toward the trees where the light was stretching across the canopy. A hush settled between them for a few seconds, the weight of unspoken memories thickening the air. Then, more pointedly, he turned back to her. "Are you doing this for Trinity? Or for yourself?"

"Does anyone fight wars for themselves?" she asked.

"I can appreciate your mindset, though we are at war with a man who will go to the ends of the earth and back for himself."

In that moment, her mind drifted to Baila. Amid the chaos of returning soldiers and Kienna's council meeting, it was reported that she slipped through the cracks of the forest and disappeared. No one knew where or why, just that she couldn't be found or felt in the forest any longer. Kienna knew instantly where she had gone, but as she sat in front of the High Commander, she was glad Baila had disappeared. Surely Baila could see which side Kienna chose by now. If she ever saw Baila again, it wouldn't be as allies.

"Meet at the training grounds the day after tomorrow," Tristian suggested. "We will train you. It's an intense program, so eat light or else you'll find most of it in the forest afterwards."

"Anything I need to know?" she inquired.

"Talon is a fierce commander of the Shardborn Battalion. He will push you to the brink. They do not use magic. Not because they can't, but because this wave is designed for silent precision. They consume their energy for raw fighting. Can you handle that?"

"I can," Kienna responded confidently. She couldn't have thought of any group to join that would have fit her better. This was where she thrived, on the brink of pure force and magicless precision.

"Good luck."

She watched him disappear into the trees, her pulse steady. The stars hadn't given her any answers, and neither had the Elvish. She didn't know if she was any closer to finding this elusive woodcarver, but she hoped she might be inching closer to finding out who she was.

Chapter 42

—Kienna—

Kienna, Danek, and Broan made their way to the training grounds nestled high above the canopies of the forest. Each wore newly issued garments. They were Elvish-made tunics and pants, fitted precisely to their forms. When an Elvish woman handed them to Kienna, she was shocked. The last time she got new clothes, Vaerin had been the one handing them to her. These were nicer than what Vaerin provided, but she hated that they made her think of him.

The fabric was unlike anything they had known. Earth-toned and modest, the colors blended effortlessly with the woods around them—soft moss, pale stone, bark-gray, and twilight brown. The material whispered against their skin, firmer than silk but lighter than leather, armor reimagined as cloth. It moved with them like a second skin. Hidden folds in the sleeves and hips allowed for fluid, rapid shifts in stance, and small pockets tucked into the inner lining held emergency supplies, almost imperceptible to the eye. For the first time, Kienna realized how much weight her former clothes had carried. This brought a wave of unexpected calm.

Moira geared up with them to go, but her skin glowed an unusual shade of green that made the others wonder if she had eaten something that didn't quite sit well. They took her to the Elvish healers, who indicated it would be best for Moira to sit out of battle training and rest a bit longer. They were sad to see their group breaking even further after Baila's abandonment, but they decided to continue without her.

They followed a section of bridges that led them to a series of floating islands that looked out over the forest closest to the elemental wind island. The Heart of Trinity rose even higher still, but being part of the clouds was like a dream. They reached the final island where hundreds of warriors clashed in disciplined pairs. At the far edge of the clearing, the group laid their eyes upon the banners of the Shardborn, rippling in the cool dusk breeze. The flag was forged from iron-black cloth, with a shattered crown at its center. It was overlaid by the silhouette of a charging stag, antlers shaped like broken crystal.

A tall figure broke from the formation and approached. His armor was functional and scarred, etched with dozens of battlefield runes. His sharp eyes were the color of storm-washed stone. "You're the girl with two names," he said bluntly.

"Kienna," she replied.

He studied her for a beat, then nodded once, addressing the rest of the group with her. "I'm Talon. You'll bleed with us, or not at all."

"We're ready," Broan boasted, stepping forward with pride.

"I'm surprised you're here in my battalion. I suspect you won't be here long," Talon said to him. "I know the others could use your strong connection to the ground."

They mused with camaraderie, something they could have only gleaned from the battlefield together. Broan boasted his chest out, hands laced through his belt proudly as the red sigil sparked.

Talon readdressed the group. "We will be going through a full day of training. We will not be eating. You must understand what it's like in battle."

"We can do it." Danek stepped forward.

"We'll see." Talon eyed them.

Danek and Broan soon learned to regret their confidence as Talon had them sprinting through the island, diving under branches, and weaving up and over the trees. Danek tried once to levitate with his magic, and he was instantly scolded by his commander and given additional laps to take as punishment.

When relief flooded them at the end of the course, Talon demanded they do it again. And again. They had run that course until their knees gave out. They panted heavily, heaving in and out for air.

Ruva sat at the edge of the battlefield, yelping grumpily in hopes of getting Kienna to acknowledge her. She eyed the wolf through breaths, but there was nothing left in her energy reserves to greet her. Still, Ruva held her place, ears flicking attentively. After one of Kienna's hard falls, the wolf let out a sharp huff. *Don't give up!* Kienna gave her the faintest nod in return, their bond tightening with each trial.

"It's a good start." Talon walked, hands behind his back. "You were formidable warriors at your old home, I see."

"We trained often," Danek heaved.

"Not like that," Kienna admitted, fighting internally to keep the light breakfast in her stomach, even after hours of grueling work.

Talon chuckled. "Stand tall." He placed the tip of his sword on Kienna's chin until she rose, face angled upward. He did the same to Broan and Danek. Their bodies ached as they inched upwards, but each obliged and tightened their formation. "Hands cusped behind your back," Talon instructed. They followed. "Good. When in the presence of a higher command, it is customary to show respect to stand in this formation."

Silence fell. Sweat dripped down over Kienna's eyes, the sting of the salt burning in the sunlight. Her heart had settled in her chest, but the fire in her lungs remained.

"Alright." Talon clasped his hands. "Let's see what you have for battle. We have a few rules when fighting—on and off the battlefield. First, in this wave, you are tested on your sheer will to fight. We do not use magic here."

"Why no magic?" Broan questioned.

"Magic is sacred and a gift from the Eternal Mother. We use magic to protect, to aid, and to heal," Talon replied coolly.

"Then why do others use it in battle?" Danek protested.

"Their duties are to subdue the enemy and to push back. Otherwise, they fight with their brute force when they have to. Our duty, in this Battalion, is to end the war. We are quick, we are brutal, and we kill when we have to." Talon paused, glancing around at the group as they all winced. "We *hope* we don't have to."

Kienna shifted her weight, a slight clench forming in her jaw. Her fingers curled inward against her palms, grounding herself as a chill prickled across her shoulders. The word "kill" sat differently on her skin than anything else they had heard today—heavier than expected. Her mind drifted to the woman in the square in River Storm when Dren had lopped off her head like it was nothing. The image still made her stomach turn.

Talon clapped once, signaling the next phase. "Now," he said, "show me what you've brought from River Storm. Let loose."

They obeyed, Broan and Danek squaring off, fists raised, while Kienna stepped cautiously into position. The trio fell into their old patterns quickly, fighting with fury, swinging wild and hard, every movement reactive and emotional. Dust kicked up underfoot. Grunts echoed off bark. Their attacks held no grace, only heat.

Talon raised a hand. "Stop. All of you." They froze. He stepped into the center and scanned each of them. "You fight with spirit but no control. That works for one swing. One punch. One desperate strike. But we don't survive on single strikes. We survive by owning the fight. Every breath, every turn of the wrist."

He motioned for Danek to stand opposite him. "This is how you displace force. This is how you survive." In one fluid motion, Talon stepped into Danek's stance, shifted his weight, and flipped him to the ground without throwing a single punch. "This is what we practice in the Shardborn. Not brute strength. We use technique and timing with strategic intent. Grappling to subdue them, then, hopefully, end them. Sometimes, more."

"Doubt I'll ever use that floppy move on a battlefield," Broan muttered, arms crossed, but he moved into the new stance regardless.

Talon showed them again, slowly this time. Each movement was deliberate, efficient, and designed to redirect force rather than absorb it. He emphasized balance, leverage, and position over power. The trio followed, stiffly and awkwardly at first. Kienna stumbled twice. Danek's footing slipped in the turn. "This still feels like dancing with an invisible deer," Broan grumbled as he tried to roll into a grapple hold. But with every cycle, their bodies found rhythm, the unnatural becoming instinct.

Kienna's breath synced with her footwork. Danek began moving with less hesitation, and Broan admitted it wasn't completely useless.

Danek offered a sheepish grin, brushing a leaf from his shoulder. "I didn't think I'd like this training, but it's different. It's like I'm learning how to think with my body, not throw it around."

Talon stepped back and clapped once. "Form up. Time to put the motions into use."

He scanned the trio and pointed. "Broan, Danek, you two begin. Kienna," his eyes landed on her, unwavering, "you're with me."

Kienna stepped forward to face her opponent, lining up and trying to walk her mind through the motions Talon had taught them. As she put mental notes of the movements and motioned through one of them, Talon disappeared and then appeared in an instant, a motion so quick, Kienna didn't have time to be shocked when her body flung to the ground.

She scrambled around for a moment, trying hard to pinpoint his location, but he had her pinned immediately, and she found herself tapping out. This happened for at least an hour. Kienna couldn't understand how Talon had enough energy to keep going at his strength, but she tried different motions each time, and each of them failed.

Her body hit the dirt, a sudden flicker of annoyance and rage engulfing her. Not to mention, the silent pangs of hunger called to her, only distracting her mind even further. Kienna slammed her fist into the ground.

Narrow your senses, Ruva whispered.

Kienna glanced up and met her wolf's stare. The wave of wonder quickly wiped from her face when Talon knocked her over and pinned her yet again. Ruva repeated herself, more tempered now.

I can't see him when he moves, Kienna said crossly. *I've never fought anyone who could move so fast.*

You don't need to see him. Sense him.

What?

Ruva pulled out of her mind and sat up. Kienna sighed. She tried once more to see him, unsure what Ruva would have meant. Clearly seeing him was sensing him, right? She was proven wrong as her ribs crushed into the ground yet again. The wolf growled.

Kienna stood, her stance going lower this time. She kept her eyes cautiously on Talon, then turned off the focus in her eyes. Her ears heightened. The breeze caressed her skin. A swift motion pushed toward her, as her hair swayed, and she moved swiftly, sticking her leg out and knocking Talon into the dirt.

He moved quickly to get up, starting the engagement with her. They wrestled around for a few moments before he pinned her down. Frustrated, yet rejuvenated by her small success, Kienna started again, holding longer strides of battle each time she tried. Talon's eyes glimmered at the hint of a potential sparring match with some grit to it.

"Come on," Talon taunted, now visibly exhausted.

The crack of Kienna's movement drew eyes beyond the ring of sparring warriors. At the edge of the field, Tristian paused mid-conversation with two other commanders. One of them, a woman in light silver mail, raised an eyebrow.

"That's the girl from River Storm, isn't it?" she asked.

Tristian didn't answer. He merely nodded, his eyes narrowing slightly. The soldiers fell quiet as they watched Kienna pivot and close the distance with Talon in a blur of motion.

She started again. This time, Kienna didn't wait for Talon to come. She jumped forward with precision, wrapping her legs around his body and pulling him to the ground. He delivered a good enough fight, but eventually she managed to slide her leg over his neck and simulate the kill strike.

Talon tapped and called for an end to the grappling. "You were excellent," he boasted. "Now that you're tired, fight Broan."

Chapter 43

—Kienna—

Broan and Danek halted. Kienna saw the sudden shift in Broan's demeanor, like he had waited for this opportunity to slam her into the ground for a long time. She tightened her body, prepared to fight.

Broan rolled his shoulders, grinning. "You sure you're up for this? I've been waiting for a rematch since River Storm."

Kienna narrowed her eyes. "Try me."

They circled. Broan lunged first, his movements heavy and forceful. The first blow hit her shoulder hard, forcing her to stumble. Kienna recovered and darted in, but he blocked her attempt and shoved her backward.

"Come on, princess! Is that all River Storm taught you?" Another swing grazed her ribs, and she winced. She'd fought Broan before, but not like this. Not without magical barriers to protect against the larger blows. And certainly not without any fuel.

"No, I've also learned how to deal with loud idiots who think swinging harder makes them better." Kienna ducked under his arm as he swung and twisted behind him. "How's that working out for you, barbarian?

"It's *Viking*, if you didn't hear correctly." Broan turned and grabbed her shoulder. Kienna yanked at his hand, but his grip was secure. "At least I'm hitting something. What'd you carve while I was off saving the realm?"

"A wolf and a weapon you're not worthy of touching." She pushed him back a step. Kienna grinned through clenched teeth. "Want me to carve you a chair so you can sit when I'm done embarrassing you?"

You two are acting like children, Ruva said. *Try to pretend you're in a war.*

Can't, Kienna said. *I'm tired of Broan not respecting me.*

Maybe just beat him, then?

It's not enough. She'd beat him plenty of times. He'd always met her with the same disdain. *Broan will hate me for everything Vaerin did in my name.*

Broan pushed his body into Kienna. Her hands splayed against his back, and she almost fell to the ground. They fumbled around, nearing the edge of the islands. Kienna didn't intend to go into the clouds. She grabbed Broan and pushed him back into the center and managed to gain enough space to breathe.

"Move faster, and you might catch me off guard next time," she taunted.

"I'm trying not to trip over that ego you're dragging behind you." He stepped in with brute strength, their arms locking in a sudden clash.

"Says the man who's been retelling the same war story for two days."

Broan scoffed. They were supposed to be fighting physically. Talon's impatience appeared to be wearing thin on the sidelines. Danek slumped like this wasn't anything new between them, but Kienna and Broan had to hash it out.

"Hey," Broan said, stepping around to catch a better angle of Kienna's legs. "Not my fault that your part of the story was back in the woods, carving cups."

Even Ruva huffed at that. Kienna's jaw tightened, fury building behind her eyes. "You're an ass, Broan. And that's why you're going down."

Broan laughed. "Try not to cry when you lose, princess. Wouldn't want to ruin all that forest dirt with your River Storm tears."

"I don't cry for River Storm," she said through gritted teeth.

Broan paused for a moment, her words hitting somewhere deep within him. Softer, he said, "Finally, some honesty. Now show me you're not the weakling the king made you."

That I can do, she told Ruva.

The wolf howled in agreement.

Gritting her teeth, she waited. She watched his breath. His stance. Then she twisted and grabbed his wrist, turned under it, and dropped to her knees. Before he could react, Kienna pulled him forward with all her strength. Broan flew over her back and slammed into the dirt as she initiated the kill strike.

"Ah, hell," he grumbled, spitting soil. "I didn't expect your dainty ass to pull me down like that."

"You've fought Kienna before," Danek reminded Broan. "We both know she is not dainty in a fight."

"You may be right," Broan muttered, brushing off his pants. "But next time, warn me when it looks like she plans to launch me like a sack of flour. I may have lost some battle glory with the men here."

Kienna assumed position next to Danek as Tristian walked forward into the field, studying them with the practiced eye of a seasoned commander. Talon mirrored his motion, standing tall but silent beside him.

"Assessment?" Tristian asked.

"They fight like savages, bicker too much, and are not nearly as quick as our standard soldier. Can't jump high enough without needing some sort of structure to jump off, but they learn quickly. Strong and resilient. The Shardborn Battalion would be honored to have them if you don't need them elsewhere," Talon replied.

Tristian studied the group, covered in sweat and dirt, their bodies visibly aching, but they held their formation strongly. "Danek. Kalyra. You will report to Talon from now on. Show up when he says. Do as he says. He is your commander now."

They nodded, though Kienna flinched at the name. She didn't know why it bothered her so much, only that it did. Was this the new version of being called princess? It hit a lot harder than when Broan did it. She shook away the distaste and kept her eyes forward, focusing heavily on something else besides her new target of anger.

Tristian waited for a response but moved forward when he did not get his audible confirmations. "Broan, I need you in the eighth wave with the Thornclad."

"Will do," Broan confirmed.

"Good work today. It's an honor to have strong warriors at our side. Go home," he demanded, moving away from them. "Get rest."

Everyone fell from their position and grumbled forward. Kienna held the line. Her body screamed for rest and food, but her feet remained planted, shoulders squared. Sweat trickled along her spine, catching the last orange gleam of the setting sun. She watched the others retreat into the soft glow of the forest. Her pulse was still steady despite the ache. There was something sacred in the silence she claimed for herself—a refusal to step away until she had truly earned the right to leave.

"Anything else?" Talon questioned.

Kienna approached. "I was wondering if there was any way I could stay and keep training?"

Talon raised his brow. "Most of our soldiers have gone in for the night. We did just finish a battle, so I think they've earned some rest."

"That's okay," Kienna responded. "I can do more obstacles or any self-driven training."

"I'll train with her," Tristian offered. His voice carried an undertone of finality that left no room for protest. Talon tensed his body, shoulders subtly straightening in a display of deference, taking his position at the command of Tristian. A flash of unreadable emotion passed through his eyes—respect, perhaps, or caution. "Dismissed."

"Thank you, High Commander," Talon said and took his leave of the battlegrounds, winding the bridges through the clouds and back into the trees. Kienna hadn't realized how beautiful the sun looked against the setting sky as it sent trails of wind blowing through her hair. Ruva relaxed into the visceral scene.

Kienna stayed in position while Tristian moved around the training grounds, removing his weapon and his suit of scaled armor. Her eyes fell on his back when he pulled his tunic over his head, revealing the hardened lines of a soldier's life. Unlike the other Elvish—slight, swift, and agile—Tristian's build was dense with strength, sculpted from years of carrying the weight of war. His muscles flexed beneath skin, weathered and worn, marred by the stories of battles past. Scars laced across his back like a tapestry of survival, some faint, others jagged and angry. One scar in particular ran from the top of his collarbone diagonally to his opposite rib, old but still raw around the edges—as though the memory of the wound never quite left him.

Tristian glanced over his shoulder as if he could feel Kienna's gaze on it, the bleeding questions that swarmed through her head.

"I'm tired," he said flatly, wiping a bead of sweat from his brow. "Less weight helps." He gave her a matter-of-fact look, but it was not unkind. "And it makes it harder for you to get a grip."

You're drooling, Ruva's voice rang out.

Hush, Kienna said, cheeks flushing.

"Let's begin," Tristian demanded.

Kienna took her position, ready to watch him as a hawk would watch its prey, to parry his quick attacks or prepare for a sweeping motion if he got her on the ground. But Tristian did not move forward. He eyed her, studying her, waiting.

Minutes passed. Kienna wondered if it were she who needed to make a move, but more so, she figured he was testing her. She held her position, dancing along as he stepped around in a circle, waiting.

As the light in the training grounds shortened, only glimmers graced the ground with gold. When he was sure that her vision had been impaired, Tristian pounced forward and swept her legs from her. Kienna stepped sideways at the rush of his movements, but he was too quick—far quicker than Talon. Her toe caught on the side of his shin, and she tripped.

Kienna was quick to claim her balance and protect her back, jumping forward to grab hold of him. Frustrated waves pulsed in her veins when she realized Tristian was smart to remove his shirt. She had nothing to grab onto but the grooves in his body, which were now laced in sweat that only made him slippery. She took hold, her hand grazing his skin before she wrapped her arms fully around him and tried to pull him down swiftly with all her might. His body budged, but he countered and pinned her down to the ground. Kienna's chest heaved in and out, her body aching.

"You're fast," Tristian noted, removing his body from hers. Kienna stayed on the ground, but Ruva urged her to stand.

"I think," she started, rolling to compose herself, "I may have broken something."

"May I look?" he asked, kneeling to her body. Kienna nodded.

Tristian pulled Kienna's shirt up and put his calloused hands over her ribs, pressing along the bones gently. She winced in pain at the visible bruises in the deep tissue, but his prognosis came out clean. Tristian helped Kienna up from the ground, her face scrunching as she moved slowly to her feet.

With all her strength, she stood tall and assumed her commanding position. "You're a great fighter."

"I was born for this," Tristian responded nonchalantly, and then pointed to her position. "You can relax."

Kienna sighed with relief. "Yeah, you're a natural."

"No, I mean, I was truly born to be a soldier. My parents had me training since I could walk."

"I don't think I was born to be a warrior," Kienna admitted shyly. She fumbled her hands around each other. "I just never got the choice."

He studied her, like the thought had been one neither of them had ever considered before. "What would you choose if you did?" Tristian pulled his tunic back over his head and collected his weapons. He resumed his appearance as the High Commander of the Trinity Army.

Kienna thought for a second. "I don't know. A woodcarver, perhaps. Or an artist."

Tristian raised his brow. "You do not love to fight?"

She hesitated to answer. Admittedly, she did love to fight—the rush of grabbing an opponent and finding a way to best them. It's why she stayed late. She was so deeply in love with herself as she moved. But fighting in war meant something different, and she couldn't get Talon's words out of her mind. A flash of heads on the ground haunted her. "I would prefer not to kill."

"How do you expect to fight with us if you're hung up on death?"

Kienna didn't respond. A tightness formed in her chest, spreading into her throat. Her fingers twitched against her leg. The word "kill" echoed again in her mind, reverberating like a struck chord. She hadn't thought that far either, fresh to the scene of battle. She had hoped it wouldn't get that far, and that, perhaps, Vaerin would stop the madness on the field, and no one would get hurt. It was a thought she knew wasn't valid, but the alternative was not one she had been willing to entertain in her mind.

"What about you?" She couldn't help but ask it. "What would you be if you weren't called to fight?"

Tristian grabbed a bag near the barracks and looked back at Kienna. He didn't even have to think long when he said, "I'd be a ranger."

"I don't think that strays away from the battle."

"No," he shrugged, "but like I said. I was born for this. And whether you like it or not, so were you."

Chapter 44

—Kienna—

Kienna rolled her eyes as Broan started into yet another story of the war he'd been fighting. It'd been one week since he got back, and she didn't know if she could stomach yet another boastful account of his journey.

"When I tell you that fucking creature came out of nowhere," he laughed, patting Danek on the back. "I about pissed myself."

"You said it looked like a shaved wolf?" Danek asked, peering over to Ruva.

Vorthakai do not *look like me. Shaved or not.*

You're beautiful, Ruva. Kienna smiled. *I'm going to find Tristian.*

Are you smitten with the High Commander?

Kienna sneered. Of course, she wasn't, but he was clearly the best soldier in this city, and if she wanted to get stronger, he was the one she wanted to train her.

I'm sorry, Ruva laughed. *Maybe it was the Blades Commander.*

Kienna turned to her. *I'm going now. Don't wait up.*

Danek, perhaps?

Kienna scoffed and walked away, back up the bridges to the islands of the Battalions.

"What are you reading?" Kienna approached Tristian at the training grounds.

Soldiers were packing for the day as the sun hit the clouds around them. Tristian glanced up from a book as his back sat against a tree swirling with wind, a cup of dark brown liquid sitting next to him. "Poetry."

This was the island of the Galeweavers. Kienna had finished another grueling training session with the ShardBorn, and Talon had told her the High Commander could be found with the wind mages before she got caught listening to Broan's story. The island itself was exactly as Kienna expected, and the breeze danced along the trees and swayed the grass. Tristian's book pages fluttered every so often.

Kienna sat next to him and peered over at the meticulously written sonnets. She didn't bother to check what it was about. She could easily guess. "Does each island fuel a different form of magic?" she asked.

"Hm? Oh," Tristian closed his book and set it aside. "Yes. We have twelve battalions that have specific magical abilities. There is an island for each of them, and then we have the larger-scale islands that are meant as temples of prayer to the Eternal Mother."

Kienna looked around. She could see the Battalion Islands easily in the clouds. The elemental islands for prayer were beneath the canopy, floating amongst the trees. The whole city was immaculate. She wished she was able to explore it with Connak, but he'd been sent away and barely had time to reach her—which made her lonely in ways she hadn't expected.

Tristian grabbed the cup next to him and sipped on it. The steam curled up with the sharp scent of crushed roots and something bitter. It was like wilted leaves and…was that thyme? Maybe dirt after the rain. It had a kick that stung the nose. Her nostrils twitched. The High Commander watched Kienna with an amused glint in his eyes, the corner of his mouth tugging upward as if he were trying not to laugh. "Care to try some? It's Viral Root."

"What's it for?"

"For drinking." A soft huff of breath escaped him, not quite a laugh, but close enough. "It's a calming root. It helps to ease the mind."

Kienna's brow arched, lips curving. "What does your mind need easing from?"

Tristian took another sip and set his cup on the ground. "Anything I can help you with?"

"I was wondering if you'd be willing to train me again."

"Is Talon not a good enough commander for you?"

"Oh, Talon is great, but I need the best."

Tristian raised a brow. "You flatter me, but I do have commanding officers for a reason. If I trained every soldier that asked, I'd be too busy to lead them."

Kienna tilted her head and glanced down at Tristian's book. Then his tea. "But you're just reading now, so—"

"I imagine I deserve a day off as much as you do."

She exhaled through her mouth and then nodded. It was a silly request anyway. He probably only stayed behind with her the last few times to see what she was made of and determine if he could trust her. That's all this city cared about was determining if she was worth being there after River Storm.

Kienna couldn't blame them. She did technically show up in the city with a mission to reveal its location to King Vaerin. Even if she'd turned from that mission, Baila hadn't. The only solace she had holding onto that secret was that Connak had to perform a specific ritual to unmask the city, one that none of them had seen. It was why King Vaerin could never find it. He didn't know the ritual either. The city of Trinity was safe.

For now.

"Enjoy your tea," she said softly and stood to leave.

Tristian grunted. "Fine. If we're going to do this again, I want to gain something out of it this time."

Kienna shrugged. "I don't know what I could give you."

"River Storm tactics. You know them, right?"

Kienna thought about it. She'd trained with the soldiers at the beginning until the king pushed for magical studies. She was younger then and not sure she retained much of it at the time, but she was certain Danek had. Maybe even Moira. She expressed as much to Tristian, to which he sent a summons for all the Guardians.

Danek, Broan, and even Moira made their way up the bridge, each with varying degrees of reluctance. Broan grumbled the loudest, clearly irritated that he'd have to leave before finishing his meal. But the High Commander couldn't be kept waiting. It was still strange how much weight Tristian's presence carried here. Revered like a king, more than the queen herself. But then again, Trinity seemed to belong to its armies.

"Ooh, I haven't been this high yet." Moira placed her hand to her heart and soaked in the sun, the orange glow forming over her body. "I'll not make that mistake again."

"Listen up," Tristian said, standing and waiting for them to fall in line. Danek, Kienna, and Broan fell in quickly, as they'd been trained for this over the last week. Moira looked around awkwardly and shifted herself to match them, but not without her brows knitting firmly together first. Tristian paced. "River Storm fighting. What do you know about it?"

"That they're fucking pussies," Broan chuckled.

Tristian squinted his eyes, and Danek nudged Broan with his elbow.

Broan cleared his throat. "King Vaerin's general used to tell us that the goal was to simulate some sort of chaos and then withdraw."

"Why?" Tristian asked.

"Could we show you?" Danek asked.

It wasn't the strongest tactic against the High Commander. Kienna knew that, but from Broan's war story across the river, Vaerin had a monster that jumped out at them at the last minute. His feigned retreat tactic was built for that.

Tristian shrugged. "Why not?"

"Keep in mind, this is a simulation," Kienna said. "You know we're here. It didn't make sense to me at first, but Broan's inability to shut up has been useful for once. It's bait. One that you almost have to fall for."

"Ha!" Broan puffed his chest.

Tristian studied them. "Bait, how?"

"Fight us," Kienna said. "Like we're River Storm soldiers. Moira will show you, but don't fight her. She's not here."

Tristian didn't protest. They all dropped into a sparring position and began pushing forward. He didn't take long proving how strong he was, pushing Kienna and Danek down with ease. Broan took some coaxing, but eventually fell as well. The Guardians picked themselves up with grit and pushed back on all fronts. After ten minutes of giving their all, they started to back away and retreat, forcing Tristian to push more energy into following them.

Then Moira blinded him with the sun.

He fell but jumped up swiftly. Of course, he did, but he'd quickly understood what they meant. "He aims to tire out our forces and then retreat to coax us into pursuit?"

Danek nodded. "So he can pick you off with whatever monsters he has, apparently."

Moira curtsied and then raised her hand. "Monster!"

Tristian squinted toward the clouds, absorbing the weight of what he'd seen. Then he nodded once. "Good work. You've done more than your part again." He shifted back to them, and he offered a half-smile to Kienna. "You've earned our trust. And my thanks."

With that, the High Commander retreated down the bridges. Kienna watched him go and then turned back to the Guardians. They stood in silence, faces tilted toward the sky where the clouds were melting in soft hues of orange, rose, and violet. Above them, the moon shimmered faintly. Fireflies began to litter the sky. Over a hundred of them, glittering through the twilight like falling stars with a melody so sweet, it could have only come from Danek's illusions.

Moira giggled, her black hair catching the fading light like the edge of a flame. The fireflies moved with her and then went and tickled Broan's face. He sniffed and swatted them away, grumbling something about the illusions making him look pathetic. But he didn't attempt to leave. For the first time in what felt like years, Kienna was enveloped in a strange warmth. No blood on her boots. No screaming. No heads rolling on the ground. Just…this.

"Come on," Danek said, his voice light with the wind. He reached for her hand.

"Danek…"

"I know," he said, tightening his grip. "Just let go for a bit. Then we can go back to reality."

A wind stirred around them, lifting the fireflies in spirals. The melody swelled, rich and alive, and before she could come up with a reason to stop it, Danek spun her gently through the light. Kienna laughed, and he grinned like he'd been waiting his whole life to hear it. Then he spun Moira, who shrieked with delight. He didn't dare spin Broan, but Broan's boot started tapping anyway.

Danek belonged here on the Galeweaver Island. She could tell in the way that wind responded to his presence, in the way that he didn't tire of swirling music and fireflies around like it was nothing. His smile brightened the entire floating island in the clouds, and by the time Kienna retreated to sit on the ledge and stare out at the stars above them, she found herself noticing that Danek was different here.

He sat down on the ledge by her while Broan and Moira lay behind them by the trees. Broan tossed rocks up and watched the wind swirl them around for fun.

"You alright?" Danek asked.

Kienna looked at him. The wind swept through, catching Danek's hair and pushing it across his sharp features. It was wild and unbothered, like he belonged to the moment. Kienna smiled and then looked down awkwardly. "Yeah, it's a weird feeling...having fun."

"I have a question." Danek paused, looking at his hands. "What's it like having all of your memories?"

Broan and Moira sat up behind them. Their bodies shifted closer.

"It's confusing," Kienna admitted. "I see things that I know are true, but I also see things that King Vaerin wanted me to believe were true. It's like a puzzle. Connak helps me piece it back together."

"Why can't he do that for us?" Moira's voice came softly behind her.

"I don't know," Kienna admitted, looking away toward her hands. She'd never truly thought about it until now that Broan, Moira, and Danek were coasting through the land with broken memories. They'd taken the news that their memories were gone surprisingly well and trusted Connak to show them the truth. The realization that they could never get their true memories back again shifted Kienna's heart back into the pits. "Our minds, mine and Connak's... He told me it wasn't magic. It just was. So, I don't think he can connect with anyone else mentally. That's all I understand about it."

"What's it like having someone in your head?" Moira asked.

Kienna glanced back at her. She was sitting up and closer to her than before. She turned to face them all. "Well, he's not *always* there. If I think enough, though, I could reach out to him, and he'd show up. I'd be able to see him like he was here in front of me."

Broan laughed, tossing another rock into the air. "I'd say you'd lost your fucking mind if the man didn't actually exist."

"What about the wolf?" Danek asked.

"She's different. We exist by our thoughts, but we can't see each other."

Silence fell between them as the glow of the moon shone down. Kienna shifted to look back out at the forest below. The clouds had drifted upward and cleared what was below. Seeing Trinity from above filled her with serenity. Like a city that had never known war. The bridges wove interchangeably like vines and branches. If she hadn't known they were bridges, they would have looked like they belonged as part of the trees. Glowing crystals kept the forest floor lit up as Elvish soldiers, and their families strolled, greeting each other and living out a normal life.

Danek shifted beside her, his leg brushing against hers. It was warm and steady. A flicker of heat rose to her face before she could stop it. It was familiar. Something she'd experienced with Connak. And maybe even Tristian.

Apparently, freedom from River Storm had come with a loosened grip on more than her memories and her magic. Her thoughts were unspooling, fraying at the edges, and wandering into places that once would've made her ashamed.

She didn't dare glance at Danek. She was afraid of what she might see.

And even more afraid of what she might feel.

Chapter 45

—Connak—

Dune's Hollow was sunbaked, half-carved from sandstone, half patched together with desert-worn wood and repurposed relics of war. Its heavy doors were splintered and crooked, rarely closed, and the heat inside was often worse than the furnace-like wind outside.

The walls, a blend of clay and baked mud, sweated in the heat of the evening, a cool breeze finally wafting through as the sun disappeared. Wooden beams groaned above, supporting a ceiling strung with bones, beads, and faded cloth. Cracked windows were covered in gritty mesh, letting in the constant moan of canyon wind.

Sand gathered in the corners like it was part of the decor. Connak sat in the middle of the tavern, hood drawn to hide his features in the evening air.

Patrons filled every inch of the hollow space. Locals with sun-scarred skin and scaled patterns across their arms lounged alongside cloaked travelers. Most bore weapons, though none drew them unless they wanted to end the night face down in the sand. The tavern ran on a tense code of survival: drink, gamble, and watch your back. Barrels served as tables. Some were singed; others split open and patched with crude nails. The chairs were mismatched. Bottles lined the shelves behind the bar, full of spirits that tasted like fire and betrayal. The most popular was Scorchroot Ale, a thick, spiced drink that burned the memory of water right out of the consumer's mouth.

Connak grimaced as the ale sank its way past his throat. He set it down gently, resolved not to take another drink of it as long as he could help it. He scanned the room like a lizard out of place in a forest full of predators.

At the center of the tavern, a sunken ring of polished stone held space for the sand dancers. Barefoot and jeweled, the dancers moved like wind across the dunes. Their feet kicked up trails of glowing dust as one brushed her hand over Connak's shoulder.

Music came from somewhere in the shadows from flutes made of bone and drums that echoed like thunder rolling through rock. It all built a pulse in the walls, in the blood. People didn't come to Dune's Hollow for peace. They came to be part of something dangerous and drink until it stopped mattering.

Behind the bar, an older woman with one good eye kept everything in check. Her name was Marnix, and no one crossed her twice. Her voice could slice through steel, and her eye saw everything. Connak liked Marnix. She was rough around the edges, but they had worked out an agreement long ago that allowed him to scope out the tavern whenever needed. In return, he never reported on any of

Marnix's doings in the pits of the desert. He laughed to himself at the thought, as if Marnix had been doing anything worthy of a Blades' attention.

Then there was her daughter, Tavren. The name still rang in his mind every time he entered Holbeck, wondering if he'd ever see her again. He'd hoped not since the memories of their last encounter ended in a knife fight.

He should have been listening, trying to source anything that could have pointed back to Vaerin's next attack, but he couldn't help his thoughts wandering back to Kienna in Trinity. He closed his eyes and let his mind wander until it touched hers.

"Where did you go?" Kienna asked, though he knew she already knew.

"Holbeck. It's hot, and I need a bath," he said, pulling her mind until he could see her sitting in front of him. She looked startled, gazing around the dust-encrusted room. "You look like you've been beaten pretty badly."

"Shardborn training. I've been doing it for a week, and I'm exhausted."

Connak winced, pointing at the bruises on her arms. "I don't envy you. Talon is a tough commander."

She tried to tug her sleeves to hide them. "These were from Tristian."

Connak stilled, his brow twitching as his jaw set. He didn't speak for a moment. His thumb tapped once against the rim of his cup, the only outward sign of his shift in mood.

"He didn't hurt me on purpose. We were sparring, and I think we got too into it."

"I'd say," Connak scoffed lightly. He skipped a beat, then the tension eased, a crooked smile playing on his lips. "You could spar with me, too, you know."

"You need to be in one place long enough to do that," Kienna said back, peering into Connak's half-filled cup. She leaned down and smelled it. Pulling back, her nose scrunched upward with tears forming in her eyes.

Connak laughed and leaned closer. "What's the report in Trinity, soldier?"

Kienna gleamed, the sudden play of camaraderie and battalion roles putting a place in her heart. "Broan and Danek can't stop boasting about how much fun it is to be here. Moira has taken a role with the herbalists. I think she likes making potions more than fighting."

"That fits Moira perfectly," Connak said.

Kienna bit her lip. "Baila is still missing."

"Missing or joined the other side?" Connak tried not to sound so accusing, but Baila might have been the biggest mistake he made bringing the group into the sacred city.

Kienna shrugged. He wondered if she'd been holding back anything in that moment, sensing the shifting weight of her body around him and the sudden lock in her mind, blocking him from seeing anything regarding Baila. Why was Kienna protecting her? The draft from the cold desert nights splashed in through the windows like a wave. She shivered.

Connak took another sip of his ale as a group of men walked by in soldiers' armor. Each one bore the crest of a serpent and ruby gems.

His eyes flicked up beneath the shadow of his hood. His hand stilled on the rim of his cup. One of the soldiers laughed too loudly. Another had the unmistakable gait of someone trained in River Storm tactics. Connak's grip on the mug tightened slightly and then loosened. He let them pass without a word, but his jaw ticked once, subtle and sharp.

—Kienna—

Kienna stared at Connak as the world began to dull. The tavern's color drained away, and the music started to sound like being underwater. Her pulse skipped. Though she couldn't see or hear anything else in the room aside from the objects still in frame, she knew his mind had wandered elsewhere. A wave of frustration resounded like a drum in her body, the beats building and building. She tried to hold onto the image of him, but it flickered at the edges.

"I think you need to get Tristian," he whispered, though he sounded faint now. His body was moving away from the table they sat at, inching closer to the dust-covered bar. "Tell him we need eight more battalions to go to Dalelry immediately. I'll send my Blades."

Connak left her mind, and Kienna found herself flung back outside on the cool, mossy forest floor. Her breath hitched. For a split second, the world spun. Colors came in too brightly, sounds too sharply. Dirt clung to her skin as if it were trying to anchor her. Her hands dug into the moss as her senses reoriented, her heartbeat racing like it was still inside the tavern. She blinked hard. Beside her, Ruva let out a soft whine and nudged Kienna's shoulder with her snout, the wolf's eyes wide and alert.

She couldn't tell what had happened, nor what Connak's cryptic message meant, only that she now held a sudden urgency that had bled into her from his mind.

Chapter 46

—Kienna—

Kienna regretted her decision to find the queen first from the moment she walked in. Elira had been groveling near the water—or she could have been praying—but she looked to be distraught as she mumbled to herself, "So many mistakes." Kienna wondered what mistakes she was talking about, but she didn't have time to mull it over. Connak sounded pressed for time when he had pulled away.

The queen's icy eyes pierced through Kienna's soul, stopping her dead in her tracks. "I'm so sorry," she whispered. "It's urgent."

"What could be so urgent that you would overstep your normal chains of command?" She looked behind Kienna and tsked. "Where are my guards?"

Kienna's breath shook as she answered, "They let me through. I have news from Connak."

Elira stood, smoothing out the grooves of her dress and brushing specks of dust from her hem. Her composure bounced back so quickly, the air shifting beneath her feet. "Have you summoned the High Commander?" Elira eyed her coldly.

"Danek went to get him."

"Well then." Elira sighed, taking a seat on one of the thick, throne-like roots, its back carved with the sigil of her clan, the great leafed crest of Belok. Around the hall, the other council seats bore the distinct markings of their bloodlines, glinting faintly in the cool, colored light from the pool. "We shall wait for them."

Not long afterwards, Tristian and Danek appeared, weary-eyed and half-dressed. Tristian rubbed a hand down his face, grumbling under his breath, but straightened immediately when his eyes fell on his queen. He took his place at her side with crisp formality, and all traces of fatigue vanished behind the mantle of command.

Danek, slower in motion but no less respectfully, steadily mirrored the stance beside Kienna, a beat behind Tristian. His chest rose and fell with effort, but his eyes remained fixed and serious, standing as Kienna imagined a warrior should.

"I assume we have good reason to be woken from our beds," Tristian said.

"Yes." Elira stood. "Please share your urgent news."

Kienna's hands began to sweat. "Connak said he needs eight battalions at Dalelry. I don't know what that means."

Tristian's face grew grim. It was as if the reaper himself had visited him.

Elira inhaled and nodded slowly to her soldier. "Can you get eight ready this quickly?"

"The Blades are already activated by Connak, I imagine. If you give the word, I'll sound the alarm and have the rest ready before dawn."

"Yes," Elira responded, sure. "I will prepare to ride as well."

"As you wish." Tristian bowed. He turned his head quickly to Danek and Kienna. "We ride in an hour. Get your armor and meet at the battle grounds."

—Danek—

Eight battalions stumbled out of their homes throughout the forest, scurrying at the ringing of an enchanted alarm. Deep within the heartwood of Trinity, ancient tree spirits awakened and released an urgent vibration that echoed through the roots, resonated in the air, and stirred the leaves like a warning carried by the wind. Glowing spores arose from moss-laden trunks, casting amber light into the canopy as the alarm rippled across the land. Soldiers burst from barracks and homes, half-armored and gripping weapons and packs with practiced urgency. They knew what the alarm meant. This was not a drill, and the entire forest held its breath.

Along the outer homes, a few villagers stood silently, some clutching shawls or pressing fingers to lips. There were no cries or pleas, only solemn nods and murmurs to the trees. They had sent sons and daughters to war before. They knew the cost. The people of Trinity were born for this. Their society, steeped in governance and battle tradition, moved like clockwork. Within moments, ranks were forming, gear was handed off, and horses were led from the stables. The pulse of war had begun to beat in their chests again.

Horses whinnied loudly at the ruckus of two thousand men gearing up with armor, equipment, and supplies. The scent of sharpened steel and sweat filled the forest air. Shouts rang through the trees. Despite their speed, everything slowed, like the final moments before a storm broke. Talon put Danek and Kienna on supply retrieval for the battalion. They scavenged water and loaves of bread, fruits, and dried meats to satisfy their soldiers. They stumbled through village homes, asking humbly for donations and made it back in time to ride out.

Frazzled, covered in sweat, and exhausted, they mounted their horses and waved back to Moira. Danek was surprised that she managed to talk her way out of battle. She was a fierce warrior with strong connections to the sun, always among the first to step forward. It was odd not to see her saddled beside them, but something in the way she stood with her hand resting near her stomach, eyes soft and distant, gave Danek pause. He said nothing, but he had to wonder. Maybe it was intuition, or he was imagining things, but something unspoken passed between her and Tislin earlier that morning. He filed it away quietly. Considering they had been heading for another desert establishment, he figured she would do well there magically. He mentioned it to Kienna while weaving through trees, but her mind had been elsewhere.

The journey to Dalelry took five tense days. The battalions rode swiftly, weaving through forest paths with the ease of generations. Danek and Kienna struggled to match their pace, kept steady only by Ruva, who flanked them loyally.

By the second day, the trees had thinned. The soft soil gave way to stone as they approached the mountain range. Soldiers dismounted their horses when the path grew too thin to herd them through the passageway. Tension hung in the air. Every step echoed with the weight of what lay ahead.

When the trail opened to the sky, Danek caught his breath and looked out. The view was breathtaking with its jagged peaks, endless sky, and rivers threading the land like silver veins. It might have felt like freedom, if not for the land of smoke and shadow on the distant horizon.

"That is Fire Storm," Talon told him and Kienna. "Don't ever find yourself over there or you'll be deeply sorry."

Danek didn't ask questions. No one did. But the name clung to him. Fire Storm. It sounded like a myth, yet the land before him pulsed with something that chilled him. A place where the sun died on approach. Even from afar, the mountains looked sharp and unnatural, as though carved by something angry. Whispers from the soldiers about Shades murmured around them. They echoed stories of shadow-born creatures who could siphon life from a man and leave behind only a shell of memory, bound to serve in the dark ranks of a cursed army. Soldiers muttered that their eyes glowed beneath cloaks of smoke, and that no one who crossed into Fire Storm ever returned whole. Danek didn't know what was true, but the unease crawling across his skin told him enough.

Crossing the river should have slowed them, but Broan, the battalion's boastful mage, conjured a shimmering path, bridging the currents long enough for the soldiers to pass. He collapsed afterward with pride bruised but intact. The real trial was the desert. The forest prepared none of them for it. Heat bore down like a punishment, turning breath to fire. Skin blistered. Throats cracked. Morale withered. They took to traveling at night, a line of motion beneath the stars. The desert wind stung their cheeks and offered no relief. Just resistance. Rest was brief, and tasks were repeated with tired precision. Danek and Kienna, along with younger recruits, were assigned to camp duty. There was no time to reflect nor space for emotion—just movement, one task to the next. It was survival by rhythm.

On the final night, they crested a ridge. Below them, Dalelry revealed itself. The desert city grew from the stone, lit by torchlight and surrounded by life-sustaining wells. There were no walls, only faith in the canyons to defend them. Tents already lined the base of the ridge, neat as blade rows. The forward battalions moved like shadows, quietly and focused. At the heart of it all, the command tent arose, its banner catching the breeze. The queen was present.

Somewhere in the distance, a hawk cried, alongside a falcon. Danek took it all in with dry, burning eyes. The campfires flickered, casting dancing shadows on the craggy rocks. The breeze cooled his sun-drenched skin, but it brought little relief. Even Kienna's lips were cracked from dehydration, and Danek's muscles screamed from exertion.

Danek turned toward Kienna, sensing the weight of her silence. "How are you feeling?"

Kienna's voice came out raspy, her tone brittle from the heat and fatigue. "Tired," she muttered. Ruva whimpered beside her, tongue lolling in thirst.

"I mean about facing war," Danek said, motioning to the site of strategically placed tents outside of the small city.

Kienna hesitated, her and Danek trailing behind. She wavered, falling onto the woven mane of her horse. "Still tired."

Danek watched the way her shoulders stiffened with each breath. Gently, he reached across the narrow gap between their horses and placed his hand over hers. She flinched but didn't pull away. Her fingers remained tense beneath his palm, but something in her posture softened.

"You know," he started again. "I think about the people of River

Storm, too, sometimes."

Kienna jerked her head to him in surprise, her hands gripping tightly to the reins again. "You were popular there," she said.

"Yeah," Danek sighed. It was a popularity he didn't care much for, but it had its uses from time to time. "More than you. But you had family there."

"Just Maren and Jacob." Kienna glanced away from Danek to the side.

He tightened his grip on her hand, hoping to pull her back to his gaze. "Jacob is a good man. He's not someone I would like to meet out here either."

"It's funny," Kienna choked. "We spent our whole lives training for something none of us thought would come, and now we're on the other side of it."

"So, you're still pretty conflicted?"

"I saw it clear as day. He killed my parents and took me from them. There was no wreckage. No rescue missions. Just pure evil. Still, how do you turn off fifteen years of loyalty beaten into you?"

Danek's arm twitched toward her again, but he stopped himself. He didn't want to overstep. Instead, he looked at his reins, trying to find the words. He wanted to understand why she carried such conflict like armor over her chest. The tension between the girl she was raised to be and the truth of who she was unraveled at her feet. Because for him, this war was not just duty. It was protection. Of the people who had accepted him and the land that had given him purpose. After a childhood of harsh orphanage walls and silent suffering beneath a tyrant, he'd found a family here. One forged in the freedom to choose, to fight for something beautiful. There had been no doubt or fracture in his identity. Only belonging.

"I have your back," he said in the void between them.

Kienna's eyes warmly rested on him. She didn't need to respond. It was the way her eyes sparkled like starlight that kept his heart beating. The way her lips shimmered above her chin, even through the cracks.

He tried to hide it. Tried not to linger on the way her face caught the firelight or how her presence steadied him. But deep down, he knew. Kienna stirred something fierce in him, something that wouldn't be easy to tame.

Chapter 47

—Connak—

Flags for every battalion flew in the night, separated in waves to prepare for which armies would march forward first and with what commands. The Emberreign flags waved with real tempered flames as they bent in the wind. Their job was to control flame and use explosive defense to take out large enemies. The Galeweavers were there and served as Trinity's wind mages. Along with them were the Thornclad and the Shardborn, both battalions known for their brute strength. The Thornclad were earth benders.

Then there were the Duskveil and the Ironbinders. The

Ironbinders forged the protection spells while the Duskveil used illusions. The Sunforged would be worthy in an attack during the day, but there was no telling when the battle would commence, so it was a gamble to choose them over the magic of the moon. The Verdent Battalion would stay behind as the healing mages.

Connak and Tislin entered the camp with stealthy precision. A large group of the Hollow Blades marched in unison behind them. Relief flooded their bodies to find rest as the unforgiving deserts between the Malintale and Dalelry nearly crushed their spirits. The cool night air contrasted with the heat of the brutal sun, and Connak was quick to dismiss his troops for rest and food. Queen Elira had been waiting. She greeted them valiantly as they passed, but her eyes locked on Connak. He was shocked that the queen was with the army, but he didn't imagine she'd actually ride into the battle.

"We need to gather the commanding leaders in the central tent," she said, her voice edged with urgency.

Connak nodded, but he scanned the camp for Kienna. He spotted her with Danek, both carrying water and supplies. She looked irritated but focused, doing grunt work with a tenacity that betrayed her distaste.

Kienna caught his gaze and smiled faintly. "You look thirsty."

"Parched." Connak took the water she offered and drank deeply. Then his eyes feasted on her, and he grinned devilishly.

Elira cleared her throat, clearly annoyed that his attention to the newcomers over his queen took priority. "Five minutes," she said sharply. "Make sure *she* is out of the way."

Her cold eyes lingered on Kienna before she disappeared into the tent.

"Ignore her," Connak muttered, but Kienna was already on her way toward Elira. Connak groaned and followed.

—Kienna—

"Why do you keep me around if I bother you so much?" Kienna demanded as she stepped through the flap. Elira looked up from a map, her face calm but unreadable. Around her, four other battalion leaders were moving pieces across a strategy board.

Tristian entered behind them and raised a brow. "Apologies, I didn't realize this was a council for lower ranks." The commanders saluted him as he passed.

"Well?" Kienna said. "Does my presence bother you that much? Have I somehow offended you by being here?"

Elira's posture remained still as she extended her pale hand, gesturing the commanders out. Her jaw tightened. The commanders exited without question. Only Connak and Tristian remained.

"Perhaps it's your explosive presence. Or your glaring inexperience in war. You're now fighting the man who raised you, and I have every reason to believe you're not ready. I do not trust you."

"Am I not your kin?" Kienna snapped.

"Are you not also his?"

Kienna flinched, her face reddening. "Hardly."

"Not hardly," Elira said coolly. "However, kinship isn't the question today. Loyalty is."

Kienna scoffed. Had she not given them her loyalty? Why weren't they hearing her when she spoke to them? It was like being in River Storm. Couldn't they see that it was their fucking riddles that made her head spin? "Do my words mean nothing to you?"

"No," she said harshly. "Your actions do, and if you can't take simple orders and follow our command, then I'm quite certain you don't fit in here."

Heat rushed across Kienna's body. She left River Storm for *this?* Granted, she didn't pledge her allegiance to the queen. She wasn't sure she could take orders from another ruler who was similar in cold command. She gave her allegiance to Tristian. Her eyes fell to him. "Am I not good enough to be here?"

"Elira," Tristian said softly, holding his hands tightly behind his back. "Connak has vetted her substantially, and he says we're in the clear. She's been helpful, and we need the soldiers."

The queen turned with precision. "And you tell me *you* trust her despite what Vaerin is to her?"

Kienna's eyes narrowed. "What *is* Vaerin to me?"

Connak stepped forward, offering a hand to steady her, but she nudged him off.

Elira dismissed her with a cold glance when Kienna tried to press again on the kinship comment. Without another word, Kienna turned and left the tent, her fists clenched.

Connak followed. Outside, he grabbed her arm gently. "You think she'll still invite us for tea next time, or should we go in with knives out and cut to the chase?"

"Who is Vaerin to me?" Kienna growled. "No more bouncing around with half-truths!"

Connak tensed his body, glancing around him before he steered her away from the open paths and toward the edge of her tent. They sat on a stone ledge tucked behind the canvas walls. The firelight from nearby camps cast flickering shadows across their faces.

A few feet away, Danek and Broan lingered beside a stack of supplies, pretending not to listen but doing a terrible job of it. Ruva lay at Kienna's feet, head resting on her paws, silver eyes alert.

Connak drew a breath. "You obviously already know your

mother, Avenna, was human. When she married Galric, they broke a lot of rules to do it. Our ancient, royal lines have been purebred Elvish lineage since the beginning, but your father didn't care. He loved her enough to break the law. He took her to the Eternal Mother and gave her a portion of its magic."

Broan's head jerked. "Those floating islands in the forest?"

"Just one at the time," Connak replied, eyes not leaving Kienna. "From their love came a different kind of magic. The islands of elemental power rose from it. You were born tied to *that* power."

Kienna blinked, heart thudding. "How does that matter regarding Vaerin?"

"Avenna had a brother," Connak continued, and Kienna's throat closed. "They were close, but when he saw the magic in her hands, and then sensed it growing in her womb, it changed him."

Danek pushed some materials aside and took a seat next to them. "Always a man ruined by what he can't have."

Connak nodded. "He was sick back then. Had some sort of disease that they couldn't cure. No one would help him, but Avenna was desperate. She gave him her magic to heal him. *He* took too much, and he drained her. It should have killed her."

Ruva let out a whine. It was like a ripple in Kienna's chest. Her body tensed. "What happened?"

"She survived only because of the child she carried. Because of you. The magic flowed back through the bond. She realized he was already too far gone into madness, and she cast him out of her life."

Kienna's throat was too tight to speak. What he was alluding to put her mind into disarray. No wonder they didn't trust her. She couldn't even begin to fathom the rest.

Connak looked at the fire, then back. "He disappeared and returned months later with an army. With dark magic. Twisted things followed him. Like creatures he pulled from a nightmare. He burned the realm. Took children—any child with magic."

Broan stepped forward. "You mean us. What for?"

"To study you. To replicate what Kienna's mother did. So he could tear open the Eternal Mother himself. I don't know. But he left us all fractured afterwards."

Kienna choked back a breath. "He's my uncle, then?"

The fire cracked. Ruva nudged her hand. In her mind, Kienna heard the beat of reassurance. *You are not him.*

But the shadow of his blood still ran in her veins, and her body went cold.

Connak looked at her carefully. "This is why Elira watches you. She's waiting for you to choose who you want to be."

Kienna swallowed hard. Her voice barely rose above a whisper. "I need air."

With that, she stood and walked into the dark.

Chapter 48

—Connak—

Connak left the others to sit in the new revelation of Kienna's kinship. It wasn't the right place to share news like that, especially when they were about to rush into a battle against Vaerin's army. They preferred their soldiers to be sharp with as few distractions as possible. But Elira insisted on coming to battle, and her vendetta against Kienna went further than her existence stemming from Vaerin. Her vendetta came from the reminder of her son, and she put their entire army at risk going after Kienna like that.

He found Tristian exiting the battle tent, lips pressed tightly. He started for the camp when Connak caught up to him. "She knows."

The High Commander studied him before realizing what he meant. "How'd she take it?"

"Honestly, not too well."

Tristian turned his head to look back at the tents. "Can she fight?"

Connak shrugged. "I hope so."

Tristian let out a measured breath. "For someone who can link to her mind, you're not being useful. What does her mind say, Connak? Because from my perspective, her heart is telling me she can't."

"We don't have time to find out. What's the charge from Elira?"

"She's a good figurehead," Tristian said lowly, glancing at Connak through the side of his eye. "But let's not pretend the charge is coming from her."

Connak smiled. The cold wind kicked sand into the air, and they both guarded their faces for a moment to avoid the sting of grain in their eyes. The Elvish did not belong in the desert with open land and nothing to protect their skin from the blazing sun. But Connak loved the instability, the sudden change of extremes to keep him on his toes.

He turned back to Tristian when the dust settled. His armor was covered in red soot. Tislin moved behind them, walking swiftly. Connak knew Tislin was trying to escape them, anything to avoid another confrontation with his brother. He wished they'd gotten along. They were going to need each other in their journey, and it would have been easier if they weren't trying to dance around their hurt pride.

Tristian reached back without looking and grabbed him by the arm. Tislin slumped forward and joined them as Tristian said, "Dalelry hasn't fallen fully, but they've been under siege for days. The outer rings are overrun. Connak, you know the desert better than any of us. What is your assessment?"

Connak's shoulders tensed. Dalelry was a weak city full of common desert folk, never prepared to have to fight anything but sandwraiths. Those were easier than a full army invading their homes. "They won't hold much longer, and I'm guessing the king's army already knows we're here. We'll need to go in now, and I mean right *now*, or the whole city will burn."

"Are your Blades in position to move first?"

Connak nodded, lowering his voice as a wave of soldiers passed by them. "Already in position. I had Tislin scouting before he walked by."

Tristian and Tislin shared a glance, like Tristian wanted to ask but wasn't sure if his brother would combat his efforts or answer in his vague responses. He straightened. "Do we have a shot in there?"

"If we strike with force," Tislin said, matter-of-factly.

"You're sure?"

"Yes, High Commander, I am. Send the Ironbinders first to cloak the flank. The Duskveil can scatter the rear lines, and the Emberreign can burn the path between the soldiers. Give it to the rest to hold. That's my assessment."

It couldn't have been a better assessment if Connak had given it himself. He'd spent years in the forest with Tislin, teaching him battle strategy. Admittedly, he was learning them himself, too, fresh to the scene of command. There were days Tislin might have known more than him, coming from a military family and having Tristian as his brother.

"Prepare your troops. I'll alert the others." Tristian turned to Connak. "Fight hard, Commander. I expect to see you alive when this is all done."

Connak saluted until Tristian dismissed him. He pulled Tislin with him. He didn't need to prepare any troops. They were already prepared and in position, scoping the city in the shadows. Disappointed that Kienna hadn't returned, he went to let Danek and Broan know. He wanted to reach out to her, to see how she was coping, but he had an entire camp of soldiers to help ready, so he shared the news with Danek and left Kienna alone to sort through this on her own.

Chapter 49

—Kienna—

Kienna's hands trembled through each breath as she paced back and forth near the rocky formations. Ever since Maren pushed her to find the people who could help her, she'd been playing different scenarios in her head of what she would learn. Nothing could have prepared her for the wrenching gut punch of sharing blood with both sides of the war.

Though it eased her own turmoil of being conflicted, in some ways it still managed to irritate an old wound that festered until it became infected. Kienna itched at her skin, twitching her head back and forth to fight off mental notes from Ruva, especially once her dungeon song started to return.

The wolf loyally sat at the base of the rocks, whimpering through Kienna's anguish. She started growling when the whimpers didn't work, and the song came back until she eventually thrust her way into Kienna's presence.

What about this is hurting you most? Ruva asked.

Kienna grunted a half-hearted attempt to pretend she hadn't been pacing and fighting off yet another attack of panic in her mind. Ruva growled again, so Kienna caved. *They keep talking about me choosing who I'm supposed to be. Not that I'm changing my mind, but if they can't give me all the information, how do they expect me to trust them either?*

I understand, Little Flame, Ruva murmured. She pancaked her body across the ground, grazing her fur through the desert brush as she inched closer to Kienna. She strategically placed her back underneath Kienna's trembling hands. *How can I help?*

"What do I do if I have to fight him?" Kienna asked out loud, lip quivering with the breeze of the night.

We pray you do not have to.

Kienna buried her face into Ruva's neck, taking in the warmth of her body as they synchronized their breaths. She was grateful for her wolf, knowing that she had someone no one else had. Ruva heard Kienna's every thought without a filter. And yet she stayed.

Ruva convinced Kienna to go back to the camp, if for nothing except the rest she needed. When they neared the tents, soldiers were already strapping horses and sheathing weapons. Clangs of metal and restless horses echoed in the night while beast and man grappled with the upcoming duties given by their commanders.

"What's going on?" Kienna turned to Danek.

He had placed his armored tunic back on, and his horse was saddled and steadied for another journey. He looked at Kienna, relieved. "I've already got your horse. Connak has instructed us to be ready for battle immediately."

"We're not even going to wait until morning?" Kienna groaned. Her neck stiffened, hand searching for Ruva to ground her once again.

Danek shrugged. "Orders changed."

"What's the charge?" Kienna asked as she reached for her armor. She yanked her dirty tunic over her head, unbothered by Danek's presence. The thin linen shift clung to her ribs, sweat-soaked and wrinkled, but it would do. Danek blushed next to her and turned his head as she pulled on the scaled armor.

You torture the boy, Ruva said.

I don't mean to.

I don't believe you.

Kienna grabbed her horse by the reins, stepping into the stirrups and flinging her body over the great beast.

"We're the last wave. So, we wait outside the city until Talon gives charge, and then we help clear the streets once our magic-born battalions run low on energy."

Kienna's heart raced heavily in her chest. Her eyes frantically scanned the Elvish men and women around her, racing to armor up and grab whatever supplies they deemed necessary for the battle. Her fingers trembled as they ran over the sword sheathed behind her back and then to her dagger. She pulled it out, holding it tightly. As she adjusted her grip, the knife slipped from her hand and clattered to the dirt. The sound cracked through her nerves. She cursed under her breath, dismounted, and snatched it up, pulse racing faster than before. Talon had urged her to grab something more formidable, but she only pushed back. Her dagger gave her room to be fast. He'd said being too close to an enemy would be as much of a liability. All she could do was smirk because Talon hadn't seen her with a blade yet, so now it was something she had to prove.

In formation, waves of armies crept forward in hushed precision. Kienna reached her mind out, hoping to meet Connak's, but she was met with deafening silence. He was leading his own battalion now, likely deep in formation, unreachable in the thick press of duty. She gulped, the absence a hollow echo in her chest.

I imagine, she said to Ruva, *that if I asked you to stay behind for safekeeping—*

I would have to consider disowning you, Ruva panted.

Kienna nodded, furrowing her brow. "Is this it?" she laughed nervously.

"I can't tell if Broan was lucky to go in an earlier wave," Danek replied. "Spirits be with him."

Kienna chewed her lip.

Tristian rode his valiant horse through the last wave. He and Talon convened in whispers for a few moments, and then he took to riding through the rows of soldiers, barking orders that were responded to with deep respect by the men ready to fight.

"You sure you wouldn't be better off staying behind?" Tristian asked Kienna.

"You said I could fight," Kienna said back wearily.

"Will you? Fight against your uncle's army? He is your family now, too." Tristian steadied his horse.

Kienna looked out at the people around her. A surge of fear coursed through her as she fought the constant haze of confusion whenever she tried to tap into anything other than her own brute force. She sighed, an approving nudge from Ruva pushing her forward.

Her body straightened. "Those people worshipped me. Maybe not the nobles or the soldiers who knew the truth..." Her mind wandered to Jacob. She pleaded desperately for him to be stationed somewhere else and to never meet him in the light of day. "I learned that a man who broke and controlled me my entire life took me so he could do just that. Then he wrapped that control in a gift box and handed it to me under the guise of love. And he did love me, in his own way. I would be lying if I said I didn't struggle with all this, but you have my word. I will help."

"This is life and death, Kienna. People are going to die." He said it as a reminder of the reality that lay before them.

"I understand. I gave my allegiance to *you*, High Commander. Please take it."

Tristian locked his attention onto hers as if he was studying her soul, and Kienna had nothing else to lose, so she let him have it. She dropped her guard and held every bit of sincerity on her face as she could. She wanted him to trust her, to let her prove that she chose against Vaerin, and she still meant it.

Danek cleared his throat.

Kienna didn't move. She locked her stare with Tristian's, both silent and watching each other. Then a warmth passed between them like sunlight in the cold. It bloomed at the base of her spine, curling up through her neck. The space between their chests pulsed with a soft glow. Kienna didn't know what it meant. Her mouth parted slightly, breath catching.

Danek cleared his throat again, louder this time.

Tristian's jaw twitched, and Kienna blinked, pulling her horse back a step. The glow faded. He forced a cough and puffed his chest, tightening his grip around the reins of his horse. "Stay with this battalion. Be prepared for an ambush while you wait. Sound the horn if you see anything suspicious. At our call, you will ride with Talon through the city."

He rode quickly, storming into battle with the third wave of his army. Magic streams soared through Dalelry, puffs of smoke and light swirling into the sky to meet the stars. Kienna watched, entranced for a moment, as each battalion's magic revealed itself like an artist's signature across the canvas of war. Crimson embers trailed the

Emberreign, arcing like fire-dancers across rooftops. The Galeweavers swept through like ghostly mist, their presence barely visible, save for the shimmer of air disturbed in their wake. Duskveil soldiers moved like shadows unhooked from their forms, disappearing into the smoke with blades that sang only when striking. Thornclad sent tremors through the streets, vines bursting from stone and wrapping around enemy lines, while the Skybinders released bursts of light like falling stars from their bows. Somewhere deep in the heart of the chaos, the ground shook briefly but unmistakably. Kienna stiffened.

Broan. He had made it to the city. For a moment, she feared for the stone beneath him as much as the enemy ahead. Each battalion was a force unto itself, and together, they were a storm.

Kienna tightened her grip on her reins. Soon, her wave would follow. She glanced at Danek, his eyes softly watching her.

"I've got your back," he reminded her calmly.

The horn called, and Talon pumped his fist with a battle cry. The Shardborn were called to duty, and they stormed forward to take the city.

Chapter 50

—Broan—

Broan pushed through Dalelry. He didn't have wings, but he felt like he was fucking flying. Creatures came out of nowhere, and his first reaction was to slam his fist into the ground and push them into the air. Then he'd summon the earth to soar through the skies until he could land near another set of enemy soldiers to do the same thing.

The rush in his bones made him feel as close to a god as he could be. King Vaerin never gave him free rein to play like this, and now that he had it, he'd never let it go. He was at war against the king to make sure he never lost it.

"You need to slow down," Connak barked at him.

Fuck Connak. Broan didn't need to slow down. He needed to keep going. The earth spoke to him and told him it would feed him for as long as he needed, so he surged, and he soared into the dastardly beasts that flowed into the rock city.

"I'm serious." Connak found him again, pulling him aside. Broan went to push back, but the Elvish man had strength beyond his frame. "It's fun until you use too much, and the Eternal Mother takes it from you."

"No time for a lecture, Dad. We're at war." Broan tried to push him off.

"It's your funeral, Broan."

Broan hated Connak for stopping him, but he fell in line behind the other earth benders and only used his magic when necessary. He learned, in time, that there was a reason behind the Elvish way of war.

Dalelry's buildings were crumbling into the caverns, some because of Broan's reckless bending. When people started running from their homes, it struck him even harder. No one had a place to hide except those buildings. Now that he slowed down to look, war wasn't as fun anymore. The rocks crashed into the red soil, catching those who were running and trapping them underneath the boulders. He ran to the rocks, pushing upward to pull them away, but he tumbled backwards when the crushed face of an old man stared back at him. It would have been enough to keep him from using magic ever again if he didn't need to slam a rock into the head of a foul beast, running on all fours like a shaved wolf that had been in the water too long.

It crumbled at his feet, bones crunching from the impact. Broan wished he hadn't seen it or the old man. The last battle out in the open riverside was more noble, pushing soldiers back and taking them cleanly. No one else had to die. Certainly not old men who just wanted to get away.

Desert flies were already beginning to swarm the old man's eye, his blood pooling into the red rocks. Broan tightened his fist and grabbed the hilt of his weapon. Connak was right. He mocked him silently for a moment before sending a prayer to his *Eternal Mother* to save the souls underneath the rocks, and he went back to work.

He motioned to move again, slamming a soldier out of his way with only his strength. Then a child ran past him, crying and screaming for their mother. What the fuck was happening? Why were the children out here? Why didn't the city move everyone out? And why did King Vaerin allow his army to kill such innocent people? The thoughts sickened him, and he wavered. War wasn't fun. War was brutal.

"Ah, fuck," Broan said and ran after the child. He grabbed him quickly and sprinted away from the fire. The child grabbed onto Broan's tunic and dug his face into his large shoulders. "If you tell anyone I went soft, I swear..."

He didn't know why he was threatening this child who was scared and still screaming, but Broan was scared, too. Scared for the child and the innocent people who got caught in this war for magic, and all they wanted to do was survive. He understood now why it had to be protected. Not for kings. Not for soldiers. But for the ones screaming in the streets.

Broan ran as far back as he could until he found another soldier in the background. Tristian sat astride his horse, having finished off another set of monsters. He had the clearest path and the fastest route away. Broan's eyes went wild. "Take this fucking kid," he barked, not caring how it sounded—not even to the Elvish High Commander. Tristian didn't flinch. He hauled the boy up and kicked into motion.

When Broan turned back to fight, he nearly tripped over the bodies strewn across the ground. Blood soaked the soil, a deep mahogany reeking of iron, thick enough to choke on. His stomach turned. They'd only begun, and already, he'd seen too much death.

He ran back to his battalion, rocks shaking beneath his feet. The city trembled and cracked at the seams. It had never been meant to withstand this kind of magic. Another creature jumped onto Broan and knocked him down into another pile of bodies. River Storm soldiers. Human. Broan knew one of them. It was that fucking kid from the actor's troupe…Akin.

His stomach clenched. He turned his head and vomited.

Tislin crouched beside Broan, his bow already loaded for an attack. Where the fuck did he even come from? It didn't matter. He turned and shot his arrow straight into another creature's head and shielded Broan from the splatter of blood. "You knew him?" he asked, eyes flicking to the pile of soldiers.

Broan couldn't speak.

Tislin didn't press. "Stand up. There's more coming."

Broan wiped his face from the splatter that passed through, the blood smearing across his hair. He would be no war hero tonight, but he would at least not let the opposition make him vomit again.

Chapter 51

–Kienna–

The Shardborn charged the city, jumping in to relieve their magical counterparts for rest. Talon and his seasoned soldiers were quick to clear the waves of the city out, pushing the opposition backward as much as they could with as little destruction as possible.

Since the city rested between small canyons, the soldiers found themselves finding different opportunities for high ground attacks, but getting the men from Vaerin's army to retreat proved far more difficult. Dalelry was a maze to them, something they didn't anticipate. Kienna could see Elvish men scaling walls to find new positions and locations to fight. She, on the other hand, weaved between buildings on her horse, so out of her element as she tried to hold on for dear life.

Relief poured through her when Danek admitted he couldn't see as well running on the horse, and he hadn't even managed to hit anyone. Horse training never happened in River Storm. Vaerin had them try once but decided they'd be more effective on the ground. They weaved into the shadows of abandoned buildings and dismounted, much to Ruva's relief to have Kienna next to her.

After safely tying up the horses, Danek tiptoed forward to scout the alleyway they found themselves in. "I think we're clear." He motioned for them to follow.

Kienna and Ruva took cautious steps out, but their sense of safety was disrupted by a screeching sound reverberating through the walls like a high-pitched siren that pinched the mind in numerous places.

Out of the shadows, a beast dropped from the wall like a dead weight and hit the ground on all fours. Kienna looked twice to make sure she hadn't envisioned it. She got her answer when Danek's stance lowered, and he pulled his weapon. The beast's skin was dark, muted gray, and its eyes were sickly yellow. Its hair was patched, falling in random, long strands that peeled back in the wind. Its jaw hung open, breath gurgling. Its head twitched as it inched closer. Its stench was like something long dead and dragged from the swamp.

"What the hell is that thing?" Danek asked, backing up quickly to Kienna's side.

Ruva bared her teeth, foam sliding from her jaws as she dipped her head to the beast in front of her. *I saw those things when Vaerin had me in chains,* the wolf growled through Kienna. *They aren't natural.*

"You mean Vaerin *did* create those things?" Kienna asked in shock, the beast contorting its body closer to them.

Kienna unsheathed her dagger. The creature circled them,

shifting from wall to wall with a sickening ease, like the shadows were throwing it forward and feeding it raw energy. Then it lunged. Kienna barely had time to react. Ruva slammed into it mid-air, jaws locking onto its throat. The beast snarled and whipped its body, flinging Ruva aside like dead weight.

"No," Kienna called, her mind surging and searching for Ruva's voice.

Eyes forward!

Kienna's heart unclenched.

Unfazed, the creature pushed its body into Kienna. Her back hit the clay buildings as burnt umber fell over her. The dust swirled into a haze, leeching into her pores and shrouding her ability to see where the enemy now stood. If it hadn't been for her training with Talon on using her other senses, she knew it would have taken her out by now.

By sheer instinct, she rolled her body away from the cracked walls in time to hear the creature slam into where she had been sitting. Her heart was a war drum against her chest as she scrambled to her feet and found Danek. The horses whinnied in panic, still tied up behind the building they destroyed.

"I don't know what to do here," Danek admitted. "I don't think anything we learned covered this."

"I don't think anything could have," Kienna panted, eyes on the falling clay around them.

Ears open, Ruva scolded.

The beast appeared from the shadows, lunging quickly for them. Kienna winced, bracing her body for another blow, but it never came. A sharp whistle sliced through the alley, and a spear tore through the beast's chest with brutal precision. It staggered, panting, then crumpled to the ground with a flood of blood pouring from it into the dirt. The panting slowed until it took a final breath and died.

"It's a shame," came a voice from above. Kienna spun toward it. Baila stood atop a crumbling wall, lowering her outstretched arm, casually twirling another spear in her hand. Kienna followed her voice, suddenly remembering when she showed up in the Malintale Forest, calculating even then. "Vorthakai have their uses. Deadly things they are, but terribly hard to train."

"Baila, thank the spirits," Danek cried. "Where have you been?"

"Vaerin would have been beside himself if we let this thing kill you," Baila continued, hopping down from the wall. She wore a tunic of dark, murky green as if the shadows had decayed her connection to life. Her eyes dimmed to match. "He is *pissed* with you, Kienna."

"You went back to Vaerin," Kienna stated. "I knew it."

"Oh, come now, *cousin*," Baila sneered, a sly smirk crossing over her face. "I could sense your turn from a mile away. I wouldn't have lasted in that damn city."

Danek shifted his eyes over his shoulder at Kienna, though he kept still and continued to hold Baila in his periphery. "What's she talking about?"

Kienna's body grew tense, her shoulders pinching into her neck as she locked her jaw and squeezed her hands into the dagger.

"I could never understand why my father loved you so much more than me," Baila pranced around them, kneeling to remove the spear from the dead Vorthakai. "When I learned you were his niece, it made a lot more sense. Especially since you, of course, came from some royal lineage in the forest and I, a bastard daughter, from some weird experiment."

"I must be missing something," Danek replied, darting his eyes between the two.

"Thank god," Baila stood, raising her hands to the sky, "that he didn't continue to reproduce. He'd have a whole army of angry children."

Kienna glared at Baila. "So, you're destroying innocent cities now to prove a point?"

"I've told you plenty of times why his side is the one worth picking. The fact that you can't see that is why you're going to lose."

"I don't think so," Kienna retorted. The tension snapped like a drawn bowstring. Kienna threw herself forward into Baila's footing, leaping over the fallen Vorthakai. Her boots barely cleared the beast's mottled flesh as she lunged, catching Baila off balance. Kienna grabbed hold of Baila's leather, sticking her foot behind her cousin's knee and dragging her to the narrow alley's dusty ground.

They tumbled hard, too hard, and rolled down another cramped alley branching off the main passage. The sandstone walls closed in, carved unevenly from red clay that scraped their skin raw as they slammed against it. Their scuffle became a chaotic, elbow-bruising fight for dominance.

The darkness thickened in this part of the city, broken only by a sliver of moonlight spilling between the jagged rooftops overhead. Dust clouded the air, stirred from the ground by their struggle. Loose stones scattered underfoot, crunching and skidding with every shift. Kienna clawed for leverage, her fingers digging into the gritty floor until her nails bent back. Baila twisted beneath her, her elbow driving into Kienna's ribs with a sickening thud, then shoved her hard into the wall. The impact cracked her shoulder against the rock, jolting stars into her vision. Baila was quick to swing herself over Kienna. Somewhere behind them, Danek's voice echoed, but he'd lost line of sight. The tight bend in the alley, the sudden drop. They'd vanished into the stone maze. He couldn't risk a shot of magic to save her.

Baila snarled and yanked her hand toward the ground, channeling her energy into the desert floor. The sand trembled, then erupted. Sharp cacti speared up around them like a trap sprung from the earth. Thorns tore through Kienna's pants and scraped her skin in a dozen places. She cried out, hot blood mixing with dust, the sting searing as her arms flailed for space between the brambles. She wailed out in pain from the tiny pricks hitting her face.

When it seemed like Baila might win, Danek appeared and

pushed his magic into her, knocking her off Kienna with a surge of wind. As the power left his palm, a blue warmth shimmered in the air, like sunlight through stained glass. It flared briefly before dissolving into the shadows. The scent of charred sage lingered in its wake.

Her body lay motionless.

"Leave her," Danek demanded, blasting another pulse of magic into Kienna's legs. His movements were sharp, almost punishing, as they were driven more by adrenaline than care. The blue light flickered from his fingertips, but it rippled with heat, his frustration bleeding into the spell. His jaw locked as he pressed his palm over her wound. Light seared through fabric and skin, stitching flesh with raw, unrelenting force.

"You knew?" he asked under his breath, not quite looking at her. The scent of charred sage thickened. "You knew she was on Vaerin's side."

Kienna hissed but didn't pull away. The pain wasn't magical; it was personal. His touch was no longer soft. The magic closed the wounds, but the silence between them didn't. "Don't do that again," Kienna warned.

They were warned time and time again not to use magic in the Shardborn. To safely secure the battle, the strongest fighters needed to hold their energy, and magic would cost them too much. It was apparent in the way Danek's shoulders dropped, and his eyes blinked slowly. Even so, the law did feel outdated. If the Eternal Mother were to give it, why were there no exceptions in these cases?

"We'll talk about all this later." He scowled. "We've wasted enough time in the shadows."

Ruva growled in agreement.

Danek and Kienna scaled the wall, emerging onto a ledge that gave them a sweeping view of the battlefield below.

The city of Dalelry stretched before them like a ripping tapestry built into the bones of the desert itself. Clay and stone buildings jutted from the canyon walls with soft edges shaped by time. Narrow alleys cut through the city like veins, flanked by desert brush and crumbling sandstone. Most of it was in ruins.

Smoke poured through the alleyways, rising in black columns toward a sky blotted with ash. Chunks of rock had torn loose from the upper ridges, collapsing into homes, pinning the unlucky beneath. People ran where they once strolled. Screams echoed between the walls. Children clung to each other, darting between shattered stalls. Soldiers from both sides clashed in the narrow paths, blades crashing against armor too close to swing clean.

Below, the Shardborn surged forward, taking full control. The earlier waves were receding, their magic dimming with wisps of color and smoke barely trailing in the sky. Where flares of power had once lit the rooftops, only smoldering glows remained. The sound of steel on stone echoed in distant bursts.

It's horrifying, Kienna told Ruva.

They need help, she whimpered.

Danek motioned to jump over and join the wave. Kienna took one final glance behind her. The dead Vorthakai remained sprawled across the dirt, and Baila was gone, leaving nothing but the shifting darkness of the alley. Her shadow slipped silently into the maze of cracks and stone, vanishing without a trace.

—Danek—

Danek hated brooding. It was unbecoming, but anger and sweat stained his tunic. He couldn't tell if it was because Baila lied to everyone or if it was because *Kienna* lied to everyone that made him worse for wear, but when they finally reached their wave of soldiers, he rejuvenated his energy enough to slam a weapon down into the armor of an enemy soldier.

He knew he didn't kill the man, but he did enough damage to force him out of play on the battlefield. Kienna glanced at him from the side with one brow furrowed and mouth agape, as if words sat at the tip of her lips but refused to come out. They approached a much heavier wave of soldiers pushing through the Elvish line. Danek could hear Kienna's breath rising. As a soldier rushed toward her from behind, Danek kicked him backwards.

"I still have your back," he whispered, but his lips pulled inward and held tightly together with tension. This only made his frustrations grow because no matter how angry she made him, Kienna would always consume him enough to throw everything on the line for her.

Kienna lunged at a soldier waving a sword in their direction, disabling his arm as he swung. She pushed him with force out of their line of sight, moving toward the next one. She moved with precision and speed that nearly matched the Elvish soldiers. Danek would have been impressed if he had time to think about it.

The battalion continued to push for what felt like hours. Soldiers from both sides fell, their screams lingering long after they had taken their last breath. Bodies piled on top of each other, burnt flesh reeking through the air. Some still twitched while others were charred beyond recognition.

Armor cracked beneath boots. Hands reached from beneath rubble, fingers curling toward nothing. A horse lay split open in the road, steam rising from its belly. And still, they pushed forward, as if momentum alone could outrun the horror.

As soldiers swung their blades at Danek, he fought the urge to wave his palm to stop the bleeding, a luxury he no longer held without Vaerin's constant source of magic feeding him. Kienna was right to scold him in the alley. It had been a shock the first time he used his magic outside of River Storm, and the immediate depletion of energy nearly drowned him in ice.

How Broan managed to surge so much magic through his stout body would forever remain a mystery to him as he spent his days trying to figure out a new way of working. Now, in battle, the frustrations crept up like tiny spiders, constantly itching and pulling his attention away from where it needed to be.

—Kienna—

Kienna threw all her energy into the movements of her body. She trained her whole life for something like this, fighting against men with bigger bodies and stronger stances. She felt oddly at home, though every move she made was strategically mapped around neutralizing her opponents and nothing more. Soldiers would writhe in pain at her feet, a much better sound than the emptiness that others had suffered during the battle.

Somewhere behind her, a man screamed, calling out for his brother. The voice cut through everything and then stopped. More screams continued. Kienna didn't look. She couldn't.

Scorched earth wafted through the city, crimson iron following suit. She thought the battle had been won, much to the relief of her fellow soldiers, all sweat-stained and muddied. The constant inhalation of dust burned Kienna's lungs. She inched forward over the injured soldiers she left in her wake. Her muscles burned. Each step was like dragging her soul uphill through sand.

The clanging of steel grew quieter. Around her, warriors slowed, blinking at the horizon as if the storm had passed. A breeze slipped through the canyon. And then, as if drawn by the hush itself, a dark wave of shadows crushed their hearts.

The Vorthakai had been formidable foes, tiring the soldiers and creating fatal wounds. They had ripped through the frontline with teeth. Kienna watched one latch onto a soldier's leg and shake until the bone snapped clean through. Another tore a man's throat open with its claws and kept going, dragging the body like it was meat. As if that weren't enough, more dark creatures appeared from the ash. Elvish men of the dead, eyes black as night and skin devoid of color.

Be careful with those! Ruva warned as she trampled over a few of the Vorthakai. *Those are Umbrin, and they've been forged with dark magic.*

Haven't they all been? Kienna hissed, trying to keep her footing.

They fought with as much force as the Elvish, with carefully thought-out movements to manipulate their opponents. It grew glaringly clear that the Shardborn was faltering. Kienna could feel it in her bones as she sidestepped the creatures, only to be knocked down and winded. She continued to get up, to fight. Other battalions rejoined, striking in the efforts to end the madness. As soldiers continued to fall, exhaustion weighed on Kienna's shoulders. Her chest heaved in and out, her heart beating furiously in her throat.

Her mind grappled with the motion of stepping over the bodies as another wave of attacks came to her. She fell again and again. Large cuts on her skin made way to deeper wounds. Blood coated her hands. She wasn't sure whose it was.

"Kienna!" Danek yelled as she fell to the ground. She struggled to stand, her breath coming in slower. "We need to push them back with magic! I can't do it alone."

No, Ruva urged.

Kienna glanced at another Umbrin shadowing its way over to her. She could see Connak and Tislin jumping from the rocks into the canyon and slicing through the evil haunting the city.

"Please," Danek pleaded. "Find the strength! We aren't winning!"

Kienna sighed, and Ruva whimpered near her. The Umbrin was now upon her, reaching to grab her soul and rip it from her chest. She descended inside herself, where pain, rage, and desperation churned like molten stone. Her breath hitched, chest tightening as a spark ignited somewhere deep. It didn't feel right at first, as if she let it go, someone would get hurt. It swarmed inside her like a dark shadow, resurfacing the torment of the dungeons. She couldn't let that magic out. Her body shook to hold onto it.

Time was running out. The Umbrin was latching its hands onto her tunic, staring with its dead eyes into her soul. A face, she realized, she would have nightmares about for the rest of her life if she managed to make it out of this. The magic stilled in her. Her fingertips tingled. The ground beneath her trembled slightly, as if the earth recognized her.

A ringing filled her ears, like a bell underwater. Light flickered along her arms. Then, a flare exploded. Flames shot out, roaring into the Umbrin and taking the creature ablaze.

But in that searing instant, something else stirred. A shadow, not her own, brushed the edge of her awareness. The flames crackled with power, yet beneath their heat was a chill. It passed quickly, almost unnoticed, but it left her heart fluttering strangely in her chest. Something had awoken with her, and it was watching.

She confidently brushed it aside to stand and pulled from the thrumming power that grew into a strong urge now, pulsing in her veins and singing how it belonged. Her eyes lit up a dark blue, and magic poured from her hands. The energy continued to build until the bright light exploded from her body, slamming into Elvish soldiers that had been near her.

Kienna flew backwards into the rocky canyon. Her head collided into the pointed rocks, blurring her vision. In that dizzy moment, she caught sight of Danek, his face twisted in panic, his mouth forming a scream she couldn't hear. He shoved past two soldiers, eyes wild and sword forgotten in his hand as he sprinted toward her. He was running, followed shortly by Talon.

Before the dark took her, she caught a flash. Connak's silhouette in the canyon haze, soaring through the wind with his blade alight. And faintly, barely audible through the ringing in her ears, a soft whimper from Ruva reached her mind like a fading heartbeat: *Stay.*

Chapter 52

—Connak—

Connak stared at Kienna's body lying with anguish in the healer's room. His jaw was tight, and his arms were crossed so fiercely over his chest it felt as if he might bruise his own ribs. A weight had settled in the hollow behind his sternum. He pulled her into this war, ushered her into battle before truly seeing if she was ready or if she even wanted it. She followed him into fire, and now she lay broken in the aftermath. A dull ache pulsed behind his eyes. He hadn't slept in days, not deeply. Each time he closed his eyes, he saw the moment her body struck the canyon wall.

He wanted to believe she would wake, but fear gnawed at him in quiet moments when no one was watching. That fear was what kept him rooted to the side of her cot—what made him pace like a caged wolf each time her breath hitched in sleep. Ruva whimpered by her side. She had to wake up. Connak couldn't bear to think about what would happen to all of them if she didn't.

The trip from Dalelry to Trinity had been a grueling journey of stop-and-go to keep Kienna in a stable state of motion. Danek begged to heal her and switched to groveling for the Elvish healers to do it, but Elira would not allow it. Energy resources were depleted to such a low level after the battle that she would never risk her Elvish life on a person who endangered them. By some stroke of luck, Vaerin's soldiers took the blast as their chance to retreat. But the brief victory meant nothing compared to the Elvish lives lost or the ones maimed by her outburst.

On the journey home, Connak tapped inside her mind, searching for a way in, but Kienna wasn't there. Her mind was black as night, and only recently a few fading stars began twinkling inside. The hints of life allowed Connak enough relief to sleep, but he kept jolting to check her breath and help the healers tend to her head wound with herbs from the elemental islands.

Finally, after days of radio silence, Connak sensed the trickle of Kienna's mind flowing like a sluggish stream through winter-dark woods. Specks of light still shimmered on the surface, but they were dim, barely pulsing. The usual warmth, the instinctive pull of her essence, had shifted. It was quiet there. Heavy.

He dipped his hand into the cold flow, and a chill shot up his arm with a dense, weighty silence. His thoughts were muted as he let himself be drawn in, his presence sinking slowly into her space. There was no welcome this time, only the echo of pain and the distant hum of a mind trying to rebuild itself from splinters.

She sat by canyons, watching the sunrise kiss the horizon as specks of pink and golden orange swirled into the sky. She wore the bright, white gown she had been placed in by the Elvish during her healing rituals, a solitude of innocence. Her hair lay softly down her back, swaying in the breezeless desert. Connak placed his body next to hers, and they sat in silence for a moment.

"My head hurts. What happened?" she asked, voice cracked and lackluster.

"You exploded," Connak sighed.

Kienna fixed her weary eyes on Connak, hands trembling against the desert rubble. She replayed the moment of her magic ascension repeatedly, trying to piece together where she went wrong. "Did I hurt anyone?"

"Yes," Connak replied.

Her focus fell from the horizon, a somber sob escaping from her lips. Her eyes grappled for answers, and her brows twitched to keep tears from flowing out faster than a rushing river. She grasped her head in pain and leaned against her legs.

"How many?"

"It's not important," he told her.

"It is," she responded through the muffling of her gown.

"Ten from our side. Three Umbrin."

"That's a lot," Kienna quivered. Connak heard the sniffling between the beats of her heart thumping through her mind. "What should I expect if I wake up?"

"You mean when?" Connak's brow rose. "I imagine there will be a debriefing. We can try to push Elira off, but she's furious."

Kienna pulled her face from the white garment, now tear-stricken. She nodded and stood from the desert rocks. As she did, dried trees caught her skin, but her body did not flinch nor pull away. Even in her mind, harsh foliage craved her skin, trying to draw a reaction. They got none.

The rocks crumbled from where she once stood. Connak visibly faltered from her mind before he was able to catch up with her path.

The world around Kienna began to shimmer. Images of Dalelry flashed into view, as it had been before the battle. Before the fire. Warm torchlights flickered in open-air markets, children ran laughing through narrow alleys, and the sandstone buildings stood golden in the morning sun. Connak watched her walk among them, unseen and unburdened.

But the images cracked. One by one, the scenes shattered like glass, catching sunlight, each joyful glimpse twisting into ash. Flames licked the rooftops. Cries of soldiers echoed down the same alleys. Blood spilled onto the desert dust. Laughter turned into screams, and children were crushed under boulders. Connak winced at the sight.

The ground beneath their feet fractured, and Kienna stumbled as the canyon itself began to crumble. Stones split and fell into a void that wasn't there before. The horizon darkened, and the wind howled like a wounded animal.

Kienna gasped, pressing her hand to her chest. Connak knew it was just her mind. Memory and grief twisted by trauma, but it felt real, even to him. Too real. His own heart beat maliciously.

Connak called out, but the sound was muffled by the roar of her unraveling thoughts. He stepped forward instinctively, reaching for her as the edge of the crumbling dreamscape cracked beneath his boots. Dust billowed around him, his form shimmering at the borders of her mind. For a brief second, his outstretched hand gripped something between her collapse and his fear of dying with her. He held steadily, refusing to let the illusion swallow them both.

—Danek—

"Would you consider Kienna a traitor?" Kaelthar demanded.

"No," Danek responded, anger lacing every word. "If you let me heal her, she can tell you herself."

Elira stood from the roots of her seat. Around the circular hall, the full council sat poised in their carved thrones of woven ironwood, robes flowing like stilled wind. Flanking them stood Talon and Tristian.

"She has Connak with her. Right now, she needs to be detained and monitored so we can figure out how big a threat she is," Alister said from his seat.

"Threat?" Danek spat back. "She's been unconscious for days! She was fighting on our side before it happened."

"You were there." Alister leaned forward. "What would you call killing three Elvish soldiers and injuring seven others?"

"An accident," Danek stated confidently.

He turned to Broan and Moira, who had also been called in to speak to Kienna's character. Moira stood, covered in the finest Elvish linens of deep blues and golds, with her face painted to match the regal colors of her garments. Her wide eyes darted nervously around the room.

Broan stood unamused, noticeably tired from a long battle and journey home, but he appeared far less beaten than the rest of the army, something Danek noticed. He used magic heavily on the battlefield, yet he was less boastful upon their return. The battle had weighed heavily on all of them.

"She wasn't even supposed to use magic." Talon stood alongside Tristian, but his voice lacked its usual conviction. He paused, as if the memory of Kienna on the battlefield softened his tone. "She trained well. Better than most. Stayed late with our High Commander to get more practice. But that doesn't excuse the risk she took, summoning it up despite our battalion laws."

"Give me a break," Danek scolded, his jaw tightening. His tension eased a little when he noticed Tristian take a step forward. "I only mean to say that she didn't mean to hurt us. She's never been good with magic."

"That was a pretty well-thought-out time bomb with advanced magic," said Seredai, the only other Elvish woman on the council.

Her skin carried a shimmer of soft silver bark, and her eyes, pale lavender rimmed in silver, studied the room. Her hair flowed like cascading water drawn from the roots of the world.

Danek cowered in her overbearing presence. "I told her to do it. She was getting tired, and I told her to do it so she wouldn't die."

"She doesn't even like magic," Broan's voice cut through the tension.

"Why?" Elira peered at them.

"She says it hurts her," Broan shrugged.

"And then there's the haze she mentioned once—" Moira started.

"Haze?" Seredai questioned, her voice cool and measured. Her eyes narrowed. "I would like to scan Kienna, with your permission, of course." Seredai nodded to Elira. She bowed in agreement, and they found an exit, leaving Danek, Broan, and Moira standing awkwardly in front of the rest of the council and their commanding officers.

"May we also go see Kienna?" Danek cleared his throat.

"No," Tristian said and left them as well.

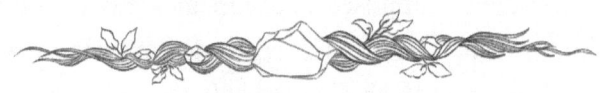

—Connak—

The world crumbled inside Kienna's mind, heaving stones from the sky into great giant heaps. Connak could barely see her as she glided through the world like a spirit trying to find its next place of rest. She wasn't fazed by the destruction around her. It was but a whisper to her mind.

He knew how much turmoil the thought of taking a life had on her soul, and Connak feared she would lose the fight to wake from her coma. He called her name, but his voice was lost in the destruction. Eventually, the pain reverberated through Kienna's brain—whether from the concussion or the regret—which started to seep into Connak.

His head throbbed, and he knew he had to get out before she took him down with her. She would anyway, but he couldn't let it happen, especially without warning Tristian. He twitched, pulling his mind in different directions, and then he yelled, "Wait for me, Kienna! I'll be right back! Please, don't let go."

Connak pulled his mind from Kienna's tether. It was a breath of fresh air after a long bout of suffocation. The air burned his throat as he gasped and choked back the turmoil in his heart. His eyes fell to the queen and the Elvish women in front of him, studying Kienna's still body.

"Elira," he cried, his eyes weary and sunken. "Please let them use magic."

The queen looked at Seredai, flickering doubt through the room.

"She won't survive my scans if you don't," Seredai agreed. The queen nodded to the Elvish woman, and she cast out her hand with a bright, lavender glow that echoed in the same hue as her eyes.

The visible anguish of Kienna's pain disappeared, something more peaceful passing as her body fell deep into rest. Her eyes, however, still flicked around, and Connak knew her mind was still not at ease.

"I need to go back in there," he begged.

"Let me scan her first," Seredai requested. "I think there may be an explanation beneath the surface for her outburst in Dalelry."

"She's crumbling in there," Connak cried back. "If I don't pull her out, she won't come back."

"Take me in there, and I will be quick," Seredai assured him.

Connak eyed her. It was dark magic she was asking him to perform, something that had not been done since the era of the Dark Priestess, but he knew better than to question her ancient ways. Her hand gently sat on his shoulder, and Connak tethered his mind to the head-splitting aura Kienna had created. Seredai looked around, eyes widening subtly, but it was not enough to stop her from her work. "Umra rineth shairen thas," she whispered, a darkness flowing outward through incantation. Connak held the tether steadily.

Seredai's magic flowed with great pulses of energy through Kienna, her mind growing with faint glimmers of purple. She passed through veils of memory, through dreamscapes that shifted like oil over water. Connak couldn't see what she saw, but he saw the tension in her shoulders and the way her magic faltered and pulsed unevenly.

A long hallway of broken mirrors shimmered briefly into view. Fractured glass glinted with dim light, and shadows moved behind each pane. One mirror cracked as Seredai approached.

Her lips parted. "These don't belong here."

Further in, Connak glimpsed jagged symbols scrawled into the walls—too sharp, too foreign for the flowing lines of Elvish magic. One gently glowed red, and Seredai flinched as if it burned her to look at it.

"Tampered," she muttered. "Twisted at the root." Seredai's face grew long, her body tensing at each pulse of magic. "I'm at the source," she told Connak. "It's tangled, like a part of it has been messed with."

"What does that mean?"

"This magic...it's hers by blood, shaped by nature. But there's something coiled around it. A charm." She moved her fingers in the air as if writing her words as she spoke. "It's reactive, not passive. Every time she uses it outside of Vaerin's will, it turns on her. Backlashes. Like a trap set to punish rebellion."

Connak's chest tightened. "How long has it been there?"

Seredai's eyes glimmered. "Since infancy, I believe. It was not nearly as severe in River Storm because she was under his control. Out here, with no anchor or walls, it grows wild. Stronger. And it's tethering him to her." Her voice dropped. "If it isn't broken soon, it will consume her."

"So, the explosion..."

"Was not something she could control," Seredai confirmed. "I must go before this tether summons the Dark Priestess. You have five minutes before you lose her, so work quickly." Seredai faded, leaving Connak in the wreckage.

He stretched his shoulders and took in his surroundings, searching for the phantom that was Kienna. The mindscape was unrecognizable. What had once been desert canyons had become a flooded ruin. Crumbled sandstone towers leaned into black pools of water, wells overflowing as if burst from within, and thick mist clung to every broken arch and shattered wall.

Connak waded forward, his breath ragged. The ground shifted beneath his feet. He stumbled through the rising flood, shoving aside fragments of splintered stone and twisted thoughts, until pain flared in his temples from the sheer pressure.

All he could hear were the muffled echoes of her cries, like distant thunder through the storm, but it was enough to tether him to her.

Connak pulled with all his might until her face appeared, beaten and bruised. He stopped in his tracks, taken aback by the sudden change, but he knew it was now or never. He grabbed her face like he did in the forest and pressed his forehead to hers.

"I never wanted to kill," she heaved, her body crumbling into his.

"You're not a killer," he gasped. "Vaerin broke you."

"We cannot blame my shortcomings on Vaerin's treacherous treatment of us," Kienna whispered. "Men died by my hand."

Connak squeezed tighter, pushing Seredai's message in pulses through her, painting the image of Vaerin taking a baby from a tree, putting her in a castle of captivity, and shredding her to the core until he found her source.

"Vaerin," Connak growled, "killed our people." She didn't say anything, but Connak could feel a weight pulling from Kienna's mind. The crashing rubble froze in place, and things went still. "Kienna," Connak said calmly. "You need to wake up now. It's time to come out of this before you can't. I won't come out of this, either, if you don't."

"I don't think I'm strong enough for this."

"You are the strongest person I know," Connak said soothingly. He knew they didn't have time to go through this, but he'd lose her just as easily if they didn't.

"I don't know if I can survive what I saw out there. The dead... they haunt me."

"I will help you," Connak pleaded, "I promise, I won't let you cope with it alone."

—Kienna—

Kienna scanned Connak's face, her icy eyes softening to a light haze of gray. She sniffled as the outside world tugged her mind. Connak faded away, and her thoughts cleared.

Eyes open, she was surrounded by Elvish healers, the queen, and an ancient woman. Connak stood from his seat and grabbed her hand with relief, burying his face into the side of her sheets. Another battle won, but for how long?

A breeze stirred the healer's curtains, soft and unexpected, fluttering the fabric like a whisper of new breath. Somewhere beyond the open window, the sounds of life resumed, quiet, distant, and steady. The world continued.

Chapter 53

—Kienna—

Kienna rested in peace for a week, relieved to hear that the army hadn't been called for another battle since then. Soldiers could rest easily and gain their strength back, as well as bury their dead. Connak sat with her in silence. Her head still ached. The wounds had completely disappeared physically now, but the bruises on her soul would take more time. Ruva rested her head on Kienna's chest, listening to the beat of her heart. She did this often since Kienna woke.

Danek came in, smiling that she was awake. "We need to walk."

She'd been in bed most of the time. Eventually, Connak told Danek and Moira they could be useful by making sure Kienna got up and restored her strength from time to time. It was Danek's turn, though Kienna protested and tried to emphasize her pain so he'd let up. He didn't, and this only frustrated her.

Ruva grabbed at the covers around her legs and nipped at her hands until she eventually let Danek help her out of bed. The wobbling and dizzy spells eventually passed after she'd done it a few times, but it didn't help the ringing in her head as she stood. Kienna winced and waited it out.

Connak's hand rested on her shoulder. "Sip some water."

Kienna waved him off and let Danek hold her arm so she could steady herself. She wanted to give up. Danek wouldn't let her, and she hated him for that as they stepped out into the forest. He held onto her tightly to give her some cushion, so she forgave him and kept stepping forward.

"We still need to talk about Baila," he whispered.

Her eyes darted away from him. "Let's go back to pretending I'm concussed."

Danek gripped her arm tighter. "I'm serious. You both lied to us."

Kienna was too eager to avoid the conversation altogether. He rolled his eyes to the trees, clenching his jaw. Ruva trotted up beside them and pushed her body onto Kienna's side for extra support.

You should tell him the truth. He'll still love you.

Stop, Ruva. Danek doesn't love me. And no one should. What if Baila has already told them where this city is?

Ruva stopped Kienna's walking. Danek motioned forward but stopped when he realized they were having a conversation. He waited patiently, the poor fool. Guilt held Kienna like a stone on her chest.

The city is designed to hide itself. There's no getting in unless you know how, and she does not know how.

You're sure?

Ruva blinked her eyes as confirmation. *They are an annoyingly cryptic people, but it helps them to stay hidden.*

"Kienna?" Danek put his hand on her shoulder more gently now.

"I'm sorry I lied, Danek." Her eyes went to the soil, but she meant it. "I felt scared of what Vaerin would do to my family in River Storm."

He nodded and placed his hand on Ruva's head. Kienna jolted, somewhat shocked that the wolf let him do it. Ruva was team Danek all the way. "Listen," he said. "I can't have your back unless I know what I have your back from."

She didn't say much but tried to show him she understood with a half-hearted smile, and then she let him walk her back to her room to rest.

Queen Elira stepped into Kienna's room late at night, a sight that startled Kienna. Many had been to see her as she healed, even Seredai, who wanted to explore King Vaerin's bond with her. It was a pressing issue that the Elvish wanted to study further, given the chance. Tristian followed shortly after. Connak, who sat reading a book in the corner, stood at the sight of his commanding officer. Tristian shook his head subtly, putting Connak at ease.

The queen's breath escaped in a sharp exhale. "You do not have to be here for this, Commanders." She looked at Tristian first, then to Connak with clear irritation. "I am only here to discuss the nature of her cursed magic."

"This knowledge is pertinent to the protection of my soldiers," Tristian said, placing his hands behind his back.

Ruva whimpered with a weary glance at Kienna. *I can growl if you want them to leave. We shouldn't put too much stress on you yet.*

We should figure out how to fix my magic. I can't let it hurt people anymore.

Ruva affectionately nuzzled her, the coldness of her nose sparking Kienna alive.

The queen stood from a distance, watching her coldly. "We will work to understand your magic as quickly as possible. We have scholars all over the Elvish realm studying the effects of bonded curses. For the time being, Seredai has created a charm for you to wear."

Kienna scratched behind Ruva's ear and watched Elira pull a bracelet from her gown. "What am I expected to do?"

"Wear it, of course." She said it as if Kienna was supposed to understand how it worked. "It will remove your magic."

"Am I no longer connected to the Eternal Mother?" Kienna put the charm on her wrist. It was a slender bracelet formed from braided silvervine and sun-hardened resin. It shimmered in the light, its weave glinting with lavender and emerald where the threads crossed. At its center was a single crystal forged from within the forest and clouded only at the edges. It was warm to the touch, beating like a second heart, and hugged her wrist snugly, molding to her skin. The humming of the forest slowed to a stop in her body. Relief and fear flooded her as the haziness dissipated. Kienna fought against the roaring river her whole life, gasping to stay afloat. Putting the bracelet on was like finally finding land where she could smell the fresh, sweet nectar of the flowers.

Tears formed in her eyes as a smile crossed her face. She laughed. *Can you feel it?*

Ruva howled with her. *Your mind is less conflicted.*

Her relief came with joy she had never experienced. She laughed out loud, cheeks reddening when she realized how silly she looked.

413

And yet, Kienna didn't give a damn. A jovial, childlike peace swayed over her. She should have been scared. Magic safeguarded her. She always had something to try if she faltered. The quiet in her body was stronger than the fear.

"Do I still need to fight?" she asked.

"You don't want to be a warrior anymore?" Tristian stepped forward and cocked his head to the side.

Even Connak sat up from the bed. *You okay?*

"I would like space to figure that out." The admission would hurt the army only by a fraction. They could certainly do without her accidentally killing people. She did more favors for Vaerin than she did for Trinity in Dalelry, and they still came out victorious. That brought her more peace because she realized she didn't have to be the Starborn for anyone. "Moira's making a difference somewhere else. So maybe I can, too, and I won't have to kill anyone to do it."

"We don't enjoy killing," Tristian argued, his jaw clenching, brows furrowing.

"Trinity is the house of governance and our sword. If Kienna doesn't want to be part of our army, then I have no use for her," Elira said. Her voice was calm, but Kienna knew the queen had slapped her in the face.

She didn't care. It felt good not to be at the top of someone's needed list. They could exile her to the forest, and she'd live out her days learning how to carve her own city. And there was no indication of a woodcarver in Trinity, so she didn't need to stay either.

"What about Silverthorne?" Connak asked. "She could go with Seredai."

Elira scowled, shooting metaphorical daggers into Connak's chest. "Silverthorne is a myth," she responded firmly, releasing the tension in her body and resuming her regal position.

At this point, Kienna had to roll her eyes. *They forget that I'm right here sometimes.*

The queen is odd.

"She could go to Dove Port, then," Tristian said.

The queen turned to him lazily. "What will she glean from Dove Port?"

Tristian shrugged. "Alliances. We need someone stationed there more permanently. She won't have to fight, but she could be our ears. Since she and Connak are connected by mind, it'd be easy to send word."

The solution did not seem to ease the queen, but what else would she do with Kienna if they didn't send her to Dove Port? Give her back to Vaerin? Elira nodded, and Kienna agreed. Dove Port had been nice with strong architecture and a craft for artistry. She could easily come to terms with waking up every morning to see the sun over the Lysiria.

Connak jumped off the bed, his shoulders pushed back. "So, you're sending her away, then? How are we going to help her if we don't have her near?"

Elira waved her wrist at him, a movement that appeared too close to the king at times. She turned to Kienna. "You will go to Dove Port. You will wear your charm at all times. I expect you to bathe with it. It does not come off your wrist. Is that understood?"

Kienna bowed, she realized, for the first time, to the queen. "Yes."

Elira stepped back, scanning the room. She cleared her throat. "Stay out of the slums of the city. Any hint of trouble from you, and I will drag you back myself, and you can rot under the roots of our trees. You leave in the morning. Take Moira."

She turned to leave, but not before giving Connak one final sharp look as a warning. Without a word, she motioned with her fingers for him to follow. Connak hesitated for a breath, the tiniest hint of a smile crossing his lips, then gave Kienna a wink before stepping past the edge of the curtain that separated the healing room from the forest. The fabric whispered and then settled into place.

Why does it always seem like he knows more than he ever lets on? Ruva asked.

Kienna rolled her eyes. *My thoughts exactly.*

"That's it then? You're pulling out of the fight?" Tristian asked.

Kienna startled. She'd almost forgotten he was there. Her fingers brushed over the emerald strands of her charm. The only other bracelet she'd ever owned was the snake Vaerin gave them, but it was not nearly as beautiful as this.

She shook her head and then looked toward him. "Surely you don't only see worth in a person by the battles they fight."

"Only when that person is worthy of fighting but still refuses. We've been sparring together. You didn't hate it, so what changed?" Tristian's hands couldn't find a place to rest. He looked so utterly disappointed in her.

Kienna groaned. "I don't know if you fought the same battle as me, but I was used as a pawn to kill ten people. Thirteen, if you want to count those undead creatures."

Tristian faltered, silence filling the space between them like fog. He exhaled sharply, the edge of his voice dulling, though his pride wouldn't let it go completely. He took a softer step toward her, voice lower. "You could still make it through this. You have potential—"

"I am nothing on the battlegrounds, Commander. You're finally getting your wish! I'm staying out of the way, so quit being such a hard ass all the time, and quit chastising everything I do!"

Tristian stepped backward, visibly shaken by her sudden outburst. His brows furrowed as if to say something harsh or to scold her for such an inappropriate turn of treatment toward him. Instead, he bowed slightly and chided, "Princess," before retreating.

That wasn't nice, Ruva mentioned, letting out a low-tempered growl in his absence.

He hasn't been nice to me! *I can't wait to be rid of him*, Kienna admitted.

Ruva shifted closer and nudged her with a heavy sigh. *He has given you more time than expected, though. And stayed late with you every night in the training grounds.*

Kienna huffed, and that was the end of that.

The firelight danced in the corner of the healing room, casting warm shadows across the wood. Somewhere in the night, a flute played a wandering melody, soft and slow. Kienna sat in silence, one hand on her charm, and for the first time in a long while, her breath was steady.

Chapter 54

—Moira—

Moira put her trinkets in tiny bags that she securely tied to her horse. The adorned jewels were unlike anything she had ever seen back in River Storm. The muted golds and bronze colors of her past suddenly didn't sit right against her brown skin. When she heard they would be going to Dove Port, Moira boasted with excitement. This would be her final journey. Dove Port was her home, with her story written all over it.

Fully packed, Moira led her horse through the clearing. She stopped immediately as voices carried in hushed tones. She peeked over to where Tristian and Tislin stood together, jaws clenched and shoulders tightly wound back.

"His name is Calder Ashfell. Don't forget," Tristian said with a tone harsher than kind.

Tislin sighed. "Yes, Brother, I understand."

"And Elowen. They'll stay with her for a bit until we find them a home. They can't be seen with her for too long." Tislin nodded. Tristian's eyes hardened. "Tislin, I'm serious. No more sacrificing your future in the shadows. This cause needs you to stay vigilant." After a beat, Tristian released his tension. With eyes still glued to his brother, he said, "You can come out from behind the trees."

Moira flushed when she stepped out and apologized, but she realized she had interrupted possibly the last conversation they would have before departing. Tristian stormed away, and Tislin relaxed.

They left as soon as Kienna readied herself, her valiant wolf trailing closely behind.

Danek was quick to send pleas to the queen to find a different path or to send him with her. Connak was content leaving them in Tislin's care, but she did think how nice it was that Kienna had men falling at her feet. A twinkle sparked in her eye as Tislin gave her his hand to help her up into a horse. As she mounted, she left her hand in his for a touch too long, and her cheeks grew hot, and she looked away.

Her mind went back to Rhior for the first time since she'd talked to Tislin about him, and she forced herself to send up a prayer that he was safe in River Storm. Her heart reached through the treacherous distance between them, but she resolved to keep her mourning at bay. She wasn't ready to talk about him again, still sifting through the feelings she now found herself having for Tislin.

Dove Port was a long day's journey. They rode quietly for most of it, but as they passed the forest opening where Kienna had found the initials of her parents, she could see her eyes darting to Ruva. They must have been having a silent conversation. Soon after, Ruva slipped away from the group and vanished with ease, as if she weren't a giant wolf nearly as big as the horses they rode.

"It can be lonely on a journey with a bonded one," Tislin said, pulling his horse back to ride with her. "They tend to forget that others are around them, too."

Moira pursed her lips together and glanced at her hands. "I didn't notice it when we had the others around. Now it's too quiet."

"Connak spent a lot of time in Kienna's mind when we were stationed in the Malintale. I spent a lot of time in my own thoughts, so I apologize if I have been ignoring you."

She gained enough courage to look at him, letting his speckled eyes greet hers. Her heart pulsed magically around her chest, a feeling she simultaneously loved and hated. Moira could barely recognize herself, falling into Tislin's company. "You and Tristian were a little tense in the forest this morning."

Tislin stiffened, his eyes shifting away from her. "He doesn't agree with me escorting you to Dove Port, but Connak didn't trust anyone else to help Kienna."

Moira's hands grew hot, which was odd. She looked at Kienna, riding on her horse as she led the way through the path, and felt an emotion that was so unbecoming for her that she had to chastise herself. "Help Kienna how?"

"I can't say much." Tislin reached his hand across their horses and caressed hers. She didn't pull away. "But we've been working hard in the shadows to get her here."

"Is she the Ashborn?"

Tislin didn't answer, but Moira knew his silence was an answer. He nudged his horse ahead of hers and took the lead, pushing them into a full gallop until they reached the clearing, and Dove Port came into view. She was relieved to see her city again, bright buildings towering in the invigorating aromas of the area. A hint of fresh flora wafted through her nostrils.

The wind blew gently against her hair as the waves pushed into the bay of the town. Ships in the harbor ebbed and flowed, the creaking sound of their planks and echoes of the seagulls ringing through the city walls.

"Ah," Moira hopped off her horse, taking it in again. "This place gives me so much energy!"

"It is your birthplace," Tislin stated, inching up next to her. "And your magic's."

"I thought all magic came from the Eternal Mother," Kienna cut in.

Tislin nodded. "Yes, but the magic you are born with is strongest when you are where you belong. Strong everywhere you go, but your energy will be less likely to falter."

The deep rays of the sun graced Moira's face, something she didn't get in strong waves under the canopies of the forest. The heat pulsed through her body, a golden ball of energy floating in her hands, warm and buzzing, tied to the weather and light. She let it dissipate before anyone could see.

"What next?" Kienna asked.

"Well," Tislin started forward, his pale skin and black garments sticking out like a sore thumb in the bright lights. "A woman, her name is Elowen, has offered to house you for a few days while her husband is at sea, but she cannot keep you for long. She's a friend of yours and wants to help."

"We could stay at the Elarent House," Moira suggested.

Tislin rubbed his hand to the back of his neck, grimacing. "Dove Port operates a little differently than the Elvish kin. While we rely heavily on working with nature and collaborating to survive, Dove Port is more of a free market."

"So, we'll need jobs," Kienna stated.

"To contribute economically," Tislin agreed.

"I love it," Moira giggled and grabbed Kienna's hand. "Imagine, two working women of Dove Port building a life for themselves."

Kienna's hesitant eyes studied her before she stepped into the streets and looked around. "Do they have a woodcarver?"

"They do." Tislin's lips curved upward, hinting that the question was almost expected. "I could speak to him while you settle in with Elowen."

Tislin stepped forward. Moira could feel it then, the creeping waves brushing over her vision. In an instant, she found herself in front of a man she'd never seen before. He was old, with dark hair now shaded and lightened by gray. His beard was full and as gray as his hair. He was bronzed like a man who had seen many days in the sun but also hardships.

He held a weathered carving knife, slicing into pale wood, but the carving bled ash instead of sap, leaking from the grain like ink until the whole block turned black. Standing next to the woodcarver was the child of her visions. She simply said, "Come, Mama."

"What is it, child? What's so important that you brought me here now?"

The child pointed to the old man, his eyes sunken in sadness. He was carving a cradle with a black shadow looming over him. The child tugged Moira's arm and whispered, "The Ashborn must carve her own fate. Beware of the blade that shaped the block."

The carving cracked, and then Moira jolted back to Dove Port, the bright lights blinding her. Her stomach swirled for a moment and then settled, but Moira was trembling. What was the child trying to tell her? Was this a warning of danger in Kienna's future? She wanted to say something, but Kienna didn't know about Moira's secrets. She held them to herself and followed Tislin. Stealing a glance backward, Kienna remained by the tree line, staring idly out toward the Lysira.

Chapter 55

—Kienna—

Hope flourished in Kienna's heart. This whole time, she'd been searching for a woodcarver in the wrong places. They passed through Dove Port once, and she kicked herself for not daring to ask if what she sought was anywhere else besides Trinity. Though she held a connection to the forest that she couldn't understand, being part of Trinity never felt like a full belonging. Part of her was split. Her heritage, she realized—as she stared at the sea raging against the rocky shore—was cracked clean down the middle.

My mother was from Dove Port, Kienna said, rubbing her hand down Ruva's neck.

You think we will find answers here?

Something inside of Kienna flickered at the thought. It was as if hidden parts of her were shattering open. Warmth coated her veins like a tempered flame. Her hand brushed the charm on her wrist to ensure it remained secure. It had worked. All the uncomfortable bits of magic were gone, every hint of Vaerin floating away. Still, something was beating underneath it all, begging to be released.

Whatever it was, it didn't feel like a curse waiting to control her. It simply felt like her.

Shall we go, then? Ruva asked, padding forward after Moira and Tislin.

Kienna turned to study the forest. Finally, her soul rested. She had made the right choice to tear down the barrier in River Storm and flee the king. Danek, Broan, and Moira were all better for it as well. They smiled more in those days, even with war knocking at their doorstep, than she recalled ever seeing them smile in the gray, decrepit city. For once, the heads stopped rolling at her feet.

Yes, Kienna agreed, running to catch up with the others. *Let's start living.*

END OF BOOK 1

Acknowledgements

Where to even start? There are so many people in my life that I've come into contact with that have been instrumental in getting this book to the finish line! First and foremost, I want to thank my husband for being my rock and supporting me through this process. Publishing a book, especially independently, takes an incredible amount of time, and he's been there for me when I felt stressed, helping me stay organized. I cannot say thank you enough to you for helping me take on this monster of a project.

Thank you to my wonderful children. Of course, they can't contribute anywhere but emotionally, but the time they let me have to write my book and do the things it takes to publish is a sacrifice they had to make. This book is for them and for our future!

I want to send a sincere thank you to all the people who read my book in its rawest form. Kenny and Cheyanna read through this story before it had the best scenes, questioning every single chapter and the motive, inspiring me to ensure I gave this story my best effort. I've learned so much from both of them!

To my editor, Charla: thank you! Thank you so much for the encouragement and walking me through this entire process. You taught me how to fight for myself and put in the work to publish. And….you may have taught me how to use a comma correctly. I'm forever grateful for your unwavering support. I cannot wait to continue our partnership through this process with all the other books I have coming down the pipeline!

For my crowbar sisters, you know who you are! You have been

amazing to talk through the struggles of being an independent author. I am so grateful to have you in my life as true friends. There is no better bunch of women I could have met that could have gotten me through these stressors, and I'm so glad this process brought me lifelong friends to hold onto. Thank you!

Thank you to Emilee and Brooke for becoming my lifelong betas and, ultimately, amazing friends. You are the people I turn to when I want to bounce ideas for my upcoming books. You are the people I send pictures to and talk about this grueling process. Your support means everything to me, and I'm so grateful to have you all in my life!

To my artist, Jennifer. Thank you for coming out from the woodworks with an inspiration to become a book artist. Thank you for making me your first client. Thank you for listening to me and stepping out of your comfort zone to try different art styles to match my vision. You are amazing. I'm so excited for us to grow together!

And finally, to my readers. Thank you for taking a chance on a debut author and reading my very first published book. I poured my heart and soul into this world and these characters, and I can't do what I do without you. From the very bottom of my heart, through the essence of my being, thank you.

About the Author

Samantha Vargas has been inventing stories since she was twelve and started writing Guardians of Alistile at sixteen. What began as a teen dream grew into the world she now shares with readers. A lifelong lover of fantasy, her shelves were shaped by The Lord of the Rings, Vampire Academy, and The Chronicles of Narnia—and yes, she once rewatched LOTR for weeks straight during an ice storm.

Sam is powered almost entirely by potatoes , water, and books. She shares her life with her husband (a fellow Star Wars and superhero nerd), her children, and their dog, Obi. If she could, she'd spend her days writing in the woods, laughing at bad comedies, and collecting cats her family is unfortunately allergic to.

For more information:
www.samanthavargasauthor.com